# The Human Family

*The Casitian Universe Series, Book VI*

**Maxwell Pearl**

# Chapter 1:
## Families' Disgrace

New Earth: November 2098
Casiti: Musb 803
Hilcyon: Sdert 1201

*"The overarching sense shared from all traditions is the love of the Divine for us, and the way the divine provides for us. For some traditions, this is without requirement. For others, the Divine requests from us some kind of sacrifice - some kind of gift from our hearts, bodies, or minds to acknowledge the love and kindness of the Divine. But the love seeps through, from texts as diverse as our 'Heart of the Carj', founding spiritual texts of those enslaved, to texts of Earth, from the Rig Veda, Bible, and so many other texts."* — Ja'lend'a, 'Spirits Alike'

### Independent Christian State, New Earth

Paul sat in the back of the church, fidgeting. He looked up to the ceiling, which he could see had tiles that were yellowed by leaks from the roof, and lights that weren't working. His father had him up there a few months ago repairing some of the lights, but more had failed since.

This was, by far, his least favorite time of year. Between Thanksgiving week, which was full of fasting and praying, with a service every single day, then on to Advent and Christmas, with more services during the week, his family was basically in church almost every day for a month. He hated it. But he basically had no choice in the matter. It was his father's church. He hadn't figured a way out yet.

Everyone rose, and he followed suit—it would be too obvious if he stayed seated. It was bad enough that he chose to sit in the back of the church instead of in front with the rest of his family.

His father, upfront at the podium, intoned, "We have sinned against God and have been banished from Heaven."

The congregation answered, "Forgive us, oh Father."

His father said, "It is only by being pure, that we can return."

"Help us, oh Father, to be pure."

"When we die, pure and sinless, we will return to Earth."

"Help us, oh Father, to remain pure until death."

He knew the prayer. It was said in every service and occasion, such as funerals and weddings, and at home almost every day. The expectation was that if you lived your life in purity when you died, you would get to go back to Earth. He stopped repeating the words years ago.

When he was young, Paul had been interested in theology, until he ran into a wall once, talking to his father, when he was about ten.

"I'm confused about something."

"What is it, son?"

"Why is it that we believe that people get to go to Earth after they die?"

"Because that is where God is."

"But I thought God was in heaven."

"Earth became heaven, son. God is there."

"When we were on Earth, where was heaven? Why don't we still go there?"

His father looked at him sternly. "Son, Earth is heaven, and we sinned and were banished here."

"But Dad..."

"Paul, stop asking stupid questions. You have to trust in God. Know His will, do His will."

After that conversation, Paul lost whatever little faith he'd had that what he'd been taught resembled the truth. It wasn't even logical. And every time he listened to this prayer being intoned just made that more clear.

Finally, the service was over. He got up and left the church building to make his way home. These days, he always left before his family. He was supposed to stay—be social with the congregation, and be a good pastor's kid. But he couldn't stand the idea of it.

When he arrived back at the house he saw the stout frame, olive skin, and dark brown hair of his mother's cousin Re'liro. He was sitting on the front stairs talking to Ke'lir, his daughter, who was a few years older than Paul.

"Re'liro!" Paul smiled. He was happy to see him. They hugged.

"Paul, you certainly have grown since I saw you a few years ago! You remember my daughter, Ke'lir?"

"Hi, yes I do." Paul hugged Ke'lir as well.

Paul said, "It's so nice to see you both."

He felt a genuine warmth inside being with them.

He asked, "What brings you here?"

Re'liro said, "Grandmother Beatrice died yesterday. We're here to invite your family to the funeral on Casiti. We've got tickets and accommodation arrangements for everyone."

He felt sad that he hadn't gotten to see his great-grandmother one more time—he'd loved spending time with her.

He said, "I'd love to go... but my family won't want to go."

Re'liro said, "You never know, Paul."

Paul was doubtful. His father seemed to revel in the feeling that he'd "reformed" Julia, a Michaelson, one of the infamous clan members responsible, from his father's perspective, for humankind's downfall and its banishment from Earth. But Paul liked his extended family and loved his great-grandmother Beatrice. He hoped the family would choose to go, but he doubted it.

"Where is everyone?" Re'liro asked.

"You know, preacher's family. Have to be social and stuff. They should be along in a while. How are things up north Ke'lir?"

He didn't really want to explain why he was here and not back at church.

They talked for a while about life for Ke'lir in the North Circumpolar Independent Zone, and her work for the New Earth Authority. Paul kept silent about his own sense of deep dissatisfaction with his life here, and his desire to be free of it. It was too tender for him.

He heard his mother's voice loudly say, "Re'liro! What are you doing here? And how could you bring your... son here?" Paul turned upon hearing his mother's angry voice, wincing at what she'd said.

"Julia. My *daughter*. And, hello."

4

"I asked you, what are you doing here? You don't belong in the ICS. I tolerate your presence when you travel with grandmother, but now..."

"It is grandmother I am here about."

"What happened?"

"She died yesterday. It was not unexpected. She was old, you know."

"Why bother to come all the way here?"

"Ke'lir and I are on our way to New Orleans to meet the family and travel together to Casiti. We wanted to tell you in person and welcome you and your whole family to accompany us to the funeral. I've even arranged all of your tickets to Casiti. We've also arranged lodging."

"You already know that I would never set foot on that horrible planet again!"

"Julia, you were born there."

"That doesn't matter. We're not going."

"Julia, the whole family is gathering. I mean absolutely everyone. Beatrice was the last of her generation, and we need to honor that. Isn't it time you mended..."

"There is nothing to mend nor honor! Please go on your way."

Re'liro shrugged. "OK, as you wish. You and your family will be missed." Re'liro and Ke'lir started to turn to leave.

Paul suddenly saw an opening, like a flash of light.

"Wait!" Paul yelled a bit louder than he wanted to.

His mother looked at him sharply. "Paul, please go into the house with your brother and sister and start preparations for the break of our fast."

Paul said, "I want to represent our family at the funeral."

Paul's father's face hardened into a mask, and his mother said sternly, "You will do no such thing."

He could feel a strengthening in his body, a sense of sureness came from somewhere.

"Mother, I turned 18 three months ago. I am an adult. Re'liro, can I come with you?"

"Of cou..."

His mother shouted, "No! I will in no way support this."

Paul turned to his mother, "It's my decision. My choice. I want to go."

Paul's father gripped his upper arm and said quietly, "If you leave this house with those heathen, you will never be welcome in it again."

It didn't take Paul long to make the decision. He shook off his father.

"Re'liro, please wait a few minutes while I gather some things."

He saw compassion and thoughtfulness on Re'liro's face. "Of course, Paul."

He could feel his father following him as he walked to his room. When they arrived, his father closed the door.

"Son, you are making a huge mistake. It could cost you your soul."

"You and Matthew seem to be so worried about my soul. Don't bother."

"We have insulated you from the wretched evil of the Casitians and the evil of your mother's family. You can't stand on your own in the face of it."

"Dad, I've heard enough about it from you and everyone. It's time for me to see for myself and make my own decisions. I know you and Mom don't respect our family and its legacy, but I do. I loved great-grandmother Beatrice—I want to be at the funeral."

"What kind of legacy is it if it caused us this destiny? It is the great sin of your mother's family."

"Dad, enough! I'm going. Let me just go, please?"

"I will morn you as lost." He turned and left, closing the door behind him.

Paul gathered a few personal belongings that he wanted to keep. He figured that he'd never set foot in this house again. There was no sadness or regret. He had been working up to this for a very long time.


Paul was challenged by the trip from the Independent Christian State through New America, into the South Central Independent Zone to New Orleans, the capital city of New Earth and the spaceport. He watched as the familiar one-story houses gave way to the cleanest streets he'd ever seen, buildings shinier and taller than he could have imagined, and smooth, quiet traffic of bicycles, scooters, small cars, and buses.

The spaceport was spectacular - all big swooping arches, tall glass windows, and lots of people coming and going. He was awed by all of it, and also angry. Angry that he'd had no idea this world existed. The Independent Christian State felt poor and shabby in comparison.

As they walked into the waiting room for the ship they would take to Casiti, he saw a muscular, young, dark-skinned man sitting alone. Ke'lir greeted him.

"Hi, Glor!"

He looked up to see them, a smile emerging from his broad face.

"Hey, Ke'lir. Where is everyone else?"

"Dad went to change the travel arrangements since most of Paul's family isn't coming. I guess the rest haven't made it here yet. We still have a couple of hours before the transport leaves. Why are you here so early?"

Glor said, "I had a meeting here in New Orleans yesterday."

"Really?"

"Yeah. I just got a spot as one of the NEA Kinder Liaisons."

"Congrats, Glor!"

"Thanks. It's a pretty low-level appointment. But I like it; it's fun work. I can do most of it from home in Zwek, but I need to be here now and again."

Ke'lir said, "I managed to make it onto the New Earth Agency Technology Committee; the NEA definitely has been reticent to include many Casitians, even though plenty of us live on New Earth, too."

Just as Paul began feeling a little ignored, Ke'lir said, "Glor, this is Paul, Julia's son. Paul, Glor."

Paul said, "You're Pkygy's grandson. Nice to meet you." They shook hands.

Glor said, "You know the family tree?"

Paul replied, "When great-grandma Beatrice visited last, we spent some time alone together. She left the family tree she'd been working on with me. I learned all of it. I liked learning about the family, even though my parents didn't really want me to."

Glor said, "Well, I'm glad you came. I'm not surprised the rest of your family isn't here."

Ke'lir said, "Dad was definitely overly optimistic. I didn't want to go to the ICS personally, but I'm glad we did. Otherwise, I doubt Paul would have gotten a chance to come with us."

Glor could see Re'liro walking toward them. He stood up.

Glor said, "Hi, cousin Re'liro." They hugged.

"Re'liro!" A shout from several yards away made them all turn toward it.

Paul saw a bunch of folks he did not recognize, except for their family resemblance, which suggested they were part of his extended family.

"Khalid!" Re'liro said and rushed toward the tall man with dark hair and a rather large nose. Paul knew Khalid was his father's age. Khalid's spouse Kira was great-aunt Leticia's granddaughter. Their adult children must be Cassie and Amadu.

Amadu clearly knew Glor and said, "How was the meeting here in New Orleans?"

Glor answered, "It was fine, I guess. I feel a little new at it, and the role is pretty low-key."

Paul was increasingly feeling left out. Although all of these family members knew each other well, he had not met most of them.

Glor said, "Hey, Amadu, let me introduce you to Paul. He's Julia's son."

"Paul, this is Amadu."

Paul stood up. "Hi, Amadu."

"Good to meet you." They shook hands.

He sat down and watched while his family—people he felt tied to, but barely knew, talk to each other animatedly about their lives. He felt bereft. Not bereft of the life he'd left, he felt clarity that this was the right choice. But bereft of a life he could have known: a life with these people. And he didn't know what he would do after the funeral. What would his life be like now that he couldn't, and didn't want to, go home?

### Hol'venif, Rel'toro, Casiti

Ro'mer z Kadarin was furiously making arrangements at their desk in the morning. Great-grandmother Beatrice's funeral was tomorrow, and they were about to be inundated with family from New Earth. At this point, most of their illustrious clan lived there, and most of them would make it back here for the funeral.

There was a lot to get done. Ro'mer had found places for all of the family to stay. Paul would be staying here, in the Kadarin family house. For some reason, their uncle Re'liro had been incredibly optimistic that Aunt Julia would come with all of her family. Ro'mer knew better, even though they'd known that their family house would have had plenty of room to house them. Having spent a lot of time with great-aunt Marianne, they knew that Julia would likely never set foot back on Casiti. They were surprised and a little concerned about Paul. He was young and an unknown quantity. Ro'mer had been told that not only had he never been to Casiti—he'd never been out of that backwater called the Independent Christian State.

Because it was winter, all the activities would be indoors. And it was somewhat of a disruption in the lifestyle of the season. Most people didn't travel much during the month of Musb. Ro'mer's pregnant co-parent had been a fantastic help. She, along with several members of their family group, handled all the food for the celebration after the funeral. It was way more food than their house had available - she was going to have to gather food from a lot of people and co-ops to make it work. But Beatrice was well-loved on Casiti, so it wasn't a struggle.

On Ro'mer's plate at this moment were the seating arrangements for the funeral. Beatrice wanted a more traditional Terran funeral, which included a time when people all sat and heard music and people speaking about Beatrice's life. And Ro'mer knew that although most Casitians wouldn't care where and who they were seated with, the Kinder and Terrans would. Great-grandmother Beatrice's children were easy. They and their spouses or current companions would sit together in the front row of the circle on one side. On the other side would be Casitian, Terran, and Kinder leadership. There were several family members in that group, including his cousin Zrel, a Terran representative and the current leader of the council, Ro'mer themself, a Casitian member of the council, and Ro'mer's cousin Hrelr, a Kinder member of the council.

Hrelr was the first of the Michaelson clan to represent the Kinder on the council. Ro'mer's mother had been the first of the clan to represent Casitians. In each case, there was some opposition to those appointments, but the family had enough influence in all three communities that it had worked out just fine. It had also helped that Ro'mer's mother was a Kadarin as well as a Michaelson descendent - the Kadarin family was illustrious on Casiti for its own reasons, spanning well before re-contact with Earth. Ro'mer's appointment as the second in the family to represent Casitians had faced no opposition at all.

It was both the great blessing and the great curse of his family. Because of their history, and particularly the history of Ro'mer's great-great-aunt Marianne Michaelson and her long-time Casitian partner Ja'el z Kadarin, and their great-grandparents Beatrice and Ngellin from Hilcyon, their family was a mixture of all three communities—all three cultures. At times, they were somehow a cohesive whole, and at other times, fractured by their differences. It seemed that somehow, the family kept trying to be the example for the unity of all of humanity, except that they often failed at it.

The worst example, of course, was Ro'mer's cousin Julia, who lived in that backwards cultish enclave that proclaimed that the sin of humanity had been to listen to the Casitians. They didn't really understand how Julia got involved there. She'd grown up on Casiti.

But then he had to remember that the ICS did have a legacy in his family. Both great-grandmother Beatrice and great-aunt Leticia grew up there, and even though they left as young adults, it still played an outsized role in their family psyche.

Ro'mer tore themselves away from those thoughts and returned to work on the seating arrangements.

After some time, Ro'mer heard a soft chime at the door. They got up and left the room to find that one of their family group had opened the door. Ro'mer felt the blast of frigid air that preceded two people, one of whom he recognized as his mother's long-time companion, Je'lin.

Ro'mer took over the door and said in Casitian, "Je'lin, come in."

She spoke in English, "I bring you Paul from New Earth. The entire family has now arrived on Casiti and is settling in."

Ro'mer smiled as Paul started to unwind what Ro'mer assumed was a borrowed heavy scarf from around his head and face.

Paul said, "It's really cold!"

"It's winter, Paul. And winter on Casiti is way colder than anything on New Earth."

He shivered. "Well, at least it's warm inside."

Je'lin switched back to Casitian, as English was not her first language, "Sorry, Ro'mer, I can't stay. Your mother is beside herself at the moment because your grandmother is inconsolable."

"I understand. Thank you for bringing Paul."

"Will you be alright with him? Everyone says..."

"No worries, Je'lin. It will be fine." Ro'mer switched back to English. "I'll see you at the funeral."

Je'lin nodded and walked out the door. Ro'mer closed it behind her.

"So, Paul, I want you to make yourself at home. This house is pretty large, but it's hard to get lost in. Let me show you around."

"OK."

"This is the gathering space where we spend time together as a family group. Over there," Ro'mer pointed toward the kitchen, "is the kitchen. Over here is what you would call the bathroom."

They walked in, and Ro'mer could feel and see the confusion coming from Paul.

"It's..."

"It's communal. Expect to find other people here when you come in."

The bath was standard for family groups. It had a huge, deep, circular tub in the center, always full of circulating hot water, with benches for people to sit on. There was a large sauna in the corner, a row of sinks, and some toilets connected to the reclamation system.

They left the bathroom, and Ro'mer pointed. "On that side of the house on this floor are the rooms for our elders, and upstairs are the rooms for the parents and children."

They led Paul down a hall and opened a large door. "Down here is the guest suite - there are several rooms. You're the only guest this week, so it's all yours—pick any room and bed you please. There is a chest next to each bed for your stuff."

"Um, are all Casitian houses like this?"

"No. Not at all. We're in a family house designed to raise children and care for elders. Most Casitian houses are much, much smaller, as they generally house only one or two people. Fifteen of us live here, plus several children of varied ages. Anyway, I'll let you settle in. Are you hungry?"

Paul nodded.

"OK, meet me in the kitchen when you are done putting your stuff in the guest room."

Paul went into the guest room, and Ro'mer went into the kitchen to see if there was something vaguely Terran to cook. Luckily, one of his family members loved sandwiches, so Ro'mer did his best to make a sandwich that Paul might deem edible.

After a brief while, Paul entered the kitchen. He was dressed somewhat strangely. Ro'mer guessed it was the dress of his region on New Earth, but he'd certainly never seen anyone dress this way. He had on a dark-colored heavy shirt kind of thing and then a lighter shirt underneath with wide triangular collars. A strange strip of cloth went from around his neck down the front of his shirt. His pants were a little more familiar to Ro'mer, although they were tighter and made of the same dark fabric as the heavy shirt—a fabric he hadn't ever seen. Paul didn't look especially comfortable in those clothes.

"Paul, would you like something more comfortable to wear?"

Paul looked down at his clothes as if he'd just noticed what he was wearing.

"Um, sure. These are my... church clothes. I didn't have a chance to change them before the trip—I left in kind of a hurry. And I didn't get to take a whole lot of other clothes with me because..."

"Don't worry. You are about the same size as I am. Sit and eat this sandwich here, and I'll get you some other clothes."

"OK, thanks. I didn't know you had sandwiches on Casiti."

Ro'mer smiled. "One of my family group loves Terran food, so there is a lot of it around. I hope you like the sandwich. It has cheese."

"Thanks!" Paul smiled.

Ro'mer picked out clothes they thought Paul could handle—nothing too Casitian. Ro'mer chose the clothes they generally traveled with when they went to New Earth. They picked a comfortable pair of pants made of thicker material so that Paul could stay a bit warmer and a short tunic and thick vest to go over it. They also grabbed one of their old coats that they never wore - Paul would need something for the outdoors, and Ro'mer figured Paul would prefer a coat rather than a cloak. They left the clothes on the bed with Paul's bag. When Ro'mer arrived back in the kitchen, the sandwich was already gone.

"Well, you made light work of that."

"I guess I was hungrier than I thought. I didn't think Casitians had cheese."

"About twenty Casitian years ago, some farmers imported goats and sheep, so there has been Casitian cheese for a while now. Anyway, third meal will be in just a little while, but I can make you another sandwich..."

"No, no, it's OK. I can wait for di... third meal. I think I want to take a little nap—my sleep cycle is completely fried."

"Yes, it will take a while to get used to the new time and the different day length."

"So short."

"Yes, compared to New Earth, it is short."

Ro'mer watched Paul leave and go to the guest room. They worried a little about what life on Casiti would be like for him.

### Hol'venif, Rel'toro, Casiti

"Thanks, Ra'el. I appreciate you letting me stay here."

"Ke'lir, it's nothing."

"Well, this whole thing interrupted your Musb..."

Ra'el smiled, and waved her hand in the air. "It's alright. The interruption will be over soon enough. Winter is a whole of your years long, remember?"

Ke'lir laughed. "Right. I keep forgetting. We don't even have winter."

"Indeed you don't. Before we decided to be companions this winter, Ve'ril threatened to move to New Earth because he was tired of Casitian winters. But I love them."

As if on cue, Ve'ril came into the room, bearing a steaming platter of vegetables.

"I might yet move to New Earth, Ra'el."

"Yes, yes, I know Ve'ril. I know."

"Some of New Earth is not so great, but where I live, up in the North Circumpolar IZ, is really nice. It is not so crowded and has weather you might find suitable. Most people find it too cold."

They sat around the table and ate, discussing the news of the community. Ke'lir always loved being on Casiti to visit, but she couldn't imagine living here full time. Winters that were a year long? Not for her. Besides, she'd miss Lake Superior. She'd heard that Loc'deher was beautiful, but it was pretty overrun by Terrans, and none of her family lived there at the moment. And, for her, family was what mattered.

After dinner, she retired to the guest room to record in her journal. Her experience traveling to Casiti with the family had had its very interesting moments, especially the conversation she, Paul, and Glor had had on the transport to Casiti. It had started with an innocent question of Paul's.

"Ke'lir, why do most people in our family have weird names, even though everyone is Terran?"

Glor said, "Everyone is **not** Terran! How dare you..."

Ke'lir put her hand on Glor's arm. "Glor, let's take this one step at a time, shall we? Paul, what do you mean by weird?"

"Well, in my town, everybody has names like Mary, Paul, Jonathon, and... you know, *regular* names."

Ke'lir said, "Yes, those are all Terran names. Further, they are all names from one particular subculture of one country on Earth."

"What do you mean by that?"

"What do you mean what do I mean? I don't understand what you are asking."

Paul looked down. "Never mind."

"No, Paul, look, I want to be able to explain it to you, but to do that, I need to get a sense of what you know."

"Obviously, I know nothing. I'm beginning to understand that I no longer know what's true."

Glor said, "You live in a little backwater that no one pays attention to anymore. That's what's true."

"Glor, that's not fair. Give Paul a break. It wasn't his choice."

"It was his mother's. His mother, daughter of the great Marianne's namesake. Her choice to live in that pit."

"Yes, OK, it was her choice. But that doesn't mean we can't help Paul figure things out."

Glor got up. "He can figure things out on someone else's time, not mine."

Ke'lir felt some degree of responsibility to Paul. A responsibility she couldn't explain but was unwilling to part with. There was time after the funeral. She wasn't planning to go back to New Earth for a while. She'd spend some time with Paul and orient him as best as she could. She knew he was going to have a rough time of it.

On the other hand, she was going to love being on Casiti. She hadn't been around for a couple of years, and she always had a fun time. She felt part of the Casitian culture, even though she grew up and lived on New Earth. Her co-parents had done everything to ensure she had a true Casitian childhood. However, she knew full well that she had more than 1/2 Terran ancestry. Ancestry that she took very seriously. Sometimes, the mix was complicated to keep together in her head, but other times, it seemed to all make perfect sense—her Casitian culture and her Michaelson family.

### North Capital Region, Hilcyon

Mrin crawled backward through the narrow conduit while dust fell off of the roof as his back scraped it. He tried to avoid getting any of it in his face. It had been many years since anyone had been through here. It would be a very long time before anyone else bothered. It was the tenth conduit he had been exploring in as many weeks. These were old conduits, long bereft of water. It was clear that the water pumping system here was not salvageable: the fusion reactor was dead, and the components were completely fried.

The last conduit he had explored had been a successful fix after several complete failures. He'd gotten the melt-pump system back up and running, and there was now a little bit more water going down into the North-central viaduct than there had been before. In the big scheme of things, it was a minor victory, and his chief was taking full advantage of it.

He got out of the conduit, dusted himself off as much as possible, shouldered his equipment pack, and started his long hike back to the maintenance building. His chief would not be happy today. None of the other water engineers had had luck, either. He was always the most successful—if something could be fixed, he could fix it. He went to the locker room and put on a clean uniform. He walked to his chief's office and knocked quietly.

"Come in." His chief had lost weight lately, as they all had. For some reason, he looked particularly haggard today. He had stubble on his head—that was a bad sign.

"Chief Jlen, bad news today."

"More bad news?"

"Conduit 34j has a completely unfixable melt-pump system. All of the units are redlined, and the fusion reactor is dead. Most of them need a new silicon triple liquid processor. The rest need some other parts. None of which we have any more of."

"There was no way to…"

"Not with this one. With Conduit 31p, there were only three bad units, and the reactor was still functioning well. I could use parts to make two of them work again, putting the whole system in that conduit back online. But here…"

"Alright. Thank you. How many more conduits are in your survey?"

"Just six more sir."

"Six. And we got only one to work so far?"

"That's correct. I hope that others have had…"

"No. None of the others have had any success. In fact, I need you to go check out Conduit 21a when you are finished with this batch. I suspect you might be able to resurrect it. Hrol could not."

"Sir…?"

"Yes."

"What is going to happen now? If we can't get more water to the North-central growing region…"

"People will starve."

"There must be another way, sir. What about contacting…"

"Supreme Chief Klef will never contact the Breft. Ever. He would rather us all starve."

"Sir..."

"Nevermind. Take a day off tomorrow; you deserve it."

"Um, thank you, sir."

He left the maintenance building and got on the tram back to his hamlet. As he looked absently at the reddish-brown terrain, he was glad he wasn't in his chief's position—but somehow, something had to change. They were in deep trouble, and he didn't want it to get worse than it already was. But it would inevitably get worse as more and more of the advanced units provided by the Breft broke. Although he was only responsible for one part of the conduits in one part of the planet, he knew that they all were sharing the same fate.

He arrived home, the home he shared with his parents and sister. He had not chosen a wife yet, and his sister had so far refused to marry. It was a good thing she spent all of her time helping women give birth. She was the most sought-after midwife in the region. It was also a good thing that their parents were secret reformers. They didn't care if either of them did what was expected. It did cause them strife with his grandparents, who were all outraged at his and his sister's delay in creating families.

He could smell the breadmufs baking in the oven. His mouth watered, and his stomach grumbled. Over the past while, he hadn't noticed his hunger much. But right now, he was ravenous. His father was sitting on a bench, reading.

"Hi, Da."

"Well, hello, son. How was your day? Any success?"

"Nope, not today. It's bad out there, Da."

"Hundreds have starved this year."

"More will starve next year. Just our section has had five unfixable conduit failures. I might manage to scrounge the parts to fix one of them, but..."

His father sighed. "Our movement is too fragile for us to step in. I have heard that some towns are starting to require loyalty oaths in order to get food. People are too scared."

"I know, Da. I'm doing what I can."

"I'm proud of you."

"Dinner is ready," his mother called from the kitchen.

"Where's Dlen?"

His mother said, "She's off delivering a baby—all the way over in Brun. She won't be back for a few days. I think she must have timed this perfectly to miss my parents' visit tomorrow."

Mrin groaned. He'd forgotten all about it. His grandparents, particularly on his mother's side, were conservative and took every chance to berate his parents about the lack of marriage of both of their children. Mrin knew that Dlen just simply didn't want to be tied down. She liked her autonomy. Mrin didn't have a good reason—he just hadn't found the right woman, he guessed.

"Well, I do have the day off tomorrow. I can help get things ready. I know it's always a big deal for you, Ma."

"Mrin, such a sweetheart!"

They sat down to eat. Mrin couldn't help but notice how meager the meal was.

"Are we getting our proper ration?"

His father sighed. "Let's not discuss this now, please?"

"Da! What's going on?"

"When I went to get our ration today, the board had only two rations for our family. When I asked why, they explained we were being punished for having an unmarried male in the house. When you marry and bring your wife into the house, they will raise the ration to five. But not before. Apparently, this is the new policy."

Mrin didn't realize that his personal reticence to marry would have such a negative impact on the family. He didn't quite know what to say. But he did admit that he now had no choice in the matter. He certainly was not going to let his parents and sister starve.

### Capital Region, Hilcyon

Jorn lost himself in the rhythm and cadence of the service. He was used to it. After more than 20 years as a priest, it came naturally to him. And his love for his people, the ritual, and the Exalted King propelled him forward.

After the service ended and he was gathering the ritual objects, Jorn saw Ylorp sitting on a bench after everyone had left. He looked troubled, as usual. Jorn knew that Ylorp wanted to dedicate himself to the Exalted King but felt stuck where he was - a married man with children. Jorn went over to Ylorp and sat down next to him.

"You look troubled, son. How can I be of help to you?"

Ylorp said, "Father, I had a meeting with Supreme Chief Klef yesterday. It's troubling me."

"How is it troubling you?"

"He knows my family history—my father, who was deemed a traitor, and my grandfather, Willm, the famous Supreme Chief. And he knows I am still unblooded.

"He told me of a group of Second and Third Chiefs that he wants me to join. This group's role is to ferret out dissent. He wants us to track dissidents and punish them. I don't know how well I can do that.

"And, while I was there, the First Chief of Food and Water, Zrok, burst in to give his report. Water levels are at dangerously low levels, and Zrok wanted Klef to contact the Breft. Klef reminded Zrok that he would never, ever contact the Breft because of the pledge my grandfather made!"

Jorn put his hand on Ylorp's arm, to steady and calm him. "The Exalted King knows your heart, Ylorp. Do the job you were given. Be obedient to the Supreme Chief, and to the Exalted King."

Ylorp nodded, but Jorn could tell that he was still troubled. Ylorp left, and as Jorn walked back to his cell for prayer, he knew he would be praying fervently for Ylorp.

Fifteen days later, a monk told Jorn about the challenge match between the Supreme Chief and First Chief Zrok. Priests never went to matches in priestly garb but occasionally went to matches in plain clothes. Even though people knew they were priests - they were the only men allowed to go unshaven, they went largely to get a sense of how people were feeling and what the challenge meant to them. It felt important to Jorn to see this one.

As he sat with hundreds of others in the main Capital Ring, where all battles for Supreme Chief were held, he was silently rooting for Zrok. He could hear others who were not so silent. So many of them knew what was at stake. They knew that if Zrok won, there would be change and perhaps less starvation. As he watched the match, he realized that Zrok was no match for Klef. The final moment, when Klef sliced off Zrok's head, was etched into his mind for a very long time.

That night, as he rose for middle-night prayers, he thought about what had happened and what was happening. He worried about his people and the planet. He prayed for all of them. And he wished the soul of Zrok speed on his great journey. And he fervently prayed to the Exalted King that change could come soon.

### Brun, Hilcyon

"Push!" Dlen was kneeling between Prun's legs. She could see the head of the baby crown. "You're almost there, Prun."

"Ahhhhhh..."

"Again, push!"

The baby finally came out into Dlen's hands. Each time she did this, she was reminded of the miracle of it—the gift of a new life. She examined the babe. It was a boy, and in fine shape. She tied off the umbilical cord, then wrapped the baby in a blanket and gave it to the mother.

"You have a healthy son, Prun."

Prun started to cry with the baby in her arms.

"What is his name?"

"His name is Ylen, after my great-great-grandfather."

"The Supreme Chief?"

"Yes."

"Such a wonderful name."

"Yes. Our family has always cherished his memory."

Dlen nodded. There were many families like Prun's. Families like hers. Descendants of the reformers that failed but somehow kept hope alive of new reforms, a new revolution. Dlen helped clean up while the dula assisted Prun. Tonight, Dlen was staying with an old friend and her husband, someone she hadn't seen in a while. She was exhausted but looking forward to spending time with Mrel tonight.

On her way out, Prun's husband pressed into her hand a small number of credit chits.

"I'm sorry it can't be more."

"It's alright. I understand." The amount, even small, touched her, given how hard things were now.

He said, "Our standard ration costs more and more these days. Anyway, thank you so much for coming all the way to Brun."

"You are welcome. I wish you and your family the best."

Dlen left, and walked the two stats to her friends' house. It was late, and there weren't many people in the streets. These days, most people stayed home when they weren't at work. Doing anything else took energy, and with the food shortages, people didn't have much in the way of spare energy.

She arrived at her friend's door. It was strange. There looked to be no one home. She knocked and knocked, but there was no answer.

A question came from her left, "Looking for Trin and Mrel?" She could see a man standing in the shadow of his doorway.

"Yes."

"They are gone."

"Gone? Where?"

"Dead. Trin died three days ago, and Mrel died yesterday."

"Died?" She couldn't get her mind to believe it.

The man spit. "The traitors refused the loyalty oath, and couldn't find food anywhere. They starved."

Dlen felt the tears flowing down her cheeks before she realized she was crying. She didn't even know what to say. And she didn't know where to go. The trams had already closed down, and inns didn't take in single women. She was momentarily confused and riddled with grief. She realized she would have to go back to Prun's. As she walked slowly, tears still streaming down her face, she remembered Mrel. They had grown up together until her father moved to Brun for a special position. They had played together, and Dlen always had a place in her heart for Mrel. She saw Mrel only occasionally, but it was always joyous and comfortable. Mrel and Trin were much like Dlen and her family, wanting change, wanting something new. It was sad beyond her ability to bear that they both were gone.

She arrived at Prun's and was gracefully taken in. She stayed there until morning, refusing their offers of food, and went to the tram to go home. Her sadness, she imagined, would be there for a very long time.

# Chapter 2:
# Family Histories

New Earth: December 2098
Casiti: Musb 803
Hilcyon: Sdert 1201

*"We were brought together from all over our home, all kinds, all shapes, all colors. The Exalted King, for reasons of his own, decided this. So we will celebrate this, this being together when we never really knew each other existed.*

*"We must be unified, and speak with one voice, be one people. We must be united, otherwise, we all suffer." Heart of the Carj, Eclogue 1*

### Hol'venif, Rel'toro, Casiti

It was dark in the guest room, but Paul could hear sounds from the common space. People seemed to be up and about, and moving around. He, on the other hand, had no interest in getting out of bed. First, it was cold. He had lots of blankets, but he could feel the cool air on his head. He was dog-tired from the trip, and time changes. He didn't even know what time it was. Casiti had a day that was just over half of the length of the day he was used to. Casitians only slept during one period of the day, which seemed weird to him. No mid-day sleep, no night-time work period.

What really made him want to stay under the covers was he was completely overwhelmed. At the time, leaving the ICS felt like the best decision, but now, he wondered. Everything was different than he expected, and nothing was familiar. The trip from his house to New Orleans was, if anything, completely surreal. He had no idea that a couple of hours away was an entirely different world. Clean, tree-lined, and well-kept streets. Buildings that were taller than any he'd ever seen, silent vehicles zipping to and fro, people dressed in all different ways. He felt like an infant, seeing the world for the first time.

And he had to urinate, but the last thing in the world he wanted to do was use the large communal bathing room. When he'd used it last night, there were several other people there, lounging around in the tub. He was embarrassed. Everyone here seemed to take nudity in stride, but where he was from, one only showed nudity with a spouse. This casual nudity was very difficult for him.

Everyone had been very sweet, friendly and helpful, which somehow made the whole thing worse. He could handle the perversion of their semi-public nudity, but to combine that with the reality of his experience in their presence was disconcerting. He found everyone to be more open, honest, and loving than anyone he'd ever met before, and he didn't know what to do with that. He expected perversion, but he had been taught that the Casitians were full of duplicity and meanness, and there was nothing like that.

Finally, his bladder won. He got up, and opened the door, and went out of the hall into the main house.

"Paul, good morning." He looked up to see Mi'nali, who he'd been introduced to yesterday. Mi'nali was Ro'mer's co-parent. The whole Casitian family thing had totally confused him.

"Good morning, Mi'nali."

"There is breakfast in the kitchen, although most of the family group has eaten. Take your time, there is no hurry. The funeral isn't for another hour."

"Only an hour?"

"A Casitian hour—I think equivalent to about four of your hours."

"Oh, alright, thanks." Paul went toward the bathing room with his head down. As he walked in, he noticed he would be all alone. He relaxed.

Afterwards, he was sitting in the kitchen, eating the unfamiliar breakfast in front of him. He had to admit that he liked it, even though it wasn't what he'd normally eat. Some sort of grain, with some odd-tasting fruit mixed in. Plus a strange-tasting hot beverage which was sort of a mix of coffee and fruity tea.

"Like the fuge?" He looked up to see Ro'mer walk into the kitchen.

"Fuge?"

"That's the hot drink you're drinking."

23

"It's good. A little unfamiliar. But I like it."

"It doesn't have the kick of coffee."

"You've had coffee?"

"Of course. We've had just about every kind of Terran food and drink imported to Casiti. Coffee was one of the early big hits, back when we still had access to Earth."

Ro'mer's casual mention of Earth, something no one casually mentioned at home, brought up a flood of feelings for Paul.

"Ro'mer, can you explain why God banished us from Earth? Everyone says it was the sins of our family."

Paul could see some struggle in Ro'mer's face, and it made him wonder whether his family was right all along.

"Paul, who you call 'God' didn't banish us from Earth. Basically, we banished ourselves."

"What? I don't understand."

Ro'mer got up, and came back with a slim tablet. He spoke into it in a language Paul didn't understand.

"Here. Read this." Ro'mer handed Paul the tablet. "It's a fairly balanced history of what was called the 'Casitian Crisis' on Earth, and its aftermath, which included our leaving Earth. Terrans and Casitians have somewhat different opinions about what happened, although I think a consensus is emerging. But read it—I think it will be educational for you. It will also tell you a lot about your great-great aunt Marianne, your grandmother's namesake, and her partner Ja'el, who was a member of the Kadarin family."

"Thanks."

"Oh, and also, when you are finished with that, you can ask the tablet to bring up a book called 'Spirits Alike' by an author named Jal'end'a. I think you'll like it."

"OK." Paul was a little puzzled, but he'd remember. It did sound interesting.

"Paul, do you need any clothes to wear at the funeral?"

"Well, I brought my black suit..."

"Black is not considered a proper color at a funeral, Paul. Not on Casiti."

"I see."

"We mostly wear white, or bright colors. Not dull colors or black. Even though Beatrice wanted a traditional Terran funeral, her children decided that since it was going to be on Casiti, it would have some Casitian elements. There are going to be some Terran and Kinder elements too."

"Well, I don't have anything white, or bright."

"I figured as much. I found an outfit for you that I think you'll like."

Later, as Paul sat in the large, circular room, he watched his family and the many others who had gathered for the funeral. He had only been to one funeral in his life. Three years ago, his father's father had died suddenly, and they had the funeral in their church. Paul couldn't even compare that to this. It had been a dour affair, and rather unpleasant. This was nothing like it. His extended family, wearing bright colors and sitting on pillows and chairs mostly in the first two rows of the circle were chatting with each other animatedly, and others in the room seemed almost happy. He couldn't quite understand it.

He was sad. He didn't know his great-grandmother very well, but somehow he knew love for her, and it was hard knowing that he'd never see her again. He realized that each time she visited, she had shown him a tiny little bit of this life—this colorful, happy life. And those visits were at an end. Then, in a rush, he realized that he could have this colorful, happy life if he wanted it. But did he really want it?

Several days later, Paul and Glor were sitting at a corner table at a small Earth-themed cafe near the Kadarin family house. Paul appreciated this place because it reminded him just a tiny bit of home. The cafes in the ICS weren't all that great. This one was far better. But it felt a little familiar.

Glor asked Paul, "Are you staying here on Casiti for a while?"

Paul answered, "I guess. I don't really have anywhere else to go right now."

"It's nice here. If you get tired of the Casitians, you can go visit Loc'deher. Lots of Terrans there, and the weather is decent. Jul'when is horribly cold in the winter, but it has a lot of Terrans, too."

"Colder than here?? Wow. Yeah, I might travel around. Are you going to continue living on New Earth for a long time?"

"Absolutely. My dad has wanted all Kinder to live together in Zwek, the Kinder region on New Earth, for a long time, and that is coming to fruition finally. I'm frankly not much of a fan of Casitians."

"The perversions?"

Glor looked confused, and Paul felt defensive. Glor asked, "What do you mean?"

"Well, you know, the companion thing."

"Oh, yeah, I don't get why they do that, it is weird. We Kinder do life partners."

"Have you found the right woman yet?"

"No. I haven't yet. I am a bit jealous of my best friend Flis, who found a wonderful man to be his partner."

Paul felt a flush and confusion. He couldn't understand why he was reacting the way he was, but he felt some deep embarrassment.

He finally said, "I thought all Kinder were normal, like us."

"What do you mean, *normal?*" Paul could tell Glor was angry.

"You know... men and women normal."

Glor got up. "Paul, you are a backwards asshole, you know that?"

"What, what did I say?"

"Fuck you. Ask Ke'lir. *She* seems to be willing to educate you. I'm not." Glor left quickly and didn't look back.

Paul felt horrible. He somehow knew he'd said something wrong, but he didn't really understand why it was affecting him the way it was. Nothing he had learned in his life seemed to be true. He didn't know what to do.

He left the cafe and went back to the family house, where he sulked around for a while. He wondered whether Glor would ever speak to him again.

A few days later, he recorded a message to Glor.

"Glor, look, sorry for what happened before at the cafe. All of this is so new to me, and I'm learning how much of what I was taught was just plain wrong. I'm confused and trying my best. I hope you understand."

Paul knew he couldn't go back to the life he'd had, and the things he'd taken for granted. But he didn't know where to turn.

## Hol'venif, Rel'toro, Casiti

Ke'lir was fidgeting. She was tired, and the service had gone on a lot longer than she thought it would. And plus, Paul, who was sitting next to her, would keep whispering questions at her, and she had to finally insist that he stop, and she would explain everything later. She could tell it wasn't satisfying him.

She'd spent some time with great-grandmother Beatrice over the years, but she was always somehow, even alive, this legendary figure, like Beatrice's two older sisters, Marianne and Leticia. And all three of them held statures that felt impossible for Ke'lir to even think about being like, but yet, she knew that her family, as well as many Casitians and humans from New Earth, expected her generation of Michaelsons to do great things. So far, though, there didn't seem much in her generation to admire. Paul was a total unknown and Glor, although he was given a position in the New Earth government, was combative and sometimes downright sullen. Liam seemed to care more about parties than politics, and Cassie and Amadu also seemed to Ke'lir to be not very serious in their approaches to life. The one exception was Tricia, ten years older than Ke'lir, who was vice president of the New Earth Authority, and likely to become it's president someday.

Ke'lir herself hadn't really figured out her path. She liked technology and had been assigned to the New Earth Agency Technology Committee. The work was engaging and enjoyable, but she didn't know how that was going to translate into something worthy of her family.

She was roused out of her reverie by a man who looked older than any person Ke'lir had ever seen. He walked into the center of the circle and stood with a stooped stature. It was still the time of remembrance, which Ke'lir thought, and hoped, was toward the end of the rather long funeral service.

"I remember meeting Beatrice for the first time when I piloted the ship that brought her home. She had just lost her first husband, Pkygy, and she was sad, but she had a strength that surprised me—the strength of character we all got to know. She had learned a lot during her time on Hilcyon, and I know that she effected change on Hilcyon—change we might not see for many years in the future."

Ke'lir remembered that strength of character. That steel in great-grandmother's eyes, and manner. A gentle and compassionate strength. She had never served on the Consej, but her influence was greatly felt. And it was she who had helped to keep the Kinder and Casitians talking to one another. Ke'lir wondered what would happen without her.

### Capital Region, Central Valley, Hilcyon

Mrin stood in front of his chief, who had summoned him urgently. He had been in the middle of attempting a repair, but Mrin was fairly sure it was a hopeless attempt.

"Mrin, I got a message from the Second Chief of water in the Central Valley region. They were digging a new tunnel to the glacier and found a huge cache of spare parts buried in a cave. It was probably left over from the uprising many years ago. Anyway, they don't have any engineers nearly as talented as you are, and they would like you to look over the cache and give them some tips about what might be there. In return, you'll get to bring back some useful parts for us."

"That's great, sir. I hope we can find a few triple-silicon liquid processors and core memory units. We could really use some of those as well."

"Go right away. Here's a ticket for the transport to the Central Valley region headquarters. An engineer will meet you there, and take you up to the cache."

"Thank you, sir." Mrin grabbed the small paper ticket from his chief.

As he sat in the transport, which was a large vehicle carrying both people and cargo on the road, he watched the hamlets get fewer and further between, then there was nothing. The headquarters of the Central Valley was a five-hour transport ride, and he settled in for the trip. He had brought a book, which, to anyone's casual perusal, was a historical account of the military exploits of a First Chief 65 years ago, who had tried to invade Nyet Grier Nro. But the book was actually a collection of the stories of Dbor. The book had been given to him by his parents a few years ago. He treasured the book, and read the stories over and over again, as did his sister. When his father gave him the book, he told the story of his grandmother Krely, who had a role in the uprising, and the mysterious Btric, who diligently gathered up the stories and started the process of having them copied over and over again, and then left to go to the planet of the Grier Nro. He and his parents were proud of that family history, although his own grandparents were ashamed of it because they felt it traitorous. His grandfather, still a Second Chief, always swore complete fealty to the Kinder way.

Eventually, he decided to try and sleep a little, and he tucked the precious book back into his bag. He was later awoken by the transport stopping. They had arrived at their destination. He got out and walked to the administrative headquarters of the Water Authority. He walked into the small building that looked to be in some state of disrepair. A man who sat at a desk in the lobby looked up as Mrin walked in.

"Can I help you? Water requests have been moved to Thirdday. So not until..."

"I'm not here for a request. I'm Mrin, sent from the Capital Region."

"Oh! The engineer. Yes, sorry. Let me take you to Jral. He's the one who will take care of you."

"Thanks." They walked down a series of halls to a tiny room with a man working at a workbench full of tools.

"Jral, here is Mrin."

"Ah! Mrin. Glad you are here. Come in." The other man left.

"I imagine you might be tired and hungry by now. It's a long, long drive up to the cave. We can do that tomorrow. You're staying with me and my family tonight."

"Thank you."

After dinner, Jral's wife was pleasant and very polite in showing him where he would sleep. He was tired from the long trip and the unfamiliar surroundings. He could tell from their dinner conversation that Jral was a traditionalist. His wife didn't even eat with them—she ate in the kitchen with Jral's young daughter. Jral's son, who was about four years younger than Mrin, had already chosen a wife, although the wedding wasn't happening until the first day of Lykl. Jral didn't say anything about the fact that Mrin still hadn't chosen a wife, but Mrin could sense judgment from both Jral and his son.

The next day, during the long drive out to the cave, Jral brought the subject up.

"So Mrin, why is a man as pleasant and good-looking as you still without a wife?"

"I guess I haven't found the right woman yet."

"What does that mean? If she's halfway pretty and can bear you at least one son, what does it matter?"

"I don't know..."

"Mrin, you know that you can't live with your parents anymore without choosing a wife."

"Yes, I know. I can't let the family suffer because of me."

"Good boy. Look, there are plenty of choices. Just make it."

Mrin nodded. He knew he didn't really have much choice, and it had been on his mind ever since he learned of the ration change. He'd found ways to eat away from home, or at least be away from home during dinner, as much as possible since then. He had considered Gren, Tyvl, and Tyrin. He liked all three of them, and Tyrin, at least was really smart, and their families shared desires for reform. He did appreciate smart women like his mother. Tyrin seemed the best choice, as he thought of it.

"All right, Mrin, we are here." Mrin looked out of the small vehicle they were driving and didn't see anything remotely resembling a cave.

"Where?"

"Five stats out that way," Jral pointed. Mrin groaned. Five stats walk would take them at least two time units.

"The ground is too unstable out there for us to drive on. We've gotta walk."

They got out, and Jral pulled a cart out of the back of the vehicle.

"This will make it a little easier to gather and transport the parts we need. What we need most, though, is your identification of the parts. You are the one who knows the most, and has had the most experience with these Breft parts."

Mrin nodded. It was an odd situation he was in. Ever since he was little, he was fascinated by Breft technology. He read everything he could find on it, and when he was an apprentice engineer, he cataloged a lot of the parts and tried to find as much documentation on them as possible. For some reason, other engineers despised working on these parts, and fewer and fewer Kinder wanted to be engineers. He was the youngest engineer by far, so it was strange to him that he was considered the most expert. But it was sadly true.

They walked toward the cave and alternated dragging the rather cumbersome cart. Mrin dragged it further than Jral just because Jral was older and seemed weaker than Mrin. In the distance, Mrin could see a small hillock appear, and then they began to descend somewhat into a gully.

"This way."

They turned sharply and rounded a curve in the gully. Mrin could see the cave entrance clearly. They left the cart at the cave entrance and went inside. Jral put a headlamp on his head, and the light shone brightly. Mrin could clearly see a door.

Jral twisted the mechanism keeping the door closed and pulled the door open, and it opened with a creak. As Mrin and Jral entered the cache, Mrin gasped. This was an amazing cache of equipment.

"Mrin, let's make this quick. Find the items we need."

"Well, I can already see a lot of this doesn't have anything to do with the water conduits."

"Well, we can ignore those..."

"But other authorities..."

"I am under strict instructions. If there are parts we can use, then we will take them. Otherwise, we leave them here."

Mrin didn't really like that, but there really wasn't much he was going to be able to do about it. He would, however, take mental notes of what was here for the future. They walked through the assorted jumble of equipment, and most of it was completely unfamiliar to Mrin. There were large cubes with complex controls with words he didn't recognize. The word "jretlr" was clearly on one of the controls. Mrin knew that was the word for "wormhole." Maybe this wasn't a cache from the uprising. Maybe this was a stash from a spaceship!

Mrin kept walking around, finding nothing really useful, although it was all interesting to him. Finally, he found a pile of assorted small parts and units in a far corner of the cave, including several triple silicon melt units, a control core, several analysis units, and some pressure valve controllers. All of these would be very useful. He saw a small unit that looked very unusual and had words on it that were not Kinder. He looked up and realized that Jral was on the other side of the cavern, looking around at something. He took the unit, which could almost fit in his open palm, and carefully placed it in his bag. He would examine it at his leisure later, but he somehow knew he didn't want Jral to see it.

After safely stashing the item, he called, "Jral!"

"Coming..." The older man arrived, out of breath.

"I found a lot of useful stuff here. We should put it all on the cart."

They spent the next time unit loading the whole pile of parts onto the cart, and Mrin did a last look around the cave. No more small mystery units, and certainly no more useful parts for the water authority.

When they arrived back at headquarters, Mrin and Jral equitably divided the parts. Well, almost equitably. Mrin noticed that Jral seemed completely uninterested in the core controllers and analysis units, so he was glad to take them. The analysis units weren't necessary, but it would be nice to have some, to at least have a sense of what was in the water they were pumping. They hadn't had a working analysis unit in all of the time that Mrin had been working on the conduits.

A few days later, Mrin was standing at the threshold of Tyrin's door. He knocked, and Mrin saw the kindly face of Tyrin's father as the door opened. He let Mrin into their cozy living room.

"Mrin! So good to see you. I imagine you wish to speak to Tyrin?"

"Yes, sir, I do. Before I do, I will tell you it is my hope to marry her. Would that meet your approval?"

"Mrin, you are a good man, and I trust you and your wonderful family. If Tyrin wishes to marry you, I certainly approve."

Mrin felt some warmth in his chest, at the same time as he was feeling his apprehension.

Tyrin's father said, "I will go get her."

Tyrin entered the living room, surprisingly to Mrin, without her father.

"Mrin, so nice to see you. How have you been?"

Tyrin was smiling, and Mrin felt his nervousness ease some.

"I'm good, Tyrin. I just got back from a trip where I was able to find some more equipment that I think will help fix more of the conduits."

"Oh, that's good to hear!"

"Anyway, I'm here to ask if you would marry me?"

He heard the way he'd asked the question, and seemed perhaps it didn't have the certainty it should have had. But she smiled broadly.

"Yes, Mrin, I will marry you. I think you are a wonderful man. And I love the idea of being part of your family."

Mrin felt the smile growing on his lips and felt relieved.

Tyrin's father and mother chose this moment to come into the living room. Mrin realized they must have been listening from wherever they were in the house.

Tyrin told them, "Mrin asked me to marry him, and I agreed."

Tyrin's mother said, "That's wonderful! I'm glad to hear you are joining his family."

Tyrin's father walked up to Mrin and slapped him on the shoulder.

"Good man! We'll arrange the ceremony to happen very soon!"

Tyrin's mother brought out some beverages and sweets. Mrin stayed for a while, sharing pleasantries with the family, said goodbye, and headed home.

The next day, at dinner, his father said, "Mrin, your mother tells me that there will be a new member of this household!"

Mrin said, "Yes, da. I've asked Tyrin to marry me, and she agreed."

"I'm glad you've found someone. I know Tyrin is a smart one."

"She is. I like that. When do you think we should have the wedding?"

"I think soon would be good. I hear there is another reduction in rations coming."

"Yes, I know. The water situation is worsening."

"Did you hear about Zrok?"

"First Chief Zrok? No. I haven't talked to anyone since I got back—I was busy using the new parts for a conduit I am trying to resurrect."

"He challenged Supreme Chief Klef."

"And...?"

"He lost. I heard it was a valiant battle, but the Supreme Chief was just that much better."

Mrin knew from the grapevine that Zrok didn't like the Supreme Chief's attitude. He, like Mrin, wanted to call the Breft and get help with their water problem. But Zrok losing would mean that someday, possibly soon, their people would starve to extinction.

Later, in his room, he pulled out the small, mysterious part he'd found in the cave. It was a large cube with rounded edges and a black square panel flush on one side of the cube. He had been mistaken in his initial quick assessment that there were no Kinder words on the device. There were some that had been clearly printed well after the manufacture of the device. These words were: "Do not, under any circumstances, activate this communications device. This device is the property of the Supreme Chief and must be only used by him."

Mrin knew that must be a device that could contact the Breft. Now that Klef was dead, there was no way Mrin would put this device in the hands of his superiors. And maybe, just maybe, he had a way to save them.

### Capital Region, Hilcyon

Dlen walked along the wall, stopping briefly at the locked gate to the temple garden. She remembered visiting once as a child when it was still open. The gate had been locked for longer than she remembered.

As she looked in, she could see that plants there were still thriving, obviously still being watered. She imagined that the priests who tended them must be limiting their own use of water to keep the garden green.

She remembered learning that so many of the plants they grew for food came directly from the Breft, and they depended on them. Something in her mind had shifted from that point on - a kind of knowledge of the inevitable—the Kinder and the Breft belonged to each other in some way. Some way still yet to be defined, she guessed.

In that moment of pondering belonging, she was reminded sharply of Mrel, who died recently. Underneath her deep grief was both anger—anger at those who forced them to starve because they would not sign a loyalty oath. She also felt deep regret. Something in her regretted not telling Mrel how she really felt: a feeling there was no space for. A kind of love there was no room for. Her heart felt heavy.

She didn't have any births to attend today, and Mrin was off in the Central Valley finding equipment for his work. She felt a sense of being untethered. She was trying to stay away from home as much as possible—finding her meals elsewhere or not eating to ensure her parents and Mrin could get enough food. She had nowhere to go today, so she headed home.

She knew that sooner or later, it was quite likely that she would starve to death. Probably sooner. They would start requiring loyalty oaths, and her parents would never sign one. Nor would she. And she knew this was likely the fate of everyone on Hilcyon, which made her angry again and then just sad. And it also made her sad to bring so many babes into a dying world.

### Capital Region, Hilcyon

Jorn sat in his monastic cell, reading aloud words from the holy book, "Secrets of the Exalted King":

"You are honored when you are compassionate.

You are honored when you give to those who are needful.

The Exalted King honors your gifts, he honors your compassion,

Because the Exalted King is generous and compassionate Himself."

The lamp on the table next to his bed flickered. The power had been spotty lately. It was almost time for midnight prayers. He had been awake for far too long, thinking about his parishioner, Ylorp, and what he was going through.

Ylorp had been following a woman who had been at a house that he was watching because it was known to have reformer meetings. She had ended up at his cousin's house.

Ylorp's cousin's father, his father's brother, had been implicated in the failed plan that had led to the execution of his father. And so he could connect the family he was watching with his cousin's family—with enough evidence to get his cousin arrested.

Ylorp had cried at having to send in that report.

Ylorp explained that the woman he had been following was Dlen Gnova Jolrs, a midwife from the capital. Jorn knew that Dlen and her father were in the reform movement. Ultimately, her being a midwife and Ylorp's cousin's wife was expecting a child provisionally cleared the cousin. But Jorn knew that the whole family was suspected, even Ylorp.

Deep in his heart, Jorn knew that Ylorp would play an important role—he just didn't know what it was. Jorn somehow knew that change would come, but he didn't understand how or when.

He heard the gentle bells for Midnight prayers and left his cell to pray with his brothers.

### Hol'venif, Rel'toro, Casiti

Ro'mer lay in bed, resisting the need to rise. They generally liked winter but found it difficult to rise well before the sun during the short winter days. But they had to rise—they had a trip planned to New Earth, which would take them away from Casiti for a few days.

One of the reasons they didn't want to get out of bed was that they would have to interact with their cousin Paul, who had become quite a challenge.

In Paul, Ro'mer occasionally saw flashes of an interesting, intriguing person, but mostly, they saw that he was consumed with his current existential crisis.

Of course, this crisis was of no surprise to Ro'mer. Paul was a teenager. A time when, on Casiti, he would be surrounded by other people his age, going on adventures and doing interesting things. Instead, he had been raised in a backward cult with little or no understanding of how things really were.

Ro'mer got up, grabbed his clothing for the day, and went into the bathing room. They saw M'nali, who was already in the tub, her increasingly protruding belly showing above the suds.

They got in, smiling, and gave her belly a gentle rub.

"How are you today?"

She smiled in return. "Doing well, although the little one feels like they want to kick their way out of my body today. Maybe it's because I have an appointment with the midwife scheduled. They want to make their presence felt."

They both laughed. Ro'mer had been to a few of the midwife appointments—particularly the ones that included imaging the fetus.

He marveled at how everything unfolded. Soon, they would have to start preparations for the birth process. It would be the first birth in the house in this generation. It was always a big party, where the whole family came back and celebrated.

Ro'mer returned to their room, packed a few things, and ran into Paul as they were going to meet M'nali, who would take them to the shuttle port.

"Hi Paul, how is it going?"

Paul said, "Uh, OK, I guess." To Ro'mer, it sounded a little sullen.

Ro'mer said, "What are you up to today?"

"Ke'lir is coming over later. Otherwise, not a lot."

Ro'mer hoped that visit would bolster Paul's spirit.

"I'm on my way to New Earth. The Consej has its quarterly convening, and I have a lot of associated meetings as well. I'll be back in about 2 New Earth weeks."

Paul nodded and didn't say anything further. Ro'mer and M'nali bundled up and walked outside to get into their family's vehicle.

Ro'mer said, "I'm worried about Paul."

"I'm not."

"Why not?"

"He's young. I had a really nice conversation with him this morning. He's lost right now, but I think he's doing a productive kind of flailing."

"I certainly hope so. I do think it was good that he got out of the ICS."

"Yes, it is a good thing. He would have been ruined and useless there."


Ro'mer's transit through the shuttle port and onto the shuttle was painless. As a member of the government, they got a comfortable cabin, which allowed them to spend the 34 hours of the transit in a setting that would provide quiet to work and sleep as they needed.

They were a Casitian representative to the Consej, the council that oversaw all humans on both Casiti and New Earth. One of their most important tasks was to transmit the results of any requests the Consej made to the Caraj, which was the body of government the Casitians had, or vice versa.

The Caraj had 12 members and was a body formed, apparently, during the period of enslavement. Ro'mer had once read a history of that august body and felt a lot of respect for it. They also knew it was full of fallible humans, some of whom were absolute enemies of any kind of change.

Many members of their illustrious Casitian family, the Kadarin, had been members of the Caraj over millennia. Their mother had been nominated at various points to join the Caraj, but because of her part-Terran ancestry, she had been rejected by the most conservative members of the Caraj. The Caraj was willing to allow Casitians with part-Terran ancestry like themself to represent Casiti on the Consej, but never be part of the governing body of Casiti.

He looked over the latest - the Caraj had requested that every item in their technology transfer from Casiti to New Earth be accompanied by an extremely detailed impact report, including environmental, economic, political, social, and even psychological! Although Ro'mer understood the concern, they felt it was a bit over the top. They knew that this primarily aimed to slow the pace of technology transfer. Ro'mer knew it would come across to the Terrans and Kinder as patronizing and demanding.

They spent the next few hours outlining the negotiation parameters. Ro'mer knew the New Earth Authority would reject this request out of hand, and it would fall to him and the other Casitian members to hammer out an agreement that the Caraj would finally agree to.

### Hol'venif, Rel'toro, Casiti

Paul was completely miserable. He'd been on Casiti for 65 days. He was counting them. He'd spent most of his time holed up in a guest room at Ro'mer's family house. Ke'lir came to visit a few times, but Paul was afraid that she'd never come back after the last visit. They'd had a terrible argument. They were discussing history, and Paul asked questions after reading the history Ro'mer gave him.

Paul said, "There is something I don't understand about why the Casitians came to Earth in the first place. My father said that you came to spread your decadence and sin. But I don't believe that."

Ke'lir said, "That's good because it's not true."

"But this history suggests that the Galactic community forced the Casitians to come to Earth."

"Well, that's an opinion. And it's subtle. I would say it was more like they *strongly persuaded* the Casitians to be involved. Casitians had been visiting Earth for many centuries before contact, and we knew Earth humans better than anyone else. It made the most sense, really."

"But the reason the Casitians and Galactics came was really the dolphins, wasn't it?"

"Yes."

"So if there hadn't been another intelligent species on Earth, would you ever have come back?"

"I don't know Paul."

"But you'd already let horrible stuff happen. For thousands of years."

"It's not that simple."

"Really, how can you say that?"

"Look, Paul..."

"Really, you Casitians are a bunch of jerks to let humanity do all that to itself before you came."

"Paul, that's not fair!"

"It is fair! You had all the technology, galactic contact, peace, and prosperity. And what did Earth have? War and strife and pain."

"You did that to yourselves!"

"What do you mean by that?"

"We had managed to evolve a peaceful society, while you all went on raping and pillaging, killing and maiming, destroying the planet..."

"And you could have stopped it!"

"Paul, you don't understand!"

She got up, got on her outer cloak and scarf, and went out, slamming the door as she did. Now, he felt regret for his angry words. But he was angry. When it was clear to him that the Casitians had let all the horrible stuff on Earth happen for so many years, he suddenly hated all of them. He couldn't understand how they could have allowed humanity to go as far as it had. And he hated that they'd allowed the ICS to exist. He really hated them, and his family, for that.

He cried for a while, feeling lost. He hated where he had come from, and he hated where he was now. He had no idea what he would do next. Somewhere in his brain, he remembered that he was going to read that second book. What was it called?

"Please give me 'Spirits Alike' by... uh, by Ja'lin... ?" He didn't remember the author's name.

His tablet spoke softly. He didn't realize it could. "Ja'lend'a. It is now available."

He tapped the icon that was the book and started to read.

# Chapter 3:
# Plenty and not enough

New Earth: April-June 2099
Hilcyon: Cfro 1201 -Mrontl 1202
Casiti: Klef 803

*"What does the Divine expect of us? What do we know about this from all traditions? The Divine demands kindness and compassion, a life of paying attention to its moments. The Divine demands, over all, that we never do to others what we hate ourselves." Ja'lend'a, 'Spirits Alike'.*

### Capital Region, Hilcyon

Dlen sat while her mother was cooking dinner for the family. Now that Mrin had wed and Tyrin was in the house, their regular rations were returned. Not that the rations were all that much food, really. Dlen could hardly remember what it had been like when she was younger, but the five rations they were getting now couldn't be anywhere near what the family used to eat. She estimated it was less than half what a family of five needed. And if Tyrin was to get pregnant... Dlen didn't want to consider what might happen. She tried to get her meals elsewhere or go without as much as she could.

Because she was in so much demand as a midwife, Dlen didn't feel much pressure to marry. That was a good thing, as she had no interest in it. She did her best as a midwife, which was a fine life for her.

"So, Ma, how is Tyrin getting along with everyone?"

"Tyrin is a sweet woman, you know. She's smart, and she thinks a lot like us. I'm glad Mrin chose her. No need to hide anything from her."

"That's good."

"One of the first things she told me was that her family had a treasured copy of the book, The Stories of Dbor."

"She wanted you to feel comfortable, letting you know she had that forbidden book."

"Yes. You'll like her."

"What's going to happen, Ma? Mrin says that eventually, all of the water conduits all over the planet will stop working. He thinks we're possibly only a year or less away from that. What happens then?"

"I don't know, Dlen. I like to think that our leaders will find compassion, contact the Breft, and save us, but I don't know that they will. Neither Dlen nor your Da thinks that will happen."

"So we all starve?"

"Yes. Or there might be a very few people left."

"How can the Supreme Chief let that happen?"

"He cares more about a principle than he cares about people, I expect. Besides, he'll be the last one to starve."

"I know. There has to be something we can do!"

"What? They hold food over our heads."

Dlen sighed. "I know. I lost Mrel to that. And I know we would never say a loyalty oath. We will starve sooner rather than later."

Her mother nodded. "But you know, Mrin is keeping us alive. Without him, I think all of the conduits would have failed already. They've sent him all over to help."

"I know. Good old Mrin."

"And his value will keep our family alive, too."

Dlen said, "Until they decide they don't value that anymore."

"Dlen, shall we talk about something else?"

"Ma, what else is there to talk about?"

### Capital Region, Hilcyon

The New Year celebration had been muted because of food shortages. Even the full rations were slim for the five of them. Mrin was hungry constantly. But he still had to go to work, hungry or not. He walked into the Water Authority building into some degree of chaos. All his colleagues were gathered around, and there was a shouting argument. He approached his bunched colleagues.

"Look, Ylon might have a more forceful style, but he'll be fine as chief."

Mrin said, "Ylon? What happened?"

Kler, who was, by far Mrin's least favorite colleague, said, "Jlen was removed yesterday by First Chief Zetl."

"What? Why?"

"Disloyalty to the Kinder way. You've seen how he feels about our current predicament. He hasn't done anything to help us become self-sufficient. He was sent to a prison colony up north yesterday."

Mrin was angry. "You don't understand anything, Kler! It's not…"

"Ah, so you are disloyal, too, eh?"

"I am not disloyal. I care about the Kinder. I don't want us to starve!"

"We must be self-sufficient. That's what Ylon will help us to do."

Mrin said, "I see. And I'm assuming you are the one going to go out on a glacier and get us water. By what? Breathing on it?"

Kler shouted, "Traitor," and swung a punch. Mrin ducked, dodged, and stepped back. "I'm going to work now. I don't know what the rest of you are doing."

Kler said, "Watch yourself, boy. You might have finally gotten a wife, but I'm watching you."

Mrin knew this to be the truth. He left the knot of his colleagues, and went back to the locker room, preparing to go to conduit 39a, which needed some maintenance. It was one of the few left working, and Mrin wanted to make sure it kept working.

A colleague entered the locker room. "You need to be careful, Mrin. They are looking for any excuse anyone can find to drop people from rations."

"I have a wife to take care of now!"

"I don't think that matters anymore."

"Yeah, I don't imagine it does."

Mrin went out to do his work, and kept his head down all day, thinking of what life would be like under chief Ylon. He didn't have so long to find out. When he arrived back, he was told that Ylon wanted to see him. He changed to a clean uniform and went to Ylon's office.

"Chief Ylon, Mrin Gnova Jolrs reporting. Congratulations on your new appointment, sir."

Ylon looked up, frowning.

"Thank you. You are being re-assigned."

"Re-assigned?"

"Yes. I'm sending a team up to Jarth Glacier. You'll be hauling ice blocks off of the glacier by cart, and dropping them into Reservoir 2a, which is currently dry."

Mrin struggled. On one hand, questioning Ylon's order would likely have bad consequences. But he didn't know whether or not Ylon understood that he was the one most skilled at fixing the equipment.

"Alright, sir. May I ask a question?"

"You may."

"I had three conduits on my list to check for repairs, and if I'm..."

"We won't be doing any more repairs. We know the equipment will fail eventually, and we need to learn how to get the water on our own. After this proof-of-concept trip, I'll be asking you to clean out the conduits of any galactic technology so water from our glacier efforts can flow."

"I understand. I wonder..."

"You are dismissed," Ylon said forcefully.

"Yes, sir."

Mrin had no idea how Ylon had in mind for them to get ice blocks from the glacier, or for ways to get water through the conduits without the galactic melters. The last time it was attempted, using solar reflectors, the amount of water they could liberate from the glacier was minuscule compared to the water generated by the melters. Mrin could not imagine carving out ice blocks would be much better.

He went home and told the whole story to his family over dinner. He was glad that all of them commiserated with him, and he felt good that Tyrin, like him, cared more about the people than whatever was defined as the "Kinder way."

### Capital Region, Hilcyon

Jorn stood up from the waking prayer with a few other priests—many priests chose to do the waking prayers in their cells alone. Jorn usually liked company.

"Jorn." He turned and saw a familiar, older priest, the assistant to Lronr, the head priest of his temple.

"Yes, how may I be of service?"

"Lronr would like to speak with you just after you break your fast."

"Do you know why?"

"Just go see him."

Jorn nodded and went to the dining hall to break his fast. After a quick meal of porridge, where the portion seemed rather meager to Jorn this morning, he walked down the long hall and up the stairs to the head priest's chambers.

He didn't often find himself here. There were many priests at this temple, and although he'd been in the priesthood for 20 years, he was still young and was also never especially ambitious.

He stood in front of the door to Lronr's chambers and knocked firmly.

"Yes, come."

As he walked in, he smelled the scent of incense.

"Jorn, thank you for coming. Please, sit."

Jorn sat in the chair facing the head priest. They were separated by a small table with a book he did not recognize.

"Jorn, you have been a faithful priest for 20 years now."

Jorn nodded.

"I have a question for you. What think you of the Breft?"

Jorn was not one of those who was especially good at being politic. He was either silent or straightforward.

"Connection with them is the only way we can survive. We must find a way to reconnect and be in a relationship. We have to heal what has been broken."

Lronr looked at Jorn with an expression he couldn't interpret, then nodded.

"That was my suspicion."

Jorn wondered whether this was going to bode ill for him.

"Here, take this book. There are not many copies, so you must take great care with it. And do not show it to anyone else."

Jorn took the book and saw the title, "Heart of the Carj."

Jorn asked, "What is this book?"

"It is a secret, holy book. One that will guide our unification with all human beings. It was written in the very early days before we were separated. Its authors are said to be some of those originally taken from Grier Nro by our parent race."

"Why are you giving this to me?"

"We have a secret society within the priesthood, Jorn. We are very large in number but work in silence. We are actively working toward reform on Hilcyon, with the ultimate goal being healing the wound with the Breft. We want you to join us."

Jorn didn't know exactly what to say. He was both excited and scared by the prospect.

"How does the High Priest see this?"

"He is on our side. He is waiting for the right moment to make our voices heard."

"Waiting? Why wait when things are so dire?"

"He worries, and I agree, that things are too precarious, and not quite bad enough. He is counseling patience and caution. He has been called by the Exalted King to this role, and I will follow him."

Jorn nodded. "What am I to do, besides read?"

"Wait, watch, and when you are given tasks, do them."

Jorn nodded. "I will."

"Thanks be to the King. Go with Him."

Jorn bowed, put his palms together, and touched the tips of his fingers to his forehead.

"You may go now, Jorn."

Jorn bowed again, got up, and left, softly closing the door behind him. He walked to his cell, knelt at his altar, and prayed. Then he started to read this book.

"We were brought together, from all over our home, all kinds, all shapes, all colors. The Exalted King, for reasons of his own, decided this. So we will celebrate this, this being together when we never really knew each other existed.

"We must be unified: speak with one voice, be one people…"

Ro'mer sat on the comfortable chair across from Gil'ern. Ro'mer was unusually unsure of themself. Partially, it was because they had always looked up to Gil'ern, who was, by far, the most revered member of the Jal'it school that Jal'end'a founded over 13 Casitian years ago. Casiti had a long history of fostering different spiritual and thought traditions in its schools. The Jal'it school was the newest school, but one that had, in some ways, the highest stature, given to it mostly by its most famous founder, who helped Casitians embrace all of humanity with her leadership.

Gil'ern said, "Thank you, Ro'mer, for taking the time to come speak with me."

"You are quite welcome, Gil'ern. I can't quite imagine what this is about."

Gil'ern smiled; the wrinkles at the edges of her eyes became evident. "I wanted to talk with you about your... cousin? Paul."

"Paul?"

"Yes, Paul. About ten days ago, he petitioned to join the Jal'it school. I could tell he didn't quite understand our structure—he seemed to think it was like conversion to a Terran religion." Gil'ern smiled.

Ro'mer was taken aback. "He did? He didn't mention it to me!"

"I don't think he wanted you to know."

"But why not?"

"Paul is a troubled young man, Ro'mer. I think he doesn't really know himself yet."

Ro'mer sighed. "Yes, I know. Will joining the school help?"

"He can't join now, he is not ready yet. First, he doesn't have the requisite education. And he's too spiritually confused at the moment. But..."

"But?"

"It is clear in our few conversations that underneath the confusion lies an extraordinary man. We just have to help that man emerge. He will be ready at some point, I know it."

"Do you have suggestions?"

"Yes, I do. He needs to find a craft. Any craft, really. Something to occupy his mind and time, and get him to focus. And he needs to live where it will be easy for him to come to our gatherings and classes so he can learn more."

"I can petition for housing on his behalf. I'm sure they will give him a dwelling. And a craft... I'll ask him what he likes to do and set him up with someone."

"That sounds good."

"Alright. Thank you so much, Gil'ern. I've been worried about him."

"Was it you that gave him 'Spirits Alike' to read?"

"Yes. I had a feeling he might appreciate it."

"That book is changing him, Ro'mer."

Ro'mer left Gil'ern's dwelling and got back into their vehicle for the trip back to Hol'ven'if. As they were riding, Ro'mer sent a message to central Rel'toro housing, requesting a dwelling in northwestern Jor'ar'lir for Paul to live. Ro'mer didn't know what it would be like for Paul to live on his own, but perhaps it was as good a time as any for it. And the craft... Ro'mer had no ideas for that, but it could wait until they spoke to Paul.

Paul had gotten several messages from his parents throughout his stay on Casiti, and he refused to answer them. Ro'mer knew that eventually, Paul would have to talk with his parents. The first sixty days of Paul's visit had been rather painful for everyone, but since the beginning of the month of Klef, Paul seemed much more mellow and less pained. Finally, he'd mended fences with Ke'lir, and they were spending time together. Ro'mer was happy about that since Ke'lir was due to return to New Earth in a few days.

Ro'mer arrived back at their house, to see Ye'losi sitting with Paul in the gathering area. Ro'mer waved, and after hanging up their outer garments, went to join them.

Paul turned to Ro'mer and said, "Hi Ro'mer. Ye'losi was just explaining the Casitian government to me. I guess I can't get my head around the idea that you don't have a hierarchy."

Ye'losi, who was serving on the Rel'toro architectural committee, explained. "There is a little bit of a hierarchy, but it's more a ladder of respect, rather than orders for how to do things or what to do coming down from above."

"Respect?"

"Yes. As people show their abilities and wisdom, they gain more respect, and are thus nominated for things that have more and more responsibility."

"Ah, that makes sense. But you still make decisions collectively?"

"We do, yes. The voice of those with higher positions carries more weight, as it were."

Ro'mer asked, "So Paul, speaking of showing abilities—what do you like to do? How might you want to contribute?"

Ro'mer could see the confusion on Paul's face. Paul said, "I want to study truth and life."

Ro'mer nodded. "I know. But you're not ready for that."

Paul looked up. "I'm not?"

"No. I had a conversation with Gil'ern, who thinks you are a marvelous young man who needs more time and guidance."

"I see." Paul looked down.

Yel'osi asked gently, "Paul, what kinds of things do you like to do?"

"Everybody always came to me with broken things. I am very good at fixing things, and learning about how things work."

Ro'mer said, "Yes, I heard you giving your tablet some pretty complex commands a while ago."

"I like technology. The more complicated, the better. It has been one of the things I've really enjoyed here—more technology!" Ro'mer saw the first smile he'd seen on Paul's face. Clearly, this was a good direction.

"How would you like to apprentice to someone who works with technology for a while? And live in Jor'ar'lir, where you can be close to the Jal'it school?"

"Really? I could live close to the school and build and fix things?" Paul sounded almost incredulous.

"Yes, really. I'll set it up for you."

"Thank you, Ro'mer. Maybe I can figure out what to do with my life after all."

*Hol'venif, Rel'toro, Casiti*

Paul and Glor were sitting again at the cafe near the Kadarin family house. They had managed to mend their fences, and Paul was actually enjoying his time with Glor.

Glor said, "So you're moving to a different part of Rel'toro? I've never been to Jor'ar'lir. And your internship sounds quite interesting."

Paul said, "Yeah, I'm kind of amazed. I'm excited about learning about technology related to agriculture. One of the things I remember from being in the ICS is how difficult growing things were for them. Here, in a much tougher climate, it seems so easy."

"Yeah, the galactic agriculture technology is quite advanced. We've been learning more about the kinds of machines we can requisition from Casiti for Zwek. We already have a lot, but we need to greatly expand our output given the increase in population."

"Oh, right! Where are your parents going to live?"

"I got them a house about three doors down from mine. Much bigger than the house they have here. Casitian houses run small, except for the family houses."

Glor looked pensive, and Paul wondered what was going on underneath the surface.

Glor said, "Anyway, the big housing push is done, and probably by the end of the New Earth year, all the Kinder will be moved to New Earth."

Paul asked, "Does that have any effect on the Kinder representation to the ... what is that again?"

"The Consej, or Human Council. The Kinder call it just 'The Council.' No. We're just stand-ins for Kinder on Hilcyon, or at least that's what my Da says. I'm not sure all Kinder agree on that."

"Sounds like you're not so sure."

"I'm not. I mean, it's likely not for a hundred years or more before they make contact, if ever. The Kinder we have need representation, too."

Paul nodded. He could understand. He remembered overhearing conversations between his father and their deacon about how important representation was in the ICS. Strangely enough, the ICS choose not to have representation to the New Earth Authority government.

Paul asked, "How is your NEA job?"

Glor smiled, "It's going well. I even got a promotion. I'm the head of that team working with NEATac on technology transfer to Zwek. I even have meetings with Ke'lir and some other family members. I like that aspect of it."

That reminded Paul of a question he'd been wanting to ask Glor.

"Glor, I just finished reading the one authorized biography of our great-great-aunt Marianne. Have you read it?"

"Yeah, I read it years ago, when I was a kid."

"Did it surprise you?"

"Um, I don't think so. Did it surprise you?"

"Yeah, it really did. I learned so much about our family."

"What were you surprised about?"

"Aunt Marianne started out as just, just an engineer no one had heard of. It was almost random that Ja'el chose her."

"I'd not say it was random, Paul, but it's true. She wasn't famous or powerful in any way."

"And she didn't like becoming famous or powerful, either."

"Yeah. I remember a story my dad told me about her once that he'd heard from Ngellin. Even well after The Event, she was still sought after—and she'd take these long camping trips with Ja'el, Leticia, and Mira, and purposefully forget any communication equipment. It drove great-grandma Beatrice nuts."

They laughed.

Glor said, "I know our family is famous, but I do think that most of us don't like to be in the spotlight. We take after her in that regard."

"I dunno, I think Aunt Tricia likes it."

Glor smiled. "OK, yes, that's one exception."

Paul said, "Anyway, I found the biography inspiring—and it was really nice to learn so much about our family. There is so much that I missed."

Paul felt like he was just getting his bearings around his family, their stature in all three communities, and where his place would be. He hadn't found it yet and felt that he was at a disadvantage, having been relegated to that backwater he grew up in. But he was feeling a lot better about everything, now.

## Pa'rai's, North Circumpolar Independent Zone, New Earth

Ke'lir was happy to take a break from reading so many reports. She'd returned from New Orleans a couple of days ago and was about to go hiking with Stacey, who Ke'lir was very interested in. She walked out of her house and down the street where she could catch one of the shuttle buses that went down that street fairly often. As one arrived at the stop, she realized she'd get to take the ride alone this time. She entered in the stop she wanted into the display at the front, knowing the bus would only stop if it detected people waiting. Her stop was the trailhead where she'd meet Stacey.

As the bus pulled away from the stop, she thought about dating Stacey, and her general conundrum about partnership, feeling her Casitian upbringing in conflict with her Terran lifestyle. She'd met Stacey at a party—one of her long-time friends in the NCPIZ was having a birthday. Stacey was her cousin and had moved here recently from New Columbia, the capital of New America. She'd been born and raised there, of parents who had also been born and raised there. Her move to the NCPIZ had caused somewhat of a stir in her family, from what Stacy had told Ke'lir.

The bus stopped near the trailhead, and as Ke'lir walked toward it, she could see Stacey waiting by her bicycle.

"Hi, Stacey!" Ke'lir said from a distance.

Stacey walked toward her, and they shared a hug.

"How was your trip to New Orleans?" Stacey asked.

"It was busy but good. It left me with all sorts of work to do, though. I'm happy to take this break. How are you? How's the new gig?"

Stacey had moved to the NCPIZ because she'd been hired by one of the new, hot, space-focused startups that were all the rage here.

"It's going really well. Working with people from all over New Earth is interesting. And the work is engaging. I had no idea how much is going on in the asteroid belt."

"I've been learning a lot about that, too, as part of NEATac. We so need the stuff from those asteroids."

"I believe it."

They started their hike, and their conversation veered from topic to topic. Finally, Stacey asked Ke'lir about what she was looking for in dating. Ke'lir had to take a breath.

"You know I was raised in Casitian culture, right?"

"Um, not really. I've heard about your family, but I didn't know that some of you were raised Casitian."

"My father was raised on Casiti; his father was Casitian, and his mother wanted him to be raised that way. My mother was full Casitian. We moved to New Earth when I was 6, but lived in a Casitian enclave here.

"So anyway, it's hard for me to figure out. It doesn't seem possible to do the Casitian companion thing here."

"I've heard a little bit about companions. Basically, you'd spend most of your time single, then just winter with a companion?"

"Yeah, that's how it works. Every winter, most people, either people who don't have children or after they've raised their children, couple up for the equivalent of a year. And they spend most of the rest of the time single."

"You mean they don't have sex outside the winter?"

"Oh, gosh, no. Plenty of sex with lots of people happens in between."

"Oh." There was an uncomfortable silence.

After a little while, Stacey said, "That's weird."

Ke'lir didn't quite know what to say to that.

She said finally, "Well, a lot of New Earth Casitians adopt serial monogamy or semi-permanent monogamy. And I know plenty who are polyamorous. Honestly, I'm not sure what I want. What are you looking for?"

Stacey, it seemed, was looking for a straight-up monogamous marriage. She apparently found any other arrangement "weird." Ke'lir may well be happy in a monogamous marriage, but not with someone as conservative as Stacey apparently was.

They finished their hike mostly in silence, parted ways amicably at the trailhead, and Ke'lir watched Stacey bike off into the distance as she waited for a bus to arrive. Ke'lir hadn't had a chance to share yet with Stacey that she'd had her sex changed when she was young. She imagined Stacey would have had a hard time with that.

She went home and, after dinner, sat down with a cup of tea and her reports. The report in front of her eyes at the moment was interesting to Ke'lir. It quantified the number of galactic technical items that Castians had been able to start manufacturing. Casitians were the only ones with enough experience with galactic technology to even think about manufacturing galactic technology.

The galactic community had been extraordinarily generous before they closed the wormhole. NEATac, only one of two bodies that kept track of technology, estimated that the technology they had been given would last more than 3000 years. In addition, they had provided a rather extreme level of documentation, but it still wasn't enough for Terrans to figure out Galactic technology.

The Consej had given NEATac the role of tracking technology use on New Earth, and tracking supplies of needed technologies. The Casitians were in charge of learning to manufacture as much galactic technology as they could manage, mostly from raw materials in New Earth's extremely rich asteroid belts. Ke'lir had read transcripts of early meetings of the Consej in its first days, debating whether it was appropriate to manufacture galactic technology. Some Casitians were adamant that they should not—that the intent of the galactic community was just that they survive with what they had until they could rejoin the community. Over time, the Terran approach won over. There was no guarantee that the Kinder would ever rejoin the rest of humanity. And if they did not, humans would remain outside of the galactic community for a very long time. Possibly forever.

And, as of yet, Casitians had been unwilling to let many Terrans learn the details of the galactic technology. This was slowly changing, and Paul's new position on Casiti would possibly help things, given their family's stature. And Paul did seem to be enjoying the work so far. Ke'lir was happy for him. He seemed to be in the process of finding his place.

## Jor'ar'lir, Rel'toro, Casiti

It had happened so fast. First, it seemed Paul was a miserable wretch, and then, he had his own place and a job! It seemed miraculous, in some ways, but his cousin Ro'mer really made it happen.

Paul had just spent his first few days as an apprentice student, working under Wer'lar with six other apprentices relatively close to his age, most of whom lived in a youth house nearby. More than 30 people were working in Wer'lar's shop. The shop specialized in repairing and manufacturing equipment related to agriculture. Paul had spent the first day working with a colleague on some equipment used to regulate the melting and pumping of water from ice. Casiti had a lot of ice, and getting the water from where the ice was to where the people were was necessary, as unlike New Earth, there was little precipitation outside of winter snow. And because of the constant exposure to water and mud, the parts didn't last all that long.

Wer'lar and her colleagues had perfected the manufacturing process, so they were now able to repair broken equipment and make new equipment when the old stuff had to finally be scrapped. Paul was starting out slowly, because most of the documentation was written in Casitian, and he wasn't anywhere near fluent in it yet. In fact, after dinner, he was going straight to the language lessons.

He walked out of the cold street of his small town into his new dwelling. It was small, which suited him fine. It had a central area in which he had a corner with comfortable pillows to sit on, a couple of chairs, and his desk. He had a small bedroom, just enough for the bed and a chest to hold his clothes. He had a small bathing room all to himself and a small kitchen. There was a greenhouse off the kitchen, and one of his colleagues had promised to visit and help him set it up. For now, he had been gifted food from a member of the Jal'it school. That felt both sweet and uncomfortable. He knew that growing one's own food was how it was done here, and he looked forward to when he could not only grow his own, but grow enough to give some away.

His work schedule was modest, as everyone's was during winter. Some people stopped working altogether, but younger people tended to work a lot during the winter. He would be working for three days, then had three off. The rest of the year, he would likely work five, and get three off. During the time off, he intended to learn Casitian, so he could read the documentation he needed for work and Jal'end'a's work in the original language. Jal'end'a's writing had come as a revelation to Paul. He finally began to understand why he had so many doubts about what he had learned growing up. And in it, he found solace and places to look for God. That made him feel like maybe he wasn't so lost after all.

He did have an unpleasant task ahead of him. It seemed that his father's threat that he would never be welcome back home was, in fact, an empty one. He had gotten six messages from them, which he had not answered, and Ro'mer, Sal'ira, and Hrelr had all gotten messages from his parents asking about him. Ro'mer finally took Paul aside before he moved to Jor'ar'lir and told him he had to send a message back to his parents. It was time finally. He sat at his desk, and pushed the icon for sending messages.

"Please record a message for my parents, Julia and Jonathon Girard, on New Earth."

"Recording."

"Hi, Mom and Dad. Sorry I haven't written back. I've been busy, and... delete please."

"Deleted."

"Record again."

"Recording."

"Hi, Mom and Dad. I know you have been anxious to hear news about me, and I'm sorry I haven't sent a message until now. I'm doing fine here on Casiti. Cousin Ro'mer has been really helpful, as has Ke'lir. I don't know how long I'll be here... I think it will be a while. Anyway, really, I'm fine. I'm a new apprentice at a workshop that fixes things and makes things, and I love it so far. I'm also... I'm learning more about our family, and history, and all sorts of things I'm sure you'd rather I didn't explore. But I am, and it's good. I promise to be better at sending messages. I hope you are both well. Give my love to Matthew and Martha. Much love, Paul."

He realized that he wasn't sure he *liked* Casiti. But he knew that somehow he *needed* Casiti right now.

# Chapter 4:
# Making Contact

New Earth: November 2099
Hilcyon: Sdert 1202
Casiti: Wend 803

*"We struggle to find the meaning to this life. We were taken from our planet, our lives, our peoples, and brought to this place. What does it mean? How can we find the way to live our lives with meaning? Perhaps we can find meaning in the toil we undertake, the effort we make on behalf of our mentors who were also our captors." Heart of Carj, Eclogue 4*

### *Capital Region, Hilcyon*

Mrin walked home, dog tired, as he had been for months. He'd been working nonstop on the glacier, helping to carve up large pieces, to be carted away and put in one of the reservoirs. It took a tremendous amount of effort, and the amount of water they could get into the reservoir was tiny. Worse yet, the last conduit in this region failed. There would basically be no water. The Central Valley wasn't faring any better. They had only one working conduit. There were maybe four working conduits in all of Hilcyon, and those were in peril, since no one was repairing them anymore.

The elevation of Zetl to First Chief of Food and Water for all of Hilcyon had been nothing less than a complete disaster from Mrin's perspective. Zetl, who was completely loyal to First Chief Klef, had this silly idea of Kinder self-sufficiency. Mrin wished that the leaders would at least use some sense. Human self-sufficiency was impossible on Hilcyon—living on this planet required galactic technology. Mrin didn't understand why the Supreme and First Chiefs didn't understand that. Mrin had read his history. During the long period when Hilcyon stopped communicating with the Breft, they were still allowing regular drops of necessary equipment every hundred years or so. However, with the last conflict, when the galactic community cut off humans, the Kinder leadership decided to go it alone. It was the wrong decision.

He opened the door to his home, to find his whole family sitting in the living room. They looked up at him, and he could tell something had happened.

"What's wrong?"

His father said, "Our chief, who had refused to implement the loyalty oath for food rations, gave in. And you know..."

"You refused."

"I refused. We have no food."

His mother said, "That's not entirely true. I knew this would happen, so I have been reserving some grain, flour, and seeds. We probably can eat for about a week."

Mrin said, "Well, we'll just starve sooner than others. The conduits are failing, they are refusing to fix them, and the amount of water we could get from the glacier over the last two weeks was, well, pitiful."

His father looked defeated. But Mrin wasn't. He decided to tell the family what he had. He got up, went into his room, and dug out the device from the pile of clothes he'd been hiding it in. He brought it out. Everyone was staring at him.

"Remember when I went to the Central Valley to assess that equipment cache?"

His father said, "Yes."

"I found this. I didn't tell anyone, but I'm pretty sure it's a device to call the Breft."

"Why do you think that?"

"Look on the side, here. It says, 'Do not, under any circumstances, activate this communications device. This device is the property of the Supreme Chief and must be only used by him.'"

"Well, let's try it, shall we?"

Mrin nodded. He looked all over the device for some sort of switch and finally found a depression on one end. He passed his finger over the depression. Nothing happened. As he was turning it over again, a red circle lit on one side. He put it down, with the red circle facing the top. Some symbols appeared in the window that was flush with one side. He didn't understand the symbols—he assumed they were Breft. The red circle turned green, but nothing else happened.

Mrin said, "I wonder if it's just sort of a one-way signal?"

They sat and looked at it, wondering whether it worked or if anything would happen. They waited and waited. Nothing happened.

Mrin said, "Well... I guess maybe we'll starve after all."

They talked for a while about ways to get food and conserve. Mrin said that he would quit his job, and try to do something to get him paid in food. His father reminded him that he'd have to agree to the loyalty oath.

Mrin said, "Da, look..."

"No, son. If you feel that you need to say the oath to eat, I won't stop you. But I would rather starve."

"I understand, Da."

They talked some more, and then they all went to bed. Tyrin and Mrin couldn't find energy for lovemaking, so they cuddled and fell asleep.

### New Orleans, New Earth

Ke'lir was in yet another meeting. She was on her monthly trip down to New Orleans to meet with various committees she was working within NEATac. She was almost falling asleep when someone burst in.

"We have contact with Hilcyon!"

Ke'lir looked up and saw a short, stout, blond woman she'd known since she was a child standing at the door with a "hair on fire" look on her face. Sandra Germain was the grandchild of Joel Martin and Laura Hernandez, who were part of her great-great-aunt Marianne's initial team.

The current NEATac chair, John Broner, said loudly, "Sandra, what?"

She said, "The communications device that has been with them since The Event was activated. There was no voice message—likely because they don't know how to send one."

Glor, who was part of this meeting, stood up. "What... what do we do?"

Sandra said, "We have a protocol. We need to call the Consej first."

John said, "I will contact Zrel and set up a meeting between the Consej and whatever group we'll put in charge of this."

Glor said, "I'm assuming this is mostly for us to give them technical support."

John said, "I'll find out how soon all of the Consej can meet."

The meeting broke up, and Ke'lir, Sandra, and Glor left the room. Sandra led them to the communications center, which wasn't used so much now that Casiti and New Earth were on the same network. There were several people in the room.

Ke'lir said, "Sandra, it's so good to see you! It's been quite a while."

Sandra said, "It has!"

Glor said, "This is so unexpected, isn't it?"

Sandra replied, "I certainly did not expect this in my lifetime."

Ke'lir asked, "How are we going to communicate?"

"We can send them a message. But the best bet is to communicate with them synchronously."

Glor asked, "How can we do that?"

"From orbit around Hilcyon."

Glor said, "But we can't..."

Sandra interrupted, "I'm assuming if they made contact, they wouldn't object to a ship."

Ke'lir said, "Yes, that makes sense. We should be safe entering their space."

John came into the room. "They have all been notified. It's still night in most of Rel'toro, and we are waking everyone. I spoke with Zrel, and he's grabbing the next train to New Orleans."

Glor's uncle Zrel was the current head of the Consej and a Terran representative. Zrel was her grandfather Pykgy's son but had chosen to live as a Terran on New Earth in Dlejon. His partner was a Terran, and he was Glor's cousin Liam's father. Ke'lir knew that Glor and Zrel got along OK, but the fact that Zrel had chosen Terran rather than Kinder culture was a bit of a sore spot for Glor. Ke'lir hardly knew Zrel. She only saw him at family gatherings.

Ke'lir said, "I'll make sure the conference room that has holo projectors is open for our meeting. We should be able to meet in three hours when Zrel arrives. In the meantime, Sandra, can you field the questions that will inevitably come from Consej members when they get the message?"

"Of course."

Ke'lir told Glor and Sandra, "Let's call Liam and get an early dinner. We'll need the sustenance. I think it's going to be a long night."

### Hol'venif, Rel'toro, Casiti

The sharp sound of their emergency message alarm woke them, and their infant's bawling got them out of bed in a hurry. They felt like they'd just gotten to sleep.

They said to the air, "What is it?"

Their system responded, "Urgent message from Zrel: 'Ro'mer, sorry to wake you. There will be an emergency meeting with the Consej at 5th hour Rel'toro time. A message was received from Hilcyon.'"

A message from Hilcyon? Ro'mer hadn't expected that in their lifetime. They had a little bit of time before the meeting. Ro'mer would wake up the house's backup infant care person. M'nali still needed a lot of rest.

The ripples and ramifications of this were just beginning to make themselves felt in his brain as they swaddled their infant and rocked them back to sleep. And they knew they would be in meeting after meeting, both with Consej sub-committees and with representatives of the Caraj. It was those joinings they were least looking forward to.

After handing off their child, getting a fast breakfast, and settling in their office, Ro'mer fired up the holo meeting to see other members of the Consej in a circle. To their right were Zrel, Tanessa, Christoph, Jayden, and Welburn, the Terran representatives, who clearly were all in the same room in New Orleans, along with Hrelr, Grynt, Masr, Glev, and Jerl, the Kinder representatives. To their left, each of them in a separate space, was Teo'lir, Samira, Kel'ora, and Ret'ir'le, the other Casitian representatives to the Consej.

Zrel said, "Thank you, especially those on Casiti. I know it's very early in the morning in Rel'toro."

Kel'ora smiled, "I've been up for hours, Zrel." Kel'ora lived in Loc'deher, a good 1/4 of the way around the planet from Rel'toro.

Zrel said, "Anyway, here is what we know—which is not much. Someone on Hilcyon, we're assuming the Supreme Chief, activated the communication device but did not leave a message. Probably, they don't know how. That device hasn't been used since Supreme Chief Ylen used it over 70 years ago.

"The going assumption is that they are likely starving. The equipment used to melt and move water from the poles is way past the end of life, and probably breaking down.

"NEA and NEATac want our approval to send a small expedition—no more than six or seven people. They can send down equipment and do repairs remotely. And they can provide food if necessary. They will stay in orbit."

Teo'lir asked, "Do we really know they are starving? Why can't we wait to find out more?"

Hrelr said, "We can't find out more until we send a ship to orbit around their planet that can read the data from all of the listening devices. Might as well send the most likely needs along with that expedition."

There were several agreeing nods.

Zrel asked, "Are there any objections to sending this expedition?"

Samira raised her hand. "I don't have an objection, but I believe we should set some conditions. For instance, under no circumstances should anything be done if the contact is not official."

Grynt said, "I'm sorry, but that doesn't make sense. It certainly seems that it's most likely that the device was activated by the Supreme Chief. But what if the Supreme Chief is corrupt in some way, and an underling activates the device because the situation is dire? Should we stand aside and do nothing?

Samira said, "Yes. We should do nothing. The only thing we should authorize is an official communication from the leader of Hilcyon. Anything else would be extremely problematic and interfere with them. They should be able to work out their problems on their own."

An argument erupted, with the Casitians and Kinder yelling at each other angrily. Only Zrel's loud "STOP!" settled the meeting.

Zrel said, "I understand the Casitians' caution. Let me make a suggestion. We will limit our work and communication if we find out this is not official."

Samira said, "I will only agree if we send an official Casitian representative on the mission. And I would like us to meet with the team beforehand."

Masr said, "And we will also have an official Kinder representative."

Welburn said, "Of course, there will also be a Terran."

Zrel said, "We've begun to put the team together. Sandra Germain, a Terran, who has been monitoring and planning for this for a long time; Ke'lir Kadarin, who has been head of a directorate for agricultural technology transfer; Glor Jror Hlad, a Kinder in Zwek, who has also been deeply involved in technology transfer. There are likely a few others we'll add. An official Casitian representative is welcome and makes sense. We will make sure to convene a meeting with the Consej and the team before they leave."

There was a little more conversation before the meeting broke up, but ultimately, it was agreed that the mission was approved with those contingencies. Signing off, Ro'mer breathed a sigh of relief. They sent a message to Zrel: "You know, Paul has become an expert in some of this agricultural technology. I doubt anyone from Casiti will want to go besides the official representative. You know that Casitians have become extremely risk-averse lately. Paul might be a good fit. I think he, Glor, and Ke'lir would work well together."

He wondered what this team would find when they arrived in orbit over Hilcyon.

### Jor'ar'lir, Rel'toro, Casiti

Spring on Casiti was a revelation to Paul. Paul knew that Casiti's seasons were starkly different, but spring was amazing. The snow wasn't completely gone, but plants were already making their way out of the ground. This was when Casitians plowed snow off their fields and started to turn the soil over in preparation for planting. Paul had taken out the 'dozer bot from the local storage shop and was watching it clear off his small plot.

His new friend Ka'li'mo had been taking it upon himself to teach Paul how to grow food. It was fun, and Paul really enjoyed Ka'li'mo's company. Ka'li'mo was a student of the Ja'lit school, and he and Paul had long conversations about God, and theology, and what it really meant to be human. Paul felt like Ka'li'mo really understood him in ways that no one had before. And the feelings he had for Ka'li'mo made him feel a little uncomfortable. He wasn't sure why.

"Paul, there is an urgent message from Wer'lar," his messaging system spoke, rousing him from his reverie.

"Play, please."

"Paul, the Kinder have contacted us and apparently are in great need of our equipment. The Consej is sending a ship to Hilcyon, and we need to send a representative. Ro'mer nominated you, I concurred, and the Consej has agreed. The ship is leaving from Casiti once the Terran representatives get here. Pack some things, and come to the shop to pick up the shipment we're preparing right now."

Paul was stunned. First that the Kinder contacted them. Second, that *he* had been chosen as the representative to help the technology transfer. He had only been working in Wer'ler's shop for 9 Terran months. He knew this technology well, though, and had repaired a lot of it then. And, of course, he was a Michaelson, which was probably most of why he was chosen. He also knew that most Casitians didn't like to travel much, and the trip to Hilcyon could be dangerous.

"Thanks, please record a message to Ka'li'mo."

"Recording."

"Hi, Ka'li'mo. I'm sorry I will miss our time together tomorrow. You might have heard by now that the Kinder have reached out, and I have been chosen to accompany the equipment to Hilcyon. I don't know how long I'll be gone. Can you do me a favor and return the 'dozer bot to local storage when it's done? It should be finished by the end of the day today. Thanks! I'll repay you with dinner at the Eagle's Nest in town when I return. Send, please."

"Sent."

"Thanks, please record a message to my parents on New Earth."

"Recording."

"Hi, Mom and Dad. I'm on my way to Hilcyon, believe it or not. I was chosen to accompany the equipment they need. I don't know how long I'll be gone, or whether or not I'll be able to be in contact while I'm gone. I imagine cousins Ro'mer or Zrel will know what's up. Love you. Send, please."

"Sent."

He hurried around his place, putting away things that needed to be put away and washing things that should be washed so he would not return to a complete disaster. He quickly packed his few clothes and some personal items. He left his dwelling and walked to the shop where Wer'lar and a few of Paul's colleagues were busy packing several rather large crates.

Wer'lar saw Paul enter.

"Ah, Paul, good." Wer'lar handed Paul a tablet. "That's the manifest. We're sending many melt-pump systems, core controllers, monitors, and analysis units. You'll see I've also included some random assorted tools and parts you might need."

Paul nodded. "Looks very complete."

"Well, it's based mostly on guesstimates. No one has actually spoken directly to them yet. I also ordered 50 remote repair units. They are now being assembled and packed in Rel'toro. That means you can send those down and do the fixes instead of going down in person. People think it might be dangerous."

Paul nodded.

Wer'lar continued, "Others have added other equipment. I know that at least some fusion micro-reactors are also being sent. I've called for an overland cargo transport. Should be here in an hour or so. You'll go with the cargo to Rel'toro, where a shuttle will take you and all the stuff into orbit."

Paul nodded again. He was still a little in shock about the whole thing. He started to help his colleagues pack the equipment, taking note of what went into what container. Before he knew it, he heard Wer'lar shouting, "The cargo transport is here, folks. Let's get this done!"

They finished up, and Paul and several anti-grav sleds piled high with containers full of equipment followed him. They all helped to get the cargo on board, and Paul grabbed his bag and jumped up into the passenger cab with the driver.

"Hi, Paul. I'm Re'qal," the person, who to Paul's eye was a woman, said in heavily accented English.

"Nice to meet you, Re'qal," Paul said in Casitian.

"Ah, you speak Casitian, at least a little, yes?"

Paul nodded, "I'm not quite... fluent yet."

Paul was getting used to the Casitian language, and he could at least tell that Re'qual had one of the accents of a true Casitian, someone whose family had lived on Casiti from the beginning. Paul knew that many Casitians still did not speak English at all. English had become like it was on Earth before the Event, the *lingua franca* of humans on both worlds.

"Well, my English is pretty rotten. So I guess we can go back and forth and get practice, eh?"

Paul smiled. They chatted amiably during the two-hour trip to Rel'toro. Even though Re'qal was in no way connected to the Consej or Caraj, Re'qal seemed to know quite a lot about him and his family. Re'qal even knew about his mother's split from the rest of the family. Slowly but surely, he had come to realize that his family was famous on both planets. He didn't quite know what he thought of that, but it didn't really matter. He just had to get used to it.

### Capital Region, Hilcyon

There was a brief prayer, briefer than Jorn expected, and the leader, the head priest of his temple, started the meeting.

This was Jorn's first meeting with the secret inner circle of priests in his temple, working not only for reform on Hilcyon but for the unification of all humans: Breft, Kinder, and those originally from Grier Nro.

But the subject of this meeting was much more prosaic: How to keep as many temples and priests as possible from starvation.

Lronr said, "Glin has talked to both Zetl and Klef. They keep demanding our loyalty, and Glin keeps reminding them that we serve a different purpose—we are outside of the politics of the chief system."

An older priest said, "And I'm sure they'd rather us go away."

Lronr shook his head, "They are not ready for the social upheaval that the end of the priesthood would generate. Too many Kinder want and need us, and they know it. In some form, the priesthood has always served an essential purpose, even before the rupture. The Breft embraced it. From what we know, their priesthood is robust, varied, and deeply integrated into their society's fabric. The Chiefs have always simply tolerated us, knowing our necessity but resenting it.

"And now, with so many suffering and starving, we are needed even more. We are an essential relief, and they know it."

The conversation went back and forth, and they made some specific proposals for simple actions. Actions they could easily do on their own. Connecting with local chiefs and connecting directly with farmers, many of whom came to services.

Lronr said, "One last thing to discuss. It's to review and revise our action plan for when the inevitable happens—the chaos that will erupt when people stop tolerating starvation."

Jorn was only moderately surprised. He listened as Lronr outlined the plan and asked for suggestions.

Jorn said, "We need to use the temples more strategically. I think they can be shelters, of course, but why not allow those who are working for reform to use them as gathering places? Their use as shelters will cover that activity."

Lronr said, "Jorn, that's a very good idea. We'll add that."

Jorn was glad he'd been recruited. He loved his life as a priest - it gave him meaning. But he felt even more of use now.

### Capital Region, Hilcyon

It was the day after her father had refused to sign a loyalty oath, and they were close to starving. Dlen was on her way to deliver another child—a child into a very uncertain future. She didn't know these parents well. She'd only seen the mother twice when her husband wasn't home.

She'd managed to eat at the house of the parents of the last child she delivered earlier in the day, but hunger was still dogging her today.

She could feel the fatigue, slowness, and fogginess in her head. And she knew the inevitable: what had claimed her Mrel would claim her.

Over the past year since she lost Mrel, she'd been working through her grief. Not only at the grief of a lost friend but the grief of a lost love.

She'd gone back to one of her favorite stories from the collection of the stories of Dbor - her most treasured book. It was one of the stories about Elfer, the unmarried, roving healer. She re-read one particular story. The one where she took another woman as a lover. It was very subtly written—one could almost miss that part of the story. But Dlen knew what it was, and Dlen often felt like Elfer.

She arrived at the house and knocked on the door. A very tall, dour-looking man looked down on her.

"What?"

"I'm Dlen, the midwife here to deliver your child."

"Alright." He opened the door, and she walked in. She could hear the woman in the back grunting and moaning.

She turned to the husband, who had followed her, and asked, "How long has she been in labor?"

He said, "I don't know. I just got home a bit ago."

Dlen nodded and put her bag down next to the bed.

The woman, whose name she remembered was Jfel, didn't look well. She'd wished she'd been able to track her more closely. Dlen was deeply worried.

"Jfel, how long have you been in labor?"

"Since yesterday morning."

"Yesterday morning! Why didn't you call for me earlier? I'm only a few stats away."

The woman was silent, looking at her husband, then looking down. Dlen turned to look up at him and saw his grim, angry face. It didn't take much to know that this marriage didn't treat her well.

She told him, "I need some towels, extra sheets, and hot water."

"I'm not your servant. Get them yourself, woman."

She realized it would take less time to do it herself than argue with him.

She turned back to the woman, "Where do you keep your linens?"

The woman pointed to a cabinet on the far wall. Dlen gathered up what she needed, having to walk around the husband several times.

She finally said, "Look, if you are not going to make yourself useful here, get out of the house, find a couple of your wife's friends, and bring them here. She's going to have a very difficult labor."

He grunted and almost started to say something, then changed his mind and walked out. Dlen heard the outside door slam. The next few hours flew by in a blur. One woman joined her and helped her out.

The baby never made it into the world. The woman had been very weak and had started to hemorrhage badly. Dlen couldn't manage to pull the baby out. In the end, both Jfel and her baby died.

She expected recrimination and anger from the father when she told him. Instead, she could see his grief. He nodded quietly and said he would call the priests and have the body taken care of.

She had hoped to receive compensation—at least in the form of a meal, but it was not forthcoming. She didn't blame him. She walked back home, sadness tugging at her heart, hunger at her belly.

# Chapter 5:
# Life and Death

New Earth: November 2099
Hilcyon: Sdert 1202
Casiti: Wend 803

*"Creation stories tell us more about the lenses with which we view the world, than the truth of where we come from. We can find in these stories such rich and deep insight into who we think we are, and where we think we will fail." Ja'len'da, 'Spirits Alike'*

### New Orleans, New Earth

Ke'lir wouldn't have time to go home before the transport to Casiti. It didn't really matter all that much, but she wished at least she'd packed a few more clothes. She would likely be away from home for weeks. The meeting with NEA, NEATac, and the Consej had been long and contentious, but in the end, it was decided that she, Glor, Paul, Sandra, and a Casitian named Pot'relo would accompany a pilot on a cargo ship to Hilcyon. Pot'relo was a member of a little-known Casitian defense organization that formed after The Event, in case any threat came to Casiti from Hilcyon. It was the first and only Casitian military organization ever, and from what Ke'lir could tell, it was tiny and didn't really do anything except model scenarios and make plans based on those models.

They chose a cargo ship first because it would seem the least threatening and second because they actually had a lot of cargo to bring. There was the equipment they assumed the Kinder would need to fix what galactic technology they had to keep them alive, including to supply water and energy. They also brought a lot of extra equipment, in case the Kinder didn't want to keep in contact. During the meeting, Zrel had told the story of how after what was called "The Betrayal of J'lec," about 1200 years ago, even when the Kinder cut off communication, the Castians would drop necessary equipment once every 10 Casitian years or so. That stopped in the aftermath of the invasion of New Earth when the Kinder decided to cut themselves off completely. They still hadn't talked to the Kinder Supreme Chief, so they didn't really know what it was he wanted when he made contact. They would find out soon enough.

As she walked through the New Orleans spaceport, she saw Glor sitting with Sandra. She sat down next to Glor.

Ke'lir said to him, "Did you speak to your dad?"

"Yeah. He's happy I'm going, but I think he wished some other New Earth Kinder could come, too."

"There's only room for five passengers on the cargo ship."

"He knows. I think he worries a little about what I might say."

Ke'lir said, "What might you say?"

Glor shrugged, "I don't know. Whatever." He looked angry. Ke'lir didn't know what was wrong, but she let it go.

Their transport was boarding, so they got on board. By now, the news that the Kinder had made contact was all over, and Ke'lir overheard a snippet of conversation.

"So what do you think is going to happen?"

"I hope they don't invade again."

"The Casitians wouldn't let that happen."

"What could they do about it?"

"Well, something, right?"

"I don't know. But anyway, that doesn't seem likely."

"Maybe they need more slaves. My great-grandfather Gary was one of those stolen teenagers."

"My great-grandmother's oldest brother William never came back."

Ke'lir's ears pricked up at that. Ke'lir doubted it was the same William she'd heard about in the family stories. The William from the ICS who landed on Hilcyon, and was the reason Beatrice's Kinder husband had been arrested and killed. Ke'lir knew that no one had ever told that family story, and William was likely long dead. It was funny how history was still sometimes alive in a moment. And this moment brought it all back to everyone.

She slept, and they eventually arrived on Casiti at the Rel'toro space center. They disembarked with everyone. They had been told their ship was already in orbit and that they would meet Paul in some small, unused corner of the space center. They walked down corridor after corridor, finally ending up at a door with the correct label on it. Glor opened the door, and a rush of cold air came through, chilling Ke'lir. It was spring but still mighty cold in this part of Casiti. She saw a cargo transport next to a shuttle in the distance, with cargo being brought on anti-grav sleds from the transport into the shuttle. They walked toward the shuttle and could see Paul overseeing the cargo transfer.

Ke'lir said to Paul, "Hey."

Paul looked up and smiled. "Hi Ke'lir, Glor…"

Ke'lir pointed to Sandra. "This is Sandra. Sandra, meet my cousin Paul."

"Hi, Paul. It's so nice to get to meet you." Ke'lir could see a slight waver in Paul's smile. Perhaps Paul had as much trouble meeting people as Ke'lir did.

"Nice to meet you, Sandra," Paul said somewhat quietly.

Glor said, "Sandra's coming with us. She's the one who has been in charge of monitoring the communications channel with Hilcyon, and she's made her life's work the study of Hilcyon's history and people. She might know even more than I do." Glor smiled. Ke'lir got the definite sense that Glor liked Sandra, which surprised her. Glor seemed to only go for women who considered themselves Kinder. Besides, Sandra must be fifteen years or more older than Glor was.

Paul said, "We're ready now. Two more cargo shipments are already on our ship. One is some remote repair units that will allow us to make repairs without having to go down to the surface. The other is apparently a lot of food."

"Food?"

"Well, the assumption is that their water system is messed up, meaning that they likely haven't been able to grow much."

Ke'lir nodded. "Ah. What kind of food?"

"Emergency rations of some sort. Apparently, hundreds and hundreds of thousands of meals. I don't really know any more than that. Also, Pot'relo is on board.

Ke'lir could still feel Glor's anger. They had had an argument earlier in the day about Pot'relo. Glor was angry that a Casitian "defense officer" was present on the mission.

Paul said, "Let's go, shall we?"

They got on the ship and greeted the pilot. This shuttle was rather bare-bones. There was a room with six bunks and space for personal effects, a small galley that also seemed to serve as a conference room, and then the main passenger space, with just two rows with four uncomfortable seats. Glor sat with Sandra in the back row, and Ke'lir and Paul sat up front.

Ke'lir asked, "How's Casiti?"

Paul smiled. "I'm having a good time now."

"I'm glad to hear that, Paul."

"I love my work, and I'm learning so much at the Ja'lit school."

Sandra said, "Isn't that the school that Ja'lend'a started?"

"It is. You've read her work?"

"Yes. A long time ago. It is amazing stuff."

"Yes, she had a gift."

Glor chimed in, "Even I've read Ja'lend'a."

Ke'lir was surprised. "Did you like it?"

"Not really. Not my thing. I mean I agree with her premise, but I rather like the Kinder Exalted King."

Ke'lir said, "Even though it's patriarchal?"

"It's not patriarchal, not really."

Ke'lir and Glor had had this argument since they were small children. For a while, it had been fun, but it had ceased to be fun quite some time ago, so they both let it go. Sandra and Glor started to discuss Kinder theology, and Ke'lir tuned them out, and she got lost in her own thoughts.

### Capital Region, Hilcyon

Mrin completely forgot about the device, so several days later, when he was in the town square looking for work, he saw his father rush to him, and he assumed something was wrong with Tyrin or his mother.

"Da!" He shouted. His father did not say anything until he reached his side.

His father said quietly, "Come home. Now. Something happened."

"What?"

His father shook his head, and Mrin followed his father home. He walked into the living room to see a three-dimensional image of a small person on the top of the device.

Mrin said, "Hello!"

With the strangest accent Mrin had ever heard, the figure said, "Hello. My name is Glor. We didn't think you'd make contact so soon."

"So soon?" Mrin was confused by the statement.

The figure called Glor said, "We didn't think you wanted to contact us at all. Anyway, we know it's dire."

Mrin nodded. He understood most of what Glor said but not every word. "It is. We have lost the ability to get water from the glaciers. We are starving."

"We can tell."

"You can tell?"

"Yes, our monitors have told us all we need to know. We are already repairing the water conduits, so water will start to flow in the next few hours."

"That is great!"

"So, Supreme Chief, we also have..."

"Wait..."

"Yes?"

Mrin didn't know what to do. He looked at his father, who just nodded as if he trusted him to do the right thing. He felt his gut wrench. What was the right thing? Lie, or tell the truth? Telling the truth seemed the best of unpleasant options, but he knew that it would likely mean he would get into a lot of trouble somehow.

"I'm not the Supreme Chief. My name is Mrin. I'm an engineer. I found this device in a cache. No one knows I have it."

"Ah. OK. We should probably..."

"He would likely execute me if he found out what I'm doing right now."

The figure turned its head and wavered.

Glor said, "We need to confer."

Mrin nodded. The figure disappeared. A few minutes later, he reappeared.

"Mrin, we cannot allow any more communication since this is not official. We can't be in any more contact. Do you understand?"

He felt his whole body drop as if falling.

"I do."

"I'm sorry."

"It's alright."

Glor nodded. "You need to return that device to where you found it."

Mrin nodded. "I'll do that."

"Thank you, Mrin. Good luck." The figure disappeared for the last time, and the unit turned off. Mrin didn't know what this meant.

The next night, Mrin looked at the inert device sitting on his small desk. He had promised to get it back to the cache, but he didn't know how he would do that without letting anyone know he had it. He expected the entire cache to be underwater by now, anyway. He might find another cache somewhere, but the first step was to get himself back in a position where he could find some other equipment stash to put it in.

It was late. He was surprised that Tyrin and his parents weren't back from the meeting. He could imagine it would be a very contentious meeting. It had been clear that the water flow would return their capacity to grow food back to what it had been a very long time ago. What would they do now that they knew this wasn't the generation that would be the last, now that they wouldn't starve? From the conversation he had with his Da earlier, there were a lot of people who were ready for open rebellion. Maybe it was finally time for that.

He heard a loud bang—it sounded like their front door. He was worried and got up to open the door, but before he got there, his door flew open, and several men ran in and grabbed him.

"Here he is! Take him!"

Mrin was scared. They put a cloth bag over his head, and he couldn't see anything. They tied him up and dragged him out. He could hear Dlen yelling something, and he fought the men, grabbing him to move in her direction. He felt a sharp pain on the side of his head and then felt nothing more.

He woke with a horrible headache. He raised his head, and a wave of dizziness made him put it down again. Finally, he could sit up and look around. He was on the floor of a dingy cell. There was a tiny window far at the top of one wall, and the small amount of light coming in suggested to Mrin that it was probably morning. The walls of the cell were solid, and there were scrawls and scratches all over it. There was a toilet and a sink on one wall, and nothing else. No bed, no chair, no pillows, nothing comfortable.

He used the toilet and washed his face. He heard the door open, and two men grabbed him and dragged him out of the cell and down the corridor to a room with a desk and a man behind it. He nodded, and the two men left, closing the door.

"Mrin Gnova Jolrs, do you know why you are here?"

"I can guess."

"How did you think you could get away with it? It was obvious *someone* called the Breft. And all it took was contacting a few chiefs to find out who might have the knowledge and access to equipment to do it. You stood out immediately. Then we found the device in your room.

"Anyway, you have been charged with treason of the highest order. You contacted the Breft without authorization."

Mrin said nothing. There really wasn't anything to say. That was precisely what he'd done, and he wasn't about to lie about it.

"Is there anything you have to say?"

Mrin shook his head. He would refrain from saying anything until he could say his last words. He knew the procedure. He'd seen treason executions.

"You have been found guilty by the Supreme Chief and sentenced to death by beheading. You will be publicly executed tomorrow in the capital square. Your father is on his way to visit. Do you have any questions?"

He shook his head.

"Alright." The man looked at him with the oddest look, like he had a question he wanted to ask but wouldn't. The two men who had brought him to this room took him, more gently it seemed and left him in a different cell. It was far more comfortable. It had a much larger window, a bed with a comfortable mattress, and a chair. He lay down on the bed, numb. He was going to die soon. Tomorrow.

### Hilcyon Orbit

Paul saw Glor sit down heavily in the chair. He, Ke'lir, Pot'relo, Sandra and Glor were in a small communications room on the cargo ship.

Glor said, "Well, what do we do now?"

Ke'lir said, "Do what we were going to do anyway. Finish the repairs and drop off the food. Then, I imagine, it's best we leave."

Pot'relo said, "I'm not sure we should drop the food. It's bad enough that the repairs are already underway. We might cause panic if they know we interfered."

Paul said, "But they are going to know we came anyway. Every single water conduit is going to be flowing. The only conclusion they can come to is that we helped."

Sandra said, "And what is the other option, Pot'relo? Leave, and let all of them starve to death? We have to dump the food."

Glor said, "You are right. We have to. But we can't do anything more until and unless we have official permission."

Pot'relo said, "I can agree to drop the food, but I will assure you no more permission will be forthcoming."

Ke'lir said, "We should wait a few days. See how things play out. Maybe they will make contact once they realize that they won't starve to death."

Sandra said, "That doesn't seem so likely, but I agree. Let's stay a bit and see what happens. Besides, our on-planet monitors have 65 years of data to analyze."

Glor said, "I must admit to surprise that the Casitians left them there."

Pot'relo said, "Monitors have been in place since before the Betrayal of Jl'ec. There were new monitors placed right before we were asked not so politely to never return."

Ke'lir said, "So I guess you, Paul, and Sandra will be busy for the next days while Glor and I twiddle our thumbs."

A day later, Paul and Sandra sat and looked at the monitoring data.

Paul said, "All conduits are flowing at full capacity. The reservoirs will be full in a matter of hours. We can scale back the flow soon."

"How long will these repairs last?"

"Well, since we had the remote units, I figured, why not just leave them here? The remote units can monitor problems and repair them as needed. Between that and the new fusion reactors, they should be OK for a hundred years or so."

Sandra asked, "And then this will happen again?"

"Yup. The remote units will start breaking down themselves and run out of spare parts. The reactors will run out of fuel by then as well."

"So we're just postponing the inevitable?"

"Is it inevitable?"

"Seems so. If the current Supreme Chief wasn't going to contact us even if all of his people died, I can't see how this isn't going to happen again."

Paul said, "Change?"

"Everything I've been seeing in the monitors suggests retrenchment since the cutoff."

"Well, we've done what we can do. We can only hope for the best."

"Yes. You've heard of the 'Betrayal of J'lec'?"

"Sure. It seems to be the major reason the Kinder and Casitians hate each other."

Sandra said, "No, the real reason they hate each other goes back much further, to when humans won their freedom from Tud'scla captivity. But this was another injury that made it worse."

"What's the story?"

"Well, that's the thing. Neither the Casitians nor the Kinder are willing to talk about it. The Kinder call the incident 'The Betrayal of Klor.'"

Paul said, "Hmmm, that's interesting."

"It is. I understand from my research that Klor was a Supreme Chief more than 1200 years ago. And my research on J'lec suggests that she was the Casitian liaison to Hilcyon during his rule. I'm 90% sure the Casitians have a written report but won't let anyone see it."

The monitoring system's voice interrupted their conversation.

"Sandra, we are hearing Mrin's name repeated many times in various places. It appears he has been arrested and is going to be executed for treason."

Paul sat up. "Oh no!"

"Let me get Glor, Pot'relo, and Ke'lir."

Sandra left and returned quickly with them.

Glor said, "He's being executed? We know this for sure?"

The system said, "Mrin Gnova Jolrs, living in the hamlet that we detected the device had been activated from, was arrested and has been sentenced to death."

Paul sighed. He said, "There isn't anything we can do, is there?"

Pot'relo said, "No, there isn't. We can't intervene."

The five of them sat there in silence. Paul was upset, but he knew they could do nothing but finish their work and leave.

### Capital Region, Hilcyon

Like everyone, Jorn was aware of the uproar because of the flowing water, and the Casitian food rations spread everywhere. Yesterday, he'd been helping other priests get rations to people who hadn't been able to get much food in the last while. He hadn't gotten much sleep last night, so he was a bit slow and groggy this morning as he sat over his breakfast porridge. Lronr's assistant came into Jorn's view as he was finishing his bowl of porridge. He looked up.

"Lronr would like to speak with you urgently."

Jorn nodded, stood up, and placed his bowl and spoon in the rack. He followed the assistant to Lronr's office.

He sat across from Lronr and heard the office door close behind the assistant. Lronr looked pensive.

Jorn said, "How may I be of service?"

"A young man by the name of Mrin did a deeply brave, but dishonorable act. He somehow managed to obtain a communications device, and he contacted the Breft."

"That is why the water flows and the food rations were dropped."

"Indeed. He was found and is being executed today at high sun. I need a priest to officiate at the execution. I know you have done this before, and it is not a task you find especially onerous, as many others do."

"I find it easy to feel compassion for the condemned and feel it important to show that compassion to others when I am doing that work. This will be harder, though—this young man saved all of our lives."

Lronr nodded.

"But I will serve."

Lronr said, "Thank you, son."


Jorn had officiated at several executions over the past years, and knew what was needed. He put on his special ritual robe: all black, with a thin, green stole around his neck, the one traditionally worn for executions. It was a symbol that all people, no matter what they had done, contained some of the purity and love of the Exalted King.

He picked up his ritual staff, and walked out of the temple toward the capital square. He found the knot of chiefs around the entrance to the jail.

"I am Jorn. I am here to officiate at the execution. It is the prisoner's right to be comforted by a priest until the time."

The chiefs knew the rules, and all but one stepped aside.

That one said, "Follow me," and led him down a series of corridors back to a comfortable-looking cell that he knew was reserved for the condemned.

The chief opened the bars. Jorn walked in and saw the chief close the bars and walk away.

Mrin looked sad and lonely but not scared. Jorn could tell there had been tears.

"How are you, son?"

"I'm alright, Father. My father and sister just left. They are sad and angry, which makes me sad. But I know I did the right thing, even if I am to die for it."

Jorn nodded. "You did a very brave deed, Mrin. You saved thousands and thousands of lives—people that would have died of hunger or of the strife that would come closer to the end."

Mrin nodded.

Jorn said, "The Exalted King will be with you, my son."

Mrin asked, "How did the Exalted King let us get to this place, Father?"

"One of our holy books says something, and it is helpful to me. It says that we are the Exalted King's hands and feet. So it wasn't Him that allowed this, it was us. And I have faith that we can change this."

"You do?"

Jorn nodded. "I do. It is my life's work to see things change."

They heard a commotion in the hall outside of Mrin's cell.

"It's time!" A loud voice rang out. "Let's go."

### Capital Region, Hilcyon

Dlen gratefully ate the chewy, rich bar. It was wrapped in a strange kind of material and had words on it she could not read. But it was the first food she'd had in days, and her body was happy. There had been a big food drop in the middle of their hamlet, and the Chief had distributed the bars to those he knew hadn't had any rations for a while. He'd given their family enough to last a few months.

Everything was chaotic. Once the news of the complete resumption of water flows in all of the conduits, even the ones that had been dry for her lifetime, there was a strange mix of celebration and fear. No one was quite sure what would happen if they showed their elation, but it was hard not to be elated. What had seemed like the certain fate of starvation for all Kinder was gone, and in its place was hope for the future—hope that many people hadn't realized they'd lost years ago. But there was deep suspicion. Everyone assumed that, somehow, someone had contacted the Breft. But she didn't think anyone, except her family, knew who it was.

Her mother, Hril, her father, and Mrin's wife, Tyrin, were out at some sort of meeting; she imagined a meeting of the new reformers. She worried about them, but she also knew that the only way this wouldn't happen again was for real change to occur. For the traditional Kinder way to finally give way to something else. Something which would allow the Breft to help them live on Hilcyon.

She thought that even though this aid was temporary, it was helpful to remind her people that they depended on the Breft after all. She knew this idea was anathema to many. But it had to be understood. Otherwise, their society was eventually doomed to failure.

She threw the wrapper out and grabbed another bar to take with her to bed. It was cold tonight, and their energy rations had similarly been withheld along with the food rations. It was nice to have food, but it would be nicer to have heat as well. She bundled up in her covers and fell asleep.

She was awoken suddenly by a big bang. She sat up in bed, and heard voices and shouts. She got up out of bed, and opened the door, only to be pushed to the ground.

"Get away, woman!"

She screamed, "What are you doing?"

"I said, *stay away* from us!"

There were men running around in the house, and several men were holding Mrin to the ground.

"Found something!"

One of the men was carrying the communications device. Dlen's heart skipped a beat. Mrin...

They took Mrin, and the device out, and slammed the door.

Later the next day, her mother, father, Mrin's wife Tyrin, and she were sitting in the living room, commiserating.

Her father said, "I can't do anything. There is *nothing* I can do to save Mrin. I wish I had made him take that thing back more forcefully."

Dlen said, "I think he thought maybe they would call back."

"They said they wouldn't call back!"

"Da, look, it's done, it's over."

Her father put his head in his hands. "I've got to be able to do something!"

Her mother put her arms around her father's shoulders. They all wept.

Several hours later, there was a knock at the door. Her father opened it and saw a tall man, grim and uniformed, standing in the doorway.

"Wlen Gnova Jolrs?"

"Yes?"

"Your son, Mrin Gnova Jolrs, is set to be publicly executed tomorrow at high sun in the capital square. I'm here to take you to see him for a last visit."

"Can my family…"

He shook his head.

Dlen said, "I'm coming."

The man said, "Alright, hurry up."

Her father nodded. "Let us gather a few things, please?"

"Make it fast."

Dlen and her father packed a few things. Everyone hugged at the door.

Wlen said, "Hril, Tyrin, remember Mrin as he was. He will always be honored in this family."

Hril and Tyrin nodded. Dlen and her father walked out the door and followed the grim man.


Dlen could hardly stand up, and she knew her father was in just as bad a shape. The last visit with Mrin had been the most difficult hour of their lives. She was prouder than she could ever imagine being of Mrin. She felt deep sadness, but all she saw in her father was anger. She understood the anger, but for some reason, right now, she didn't have access to it in herself.

They had argued last night after the visit. She felt compelled to witness Mrin's execution. Her father didn't want her to see it. And during that argument, she learned how angry her father was.

She had asked, "Da, I'm going. That's that. Why are you so angry with me?"

He took a moment, then sighed, and his shoulders slumped. "I'm not angry at you, Dlen. I'm angrier than I have ever been in my life that Mrin's life is going to end this way. It's unjust. It's wrong, and I can't do anything about it."

They were behind the first row of onlookers. A huge crowd had gathered to see the execution. Dlen decided that the mood of the crowd was strange. It wasn't the mood she usually felt at public executions: the mood of proud retribution for wrongdoing. No, this was a different mood altogether. Many of these people were angry, perhaps angry like her father.

When they brought Mrin out, Dlen could see that he was holding his head high. Shouts and cheers rose from the crowd. "Mrin, Mrin, Mrin, Mrin, Mrin!"

She looked around. Yes, they felt the same injustice as her father. They *knew* Mrin had saved all of them, and they were angry that he was being executed.

A first chief shouted at the crowd, "Quiet! Be Kinder!"

But the crowd only got rowdier. Dlen was sure there was going to be a riot. But then, the Supreme Chief appeared. The crowd went silent.

He spoke in a loud, commanding voice. "We are here today to carry out justice. Mrin Gnova Jolrs committed treason by contacting the Breft on his own. He has gone against the Kinder way of self-sufficiency. He must *die* for his treason, as *all* traitors of the Kinder must die."

The crowd was completely quiet. Mrin was brought forward. A priest stood next to him and prayed over him. Dlen noticed something in the way the priest acted. It wasn't perfunctory—she felt he had genuine compassion and admiration for Mrin.

The priest asked, "Do you have any last words, Mrin Gnova Jolrs?"

"I do," Mrin spoke clearly and with determination. Mrin looked up, and saw Dlen and her father looking at him. He smiled, and Dlen felt the tears flowing down her face. They were tears of pride as well as sadness.

"I care deeply about the lives of the Kinder, which is why I did what I did. I won't live to see tomorrow, but I die gladly, knowing that many Kinder will live to see another day, another year, and the rest of their lives. We cannot live on this planet without help. My dying hope is that our leaders understand this before all the Kinder die."

The crowd was stirring. Mrin was pushed down on his knees in front of a block, and someone held his head down on it. The executioner raised his sword, and Dlen had to turn away and leave. She could not watch the stroke fall. She noticed her father was close by her. As she walked, he heard the loud thunk, and felt the life of her brother leave her heart. The crowd surged by them, and they both struggled to keep up, to move away from the center of the square as quickly as possible.

It would indeed be a riot, and the last thing they wanted was to be caught in it.

They managed to make it out before things really got ugly. She could see a large cadre of men with swords and other weapons flowing into the crowd. The Supreme Chief's men. She knew many in that crowd would not survive the night; many women would be without their husbands and children without their fathers.

They managed to catch the last tram back to their hamlet from the capital. Even though few other people were on it, Dlen could feel the somber mood. Dlen looked over at her father and saw a kind of grim determination she'd never seen before.

"Da, what are you thinking?"

"Mrin will not die in vain. I will make sure of it."

### New Orleans, New Earth

Ro'mer had made another special trip to New Earth, alongside the rest of the Casitian members of the Consej, to meet with the team returning from Hilcyon. They were glad that the team had obtained a lot of information from the listening devices on Hilcyon. There would be years of analysis ahead.

As they walked into the large conference room and looked around, he saw Paul on one end, talking animatedly to Glor. To Ro'mer's eye, he looked more engaged and confident than he'd ever looked. It was as if Ro'mer was looking at a different young man. The months on Casiti, this project and travel seemed to have grown Paul quickly.

Zrel rang the bell as people started to filter into their chairs and in from outside.

Zrel said loudly, "This meeting of the Consej and the team returning from Hilcyon will come to order!"

After some rustling and shuffling, the room became quiet.

Zrel said, "You've all had a chance to read the final report generated from the team over the past few days, as well as the interim reports sent while they were in orbit. The purpose of this meeting is two-fold: one, to answer any questions Consej members might have of the team, and two, to establish next steps, if any, so that structures are in place for any official contact."

Several Kinder and Terran representatives had questions about the data and about the execution of Mrin, the engineer who had made contact.

Then, Zrel said, "I will now hand it to Samira, the lead Casitian representative. Samira?"

Samira said, "Thank you, Zrel. I have several questions. First, why did you take action to repair their systems *and* drop food before you knew this was not an official contact?"

Glor said, "We assumed the contact was official. So we started repairs immediately. We were all taken by surprise."

Samira said, "But you knew it was possible that it wasn't official. Why didn't you delay the actions?"

Sandra said, "It was obvious once we got into orbit and looked at the quick analysis of the data from the listening devices that they were in dire straights. They'd had a 35% decrease in population since the devices were put in place, with an 85% decrease in growing crops. They would have all died."

"But you were clearly instructed that we were not to interfere without knowing that the communication was official!"

Po'tre'lo broke in, "I decided it was important—we couldn't let them starve. We did nothing further to interfere."

Samira was obviously angry. Ro'mer could see the set of her mouth and the tightening of her fists.

She said, "You did not follow instructions, Po'tre'lo! No actions were to be taken unless it was official communication. Not only was it not a competing faction—it was a lowly engineer! What were you thinking?"

Po'tre'lo held her ground. "It looked very clear that unless we did something immediately, most, if not all, of the Kinder on Hilcyon would starve to death within a year, perhaps less. It would have been inhumane not to act."

Ke'lora said, "It is clear that Po'tre'lo did not follow instructions and made an unfortunate choice. No action should have been taken."

Hrelr stood up. "How dare you! Are you suggesting that all of the Kinder on Hilcyon should have starved to death?"

Ke'lora said, "If that was their choice, yes."

The room erupted. Ro'mer watched this unfold - the Kinder understandably upset at what they felt was the aloof and unkind approach of the Casitians. At least right now, the Terrans seemed to be siding quite solidly with the Kinder.

Then Paul's loud, strong voice, quite surprising Ro'mer, said over the din, "We did what we did. What we need to focus on now is what we will do in the future."

The room got very quiet, and people settled down. Zrel said, "Well said, Paul. What's done is done. It is unlikely that the Kinder will contact us again in our lifetimes, now that they won't starve and will be able to survive another hundred years or so."

Samira said, "The Casitians will never agree to intervene without official contact again."

Grynt, another Kinder representative who rarely spoke said, "I think that's obvious. But that doesn't mean that you will get your way. We Kinder are united in our stance that we need to do whatever it is that we can to work toward unification—even if that means we work in unofficial channels."

There was silence in the room. Ro'mer wondered whether the Casitians felt chastised by Grynt's statement. Ro'mer felt he needed to say something.

"I don't think all Casitians on this body agree with Samira. I believe unification is our most important goal. I, at least, am not in agreement with Samira on this."

Samira laughed. "Of course you are not, Ro'mer. You aren't really Casitian."

Ro'mer stood up, angry. "I am a Kadarin—as much Casitian as you are, Samira."

Zrel said, "OK, let's calm down everyone. This isn't getting us anywhere. I will put together a small subcommittee to work on the question of the next steps. They will have complete access to the team and come up with recommendations."

Ro'mer knew that neither Samira nor they would be on that committee.

The meeting came to an uncomfortable close, and Ro'mer made their way to the house - they still had a few meetings before they could take the shuttle back to Casiti. And back home, a very uncomfortable meeting with the Casitian representatives of the Consej with the Caraj, which had much more staunchly non-interventionist members than Samira and Ke'lora, if that were even possible.

# Chapter 6:
# New Beginnings

New Earth: December 2099 - January 2100
Hilcyon: Sdert - Lykl 1202
Casiti: Wend 803

*"Leadership should be seen as a gift of honor to be given, not a privilege to seize." Heart of the Carj, Eclogue 23*

### Hilcyon, Sdert 32, 1202 (December 10, 2099, New Earth Time)

Dlen, Hlir, and Tyrin were sitting around the table, waiting for Wlen to arrive. Dlen was glad that Tyrin accepted their offer of living with them—they had come to love her and consider her family, even though she and Mrin had only been married for a few moons.

The front door opened, and Wlen walked in. Hril got up to greet him.

"How are you tonight after training, husband?"

"I'm less tired tonight; I think that's a good sign. I am mastering my short sword."

"Good, good. Wlen, I don't want to lose my husband and my son in the same year."

"You won't, wife. I will win this." Dlen's mother smiled. She was supportive, although they all knew she was scared, and wouldn't show it.

They all sat at the table, and she helped her mother serve dinner.

Dlen knew that the first ten days or so of training had been utterly brutal. He would come home sore and bruised, and wake up so stiff the next day that he couldn't imagine returning to training. But that grim determination that Dlen had seen in him the day Mrin was executed would be in his eyes and face, and he'd go back to training the next day, no matter how he felt.

Her father had never been a chief. He had told her that he had hated the chief system from when he was a little boy. But Dlen knew he had always liked physical exertion and was very healthy. When he told them that he had decided to challenge Klef, they all thought he was just too stricken with grief and anger, and the notion would pass. But he had kept training, and Dlen now knew that he would do it.

Klef had done a good job of keeping all of his First Chiefs in line—none of them would challenge him. Although it was extremely rare, it was possible for a non-chief to challenge even a Supreme Chief for leadership. Her father would be ready, and Supreme Chief Klef would be taken completely by surprise. Dlen hoped that would be enough.

Wlen asked, "So how goes the resistance?"

Dlen said, "I was elected to go to the capital and represent our hamlet."

"Dlen! Wonderful."

"I'm leaving tomorrow, Da. I have a birth to attend in Swet, which is quite conveniently on the way. I'm assuming whoever is watching me won't bother to follow me all the way to Swet."

"Let's hope not."

### Independent Christian State

Paul sat on the bus, watching the landscape change as they crossed the border into the ICS. He was reluctantly visiting his family for the Christmas holidays. His paternal grandmother was dying, and no one thought she would live to see the new year. He didn't especially like his paternal grandmother, but his father asked him to come home to visit, and he agreed. He figured he'd stay through the funeral.

He thought he was prepared to see the ICS again, but as he watched the streets get rough and grimy and looked at the buildings that were a hodge-podge of different kinds of hand-built houses and low buildings, he realized how much the year had changed his perspective. The ICS was a backwater, and it surprised him how bad it looked in comparison to where he had been for the last year.

He'd read a lot of history since he landed on Casiti, and he felt like he had a better handle on why things were the way they were. He'd known that his paternal grandmother's grandfather was one of the founders of the ICS, Thomas Martin, who had basically been forced to leave Earth well before The Event, because they were not willing to acquiesce to the demands of the Casitians. However, as Paul kept reading, he realized that the demands of the Casitians were quite reasonable and wouldn't have interfered with the practice of the Christian faith. In his childhood, Paul had been taught so much that was so wrong. In learning more from Jal'end'a's writing and attending classes at the Ja'lit school, he understood better why the people in the ICS had developed the theology they had. Banishment from Earth was truly a big deal, and Terran subcultures had a variety of ways of dealing with it, and Paul knew his community's was one particularly extreme version. But he couldn't help but hate it.

It was going to be a hard trip for him. He knew his family would want him to stay, but he knew he could not. For one thing, he had an important role on Casiti, now, since his visit to Hilcyon. He had been given a spot as a student in the Casitian group whose role was to strategize the long-term process of sending needed supplies to Hilcyon, even though they probably didn't really want them. There was so much they learned from that visit, information they would put to work in crafting the next steps.

The bus stopped at his hometown's stop, and he grabbed his bag and walked out of the bus to see his father and brother awaiting him. His father came to hug him.

"Paul!"

"Hi, Dad. Hi Matthew." He hugged them both.

"You look good, son. Those Casitians are treating you well?"

Paul nodded, not wanting to get into anything right at the moment. They walked the mile or so to the house, and his father and brother caught him up on the family news: one engaged cousin, a birth, and, of course, his dying grandmother. They were going to visit her the next day. Paul was quiet with the varied news, nodded when it seemed appropriate and didn't comment or say much.

Matthew asked, "So Paul, what was Hilcyon like?"

"Well, I didn't really see it. We didn't go down to the surface. But it is so unlike New Earth—it is extremely dry and a lot colder. Casiti would be very hard to live on without galactic technology, but it would be at least possible. Uncomfortable for years at a time, but doable.

Hilcyon is really not livable by humans without galactic technology, so when the galactic technology wore out, they were in deep trouble."

"How long have they been on that planet?"

"As long as the Casitians have been on theirs, but until the Event, the Casitians had supplied them with needed technology."

"Does anyone think they will actually decide to have contact with the Casitians?"

"I don't know that anyone really knows. Things were in upheaval when we left—we are monitoring the situation, but it's hard to know exactly what's happening right now."

They arrived at the house, and Paul was greeted heartily by his mother.

"Paul! It's so good to see you." She gave him a big hug.

"Where's Martha?"

"She's with her fiancée. They'll be by later."

"She's getting married? To whom?" Paul was surprised his father and brother hadn't told him on their walk.

"Franklin Martin."

Paul was taken aback. Franklin Martin was not only Paul's third cousin but also heir apparent to Franklin's father, the current Bishop of the ICS. Martha was most definitely marrying up.

"Wow. That's big."

His mother said sternly, "You will not mention Casiti, or your trip when he is present, do you understand?"

"Martha didn't tell him…"

"No. He knows of the sins of the Michaelsons, but…"

"Mom! Stop it! Do not talk about your family in those terms, please."

"They are not my family anymore! Jonathon's family is my family now."

"Well, then, don't talk about *my* family that way."

That tense exchange was the last they spoke of the rift between them. The rest of the day sort of blurred together for Paul. He spent some time with the whole family and Franklin Martin but said virtually nothing. He then made a lame excuse to go to his room and take a nap, as he could not mention that his body was on a totally different time than ICS time.

His sister's decision to marry Franklin meant that his immediate family was soon to be at the heart of things in the ICS. Franklin's father was ailing, and the wedding was being held in early January because of that. Paul knew there would be no way he couldn't stay for the wedding, but he was not at all looking forward to spending three full weeks in the ICS with his family. When he got to his room, he grabbed the new phone he'd gotten for his stay on New Earth, and called Ke'lir.

"Hi, Paul. How's the visit so far?"

"You wouldn't believe it. My sister is marrying Franklin Martin."

"Who's that?"

"The heir apparent for ICS Bishop."

There was silence.

"Ke'lir?"

"Really?"

"Yeah. I have to stay for the wedding on January 9th."

"I'm sorry you have to stay that long, and what are you going to do about..."

"I don't know. My mother has asked me to keep a very low profile. The Martin family does not know that I live on Casiti. I imagine they would not be happy to hear it. My mother doesn't want them to know about it before Martha gets married. I can understand that—I don't want to ruin things for my sister. So I'm going to keep quiet, then leave, and I imagine probably never come back—I'm sure I won't be welcome anymore, once Franklin becomes Bishop. Anyway, look, I'm going to need a break. Can you meet me in New Orleans, maybe in a week? I can come up with some excuse related to my role."

"Sure, I'll call Liam, too. We'll hang out for a while, save you from your family."

"Great. Thanks!"

That next week, Paul was sitting across from his cousin Liam, and next to Ke'lir at a bar in New Orleans. Glor had gotten up to get them a new round of beer. Paul liked alcohol. Drinking was not allowed in the ICS, but he had been introduced to it hanging out with Ke'lir and Glor. There were quite a number of Terran-themed bars and restaurants on Casiti that served alcohol as well.

Liam said, "Oh, man, I am so sorry about what's happening with your family, Paul."

"It's messy right now, for sure. My grandmother died the day before Christmas, which set everyone on edge. Then, I got cornered at the funeral by my sister's fiancée, who was convinced I had not spent the last year on the other side of the ICS studying theology as my parents had told him. Of course, I had to tell him the truth—how could I lie? Now everyone is mad at me, because I exposed a lie *they* told, and Franklin's family is considering revoking the marriage offer."

"Do you think they will really do it?"

"No. I think it's posturing. When I talked with Franklin, it was pretty clear that he'd learned that I had been on the trip to Hilcyon. Unlike the rest of the ICS, I guess he reads the news feeds. I don't think it bothered him as much as it bothers his father. He really loves Martha and wants to marry her. He just had to let his father bluster."

"Ah, I see. Still, that's annoying."

"Yeah. Far more family drama than I want to deal with right now."

Glor came back with the second pitcher of beer.

Paul said, "So Liam, I hear Tricia wants you to work for her in the Vice President's office."

"Yeah. It's a high-stress job. I'm not sure about it. But I'm thinking about it."

Ke'lir said, "And make something of your life, finally?"

"Ke'lir, that's not fair!"

"It is fair, Liam. You're what, 23?"

"I turned 24 last month."

"Well, then."

"I know. It just feels so fucking intimidating to be in this family, you know? All of these high expectations from our parents to be leaders, like them, and like their parents, and the *great Michaelsons*. I felt like maybe I was better off just staying at home doing nothing."

Paul listened to Ke'lir, Liam, and Glor commiserate, but he couldn't really relate. He wished he'd grown up with all the advantages these three were railing against. He realized, though, that even though he hadn't grown up with the advantages or the expectations, he occupied a space of privilege he hadn't expected.

They finished their beer and went back to Liam's, where they all stayed for the night.

He'd enjoyed his little sojourn to New Orleans. He liked his cousins, and it had been nice to get a break from his family crisis. When he arrived back home, Franklin and his father were sitting in his parent's living room with his parents and Martha. He tried to slip past to return to his room without making himself obvious, but Franklin stopped him.

"Hi, Paul. Welcome home."

"Hi, Franklin. Thanks. It looks like you all are busy..."

Thomas Martin III, grandson of the founder of the ICS, Thomas Martin, looked at Paul and said, "Paul, sit down a moment, please, will you?"

Paul nodded and sat in one of the chairs.

"You know that your trip to Casiti is quite a concern for our family. I don't want the taint of the Casitians to touch us. We must remain pure. I'm sure you'll be able to toss off what you've learned now that you are back to stay."

Paul didn't know what to say. He felt insulted and angry but knew he couldn't express that. He closed his eyes for a moment, using the technique he'd been taught at the Ja'lit school to quiet his mind and open himself to the wisdom of what the Casitians called "re'es," which translated to "Spirit." Paul thought of "re'es" as God, but different than the God he'd known growing up. He now knew what to say. He opened his eyes to see everyone staring at him. His mother looked very worried. He smiled.

"Sir, I understand and appreciate your concern. You needn't worry about our family. God is with us." It was an easy truth to tell, while leaving out what didn't need to be said.

Thomas Martin nodded, satisfied. His mother, who knew full well that he would be leaving to go back to Casiti after the wedding, looked at him with a mixture of pleasure and perplexity. His father's face was unreadable. After some pleasantries and the assurance that he would let the wedding go forward, Thomas and Franklin left. His father faced him.

"That was masterful. Where did you learn to talk like that?"

"I don't know that I learned, Dad. I'm learning these interesting mindfulness techniques at the school I'm attending, and I just opened myself to God, and asked God what to say. That was what came out."

His father looked somewhat surprised but didn't ask anything else. Paul was glad that he'd been right about Franklin and glad his sister's wedding was back on.

### Pa'rai's, North Circumpolar Independent Zone, New Earth

Ke'lir was glad to be back home again after her trip to New Orleans. She liked spending time there, but she loved home a lot more. It was quiet, and her house had a view of Lake Superior. The NCIZ was, alongside the SCIZ, the least populated part of New Earth. Her town was small, had a sizeable Casitian population, and everyone knew everyone else. She lived in the same house that Leticia Michaelson and Mira Michaelson-Kline had shared many years ago. It had been occupied by their granddaughter Kira until Kira married Khalid. Various family members had used it as a vacation house for many years until Ke'lir asked if she could live there. Ke'lir loved it. It was a little large just for her. Sometimes, she felt herself rattling around in it. She thought she'd find someone who perhaps wanted to live here with her someday. But she hadn't found that person yet.

Ke'lir had a big report that she had been procrastinating on. She was supposed to look over the plans that had been in place for many years for technology release to the Kinder on Hilcyon and do her best to square it with the reality they had seen when they were there. Of course, she could basically write one sentence that said, "There has been no official contact with the Kinder. Thus, this plan is irrelevant." Somehow, that seemed like not what her managers would want to hear. So she buckled down to write something much more detailed.

She got sidetracked in thinking about an interesting conversation she and Paul had while visiting Liam in New Orleans. She could see that Paul had grown in the year since he'd left the ICS, and she'd wanted to ask him about his experiences.

She'd said, "So, Paul, it seems like a lot has happened in the last year, huh?"

He nodded. "I'm not sure I can keep up with it all. Move to Casiti, start a job, learn Casitian, learn to grow my own food, get called to go to Hilcyon... It's a bit dizzying. But I'm managing."

"You seem to be more than managing..."

"The mindfulness techniques I've been learning have helped a lot."

Ke'lir knew those were the techniques all Casitians learned as children. She'd learned them as well.

"They help?"

"Yes. And I'm trying to get over my anger about the ICS. I think it's working." He smiled crookedly. "I don't know how much I really like Casiti or the culture, but it seems that's the place for me right now. And I'm making friends."

"You are? That's good."

"Yeah, one of my co-students in the manufacturing lab is a really nice guy. We've been hanging out together. His name is Ka'li'mo. He's teaching me how to grow food and helping me with some aspects of being on Casiti. I like him a lot, and he's sweet."

She asked innocently, "That sounds nice. Might you be companions next winter?"

Ke'lir could feel the great tension coming from Paul. She had completely forgotten about the norms of the culture he was raised in, and his tension was a surprise. She backpedaled. "Well, I'm really glad you have a new friend." She felt him relax.

"Yes, thanks."

Ke'lir thought back on that conversation and wondered whether or not Paul had really considered what his feelings were. He had waxed so eloquently about how much he liked Ka'li'mo. She remembered how she'd felt about a new friend she'd had several years ago—the friend who became her first companion. Mari'sol had been born on Casiti, and she was fully committed to the Casitian way of doing relationships. They had lived together for a Casitian winter, the equivalent of a year. Then Mari'sol left to move back to Casiti, and Ke'lir moved into this house in Pa'rai's. Ke'lir hadn't been so happy to part with Mari'sol, and they were still friends. Even though Ke'lir was raised on Castiti by Casitians, she still couldn't quite get with the Casitian relationship program. She wanted a partner like Leticia had in Mira. Yet sometimes, when she was with Terran women, who would be more oriented that way, she felt too Casitian. It was a conundrum she had not yet found the answer to.

### Hol'venif, Rel'toro, Casiti

Things had finally settled down, and Ro'mer felt they had time to re-orient themselves to family and home. The past month had been full of meetings and conversations, and he felt constantly defensive and embattled.

All of the other Casitian members of the Consej and virtually all of the Casitian governing council, the Caraj, found Ro'mer to be problematic. They felt that because Ro'mer wasn't 100% Casitian, but merely 75%, with some Kinder thrown in through his great-grandfather Ngellin, Ro'mer was suspect.

Ro'mer never felt anything else except Casitian. They had grown up on Casiti, with two parents who considered themselves Casitian. Further, they were a part of the illustrious Kadarin family—a very old and well-regarded family on Casiti. They were puzzled and upset by the way they felt the Casitian leadership was treating them.

Not that this was necessarily new. They and their mother had both been passed up for consideration as a member of the Caraj, a position they both could earn, given their status.

The best news of this entire mess was how much their cousin Paul had grown in the last several months. It was remarkable to see. He had changed from a sullen, confused teenager into a confident, able young man. Ro'mer was glad for whatever role they played in that transformation, but they suspected that once Paul had been removed from that backwater he grew up in, he would have blossomed anyway.

They were holding their firstborn, Jel'iro, who had become quite a handful now that they were crawling and moving around. Ro'mer couldn't put them down and expect them to stay in the same place. Their co-parent M'nali was off on a trip to Loc'deher for work, so

Ro'mer was in place as primary caregiver, although there were always folks at home who could take care of Jel'iro if needed.

They were glad to be home and spend time with their offspring and family group. They hoped the quiet would last a while.

### Capital Region, Hilcyon

When Jorn heard that Wlen, Mrin's father, had challenged Klef to become Supreme Chief, Jorn knew he had to go to the ring and watch. He didn't relish seeing someone die, but he knew this was important.

Ylorp had been following Dlen, Wlen's daughter, for months. He had only reported a small fraction of Dlen's activities: basically, only the births she attended, none of the meetings and such. Ylorp worried that he'd be discovered, but Jorn knew Klef was not as in touch with what was happening with the people as he thought he was.

He arrived at the entrance of the arena. He was part of a stream of people—the arena would be packed full. He was glad he'd arrived early. He'd never seen it this full.

After a while, the doors for the challenger and defender opened. Both Wlen and Klef were wearing the traditional fighting uniform: it had a top that wrapped around their torsos, with a fabric belt. Jorn saw that Wlen had chosen a short sword. A very wise choice; it was one of the best weapons against Klef's circle blade.

As Wlen reached his bench, one by one, the crowd stood with their right hands at their heart. Jorn joined in. It was a great sign of respect.

He saw Klef scowling and heard him say, "Let's get this over with, shall we? I have things to do."

Wlen nodded. They moved to the center of the ring, did the traditional bow to each other, and Wlen backed up; Jorn imagined it was to get a measure of Klef. Jorn knew that the last fight Klef had was more than a year ago, and he doubted that Klef had been training. Jorn thought that it was likely that Klef didn't take Wlen seriously. This was Wlen's major advantage.

Jorn saw Wlen scramble out of the way of Klef's swings and even tripped twice. Jorn wondered whether that was on purpose. Klef started to laugh. Klef swung his circle blade, a wicked curved blade on the end of a long pole, and Wlen would duck or jump to avoid it. Wlen let Klef get closer and closer, and Jorn bet that he was making him think he was coming in for the kill.

Klef swung in a wide arc, slicing Wlen's leg badly, and it caused Wlen to stumble. Klef used that moment to swing the back of the pole into Wlen's head. But unexpectedly, Wlen bent his body sideways and then swung his right arm, which held the sword, over and up and plunged the sword into Klef's exposed chest. Klef looked up, surprised, and fell over, dead. The crowd erupted.

Jorn watched as the crowd flowed over the seats into the arena. He saw Wlen collapse. His fight attendant lay him down and started to put bandages on his leg. His attendant and two others carried him out of the arena. The crowd was chanting, "Wlen! Wlen!" Jorn couldn't help but join them. He was elated. Perhaps, maybe, things would change for the better. He would talk with Glin. Perhaps it was finally time to connect the priesthood with reformers.

# Chapter 7:
## Intermezzo

New Earth: April 2100
Hilcyon: Cfro 1202
Casiti: Nird 804

*"Death is the greatest unknown, and we can't help but attempt to understand and guess what is to come afterward. But the most important thing is honoring what the dead offered us in life."* Je'lend'a, 'Spirits Alike'

### Jor'ar'lir, Rel'toro, Casiti

It was Casitian New Year. Yesterday and last night was the somber remembering of everyone who had died during the year. Paul had been at the Ja'lit school, taking part in the traditional rituals of the day. He felt embraced by those rituals, and held, in a way. He mourned again for his great-grandmother Beatrice, and even his grandmother Margaret, who had died on Christmas eve.

The day of the New Year was spent in creative pursuits, to bring in the spirit of the year to come. Many people were outside, making sculptures. Many were painting the outside walls of their houses with riotous patterns or making mosaics for their front stoops. Paul had decided that it would be fun to paint his door, and he stood back to look at his handiwork. He didn't know how whether it measured up to Casitian standards, but he liked it. It had a sunburst on one side, and rays of sun projecting down and out. It had a deep blue sky, and a green landscape on the bottom.

"Hello, neighbor!"

He turned to see his next-door neighbor, one of the few other Terrans living in Jor'ar'lir. Paul remembered her name was Jaimee Waters.

"Hey Jamiee! Blessed New Year."

"Blessed New Year to you, too. Nice door! I made a sculpture in my backyard."

Paul knew that many Terrans living on Casiti tried their best to join in on the Casitian cultural activities, but amateur public art was hard for many Terrans. Somehow, it hadn't been for him.

"Well, I'll have to come see it sometime, but now I need to cook dinner for a friend."

"Have a good one!" Jaimee started to walk on. It looked like she was on her way somewhere else, anyway.

"Thanks! See you soon." Paul waved.

He had invited Ka'li'mo over for dinner and to see his handiwork. Also, to eat his handiwork. Paul planned a fairly ambitious meal for Ka'li'mo: a mix of Casitian and Terran food. He hoped he was up to the task. He went inside and grabbed all the ingredients he needed for dinner. As he cooked, he couldn't help but remember his conversation with Ke'lir when he was in New Orleans. Her suggestion that Ka'li'mo could be his companion had sent him into a tailspin. Paul had been taught that men with men was a perversion and only men and women should be together. A part of him still believed that. But Paul had always known that wasn't the right thing for him, but he hadn't really spent much time dealing with his feelings for other boys—he'd just stuffed them.

Coming to Casiti and living in a culture where there were no such ideas at first felt really threatening to him. And as he got to be friends with Ka'li'mo, he knew things were going on inside of himself. When Ke'lir made that innocent remark to him, he realized he had to deal with it. He spent days avoiding Ka'li'mo; then, finally, he had to go talk with one of the teachers at school, who helped him understand what was happening and how to separate his own feelings and beliefs from those he grew up with.

Poor Ka'li'mo had been completely mystified about what was happening, and finally, several days ago, Paul had a conversation with him.

"Ka'li'mo, I want to apologize for how I've been lately."

"It's not a problem, Paul; I just want to know what's going on."

"I… I've learned that I can't ignore my feelings for you, even though they feel dangerous to me."

"You grew up in a different culture. I understand that."

Paul couldn't help but reach out and touch Ka'li'mo's arm. "You are such a wonderful man. I'm sorry if my behavior has hurt you."

Ka'li'mo had smiled this smile that made Paul just light up inside. "You haven't hurt me, Paul. I'm glad you are sorting out your feelings."

Paul took a breath. "I am. I have come to really appreciate you, Ka'li'mo, and…"

"And…?"

Paul didn't really have the right words. He knew Ka'li'mo wasn't fluent in English, and he still had a ways to go in the Casitian language. "I want to… I want to be your companion."

Ka'li'mo smiled. "Well, Paul, just so you know, Casitians don't consider lovers between winters to be 'Companions.' That's reserved for the winter."

Paul was confused, but Ka'li'mo patiently explained the word he was using and Casitian culture to him and then expressed his own interest in being with Paul. Paul was relieved to have finally told everything to Ka'li'mo, and he was happy that Ka'li'mo was as interested as he was. Ka'li'mo was due here in just a while, and Paul smiled as he chopped the onions and garlic. He was happy, in a way he couldn't have imagined being just a New Earth year ago.

A chime roused him from his thoughts. He stopped chopping and went to his desk to see an incoming message from his father.

"Thanks, Play message."

"Hi Paul, it's your dad. I just wanted to let you know that Martha's father-in-law died last night. Franklin is set to be installed as Bishop tomorrow afternoon sometime. Franklin wanted me to let you know that he will be contacting you. Anyway, I hope you are doing well."

Of course, his father had no idea it was Casitian New Year, so Paul didn't feel insulted that he'd not mentioned it. It was strange that Franklin was going to contact him. He couldn't even imagine when the last time the head of the ICS called someone on Casiti. Perhaps it had never happened before. But then, Franklin was Paul's brother-in-law, which was a bit different. But still, Paul could not imagine why Franklin would want to talk with him.

### Hol'venif, Rel'toro, Casiti

Ro'mer wasn't exactly sure why they had been summoned by the leader of the Caraj. They and Trel'or'li had a long history together, including having been companions the one winter between his leaving the youth house, where they had met, and Ro'mer's decision to raise children. Of late, they and Trel'or'li's relationship had been antagonistic. Trel'or'li's position around Hilcyon reflected the conservatism of the mainstream of the Caraj.

The building housing the Caraj and its associated offices was one of the oldest buildings in Rel'toro, which meant it was one of the oldest buildings on the planet. As they approached it, they were awed, as usual, by the building's grandeur—an unusual feature of buildings on Casiti. It was quite tall, more than several stories. Ro'mer had been in the building several times, and as they entered the grand main entrance, they looked up to see the high ceilings, with many exposed beams above, hosting sculptures and paintings of all kinds, many of which were thousands of years old.

They walked down the main corridor leading to the large back office of the leader of the Caraj. It was quiet today. Not many people are in the offices or moving about in the corridors. Ro'mer entered the door to the leader's office and was greeted by a junior Caraj student.

"Good morning, Ro'mer. Trel'or'li is in a joining with the architectural committee, and she will be done soon. Please sit."

They sat in a comfortable chair outside Trel'or'li's office, while the student offered them drinks and sweets. Ro'mer was nervous. Finally, the door to the office opened, and several people they did not recognize emerged and nodded to him and the student. The student indicated he could enter the office.

Tre'lor'li was standing next to her desk. As Ro'mer walked in, she moved toward them, a little haltingly, but they embraced, as usual.

"Ro'mer. Thank you so much for coming."

"I'm happy to be of service to the Caraj, you know that."

Trel'or'li nodded. "I do. And I know that there are times that we disagree on what's best for Casiti."

Ro'mer said, "Yes, that is true. Anyway, how may I be of service?"

"I have heard from a scholar who studies Hilcyon and its history. After they analyzed the data the team brought back, they are fairly convinced we will be contacted again officially sooner than anyone thinks. Perhaps even in the next 25-30 years."

This surprised Ro'mer. The assumption of everyone they had discussed this with was that it would be another 100 years or more: when the equipment the team fixed failed again.

"Tell me more about their thinking?"

Trel'or'li shook her head. "They don't have much to go on—it's a hunch. They think the increasing instability of the leadership structure means they will contact again before the equipment fails."

"Can you give me the contact info for this scholar? I would like to speak to them and get them in contact with the team."

Trel'or'li nodded. "Yes, of course. They are rather old, and I'm sure they are not interested in traveling to New Earth. But I'm sure they will be willing to speak to your team remotely.

"But more importantly, Ro'mer, I am urging the Caraj to set in motion some specific plans that can be implemented in a much shorter timeline, like 20 years. We must have a set of policies in place, potentially encompassing all possibilities, including fractured government, another rogue engineer, etc."

"That makes sense."

Trel'or'li looked stern for a moment. "We cannot have happen what happened last time."

Ro'mer said, "What do you mean?"

"The Caraj is deeply committed to zero intervention in Hilcyon politics. The Kinder must come to unification themselves."

"Trel'or'li, with that commitment, we may *never* unify. We have to provide avenues for the Kinder on Hilcyon to find their way into communication with us for the long term."

"You realize, don't you, that most Casitians still call the Kinder 'Za'aref'?"

Ro'mer knew that term; it meant "accursed." They sighed. "Yes, I know. And I know that most members of the Caraj have little interest and less hope in unification."

Trel'or'li's voice got hard. "That is not fair, Ro'mer. Every member of the Caraj is committed to unification before the 1000-year deadline. But we will not sacrifice our values to make that happen!"

Ro'mer took a breath, realizing they were treading into dangerous waters. They didn't want to rehash arguments they had had with Trel'or'li over the years.

"I understand your perspective, and we, of course, differ. In any event, let me know how we and I can be of assistance. You also know that the balance of the Consej will not be in your favor."

She nodded. "Yes, I know that. And we will have to take that into consideration as we craft our own policies. We understand that the Consej and New Earth might go in their own directions."

Ro'mer saw, potentially in the future, another retrenchment. A retraction from human politics that had happened before. It was almost cyclical. He sighed.

"I understand."

Trel'or'li stood. "Thank you for coming, Ro'mer. It's good to see you."

The bond between her and Ro'mer was enduring, even with their profound differences. Ro'mer stood, and they embraced. As Ro'mer walked out of the offices and out of the building, they pondered what the future might hold, and what they might see of it.


### Capital Region, Hilcyon

"Da! Be careful." Dlen grabbed her father's arm to support him as he stumbled while walking to the desk. "Your leg is still healing."

"I know. I'm just impatient and have so much to do." Dlen saw her father sit down heavily in the chair behind the desk.

"Da, there is time. You have one month of complete peace. No one can challenge you. And if you don't take it easy, you won't be healed!"

"Alright, Dlen, alright. Has Rtlir made it to the capital yet?"

"He has. He's waiting outside the door."

"Ask him in."

Dlen went to the door and ushered in Rtlir, who was her father's oldest friend and a fellow reformer. He walked in and smiled broadly.

Rtlir said, "I never could imagine this day, Wlen. You as Supreme Chief!"

"I never could either, Rtlir. I need you."

"Yes, you do. I'm here."

"I need an attache."

Rtlir nodded. "I'm happy to serve, sir." He smiled.

"Don't 'sir' me, Rtlir!"

"Wlen, I must. You are Supreme Chief. Especially when there are others in the room." He turned toward her and smiled. "Although Dlen is an exception."

Dlen had always liked Rtlir. Wlen nodded, and Dlen could tell her father was reluctant to accept the reality.

"First, I must know who is with me and who is not."

Rtlir said, "Just so you know, I've already heard that four First Chiefs are being challenged. Some by non-chiefs. You have set a precedent."

"What are their chances, you think?"

"I don't know yet, but I will find out. You will know in a few days who is with you and who is not. When are you meeting with your First Chiefs?"

"Tomorrow, but maybe..."

"I would wait until the dust settles a bit."

"That makes sense, Rtlir. I already have a long list of people who want an audience with me. That will keep me busy for days."

"Finally, a Supreme Chief that really listens."

"Yes. And I fervently hope to be our last Supreme Chief. If I can manage that..."

"I have some ideas..."

Dlen saw her father smile. It was time for her to go.

"Da, I must go."

"Yes, I know. Go get settled in our new dwelling with your mother and Tyrin. I promise I won't overdo it, OK?"

"Yes, Da. See you later."

Dlen left the office and walked down the hall of the Supreme Chief's wing of the capital building. Everything seemed unsettled. Dlen knew that most of the staff here in the capital were wondering whether or not they would still have a job in a few days. Dlen imagined many would not.

Men here were clearly not used to seeing women in these halls, and she was the subject of stares and whispers, but she ignored them. She walked out of the capital building and across to the Supreme Chief's dwelling. It was the largest dwelling she'd ever seen. It was imposing, with a large entrance, a broad staircase going upstairs, and more rooms than she could count. As she walked in, there were still men carrying belongings from the previous Supreme Chief's family. Their own belongings weren't arriving until tomorrow, but much was left behind: legacies of previous Supreme Chiefs.

When they arrived late last night, after Wlen had won his challenge match, Klef's wife and children were still in the house, packing their things. Dlen was learning that the transition in leadership was sudden and somewhat chaotic. And, for Klef's family, more than tragic. The family of a Chief who lost his challenge match was stripped of all of the trappings they had gotten used to while the Chief was in power. Now, Klef's family had nothing. They were returning to Klef's wife's home hamlet and moving back in with her father and mother. Dlen knew that life would be hard for them—the widow's life was unenviable. Dlen knew then that this was something she wanted to help change.

"Dlen!" Dlen turned to see her mother, followed by several women.

"Ma."

"Dlen, this is Grev, Tylr, and Proglr. They are here to help us with anything we need."

Dlen looked at them. They seemed friendly enough.

"Hi. Nice to meet you."

One of them said, "Nice to make your acquaintance, ma'am. I am Grev, head of house staff. I understand you have not chosen your room yet. Tylr, here, will show you the options. There are many."

"How many rooms are there in this house? It seems huge."

"It is quite large, yes, ma'am. There are six suites, with twenty-five bedrooms total."

Dlen was taken aback. "Twenty-five? Really? What are we going to do with twenty-five bedrooms?"

"Of course, most are not used. But some Supreme Chiefs have extended family live here. And, of course, as lovely as you are, you'll be having a family soon."

Dlen didn't say anything in response to that comment. Dlen hoped that her father and mother didn't want to have their parents live here. Dlen thought that would be a nightmare. However, with their son and son-in-law as Supreme Chief, maybe they would finally get over the issues they had with her parents. Then again, once they knew what her father planned...

"Alright, Tylr, let's go pick a bedroom for me, shall we?"

Tyler curtsied, and said, "Please follow me, ma'am." Dlen wasn't sure she was going to ever get used to being curtsied at and called "ma'am." They went upstairs, and went from room to room, with Tylr explaining the history of each room, which was utterly fascinating to Dlen. This had been the dwelling of every Supreme Chief for the last two thousand years, so there was a lot of history.

"Tylr, were you trained specifically in the history of this building for your job?"

"No, ma'am, I just find it of interest. I like to study history in my spare time."

"You do? So what else can you tell me?"

"Well, this suite here..." Tylr pointed to the next door they were about to come to. Tylr opened the door with some difficulty—it clearly hadn't been opened in a very long time. They walked in. It was completely empty, except for a lot of accumulated dust on the floor. Dlen could see several doors leading to other rooms.

"This suite?" Dlen asked.

"This suite has been empty for over 1200 years. It was where the Breft would stay and work when they visited Kinder Home. It has this large parlor, an office over there," Tylr pointed, "and four guest bedrooms and a communal bathing room, as that was what the Breft were used to."

"Really? Wow."

"Yes. It has been kept empty to show..."

"Indeed, I understand." Dlen had an idea. She would furnish this suite and prepare it with her father's permission. It was a perfect sign of the change to come.

### Pa'rai's, North Circumpolar Independent Zone, New Earth

Ke'lir looked at her date across the restaurant table. They were eating appetizers and had just finished the initial "getting to know you" small talk. Ke'lir had learned that her date grew up in the NCPIZ, and was a doctor, and currently worked at the medical center her great-great-aunt Leticia and her partner Kira founded many years ago.

Ke'lir could tell that her date was having a hard time not being a bit awed by her—which was a familiar feeling. She liked the privileges that she gained by being a member of her family, but she didn't really like some of the other things that came along with those.

And this woman was a chatterbox. Ke'lir didn't know whether it was nervousness or her nature.

She continued, "Anyway, this is the first date I've been on since I broke up with my ex three weeks ago. I'm trying to get out there, you know?"

"How long were you together?"

"Six years. It was a tumultuous relationship. She was a controlling type, you know? It was challenging. I finally had enough when she didn't want me to get another car."

Ke'lir was confused. Most people on New Earth didn't own even one car. *"Another* car?"

"Well, yes. I have a standard 2-person commuter and wanted a sports car."

Ke'lir said, "Why not rent a sports car when you want one? That's what everyone does."

"Well, I'm not *everyone*! I wanted one for myself."

The waiter came to their table with their entrées just at that moment.

"Cultured Tilapia with couscous and grapeberry coulis?"

Ke'lir said, "That's mine."

"Fried Gumbys on mashed tato root, and psuedopepper hash?"

Her date nodded. "So anyway, she didn't want me to get the sports car. Which was a lot like her."

Her date launched into a long diatribe about how controlling her ex was, and all of the stories just sounded to Ke'lir like someone trying to be somewhat reasonable in the face of this unreasonable woman. She took the attitude of enjoying her food and taking in the story as if she were watching a show on the net. There was no way there would be a second date, so this could just be entertainment.

She got home after unceremoniously battling off the woman's attempts to kiss her and bring her home. She thanked her lucky stars for getting over the phase of trying to save or change her partners. This one would have been a prime candidate.

She sat down on her couch and looked at her tablet, where she found an email from her cousin Ro'mer. Ro'mer had just met with the head of the Caraj on Casiti, explaining that there was a Casitian historian who thought that the Kinder would be in contact within their lifetimes. They were also expressing their concern about the Casitian perspective on contact with Hilcyon. They suggested that the team meet with the Consej and try to craft their own set of policies for handling another contact situation.

Ke'lir knew that was going to be contentious. The Casitian members of the Consej, except for Ro'mer, were conservative and would go along with whatever the Caraj drafted. And the Kinder would be going in a completely different direction. Ke'lir wasn't sure how they were going to come to a compromise between those two radically different opinions.

But she agreed that it was worth an attempt. If indeed they would be in touch in less than 100 years from now, they should have some of their ducks in a row well before they made contact again.

### Capital Region, Hilcyon

Jorn was honored to be accompanying Glin, the High Priest, to a meeting with Wlen, the new Supreme Chief. Jorn thought that Glin had chosen him primarily because he had been the priest who officiated at Mrin's execution. But Jorn also was an up-and-coming member of the secret society within the priesthood and had been doing a lot of work around strategizing for reform.

A tall, broad man, somewhat breathless, came out of the Supreme Chief's office and introduced himself.

"Hello, I am Rtlir, Wlen's attache. Thank you for coming to speak with the Supreme Chief."

Glin said, "I believe this is the first time in a long time that a Supreme Chief has requested a meeting with the High Priest. I generally had to beg and plead for an audience."

"This Supreme Chief is different—he wants to hear from all constituents. Anyway, please, come in."

As they walked into the room, Jorn saw Wlen limp from behind his desk. He was still clearly healing from the fight a few days ago.

Wlen looked up. "Please, have a seat. I'm glad you are here."

Glin looked surprised but pleased. They sat.

Wlen said, "I especially wanted to talk with you. I want to hear what the priesthood thinks about modest reforms in our government."

Glin asked, "What kinds of modest reforms are you suggesting?"

"Elimination of loyalty oaths, to start. I've already dismantled all operations spying on our people. I plan to start an engineering training program so that we can build a cadre of people who can fix the Casitian technology. Those are the beginning things I have planned."

Glin said, "I suspect you have more in mind."

Wlen was silent, and Jorn had the sense that he was figuring out how much he wanted to say.

"Well, yes. I would like to initiate consistent communication with the Casitians."

Glin nodded. Jorn was also sensing that Glin was measuring his words. "Yes, all of those make sense to us, and we are in full agreement with those ideas."

Wlen asked, "Would you go further?"

Glin nodded. "Yes. We would."

"How far?"

Glin paused. "Ultimately, the priesthood, at least most of it, is in favor of full unification at some point in the future."

Wlen looked shocked. "Really? I had no idea!"

"It's a well-kept secret, and I would ask you to keep it that way. I'm choosing to trust you, based on what I know of you. But we have been dedicated to, and working toward, unification for hundreds of years."

Wlen was silent for a moment. "I see. Honestly, that's further than I would have thought possible."

Glin nodded. "It will take time for our people to get used to the idea."

"Yes, it will, but it is a future I am interested in working toward. I intend to see the end of the trial-by-combat system."

"It is long since time for that to end. It should never have started. Anyway, how can we best be of service to you?"

"I'd say keep doing whatever it is you've been doing. You'll find no resistance from me. I look forward to seeing how our efforts can work together for a new future."

Wlen stood, and clearly, the meeting was over. But before he said anything, he looked straight at Jorn, as if he hadn't seen him just now.

"You. You are the priest who blessed my son at his execution."

Jorn nodded. "Your son was a brave young man."

Wlen said, "Thank you for the dignity you gave him. I could see your compassion and regard for him."

"I was glad to be of service to him. We had a good conversation before he died."

"You did? What did he say?"

"He said that he had no regrets. He was happy he did what he did and glad that it saved lives. I told him the Exalted King was with him."

Wlen nodded, and Jorn could see a tear forming in Wlen's eye. "He was a brave boy, my son. I will do everything I can to make sure that his death won't be in vain."

# Chapter 8:
# Reaching Out

New Earth: January 2101
Hilcyon: Lykl 1203
Casiti: Hevl 804

*"We can't see or feel the Divine. But it is with us in each moment. We can notice and be aware of its presence." Heart of the Carj, Eclogue 43*

### Capital Region, Hilcyon

Dlen was on her way to her father's office to give him her report. He had given her the task of paying attention to the agriculture reports and keeping him up to speed since he had so many other things to do. Her life as a midwife had changed with her status, and she was only attending about half of the births she'd attended before.

She had been reading the last report from the farm regions. At least one thing was going right. There was more water for irrigation than there had been in a very long time, and there was, finally, a real surplus of food. Everyone on Hilcyon would have their fill, and the warehouses would be full with a surplus. She knew that Wlen had already set aside the New Year, two months hence, as a big feast day. No one would have to work, and everyone would celebrate the end of the famine and danger to Hilcyon.

As she walked down the halls of the Capitol, she thought of how the last eight months had been so difficult for her father. He had had a few months of respite, then three First and Second Chiefs had challenged him, and he had to win each one. The last was the most difficult—he'd come very close to losing. After that, and the resistance to even minor changes he had tried to implement, it was clear that the change they wanted wasn't going to come any time soon. In fact, they had begun to realize that change might not come at all if her father lost another challenge. He had only one half-month of respite left, and each battle had been more difficult than the last.

They'd had a conversation about this last night, and Dlen and her mother had convinced him to call the Breft using the same communications device that Mrin had used and died for. Wlen had finally realized that everything he and Mrin had worked for would be for naught if he lost the next challenge.

She walked into his office to see Rtlir standing in front of her father's desk and the communications device that Mrin died for on the desk near her father.

Her father looked up at her and then pointed to the device. "It's time."

She nodded.

Wlen picked up the device, found the button Mrin had pushed, pushed it, and then put the device back on the desk.

Wlen said, "It will take a while before they contact us."

They were all surprised to hear a voice speaking in a relatively decent accent.

"Hello! Do you have a message?"

Wlen said, "Yes. This is Supreme Chief Wlen Gnova Jolrs. I would like to invite the Breft to a meeting here on Hilcyon."

"Message relayed. There is an approximately 1.5-day delay before you will receive a message back."

"Thank you."

"You are welcome." Nothing more came from the device.

Wlen said, "I guess we wait."

Rtlir nodded, and Dlen wondered what would come of this.


That evening, Dlen was called to a birth in the outskirts of the capital. Somehow, even though everyone knew that her father was a reformer and the father of Mrin, even traditionalists wanted the honor of Dlen, the daughter of the Supreme Chief, attending their births. This birth was to the wife of a very prominent Second Chief, one Dlen suspected might be next in line to challenge her father.

It was an easy birth, and Dlen was compensated handsomely for it. As she was taking her leave, the Second Chief stopped her.

"Dlen, thank you for helping my wife."

"You are very welcome, Chief Hwel. I am happy to."

"May I ask you something?"

"Certainly."

"Why does your father continue to allow you to stay unmarried now that you could have virtually any single man in the Capital?"

Dlen didn't like the question, but she didn't really know how else to answer it. "He values my work and lets me make my own choices."

"He thinks women have the capacity to make choices? You are too beautiful to be allowed to remain unmarried." There was a dripping acid tone to his voice. She ignored him.

"Excuse me, Second Chief, I must leave now. I hope your wife and daughter do well."

"*Daughter*, you see, that's the problem. This is her second."

Dlen slipped past him and out the door. Change couldn't come quickly enough for her.

### Pa'rai's, North Circumpolar Independent Zone, New Earth

Ke'lir had been interrupted at a rather inopportune moment. She'd been in a very long conversation about Casitian culture—particularly the culture around relationships, with a Terran woman she'd started dating. Unlike most of the Terran women she'd dated, this one was polyamorous. Ke'lir really liked and was attracted to her and expected that they'd have sex, but Ke'lir was beginning to realize that perhaps she herself was more monogamous than she'd suspected.

Her AI chimed its insistent emergency chime.

Ke'lir said, "I'm really sorry, excuse me please, this sounds like an emergency."

She got up, entered her office cubby, and asked her AI to play the message.

"Hey Ke'lir, this is Sandra. Believe it or not, the communications device was activated again, this time by a new Supreme Chief. I'm in Zwek but I'll be returning with Glor to New Orleans right now. We're convening a meeting in New Orleans tomorrow at 8th hour."

Her first thought was that she'd have to be on a transport during her night sleep period—that was her least favorite thing. Her second thought was that it looked like she wasn't going to get laid tonight. Her third thought was, "Sandra? With Glor in Zwek?" Only after those thoughts did the surprise of the contact from Hilcyon register. Even the least conservative estimates out there said it would be 20 years before they heard from them again, not in only one year.

She bid her date good night with apologies, packed what she thought she'd need, and called a taxi to take her to the Pa'rai's transportation hub, where she'd pick up transport to New Orleans.

She'd managed a little sleep on the transport. She'd booked a luxury berth with a bed. The transport arrived in New Orleans at 5th hour, so she had a few hours to kill before the meeting. The Michaelson family had a house in New Orleans where no one lived but where family members would stay when they needed to when visiting. It was where Ke'lir almost always stayed when she was in town, unless she was hanging out at Liam's ample house. She even basically had her own room: it was rare that anyone else needed to use it. The house had quite the history - it had originally been built for her great-great-aunt Marianne and their team during the initial phases of settlement, and it had been used by many family members since. Pictures and memorabilia were on the walls of most of the rooms. Even though it had never been home for Ke'lir, it kind of felt that way because she'd spent so much time there.

She dropped her bag on the bed in the second-floor bedroom, walked back downstairs, and brewed a cup of coffee. There were some basic essentials in the refrigerator and freezer, and she made herself an omelet and toast.

As she was eating, she heard the door lock chime and heard voices in the front part of the house. She recognized the deep voice of Glor and the gravelly voice of Zrel. They appeared in the kitchen, along with Sandra. Ke'lir got up, and they all hugged.

Glor said, "Ke'lir, you got here ahead of us."

She said, "Yeah, transport from Pa'ra'is arrived at 5th hour."

Sandra said, "I despise taking transports over night sleep time."

Ke'lir nodded. "Me too!"

Zrel said, "I'm glad I don't need to travel like that much."

Ke'lir said, "Zrel, why are you here so early?"

"I knew you all were arriving early. I wanted to be here when you got here."

Sandra said, "It's been forever since I've been in this house. It looks pretty much the same as when I was younger."

Sandra had been a fixture in their lives, as had many of the children, grandchildren, and great-grandchildren of that initial team that had been pivotal in The Event. Ke'lir knew that Sandra had spent time in the house with her grandfather, Joel, on some occasions. It was how they'd met when she was a child. Ke'lir felt that, in a sense, Sandra, like the others, was part of her extended family. She also saw so many of them quite often, as they were, like her, in leadership positions in government.

Ke'lir asked, "So Sandra, what do we know about the contact?"

"Just that it was someone named 'Wlen,' who is currently Supreme Chief. He is inviting us back. We don't know anything more."

Zrel said, "The Consej is going to meet later today once those in Rel'toro are awake."

Ke'lir asked, "What do you think the Consej will say?"

Zrel shook his head. "I have no idea. We were just talking about the very beginnings of planning for the next contact. We don't have a plan. I know the Casitians, except, of course, for Ro'mer, will be hesitant."

Glor nodded. "I think it might be messy. Glad it's not my job to wrangle that."

Zrel chuckled.

### Hol'venif, Rel'toro, Casiti

Ro'mer was in the main living area of their family house, looking after the two infants in the house. Their own child was napping peacefully, and the other child was beginning to squirm a little and make faces. Ro'mer knew that meant they needed to get taken to the bathroom.

As they were going about the process of helping the child eliminate and cleaning up, they couldn't help but think about Hilcyon and wonder what was happening there.

Just as they were finishing cleaning up, their co-parent, M'nali, came into the bathroom.

"Ro'mer, your message system has an emergency message for you. I'll take the children."

They nodded and handed the infant over, and rushed to their office.

They asked their message system, "Who is the message from?"

"Consej chair Zrel."

"Play, please."

"Ro'mer, hey, so you probably can't believe this, but I just got word from the communications office on New Earth that the Kinder activated the device again. They have confirmed that it was the Supreme Chief who made contact this time. We obviously need a Consej meeting to determine the next steps. I'm in New Orleans with the team and convening a meeting in two New Earth hours."

Ro'mer couldn't really believe it. Everyone was saying contact in 20 or 30 New Earth years would be the most likely scenario instead of 100. No one thought contact in just over one year, or basically one Casitian season, was even possible.

After getting some breakfast and arranging infant care with M'nali and others in the house, they returned to their office and got ready for the meeting. They were pretty sure where Samira and Kel'ora stood. Ret'ir'le and Teo'lir were more of an uncertainty, but Teo'lir tended to follow Samira's lead. Ret'ir'le could be a wildcard.

As the holo imager fired up, the images of his fellow Consej members appeared. The Terrans seemed to all be in the same meeting room, as usual, along with most of the Kinder. Three of the kinder representatives seemed to be meeting from home.

Zrel said, "I'm bringing this emergency meeting of the Consej to order. Our agenda is pretty straightforward—we need to consider sending another mission to Hilcyon, in this case, potentially sending people to the surface. The team has requested a crew of six, all people who have gone before, plus one medical crew member. We will take comments now."

Predictably to Ro'mer, Samira weighed in first. "Pot'rel'o will not be on this next mission. The Caraj has been clear that they wish to send a new representative."

Glev, a Kinder representative, asked, "Why? She seemed to have done a good job last time."

Ro'mer braced themselves for a possible explosion.

Samira said in a clipped tone, "She did not follow the instructions of the Caraj. We do not wish something like that to happen again."

Zrel said, "I think we can agree that it is up to the Caraj to send whatever representative they wish. Is there anyone who is opposed to sending a mission?"

Teo'lir said, "I'm not opposed, but I believe it should be limited to speaking with the Supreme Chief while in orbit, and assessing, then getting back to us, and having us determine the scope of their work."

Christoph, a Terran representative, said, "That's ridiculous. It's clear this contact is official. They should be able to go to the surface and assess what's needed. If they made contact, they obviously need something from us—we should find out what it is, and that's easier assessed on the ground."

A heated debate ensued, but it was clear to Ro'mer that the people in favor of letting the team go to the surface and determine what was needed on their own would win the day. Surprisingly, Ret'ir'le was firmly in favor of allowing the team to go down to the surface.

Ultimately, the Consej voted 10 to 5 to approve the mission and give the team autonomy. Ro'mer wondered whom the Casitians would want to send along with the team and what effect that would have.

### Independent Christian State, New Earth

Paul couldn't quite believe it. He was sitting in the office of the Bishop of the ICS. And he was glad to be here. It had been a strange visit. First, he had surprised himself by wanting to go back home for another Christmas visit. He had been having a lively written conversation with Franklin, his brother-in-law, who was now the Bishop of the ICS. Franklin didn't want the ICS to be a backwater anymore—he wanted it to return to being a full participant in the life of New Earth. And being a full participant in the life of New Earth meant communicating with Casitians. Franklin had a theological task, not only a practical task.

Paul had read a very detailed history of the theology of the ICS, written by a Terran researcher about 25 years ago. It explained how the ICS started with a theology that resembled very closely the conservative Christian ideology of the 20th and early 21st Century on Earth. But after The Event, when many Christians decided to leave the ICS, and not settle there because of the much more primitive conditions, the theology of the remaining citizens took some strange turns. The initial reasons why Casitians weren't allowed into the ICS had to do with a political stance. But that progressed into a theological stance of Casitians as a manifestation of the evil of Satan.

Franklin had never believed that, and, of course, neither had Paul. In fact, Paul knew his opinion was fairly common in the ICS. But it was definitely not the party line. Franklin had to shift the party line somehow.

"Thanks for coming here, Paul."

"I'm glad I'm here. I can't quite believe I'm here. Your father is likely rolling in his grave."

"Yes, I'm sure he is. I need some help. I've been tired of the state of things in the ICS since I was a lot younger, and now that I'm Bishop, I see it in numbers. We are dying, Paul. There are few jobs, and we export nothing. There are people in the ICS who are poorer than anyone on New Earth would imagine or accept."

"I know."

"But I don't even know where to begin."

"I'm not sure I know either, Franklin, but I would suggest that a good first start is to send a representative to the NEA."

"I don't think I can. There are all sorts of requirements for countries and independent zones that we can't meet."

"Look, let me talk with some folks and see if there is a way that you can be brought in without those requirements. They have to be willing to start somewhere. I think a representative is a good start. Begin the conversations necessary. Also, didn't you used to have an ambassador from New America?"

"We did, but that ended more than 40 years ago."

"Bring it back. Ask for an ambassador and send one. Most countries now have ambassadors to most other countries. Even the zones do, too. My cousin Khalid is the NCPIZ's ambassador to New Aard."

"Those sound like very good ideas, Paul. Honestly. I must tell you, I'd love it if you returned to the ICS and worked with me."

Paul figured this was coming, and he had an easy answer. Coming back to New Earth was a possibility for him, but coming back to the ICS was not. He'd like to help the ICS move forward, but he would have to do it from a distance. Besides, he loved his studies at the Ja'lit school and his work.

"I'm sorry, Franklin. I won't. I have work that I love on Casiti, and I am studying there."

"Studying?"

"Yes. I will officially be a student of the Ja'lit school later this month."

"Is that a technical school?"

"No. It's the Casitian equivalent of a seminary. It was founded by the great Ja'len'da, who studied many Earth traditions."

Franklin got a strange look on his face. Paul realized that perhaps the reform was not as deep as Paul might have wanted or expected. He decided he probably didn't need to play his trump card, Ka'li'mo.

"I see. Well, I'm sorry you won't consider returning. Perhaps in the future."

"Perhaps."

"Will you marry a Casitian?"

Paul was surprised by this question. "Casitians don't marry, Franklin. At the moment, I have no plans in that direction." This was most definitely true.

Franklin nodded.

They talked for a while further about strategy, then Paul took his leave and went back to his parents' house. He would be leaving in the morning.


Several days later, Paul sat in meditation in the hall of the Ja'lit school. It was beautifully decorated and always made him feel at home. This meditation session was one of his favorite techniques Jal'end'a had brought this from Earth. It was called "Centering Prayer." It was different from a lot of techniques, but the idea was to bring to mind a holy word and open oneself up to the wisdom of the Divine using that word.

The contemplative techniques of the Ja'lit school were collected from a variety of sources, some Casitian, but many from the varied traditions on Earth. Some were of Buddhist origin, and others, like this one, were Christian. Some were from Judaism, or Sufism, or other traditions. Paul really loved the eclectic nature of what he was learning.

But today, his focus on the holy word was wavering. Ka'li'mo, who sat near him, was in his mind constantly. Their friendship and relationship had blossomed, and Paul felt happier in his life than he'd ever been.

The light gong sounded, and Paul was stirred out of his reverie, feeling a little guilty for his lack of focus. Then, he remembered his self-compassion lessons and felt better.

Ka'li'mo came up to him. "I'm really hungry. If it weren't for your offer to take me to that Earth restaurant tonight, I would dive into my freezer for the soup I made months ago."

Paul smiled. He'd learned so much about Casitian culture in the past while, and it always surprised him that they never developed restaurants or takeout. Even at home, where his mother almost always cooked, they went out to eat on occasion. Restaurants were an Earth import.

Before they could leave, one of the staff of the school ran up to Paul.

"Paul, I'm sorry to interrupt. You have an emergency message from Sandra Germain."

He followed the staff member to the office and retrieved the message from his mailbox.

"Paul, we got contact again from Hilcyon. The Consej has met and approved most of the team we had before to return. There are a few details to iron out before we leave. I'll keep you posted, but I'm assuming we'll be leaving from Casiti in a few days."

He left the office to find Ka'li'mo waiting.

"Sorry! Let's head out. I'll tell you more at the restaurant."

He woke early and saw the sleeping form of Ka'li'mo in the bed next to him. He was constantly surprised at the pleasure and joy he found in Ka'li'mo's body and their connection together. Sometimes, when he reflected on what he'd been taught as a child, he was struck by how uselessly awful it was. Why keep humans from the pleasure of our bodies, the bodies the Divine gave us?

He didn't look forward to his next visit to his family's house. The distance between what he believed, how he was living, and what his family believed was growing all the time. He was having a hard time reconciling them.

His mind then went to Hilcyon and wondered what would happen. What would it be like to be there, and how would it unfold? It was staggering, in a way, that he was a part of it. He almost thought, "When will the adults step in?" But he realized he was the adult. He'd been there before. He had experience.

Ka'li'mo stirred and opened his eyes. He smiled when he saw Paul looking at him.

"Been awake a while?"

"No, just a little bit."

Ka'li'mo responded by reaching out, and caressing him, and kissing him deeply. He got lost in his touch.

### Capital Region, Hilcyon

Jorn made his way to the High Priest's office in a different temple than his. It was a bit further away from the Capitol buildings. He wondered what this was about—they had just made some good decisions at the reform meeting the other night, and although Jorn had a list of things to do on his plate, they weren't things that needed attending to in an immediate sense, and certainly not from the High Priest!

He was greeted at the door of the High Priest's suite by a priest familiar to him from the meetings.

"Father Jorn, glad you could come. The High Priest is ready for you."

Jorn nodded and entered the opened door. There was a small ante-room, and Jorn saw a large office with an open door on the left. He walked in.

He noticed how *old* the ephemera on the walls were and how many old books were on the shelves. These must have belonged to many, many High Priests over the years.

Glin, the High Priest, was sitting behind a massive desk—probably the largest desk he'd ever seen. It, too, was *old*. He couldn't even imagine what kind of wood it was made of. There were some very small trees that grew on Hilcyon, but they were not enough to ever use for furniture. All of the furniture was made of a processed version of a reed that grew in the equatorial regions. This was clearly not made of any processed product. Jorn wondered whether it might have come from materials from Casiti, which he had read had abundant large trees.

"Blessings, Your Holiness. I am at your service."

"Father Jorn, thank you for coming. Please be at ease. Have a seat."

Jorn sat in one of the chairs in front of the desk. It was surprisingly comfortable.

"I wanted you to know that Supreme Chief Wlen has contacted the Casitians. We don't know any details yet, but we expect them to send a team to the planet to meet with us."

Jorn was surprised and pleased by this. He'd wondered how long Wlen was going to wait, and at some point, it seemed Wlen was resistant to starting the process of contact. But apparently, he changed his mind.

"That is wonderful news, Your Holiness! I am heartened by the idea that we can start our process."

The High Priest nodded. "Yes, I am as well. And I would very much like you to take part in this. You have shown yourself to be a steady, intelligent hand at planning, and I think you would be the right person to be a liaison between me and this team."

Jorn was taken aback. "Me, Your Holiness? There are so many priests my senior."

"Yes, yes, I know that, but it is my instinct that a young hand is the right pick."

"I much appreciate your confidence in me, Holiness."

"Wlen is awaiting communication from the Casitians about when and how they are arriving. I'm assigning you to the Capitol for the time being."

"Thank you, Holiness. I won't let you down."

He smiled. "I'm sure you won't, son."

# Chapter 9:
# An Opening

New Earth: January 2101
Hilcyon: Lykl 1203
Casiti: Hevl 804

*"When we look out at the stars, what do we see? For so much of Earth's history, spiritual traditions made stories about the stars—the gods and epic tales spun from the stars' positions in the sky. And, of course, there have always been epic tales and beings who are like gods in the stars." Ja'lend'a, 'Spirits Alike'*

### Capital Region, Hilcyon

Dlen was sitting at the table with her mother, father, and sister-in-law Tyrin. It had been several days since they had activated the device, and Dlen had not heard anything. They had dinner together alone a few times a month. Mostly Wlen had to entertain this Chief, and that priest, and that guest, and when that happened, all of the women of the house ate separately in the small dining room. Dlen was happy that her mother no longer had to cook or clean, but sometimes she thought that perhaps she was bored. She did help to coordinate the house, and was also entertaining wives of Chiefs.

Dlen enjoyed her work, but unfortunately, she had a surfeit of suitors now that she was the Supreme Chief's daughter. She could begin to feel the pressure to wed—not from her parents, but from others. But she had no interest in doing that—Dlen couldn't see herself as a wife and mother.

Now that her father, as a reformer, was Supreme Chief, perhaps there would be more room for Dlen to be on her own, doing what she wanted to. But Dlen worried about him. He had been challenged at the end of each month of respite, and the last time, he almost lost. She looked at him. The weal on the side of his face was still clear, and he limped around most days.

Her father said, "So, more news."

She looked up. "What, Da?"

"We heard details back. They will send a contingent, which will arrive in several days."

Dlen asked, "Are you going to announce anything?"

"I must, at some point. I don't quite know how, yet, but I need to stop the challenges."

Her mother leaned over to Wlen and put her hand on his shoulder. "Well, husband, I will be happy if you won't have to fight again."

He nodded.

They finished dinner, and Dlen planned to finish setting up the suite that had long been disused for the Casitians. Tylr had been a real help in finding furniture from various places in the residence and Capitol building to place in the suite. Dlen wanted to add some finishing touches, like lighting, pictures, and other things that she hoped would make it more comfortable for them.

That evening, and over the course of the next few days, as she found herself engaged in preparations for them, she wondered what this group coming would be like and what changes they would bring with them. Part of her felt hopeful, but another part of her was skeptical. There was so much opposition to reform in many quarters of Hilcyon. She didn't know how this would play out.

### Hol'venif, Rel'toro, Casiti

Ro'mer had commandeered a conference room in the satellite Consej building. It was used at times for the Casitian representatives and also had offices for the students who served the Consej.

Paul, Sandra, Glor, and Ke'lir had arrived from New Earth, and the ship that would take them to Hilcyon was being prepared. It was a courier ship rather than a cargo ship, although it didn't really have all that much more room for crew.

The Caraj had chosen their replacement for Pot'rel'o. A stout man who seemed, to Ro'mer anyway, to have a fairly dour personality. His name was Li'more. In addition, the Caraj had offered a very highly trained medical crew member, Cre'relo, with whom Ro'mer had interacted on occasion for other projects. Ro'mer respected them and thought they were a good fit for this expedition. In addition to this crew, the ship would have two pilots and two security crew.

Ro'mer had been tasked to gather this group together and answer any questions they might have about the directives of the Consej and Caraj regarding what they could and could not do once they got on the ground.

Once everyone had arrived in the room, Ro'mer rang the bell.

"OK, everyone, let's get this started. You are scheduled to leave first thing tomorrow morning."

The crew from New Earth looked a little bleary-eyed. They'd arrived only hours ago, and who knew what New Earth time it was.

"I have some clear directives from the Consej and Caraj, and Li'more can add more nuance as he has been given those orders in great detail.

"You are there to *assess*. We need to understand how stable the government is and how ready the whole population is to open up contact on a regular basis. Also, you are tasked with assessing their needs for materials and the extent of technology transfer that might be appropriate.

"I want to make it clear that although the Consej has given you some autonomy, for almost any action, you'll need to wait for Consej approval before moving on it."

Ke'lir said, "But what if something is really obvious to us that is urgent?"

Ro'mer said, "You have been given some autonomy, but please use your judgment. Make sure you consider the long-term effects of whatever decision you make."

Li'more said gruffly, "I'll be there to make sure that whatever we do can be aligned with the Consej and Caraj's ideas of our limitations as a team."

Ro'mer knew well that Li'more was following the Caraj's lead far more than the Consej, but they didn't bother to say that. It was self-evident to everyone in the room. Li'more was there because Pot're'lo hadn't been directive enough.

Paul asked, "What kind of permission do we have to talk to different constituencies while we are there? Can we find other organizations and people to talk with? The Supreme Chief has his ideas, but we might want to hear from others."

Ro'mer nodded. "Yes, definitely. Make sure that you are transparent with the Supreme Chief who you will be seeking information from. If he is as reform-minded as we hope, he will find this a great opportunity to bring more people to the table."

They fell into an easy discussion of detailed logistics regarding what they were bringing and how long they would likely stay. Ro'mer felt mostly good about this team, although they worried a little about how Li'more would work with everyone else.

### Hilcyon orbit, Hilcyon

Ke'lir entered the small conference room. They had just arrived and were in orbit over Hilcyon. The next step was to contact the new Supreme Chief and discuss the next steps. They really had no idea what he had in mind, although given that he was in contact, it suggested a desire for ongoing connection. This time, they had come in a somewhat larger ship with a larger team of people, although not all of them would go to the surface.

Sandra said, "OK, it's time to make contact. Glor?"

Glor, who was standing on one side of the room, nodded. Sandra said, "Communication on."

The communication started, and the image of the Supreme Chief and one other person materialized near Glor. The voice of Ke'lir's translator was in one ear.

"Supreme Chief, my name is Glor Jror Hlad. I come from a planet we call New Earth."

The Supreme Chief nodded. "Yes, I know of this planet. My grandmother Krely knew a woman named Btric, who came from your planet."

"Your grandmother knew Beatrice?"

"Yes. You sound surprised."

"Beatrice was my great-grandmother."

"How did you come by that Kinder name?"

"Great-grandmother Beatrice married a Kinder man, Ngellin Yolse Marn."

Wlen looked surprised. "How could there be Kinder on New Earth?"

"About 2,000 Kinder soldiers deserted during the invasion. They settled first on New Earth, then many went to Casiti."

"Really? I had no idea so many..."

"I imagine that was kept from the leadership at the time. Anyway, Supreme Chief..."

"Wlen. Call me Wlen."

"Wlen. How can we help?"

"It is time for the Kinder to rejoin the rest of the people. Change must come. Unfortunately, there is resistance to this idea."

"Resistance? In what form?"

"I am being challenged for my leadership each month."

Glor said, "I don't understand."

"Here, if someone wants to be promoted, they challenge the one above them to battle in the ring. The winner gets the job. The loser dies. The winner cannot be challenged for one month."

Ke'lir could feel the emotion in the room change. Even though they all knew about how the Kinder chose leaders, hearing it again was shocking.

"I see. So at the end of that time, you are being challenged by people who don't want the reforms you seek."

"Yes. And I will lose. If not the next one, the one after that. I wish to be the last Supreme Chief. I want the people to be able to choose their leaders. I must change this system, but to..."

"You need our presence."

"Yes."

"We understand. We are prepared to send down a small team at first, and then continue discussions. We also have to confer with our leaders at home about the best way to approach this."

Wlen's expression changed, and there was a pause. "Yes, of course. When can your team arrive?"

"We will send a shuttle down to arrive mid-day in the Capital. Is there a preferred place for us to land?"

"The Capitol Square. We will meet you there."

Glor nodded. "See you tomorrow. Communication off."

Li'more said, "This is not the situation we expected. I'm alright with us going down, but we have to be very careful what we do."

Ke'lir nodded. "We have very clear directives to assess, and only do what the people of Hilcyon ask us to do. Yet, there is clearly differences of opinion."

Glor said, "But the Supreme Chief is the spokesperson for the people..."

Ke'lir said, "Yes, but he probably would be replaced in a month or two if we don't intervene. But if we don't intervene..."

Li'more said, "We will bring the security team. We talk with Wlen, and we will also wait to see what the Consej will say."

Ke'lir said, "This is going to cause an uproar in the Consej!"

Glor said, "Let them be in an uproar. We're here, on the ground. The overall goal is to have the Kinder rejoin the rest of humanity. Our involvement will help assure that."

Li'more said, "But we have to respect the directives of the leadership."

Sandra said quietly, "But what if this causes a big backlash? We need to know how strong the resistance to reform is. If it's stronger than the reform movement..."

Glor said, "I doubt it. The people know how they were saved from famine and near extinction."

Sandra nodded. "Yes, this is true. I guess we'll have to find out."


### Capital Region, Hilcyon

Paul squinted in the unfamiliar sun. The sun of Casiti was pretty similar to the sun of New Earth, just a little further away. This sun just seemed different from either. It definitely was colder. Paul knew from briefings that the mean temperature for most of Hilcyon was a little lower than the mean temperature for Casiti. Casiti was tilted much more than Hilcyon, so it had periods of pretty warm weather. Hilcyon wasn't tilted, and the mean temperature was not so far above freezing most of the year. The temperate zones near the equator were better, but it never got really warm on Hilcyon. Between that, and the lack of rain, Hilcyon was a forbidding place.

He was with Ke'lir on one side of him, and Li'more on the other. Glor was in front of them, greeting the Supreme Chief. Paul looked around. There was a huge and growing crowd. They seemed mostly friendly and curious, which was a relief. Li'more and the security team had given them all some defensive devices in case of a riot.

He heard his translator's voice, translating the conversation Glor and Wlen were having.

The Supreme Chief said, "I welcome you and your team to Kinder Home. You will be staying with my family, in our house. There will be a welcoming dinner and reception. Tomorrow, we will start discussions of our exchange."

This seemed to be very careful talk from the Supreme Chief.

Glor said, "I wish to thank you for your gracious welcome and hospitality. We look forward to meeting your family and more Kinder Chiefs. We also look forward to our conversations about the relationship of Kinder Home, New Earth, and Casiti."

Paul thought it was diplomatic of Glor to put New Earth first, but then Paul remembered that Glor really was of New Earth, not Casiti.

They walked away from the shuttle, and the pilot took off to return to the ship. The group of them, both the team from the ship as well as a group of Kinder, walked down some streets, and toward a pair of rather imposing buildings.

Wlen said, "This building on the left is the Capital. That's where I have my offices, and where the First Chiefs and staff have their offices. On the right is my residence. Come."

They followed him and his entourage into the large residence. There was an enormous entryway, and Paul could see a large room to the right with tables where there were people bustling about, obviously preparing a feast. Several men and women approached them.

One tall, striking woman, with a shorter haircut than any other woman he'd seen so far, was introduced to them as Dlen, Wlen's daughter. Paul noticed that Ke'lir was staring at the woman with an odd expression.

Dlen said, "Welcome to our house. If you'll follow me, I'll take you to the suite where you will stay. It was designed for the Breft when the residence was built, but had remained empty and unused since…"

Ke'lir said, "Since the Betrayal of Klor."

Dlen smiled at Ke'lir, and nodded. "Yes."

They walked upstairs, down two halls, then into an open parlor.

Dlen said, "This is the parlor. That room in the far back," she pointed, "is your office space. Its windows look down on the atrium between this building and the Capital. Over there," she pointed to the left "are two of the guest rooms, and bathing room. To the right over there are the remaining three guest rooms. One room has one bed, and the other four have two. We didn't know how many you would be. Is it just you eight?"

Ke'lir said, "At the moment, yes. This will be fine, thank you."

Dlen said, "You are very welcome. This is Tylr, she will see to your needs. Feel free to ask her to find me when needed." It seemed to Paul that she said that directly to Ke'lir.

Ke'lir smiled. "Thank you so much, Dlen. This is wonderful. We'll see you at dinner?"

"Yes, you will." She turned and left them then, but before she walked completely out the door, she turned to look again at Ke'lir.

Glor came back from walking around. "Sandra and I can share the room with one bed—it's a full-ish sized bed."

Li'more said, "I'll share a room with Cre'relo, and the two security team members can share a room. Paul and Ke'lir can have their own rooms.

Paul was grateful of that.

Sandra said, "Uh, folks, I know you Casitians grow up with communal baths, but the rest of us didn't. Can we agree this isn't communal? When the door's closed…?"

Paul was greatly relieved when the Casitians agreed. He'd get his own room, and get to use the bathing room alone. Things were looking good.

## Capital Region, Hilcyon

Jorn noticed that he was going through the motions on the 6th hour prayers today. He was glad it wasn't First Moon rise, so there were only his fellow monks to witness what he felt was a mediocre performance of the prayer.

But his mind was on the Breft, who would have just arrived on Hilcyon. He had been invited to the introductory dinner this evening, and he had also arranged with Wlen some individual time to meet with this team. He was eager for it.

He had spent the last few days in planning for their arrival. He wanted to make sure that they understood the role of the priesthood, and it's overwhelming support for re-contact and eventual reunification. He understood that they would see clearly the divisions in the chiefs. He wanted them to see the broad agreement of this fundamental part of Kinder culture.

Later, as he walked to the Supreme Chief's residence, he saw the activity around the Capitol and residence, and knots of people, some clearly chiefs, talking, some in whispered tones he could not hear, others shouting in argumentation.

One man, a short, fat chief who was bulging with muscle, and another, who surprisingly had a tiny tuft of hair growing under his lower lip, were in a heated argument.

The fat one said, "Wlen is endangering us! Our culture cannot stand in the face of the Breft. We separated from them for a reason. We need to keep separate!"

"I'm not eager to mix with them, but I want my children, and grandchildren, to live and thrive. We cannot live on this planet by ourselves, we need their help!"

"We don't need them!"

"We almost starved, Hton. The only reason we've survived here as long as we have was the generosity of the Breft."

"Generosity? Pfah! They want us dependent on them. Willm did the right thing by cutting off all contact with them."

"And then we almost starved. Without their help, we all would have died. Get your head out of a rock, Hton."

Jorn had heard many versions of this argument among the parishioners of the temple. And he knew for certain that the man was correct—the Kinder could not live alone on Hilcyon.

Jorn had read the histories, unlike many. He knew that the reason they had been settled on this planet was because they had refused to join the Casitians on their planet, and had been given second-best. The priesthood had hoped that the reliance on galactic technology would keep them in contact with the Casitians, but between the Betrayal of Klor, and Willm, the Supreme Chief with the secret of being from Grier Nro, contact between the Kinder and Casiti had grown more distant, not closer. Jorn hoped that this would finally be the opening they needed.

# Chapter 10:
# Introductions

New Earth: January 2101
Hilcyon: Lykl 1203
Casiti: Hevl 804

*"We lost so much when we were taken from our homes. We need to work together to re-claim and re-discover what was lost. And we need to create things anew—from a shared sense of what it means to be human." Heart of the Carj, Ecologue 98*

### Capital Region, Hilcyon

Ke'lir dropped her bag on the bed. It was a small bed. Large enough for her, but she was used to more spacious sleeping surfaces. She sat in the chair that was facing a small window. The window looked out onto a courtyard, and there were people moving back and forth across it.

She couldn't help but think back on Dlen. Dlen was, of course, quite beautiful, but it wasn't really the beauty that struck Ke'lir—it was the way she carried herself. She seemed sure of herself, and strong, in ways the other women she'd met so far didn't appear.

Ke'lir knew this was a patriarchal society, so she had no illusions about what life was like for women here. But she did wonder what Dlen's life was like. She imagined it was likely different than most. She reminded her of the character of Elfer in the Stories of Dbor she'd read so long ago. She was looking forward to learning more.

Ke'lir also worried about Dlen. Ke'lir had no idea how this endeavor was going to go, and it certainly had dangers for anyone associated with this reformer Chief, particularly his family. When most of them eventually left, which they would have to, what would it be like? Would he lose his place? How could they prevent that?

She knew that at this very moment, on New Earth and Casiti, there were raging arguments about what to do, and how much to intervene.

But they were here, on the planet, and she wasn't sure she knew. She wondered whether Dlen might have some insights.

Ke'lir got up, and went to the parlor, and left the suite, to find Tylr sitting in a small alcove sewing. She jumped up.

"Ma'am, how can I help you?" Ke'lir heard in her translation earpiece. She subvocalized, and the response in Kinder came into her ear. She repeated it.

"I wonder if you can find Dlen for me. I need to ask her something."

"Certainly Ma'am. I'll be right back." Tylr ran off before Ke'lir could say anything. In just a few minutes, Tylr came back with Dlen in tow.

Ke'lir said, repeating her AI's translation of her intended statement, "Hi Dlen. I'm sorry to interrupt whatever you were doing…"

"It's fine. Come, let's find a place we can talk."

Ke'lir followed Dlen to a small library, with walls of books. The sat down.

"This is one of my favorite places to spend time. You would be amazed at what books are here. Luckily, the previous tenants simply ignored this room."

Ke'lir smiled. "First, I need to apologize for my language skills. I have a translator earpiece, so I will be slow in speaking."

"Translator earpiece?"

Ke'lir pointed to her ear. "This kind of hears me think, and then translates for me."

Dlen said, "Hears you think?"

"Well, that's an exaggeration. I speak without sound, and it can hear it."

"Ah, I understand. Like when we learn to read silently as children."

"Yes! Exactly."

Dlen smiled. Ke'lir could feel her heartbeat get faster. She was captivated by Dlen's eyes, and face. She loved the way her hair… Ke'lir could feel herself blush, and she re-focused herself.

"Anyway, I thought it would be good to get your view of what you think would be best for us to do here. You know the inside of this society, more than your father can tell us."

"When you first came, and fixed the water, and sent food, people were happy. They thought of my brother as a hero."

"Your brother was Mrin?"

"Oh, I thought you knew."

"No, we had no idea the new Chief was the father of Mrin. We knew Mrin got executed for talking with us."

"Da didn't want Mrin to die in vain. So he trained and trained and challenged Klef. And won."

"I see. Keep going."

"But the people think the Breft are evil. They have for many, many years. Since the beginning, really."

"The Casitians called the Kinder 'accursed' for a long time. But since The Event, Kinder have lived on Casiti, and the Casitians have learned more about them."

"The Event?"

Ke'lir realized that Dlen likely had no idea what had happened. She asked, "What do you know of Earth?" She spoke the translation, "Grier Nro."

"It was the origin of all of our people. The Exalted King wanted us to return there, but we were refused by the galaxy. I don't really believe in the Exalted King, and I'm sure the history is complicated."

Ke'lir nodded. "Sixty-six years ago, the Galactic government cut us all off from Earth for 1000 years. That is what we call The Event. All Terrans had to leave Earth. My family includes some Terran, and some Casitian and some Kinder."

Dlen said, looking overwhelmed, "Ah, there is so much to learn!"

Ke'lir said, "OK, so back to where we were. What can we do, do you think, to sway the people?"

"Sway the women. Although women don't have any political power, they do have a lot of influence on their husbands, fathers and sons."

"And how can we sway the women?"

"Make their lives easier. First off, make childbirth less dangerous. I lose too many women and babies."

"*You* lose?"

"I'm a midwife. I attend the births of about ten women each moon. I lose six or seven a year in childbirth. And there are many more babes that die, too."

Ke'lir was frankly shocked. "Six mothers out of 100?"

"How many do you lose?"

"This is not my field, but I don't think any women die in childbirth on Casiti. There are some areas of New Earth that have fewer and less developed medical facilities than others, and they might lose some on rare occasions. But in most areas, I don't think they lose any. It seems we need to start with medical assistance."

"Yes."

"Do you have any births soon?"

"There are a few women I am waiting on. Why?"

"Can I bring a doctor? We brought one with us. To observe, and get an idea of how best to help."

Dlen nodded. "Of course. That would be wonderful. I'm sorry, I must go back to the preparations for the feast. It will start soon."

"Oh! I'm sorry, I didn't mean to delay you."

Dlen smiled, the smile that was melting Ke'lir's heart. "Not a problem. It was nice to talk with you."

"I enjoyed our conversation, Dlen. I look forward to more."

"There will be more, you can count on it."

Ke'lir watched Dlen walk out of the room, her heart finally stopped beating quite so quickly. Ke'lir could feel that familiar feeling, like how she felt when she first met Mari'sol. But Ke'lir had to remember that Dlen wasn't Casitian, or even Terran.

### Capital Region, Hilcyon

Dlen walked away from Ke'lir on her way back to the dining hall bemused. Ke'lir was such a mystery to her. She was clearly unmarried, yet old enough to have married and had children a long time ago. Dlen found herself thinking back to Mrel, and how she had felt for so long about Mrel. Some of the same feelings were emerging when she thought of Ke'lir.

But Ke'lir wasn't Kinder, and didn't know or understand their culture. And would be leaving eventually. Dlen shook her feelings away, and put herself back into preparation mode.

A little later, as she was laying out the cutlery, which included two kinds of spoons, a knife, and pick that was only used for special occasions, she couldn't help but think back to Ke'lir over and over again. She sighed.

Her mother, who was unseen at her elbow said, "Are you alright, Dlen?"

She spun, surprised. "Yes, Ma, I'm fine. Just thinking about this dinner, and how unusual it is."

"I know! Wives and children dining with their husbands and fathers is almost unheard of. But we had to do it—first because the team that came have women, and also we wanted to show boldly which direction we were going in."

"I do hope that the presence of the families will mean the chiefs will behave themselves."

"I hope so too, Dlen."

Her mother said, "I think we're about as ready as we're going to get. The kitchen is doing great, and everything is on schedule. Why don't you go up and change? And perhaps help your father. He has a new set of clothes to try on."

Dlen nodded, and walked out of the dining hall, and up a set of stairs to the main residence area. She turned toward her left, the direction where the Casitian group was staying, and could feel her desire to see Ke'lir again. She took a breath, turned right, and went back to where her father's rooms were.

He was standing next to a tailor, who was doing last-minute adjustments to his new clothing. He had on a deep blue tunic, loose pants of a brushed fabric, and a traditional elaborately woven multi-colored belt.

"Da, you look so wonderful!"

"Your Ma was insistent that I wear something new, and got something for me. You like it?" He spun around.

"Very sharp!" Dlen said.

Her father smiled. She said, "It looks like you are in good hands with the tailor. I'm going to go get dressed."

"We'll see you downstairs."

Dlen was torn about what to wear. She had obtained a couple of very nice bltynon, the traditional Kinder women's clothing, with expensive fabrics. She also owned one nice set of gythry, which were like pants, except they were very flowing, and resembled a blytnon if you weren't walking. She decided to wear the gythry, and add her own deep blue tunic and embroidered belt. It wasn't at all traditional, but it felt good.

As she walked into the dining hall, a few chiefs and others had begun to gather and were amiably talking with each other. She noticed a few mild glares in her direction, which she was well used to.

"Daughter! You look marvelous!" Her father said loudly, so that almost everyone could hear.

"Thank you, Da."

She joined him on the dais, sitting to his left. She could see four chairs to each side for the Casitian team.

She thought she should probably stop calling them that in her head. She was aware that they were not all Casitian. Many were Terran, and one was even Kinder!

### Capital Region, Hilcyon

Paul entered the large hall with the others, marveling at the size. There were people beginning to gather at long, narrow tables, and he could see a raised dais where Wlen, his wife and family were beginning to sit down. There seemed to be seats to the left and right of his family, and Paul assumed that was their place to sit.

As they walked closer, Wlen stood up.

"Welcome! Please sit up here with me and my family."

Paul and the others nodded, and walked up the stairs on one side of the dais. There were some murmurs around them, and he looked around to see many staring at them.

They arranged themselves, Glor, Sandra, himself and one security officer on one side, Ke'lir, Cre'relo, Li'more and the other security officer on the other. Paul noticed that Ke'lir took the opportunity to sit next to Dlen.

Wlen said, "Welcome. We are looking forward to having you taste the bounty of Hilcyon, which you made possible for us."

Glor said, "We are glad to be here, and look forward to that."

Paul watched people filter into the hall, and eventually, everyone was seated. Wlen rose.

"Chiefs and families of Hilcyon, welcome to this dinner. We are here to give our thanks to this team for their help two years ago. And we look forward to fruitful conversations about how we might gain more technology and assistance. In return, we look forward to you learning more about Hilcyon, and the Kinder people, and understand our strength and stamina."

Wlen turned to Glor, and sat. Glor rose, and Paul knew he spoke Kinder without translation. "Thank you, Supreme Chief Wlen for the opportunity of this visit, and the chance to reconnect, and learn more about the Kinder here on Hilcyon. And we look forward to find ways we can be supportive."

While Glor spoke, there was a lot of murmuring. People could tell that Glor spoke fluently and appeared, to their eyes, to be Kinder. Glor then sat, and the servants began serving food, and small conversations started to break out at the tables.

Li'more asked him, "So what do you think so far, Paul?"

"I'm not sure. I get the definite impression that some number of chiefs are here somewhat unwillingly, but are on their best behavior. I also get the impression that this dinner is unusual."

"Yes, I get that impression as well. I hope we'll have a chance to meet with as many of the first chiefs as we can—even some of those who are against reform. We need a sense of how strong the reform movement is, and how strong its opposition is."

"Yes, that makes sense."

Paul thought the food was wonderful. It reminded him a lot of Casitian food. Clearly, the vegetables and grains were almost all the same. There was one chewy grain that was unfamiliar to him in taste. He wondered whether or not it was native to Hilcyon. The food, unlike Casitian food, had virtually no spicing. There was an aromatic, somewhat similar to onions that Paul was familiar with, and that was almost ubiquitous in the food. There was also a liberal pouring of a local alcoholic beverage. Paul was sure to be careful with it. He didn't want to end up drunk.

Toward the end of the dinner, an argument broke out at the end of one of the tables. It was quickly quelled, but Paul definitely heard the term "Breft" shouted several times by one person.

Wlen apologized for the outburst, and seemed to take it in stride.

As the dinner ended, and they started to get up to return to their quarters, Wlen said, "I think that was more a result of too much drink, than anything else."

Paul wasn't so sure.

### Capital Region, Hilcyon

Jorn was seated at the back end of one of the long tables, where a few priests had been given seats. He was sad that he wouldn't get a chance to speak to any of the team this evening. But he understood why it was set up this way.

Wlen knew the priests were completely supportive of what he was doing. But he couldn't give them any more social positioning than they normally received. The priesthood was generally the lowest status group, as they were men who did not participate in the chief system. They were even below men who were not chiefs at all, because some men could have the potential to become chiefs—priests never would. Their status was only very slightly above women.

And speaking of women, it had been a surprise to Jorn that the banquet included the wives and children of the first chiefs. He thought that was a good idea, but could also be a provocation.

He enjoyed the richness of the food. He hardly ever got food like this. The fare at the temple was simple and plain, even after the end of the famine.

Toward the end of the dinner, he heard the beginnings of an argument at the end of the table next to him.

"And they have us bring our *wives* here? What does Wlen think he is doing? The Breft will ruin us!"

"Hush, Msrotl."

"Don't tell me to hush!" The person named Msrotl was getting more agitated. He rose, and banged his fists on the table.

"The Breft will ruin the Kinder!"

Jorn and two other priests got up and were on both sides of Msrotl, trying to calm him down. Eventually, they escorted him out of the hall.

"Leave me be!" Msrotl shouted. A woman Jorn assumed was his wife was trying to calm him down. A child, who was probably Msrotl's young son, stood back away from his father. Jorn went to him.

"What's your name?"

"Plir. My Da is angry."

Jorn said, "Yes, Plir, he is. But it's probably because he's had a little too much to drink. You and your Ma can take care of him."

Jorn could see Plir shy away. He wondered about the relationship between this sweet boy and his father.

Eventually, Msrotl and his family left the residence. Jorn decided he would return to the temple. He knew the schedule tomorrow. He would have the opportunity to finally meet the team, and talk with them. He was very much looking forward to that.

### Hol'venif, Rel'toro, Casiti

Ro'mer was quickly packing. They had a headache. They had just finished a holo call with Samira, who was livid. The team on Hilcyon had sent a preliminary report, which included the news that the current Supreme Chief was under threat, and likely would not survive another challenge to his leadership.

Samira was adamant that the mission be aborted immediately. Luckily, no one else on the Consej agreed with that stance. Zrel had asked Ro'mer to come to New Earth to help support him and the team from there, and they had agreed.

M'nali entered the room, her belly protruding. She was pregnant again, with their second, and final child, expected in just a few weeks. Ro'mer turned to her.

"I have to go back to New Earth again. Zrel needs support. We have a bit of a crisis brewing."

"Ter'olo and Cri'stia are on board to take care of things where needed. We'll all be fine."

"I know, but I hate to leave so close to your time."

M'nali smiled. "Well, if the last birth was any example, you'll have plenty of time to get back for the birth."

M'nali had had a very long labor last time. Ro'mer hoped to return well before she even entered labor.

They hugged, and M'nali left them to their packing and their thoughts.

The Casitian shuttle arrived in New Orleans at an absurdly early hour of the morning, and Ro'mer made his way to the Michaelson house to get a little sleep and freshen up before they showed up at Zrel's office.

When they got up from their nap, and made their way to the kitchen, Ro'mer found Tvor sitting drinking a cup of coffee.

"Tvor! So nice to see you!"

They hugged. Tvor, Glor's younger brother, was newly employed by the NEA, having just graduated from university.

"It's good to see you too, Ro'mer! How's the kiddo?"

"They are doing great. Walking already! And M'nali is ready to birth her second."

"Cool!"

"How's the new job?"

"I love it. I'm learning so much about politics and how the NEA interacts with all of the zones and countries, including Zwek. I've met so many interesting people!"

"Do you get to see Tricia much?"
"No, not at all. Aunt Tricia is in a different building. Besides, she's super important! I'm just a lowly clerk at this point."

Tricia was technically Tvor and Ro'mer's second cousin once removed, but Ro'mer guessed "Aunt" was as good a term as any.

"How long are you in New Orleans, Tvor?"

"A couple of months. I get to go back to Zwek after a training period. The job requires me to be here 3 days every 10."

"That's not too bad an arrangement."

"No, it's OK. I will probably end up living with Liam when I need to be here—he'd like some company, and his place is huge."

Ro'mer recalled that Liam's father Zrel had inherited the house that great-great-Aunt Mira's co-parent Kurt had lived in after he was

President of New America. Zrel never liked that house, so he gave it to his son.

It had been nice to have this distraction. They weren't looking forward to the next few days. They made some more coffee, helped Tvor make breakfast for both of them, then made their way to Zrel's office, dreading everything.

# Chapter 11:
# The Simple and the Complex

New Earth: January 2101
Hilcyon: Lykl 1203
Casiti: Hevl 804

*"Ultimately, we are all humans. Casitians must remember that there is so much we share - especially the grief of not being able to return to the planet of our birthing." Ja'lend'a, 'Spirits Alike'*

### New Orleans, New Earth

"And this, *exactly*, is why we should have never, *ever* agreed to allow Terrans to represent Casiti on the Consej!" Samira's angry voice boomed above the din.

Ro'mer sat at the table, feeling relatively calm, although Ro'mer knew that what was happening now was the conflict that they knew had been coming, ever since the second call from Hilcyon. The report from Glor's team made it clear that the situation on the ground was going to be very complex. What degree of interference in Hilcyon's government should they have? How could they assure that the current reformer Supreme Chief remained in power?

All of the Kinder representatives felt it necessary to intervene and assure the continued leadership of the reformer Chief. The Terran representatives, including the current chair, his cousin Zrel, were evenly split. The Casitians, save Ro'mer were dead set against any interference, and they were going to tip the balance. Ro'mer thought intervention was wise. It would have been a deadlock, assuring no intervention, had Ro'mer not been on the Consej.

It had been a major concession of the Casitians 50 years ago to give up consensus decision-making in favor of majority rule, since neither the Terrans nor the Kinder had that tradition. Ro'mer imagined that they were regretting that concession greatly at this moment. But it didn't matter. The Consej had decided that they would intervene. The question now was how much.

Zrel rang the bell repeatedly. "Please settle down. The vote is complete. We have decided that we will intervene in Hilcyon's process, for two aims. First, to assure their continued well-being, and second, to assure the eventual peaceful re-unification of all humans. But we need to decide on the parameters. Let's each go and confer with our communities and committees, and come up with a series of proposals, to create a plan. Our team on Hilcyon is going to need guidance, and the sooner we can give it, the better."

Ro'mer did not look forward to the meeting they knew would happen right after this one, with the Casitian representatives of the Consej, and the Casitian council, the Caraj. Ro'mer had several friends on the Caraj, but the Caraj had never been open to representatives that had even a small amount of Terran ancestry. Their mother was nominated to the Caraj just a few years ago but was not invited by the Caraj to join.

Several days later, after returning to Casiti, Ro'mer sat on some pillows in the room they shared with Mi'nali. They were exhausted and deeply troubled. After Ro'mer's vote broke the tie on the Consej for intervention into the politics of Hilcyon, all hell had broken loose. The Caraj, who were responsible for nominating Casitian members of the Consej, came to consensus that no one with less than 63/64ths native Casitian heritage could serve as a Casitian member of the Consej. Given that only 67 years had passed since Terran presence on Casiti, it eliminated everyone with any Terran relatives. No member of the Michaelson family would again serve on the Consej as a Casitian representative for many, many years, if ever. They also decided to revoke Ro'mer's position, so Ro'mer was about to lose their seat. This would virtually assure that any assistance that they would have given to the current Supreme Chief would not be coming.

Even worse, the Caraj was even considering asking the Consej to bring the delegation back home immediately. From Ro'mer's perspective this would be a disaster. It would have the certain affect of weakening the hand of the reformer Chief, potentially reversing the reform movement.

Ro'mer could see the somewhat hidden undercurrent of suspicion of their family, not only on the Caraj, but among Casitians in general. There were some number of blended families by now, but none were nearly as well-known as the Michaelsons. And very few contained members of all three branches of humanity. Ro'mer could see the beginning of the erosion of the long work of their family, and of the peaceful coexistence fostered by Jal'end'a and others during and after The Event.

Well, there was no point in rehashing these events. There wasn't much Ro'mer could do about them. They didn't know when Glor, Ke'lir, and Paul would be returning. They hoped at least that the Consej would give them time enough so that some good could be accomplished. And Ro'mer needed to get busy shoring up their family's position.

### Capital Region, Hilcyon

Dlen washed off her hands, while the doctor that Ke'lir had brought with them took care of the mother and baby. Dlen knew that both would have died without this help. She had worried about Hjirn's pregnancy for months, and when they had arrived during her labor, she was sure that Hjirn could not survive it.

Dlen walked to the side of the room where Ke'lir stood, watching.

She said, "Ke'lir, I wish to thank your doctor for saving Hjirn's life, and the life of her son. Her husband Ylorp will thank you both."

Ke'lir nodded. "I'm glad we were here, Dlen."

Something in the way that Ke'lir looked at Dlen made her heart flutter. But she needed to focus on the tasks ahead.

"Can you bring more doctors? How can we save more lives?"

"We only have one, Dlen. I've been talking with her, and she has a training plan in mind. We'll be able to leave you with tools and instruments that you need, and train you to use them."

"So you'll stay for a while?"

Dlen could hear something strange in Ke'lir's voice. Ke'lir had gotten better and better at speaking in their language, but Dlen could tell there was some hesitation.

"Dlen, we have been told we need to leave soon. We can't stay as long as we originally thought. Glor is speaking with your father about this. We have been ordered not to intervene in your governmental process. I'm so sorry, I wish things could be different."

Dlen felt her heart drop out of her chest. She had been so hopeful. Hopeful that her father would survive, and hopeful for the reform effort. Now, she knew. There would be war. She looked at Ke'lir, who looked sad, and had tears in her eyes. Dlen knew that Ke'lir cared about them, but she had no idea it was so much. She reached out to Ke'lir, and touched her arm.

"I know you would do everything you could do to help us, Ke'lir. Perhaps it is right that we have to be the ones who will work this out on our own."

"But I don't want you to be in danger…"

Dlen said quietly, "We'll be alright." But Dlen didn't believe that. The reformers would take to arms to keep her father in place as Supreme Chief, and Dlen wasn't at all sure they could survive the war. But she would do the best she knew how.

Ylorp, Hjirn's husband, and father to the newborn boy, approached Dlen and Ke'lir. He looked at Ke'lir.

"I know my son and wife would be dead if it were not for you. We had tried so hard, for so long, to have a child, and when this pregnancy was so difficult for Hjirn, I had little hope."

Ke'lir said, "I'm glad we were here to save these lives. There are many more we could help."

Ylorp nodded. "I wish to help spread your knowledge to assist more families. But I am in a precarious position."

Ke'lir said, "You all are. But why are you particularly?"

"I am in a unit that is secretly dedicated to stamping out reform. It was openly before Wlen became Supreme Chief, but now, my Second Chief is secretly working against Wlen. I knew of Dlen a long time ago, and each time she came to this hamlet, I watched her. If my Second

Chief knew that she had delivered my son, he would probably have me killed—but I knew she was the only hope we had.

"And I am carefully watched. My father was a rebel, and was executed for sedition when I was a child. My grandfather was the great Supreme Chief Willm. I am watched from both directions."

Ke'lir said, "Willm?"

"He was from Grier Nro, but that is a closely held secret of our family."

"William! He became Supreme Chief?"

Dlen was astonished that Willm had been from Grier Nro. She said to Ke'lir, "He is considered the most revered of Chiefs in the current era. He re-united all of Hilcyon after the rebellions. You know of him?"

"Yes, from my own family history. Most on New Earth don't know his story. Beatrice, or Btric as you called her, found out he was on Hilcyon. But no one knew he became Supreme Chief."

Ylorp said, "He pledged to never contact the Breft."

Ke'lir said, "Of course he made that pledge. If we were contacted while he was still alive, his secret would have been exposed!"

Ylorp nodded. "And he would have been killed for his treachery."

Dlen said, "We must go. It would not be good to be here too long."

Ylorp nodded. "Thank you again."

Dlen nodded, and Ke'lir and the doctor joined her at the door. They left, and walked to the edge of the hamlet where the shuttle was. They took the shuttle back to the capital, and walked to the Supreme Chief's mansion.

Ke'lir said, "Dlen, I know it's late, but can we talk? I need to discuss some things with you."

"Certainly. Let's go up to the library."

As they settled in to chairs opposite each other, Dlen had another look at Ke'lir. She realized that not only had she come to greatly enjoy Ke'lir's company, but the idea of losing it was wrenching. She took a few breaths, to settle herself.

Ke'lir started, "Dlen, I don't know how much time we have, but we need to train you, and as many other midwives as you can gather, on how to use the equipment we have. I've talked with our doctor. If we had more time, we would take you all through a normal educational process, but we don't have time for that. We also don't have time to translate all of our medical documents into your language. Our translators are working hard, but we need your help. We don't have any relatively modern language guides."

"I have four midwives in mind already. They are smart, and fast learners. We all can help you translate. I've already set aside some rooms for us all to work."

Ke'lir smiled, and Dlen felt herself get warm. It was an unusual feeling, one she hadn't had in a very long time. She realized that she'd felt this way with Mrel. Sadness and fear overtook her for a moment, until she felt calmed by Ke'lir's touch on her arm.

Dlen needed for this moment to end. "It's late—I have much to do, and need rest. Let's reconvene tomorrow."

"Yes, I'm sorry to keep you up. Tomorrow." Ke'lir got up, and left the room. Dlen watched her leave with sadness.

### Capital Region Hilcyon

Ke'lir walked into the parlor, and saw Glor and Paul, sitting. Ke'lir greeted them, and then started to tell the story of the woman their doctor saved from dying in childbirth.

Ke'lir continued, "So I think the more we can support women in childbirth, and their infants early in life, the more women will appreciate our presence here, and the more they will influence their husbands, sons, and fathers."

Glor said, "I don't know, Ke'lir—this is a pretty patriarchal society. Will the women have that much influence?"

"If more of men's sons survive, Glor, that will make a difference to them."

Paul said, "The Consej isn't going to limit how much medical and humanitarian aid we can provide, are they?"

"No, I don't think so. Most of the Casitian representatives want us to leave, but enough of them are willing to have us help for a while. We can stay for another 20 days."

Ke'lir said, "That's not enough time to train the midwives..."

Glor said, "Can't you train Dlen, and a few more enough so they can train others?"

Ke'lir could feel herself getting angry. "Glor, these people are using 19th century Earth level medicine!"

Glor sighed. "Ke'lir, I can't fix this. We have 20 more days. There is nothing I can do."

"We have to stay longer, Glor! Besides, no one at home is going to..."

"You want to threaten all of our careers? Ro'mer was clear—our family *reputation* is in peril."

Ke'lir was infuriated. "These *people* are peril, Glor!"

Ke'lir got up, and walked out of the room, slamming the door. She was angry, upset and sad, and she knew her feelings were out of proportion. She realized how scared she was for Dlen. She sat down heavily on the bed.

"Knock, knock?" Ke'lir looked up.

"Yeah, come on in."

Glor sat down on the chair, and said nothing for a minute.

Ke'lir said, "Look, Glor, I'm sorry for storming out like that. Dlen has been giving me a lot of information, and I'm learning a lot. This society is on a kind of cusp. If we can't intervene, and give support to the reformers, things will get bad. Dlen knows a lot of reformers, and they are ready to take up arms to support her father. There will be war."

Glor said, "I know. I wish I knew a way we can prevent that, but we can't. The Casitians are really clear—they don't want us to intervene, and a lot of Terrans don't want that either. There isn't anything we can do."

"I don't want to go against orders. I just..."

Glor said, "Let me know if there is any way I can help with anything, Ke'lir. I'll stretch our orders as far as I can."

Ke'lir looked up. "Thanks, Glor."

She still felt devastated.

*Capital Region, Hilcyon*

Jorn looked around him at the people who had traveled to Hilcyon to help them. There was the one named Glor, who looked almost Kinder, except for the small tuft of hair on his chin and a strange accent. Then the young one named Paul, who was much lighter skinned than Glor, or any Kinder, who seemed older than his years. There was the woman, Ke'lir, who had the skin complexion of Kinder and Casitians, and was, from what Jorn knew, unmarried. There was the dour, stout one named Li'more, who he heard was from Casiti itself.

They had all introduced themselves, and Jorn was beginning to explain the priesthood, and more particularly, the secret society within the priesthood.

Jorn continued, "Our inner group has been working on reform, but it's been slow. The Kinder chiefs allow the priesthood but don't respect us, so we have little influence."

Paul said, "I'm impressed that you've been working underground for so long. How many Kinder are aware of your efforts?"

"Not many. We realized a while ago that being open about our efforts would lead to reprisals. So we only tell those we really trust."

Paul asked, "Is the entire priesthood on the same path?"

"Mostly, yes. There are some orders that are very conservative, but they are small, and hold little influence."

Ke'lir asked, "We have been asked to assist midwives with medical issues relating to reproduction. Does your priesthood support that?"

"Although as of yet, no women are allowed to be priests, we together with women are the essential parts of Kinder society that the chiefs either ignore, or resist. We support anything you can do to help women."

Paul asked, "As of yet?"

"There are more liberal orders that have been considering including women in the priesthood. It just hasn't happened yet."

Glor said, "We have a priesthood as well. I have been to services a few times. I'd love it if I could go to services while I'm here."

Jorn was surprised. "I don't understand, how could there be priests among the Kinder there?"

"My understanding is that a few of the soldiers left on New Earth had been recruited from the priesthood, and they created an order, and trained priests."

Jorn couldn't imagine how that could have happened. He would ask Glin. He knew Glin had access to historical records and information that could hold the key. It reminded him of another question.

"When you say, 'left on New Earth', what do you mean? They were abandoned by their chief?"

Jorn could see Glor hesitate, then make some sort of internal decision.

"The Kinder who were on New Earth were deserters. About 2,000 Kinder men deserted during the invasion of New Earth. A small number of them, I think it was about 200, went back when the reformer Supreme Chief at the time who had taken over asked them to return to help with reform. I don't blame them. New Earth is paradise compared to Hilcyon. It's sort of amazing more of them didn't desert."

Jorn was torn, but he realized he needed to explain how bad this situation was.

"Glor, forgive me, but I think you don't have a full understanding of the gravity of this situation. You, and the Kinder you represent, are descended from deserters. Desertion from one's duty is considered one of the most severe forms of dishonorable behavior. Deserters are sentenced to death here."

Jorn could see Glor's face show confusion and fear.

Jorn asked, "Who was the deserter you are descended from?"

"My great-grandfather's name was Ngellin Jror Hlad. He became the leader of the Kinder on New Earth, eventually participating in the government."

"So you, Glor, are the great-grandson of not only a deserter, but the *leader* of the deserters?"

Glor was silent.

Jorn said, "Glor, I will not share this widely, nor should you, but you and your people need to take into consideration that this will be a big hurdle for us. I mean, it's not a hurdle for me, or the priesthood, but the chiefs may well find it impossible to move forward."

Paul said, "Thank you, Jorn, for your honesty. We had no idea this would be an issue."

"Honor is not important to you?"

Glor said, "Honor is important—but even for us Kinder on New Earth, honor is not defined as obedience. Honor is a combination of factors: integrity, honesty, and willingness to do the right thing. Disobedience can be honorable."

Li'more added, "For Casitians, honor includes respecting those who have more standing, but not blindly just because."

"Ah, so for all of you, Mrin was honorable?"

Paul said, "Oh, yes, very much so."

"Alas, not for us. Although many consider his act to be brave and are grateful for it, everyone agrees he was not honorable."

Jorn watched the whole team take that in. "I will be happy to work with you to figure out how we all might navigate this, but it *will* be a factor.

"On a different note, in two days First Moon rise prayers at the 12th hour will be happening. It's a major ritual. I would love to invite you to our temple for it."

Paul nodded, "Yes, we'd love to attend."


### Capital Region, Hilcyon

Paul was walking with the rest of the team back from the temple to the Supreme Chief's residence. He was deep in thought. He had been much more deeply touched by the rituals and prayers than he thought he would. He realized that he'd kind of expected something similar to church at home, but this was utterly different. There felt to be something much more transcendent and unifying, somehow. He didn't quite know how to explain it.

He was still mulling over so much that had happened over the past few days. Ke'lir's connection with Dlen, his budding friendship with Jorn, who he'd gotten to spend some time with after their last team meeting, and Glor, who was feeling increasingly conflicted after the conversation with Jorn about honor.

They were in a rough spot. It had not occurred to anyone that it might matter that the Kinder from New Earth were deserters. And further, putting Glor in the leadership position was seeming, at this moment, to have been a bad decision, because of who he represented.

And there was nothing they really could do about it now: they only had 17 more days here, to do what they can, and meet with whoever they can. They will then have to leave. It gave Paul heartache that they couldn't stay, and he didn't really quite understand it, but they didn't really have a choice.

In a couple of days, he had a meeting with a group of chiefs who didn't want reform. That should be interesting. They had refused to meet with Glor, which hadn't helped Glor's mood at all.

He caught up to Ke'lir, who seemed to be brooding as well.

"Hey, Ke'lir, what did you think?"

"Of the service?"

"Yeah."

"It was interesting. I was kind of surprised how much I liked it."

"I know, me too. There was something really special about it. But maybe just because it was really novel for us."

"No, I think there's more to it than that. I wish Ja'len'da were alive to see it."

"Me too! I thought of her a lot during the service."

They continued to walk together in companionable silence.

# Chapter 12:
# Unfolding

New Earth: January - February 2101
Hilcyon: Lykl 1203
Casiti: Hevl 804

*"Love must be the pillar and the foundation of our lives. Without love, we have nothing." Heart of Carj, Ecologe 231*

### Capital Region, Hilcyon

Her father had asked Dlen to be at this meeting to give the news that she'd heard from Hjirn. Wlen sat with his attache Rtlir, and several other extremely loyal associates—most of whom she knew well. Her father asked her to explain what she knew, and how she knew it.

"Recently, I saved the life of Second Chief Ylorp's wife while in childbirth. He has pledged to feed information to his wife, who will feed it to me. I have learned that there is a rebellion planned at the dinner in two days."

Rtlir asked, "What kind of rebellion?"

"Ylorp didn't have details, he just knew that they were mobilizing. He had been largely excluded from the planning process. He also said that Msrotl thinks that the Breft aren't ever leaving."

Wlen said, "Thank you, daughter. I'm not really that surprised. I've been seeding to specific chiefs who I am suspecting of disloyalty. Can you relay this information to Glor?"

Dlen nodded.

"And daughter, please ask your mother to heavily water the drinks that night, please? We'll need to be sharp!"

Dlen said, "Yes, father. That's a very good idea."

As she left that office, knowing that they were planning their defense, she was sure that even after they fought off this rebellion, there would be more to come. War was inevitable. There was too much of an even match between the numbers of reformers and traditionalists. The only way out was going to be war, now that the Breft were not going to intervene.

Dlen wondered if her father wished that he'd never called them. She wondered whether any of them would survive the war to come.

## Capital Region, Hilcyon

Dlen, Ke'lir, the Casitian doctor, and several midwives had been busy at work all day. Between training the midwives and help with translation of documentation, they had had several long days already, and they would have more long days until Ke'lir and the rest of them finally left.

In the morning, Dlen had alerted them that there would be an attack in two days, at a big dinner that had been planned for some time. Glor said Wlen was confident they could defend themselves, but Glor had made sure the security staff were prepared.

Ke'lir had been in a terrible state but was trying hard to not let anyone know it. She had irretrievably fallen in love with Dlen, but, of course, she hadn't told Dlen. And spending time with Dlen was exhilarating and deeply painful at the same time. At the end of every day, she spent most of the night sleepless and crying.

Ke'lir tried to focus. She was working with Dlen and the automated translators to translate, and then further explain, the Terran medical documentation they would be leaving behind. Ke'lir had decided that basic Terran medical documentation was going to be easier for the Kinder to understand, even though they also would be trained to use the Casitian medical equipment without understanding much of how it worked, since Casitian medicine was much further advanced than Terran medicine was.

Dlen said, "This translation doesn't make sense. The translator got caught on this word, and I can't pronounce it."

Ke'lir said, "Let me see." Dlen pushed the tablet toward Ke'lir, and pointed the word out.

"Spleen."

Dlen tried, "Splin."

Ke'lir smiled. "That will do." Ke'lir had encountered how difficult vowels, especially long vowels, were for the Kinder.

"What is it?"

"It is a relatively small organ, to the left of the stomach."

"Oh! We have a name for that. I'll have the translator replace the words."

"Thanks!"

After a few minutes, Dlen said, "Speaking of stomachs, I'm rather hungry, and I'm sure you are too. I'll go get someone to bring us all some dinner."

Ke'lir nodded gratefully. She was hungry, and between the work, and trying hard not to let her distress show, her appetite hadn't shown up. But now that food was on offer, she realized how little she'd eaten all day.

After the dinner break, and another time unit of work, the other midwives left to return to their families, and Ke'lir and Dlen were left alone. The last thing in the world that Ke'lir wanted to do was leave and go back to her room. But her brain was pretty much done, and focusing on work had become impossible.

Dlen finally interrupted Ke'lir, who was repeating herself a few too many times.

"Ke'lir, I think it's time we stopped for the day. It's been a very long one, and you look so tired. Are you sleeping?"

Ke'lir looked up at Dlen and saw the concern in her face. She felt a tear drop down her cheek. She wiped it off "Sorry. I've been under a lot of stress."

Dlen reached for Ke'lir's hand and folded hers over it. "I can see how much you care about us."

Ke'lir was fighting with herself. She wanted more than anything to tell Dlen how she was feeling, but she knew there was no purpose in it. What could it matter how she felt? They had no future but the next fifteen days.

There was silence between them for a while, then Dlen said quietly, "Ke'lir, what are you not telling me? I can feel it—the conflict you have inside of yourself. Please, tell me. I won't tell anyone."

"It's not about..." Ke'lir took a breath and looked into Dlen's eyes. She came to a quiet conclusion. If fifteen days was all they had of a future, it was better than nothing.

"Dlen, I know that your culture is very different than mine. In my culture, there is space for two women to love each other, to be intimate with each other... to live with each other, make a family together."

Dlen nodded but said nothing. Ke'lir forged ahead.

"I've read the stories of Dbor, and know of the story of Elfer, which I imagine you are familiar with. Anyway, over the past 10 days, we've worked closely together, and I feel as if I've gotten to know you well. You are a beautiful person, smart, deep, fascinating... I..."

She was struggling with the language. She subvocalized words to her translator, and finally, it gave her the words to say.

"I have fallen in love with you. I don't know whether you feel anything for me, and I know we can't have any sort of future together, but..."

Dlen said nothing and got up from the table. Ke'lir was afraid she had offended Dlen.

"I'm sorry... I didn't mean..."

Dlen said quietly, "Don't be sorry." Dlen took Ke'lir's hand, and led her through the corridors back to the library, their favorite place to spend time together. Dlen closed the door and motioned to have Ke'lir sit on the large, plush window seat.

"We won't be disturbed here." Dlen sat next to Ke'lir, their bodies in contact. She put her arm around Ke'lir.

Tears were flowing down Ke'lir's face. She couldn't help it. She felt undone.

Dlen said, "I treasured the stories of Dbor, and, yes, the story of Elfer. When I was a girl, I had a friend. Her name was Mrel. We played together all of the time, and sometimes we played at being husband and wife together. I never really knew what that meant, but I knew what I felt for her, and I knew there was no room for what I felt. When I met you, I felt the same way again, but I didn't really admit it to myself—I couldn't admit what it meant."

Ke'lir wiped tears from her face and looked at Dlen. She moved toward her, and gave her a gentle kiss on the lips. The kiss became less gentle, and more urgent, the longer it lasted. Dlen and Ke'lir lay down finally on the seat, aware of nothing else but the movement of their bodies together.

## Capital Region, Hilcyon

This morning, Paul had gotten up early and was sitting in the main room of their suite, reading his tablet before breakfast, which was due soon. He had felt a little bit like a fifth wheel over the past few days. Ke'lir was busy with Dlen and the midwives, Glor and Li'more were busy with Wlen and security concerns, and Sandra was busily studying every book and archive she could get her hands on in the capital.

Paul had several meetings with engineers, hoping to do some degree of technology transfer, given the reality that they were leaving, not to return until things settled out and they were called back. The problem was that there just wasn't the expertise to handle the information. Mrin had been the last engineer who understood or cared about galactic technology, and no one else had nearly the experience and knowledge he'd had. After discussions with Glor and Ke'lir, they agreed that at least for now, technology transfer would be limited to medical technology.

He'd also had one disastrous meeting with some chiefs who were against contact at all. They let him know in no uncertain terms that they had been deeply insulted by Glor's leadership once they discovered his heritage, and refused to say anything more.

So that left Paul with helping Ke'lir, but there wasn't a lot to do. He was getting bored. But he had brought a very large collection of Casitian theology texts with him on this trip, so he could keep his mind occupied to some extent. And he had planned a few meetings with Jorn, and he looked forward to those conversations.

He also had his continued correspondence with Franklin Martin to keep him occupied. Franklin had, at his suggestion, sent an ambassador to New America and accepted one. He had also sent an ambassador to the South Central Independent Zone. They had not yet sent an ambassador back, but one was promised. In addition, due to

Paul's coordination, the New Earth Agency was considering taking a representative from the ICS. It was a step in the right direction.

But Franklin was facing a lot of opposition, although interestingly, his parents were an unexpected source of support. His father, largely because of his father's family connection to the founder of the ICS, had been a staunch traditionalist. But over the past year, he'd seemed to moderate just a tiny bit and had been supportive of the changes Franklin was making.

He had also been in contact with Ro'mer, who was busy doing their best to keep their family reputation intact now that the Caraj had made the drastic decision to revoke his place on the Consej and prevent anyone with any degree of Terran heritage from filling a Casitian slot on the Consej. Ro'mer felt that they could see and hear the Casitians closing up again, after the open period after The Event. That worried Paul, quite a lot. The hope of a re-unified human species depended upon Casitian openness.

He heard the front door open, and he was surprised to see a somewhat disheveled Ke'lir enter instead of their breakfast.

"Hi Ke'lir. Did you work all night?"

"Uh, um. No. I gotta get a bath. Breakfast not here yet?"

"Nope. Should be here momentarily."

He watched her go into her room, get a bundle, and then go into their bath. Paul was a bit puzzled, but when the door opened again, with one of the women of the house bearing a cart with breakfast, he forgot all about it.

### New Orleans, New Earth

Ro'mer sat with some Terran and Kinder members of the Consej, along with several other members of the Michaelson family. It was a strategizing meeting to try and move the Consej back to a position of intervention before Glor had to bring everyone home. Ro'mer was cautiously optimistic.

Tanessa Bird lived in the South Circumpolar Independent Zone, which had a very large Casitian population, and followed Casitian culture fairly closely. She had been dead-set against intervention of any kind, and Ro'mer didn't think this conversation was moving her position at all. Christoph Kim was from the North Central IZ and had been supportive of some kind of active intervention to keep the reformers in place. Jayden Rush was from the South Central IZ and would likely change their vote to agree to intervention. Welburn Snider had also voted against intervention but was leaning toward changing his vote, too. This meant that two new votes could go in favor of intervention.

Ro'mer's cousin Zrel, a Terran representative to the council and its current chair, had called this meeting. He had hoped that the information Ro'mer had to share about what was happening on Hilcyon might sway some votes, especially since they didn't really have enough time to do enough knowledge transfer to save many lives. Welburn hadn't been sure.

Welburn said, "Look, they have been living and dying without our help for a long time. I'm leaning toward intervention, but maybe they are better left alone."

Ro'mer said, "But Welburn, that's just it; they need help. They can't live on Hilcyon without our help, as was proven just last year. We had to fix their equipment and send down food, or else they all would have died! Our support can help them even more, which might, in time, lead them to be more willing to stay connected to us."

Tanessa said, "Some Casitians argue that letting them all die might be the best alternative. Let them die off, then, when they are gone, re-populate Hilcyon. When the galactics return, we'll be unified."

Ro'mer said, "Oh, and you think the Galactics won't be able to tell we just let them all die? I'm sure when they learn that, they are going to lock us in here and throw away the key for good!"

Tanessa sighed, and everyone was quiet for a while.

Zrel spoke, "Welburn, Jayden, can we count on your changed votes?" They both nodded assent. "Tanessa?"

She shook her head. "I'm sorry, Zrel. My people in the SCIZ would never forgive me. They just don't agree. And I don't either."

Zrel nodded. "OK. Thank you all so much for coming. The Casitian members of the Consej are likely going to put some procedural blocks in place. I hope we can get this vote going before our team has to leave Hilcyon—it will make things so much easier."

When Ro'mer and Zrel returned to the Michaelson house, they discussed the current situation.

Zrel said, "As you know, the Casitians are not happy right now."

Ro'mer said, "You would not believe the meeting I had a few days ago with Trel'or'li. She has been doing everything she can to strip power and influence from the Casitian arm of our family. My mother has had her official role reduced dramatically. I'm pretty sure Paul will be removed from his role when he returns, which is going to break his heart. And it's not just our family. Every blended Casitian/Terran or Casitian/Kinder family living on Casiti is feeling the heat. I think they want us all to just go away."

"I've heard they are now decreasing visitation permits for Terrans."

"Yeah. They are seriously retrenching. I'm not even sure how long Terrans will be able to be residents of Casiti. Several measures are already pending in the Caraj to greatly reduce the Terran population, especially in Rel'toro."

"It's hard to think we might witness a breach or separation. I don't know what to do, Ro'mer. I don't know how to keep this together. If the Casitians want to separate, they will, and there isn't much we are going to be able to do about it."

Ro'mer silently assented, feeling depression move over him in a wave. All of the work he and his family had done for so many years to bridge the gaps between the Casitians and others seemed to be turning to dust. He was glad grandmother Beatrice wasn't around to see it.

### Capital Region, Hilcyon

Jorn sat across the desk from Glin, who looked thoughtful. Jorn had just finished his report on his meetings with the Casitian team and his time with Paul separately.

Glin said, "I appreciate the openness with which this group is approaching us. It must be clear to them that the Kinder are having a hard time matching it."

Jorn nodded. "It seems they, like the priesthood, are committed to eventual unification. But the rest of the Kinder... they can't even seem to agree on continued contact."

"They do seem willing to work with us at our pace."

"Yes, your Holiness. I just wish we knew what our pace was! I've been hearing all sorts of chatter from our congregation. I'm worried something bad is going to happen."

Glin nodded. "I've heard from Wlen that he heard from a back-channel that a revolt is planned for tomorrow, during the big dinner. I think we should try to be prepared."

"What do you suggest?"

"I've tasked a number of priests from your temple, and the two other capital region temples to hang out around the Capitol and Supreme Chiefs residence during the dinner. I'm hopeful they can be instrumental in heading anything off."

Jorn said, "That's a good idea, your Holiness. As you know, I've been invited to the dinner, so I'll be there."

Glin passed a sheet of paper. "Yes. I've planned on that. Here is a list of the priests I've assigned. You know many of them."

Jorn looked at the list. A very logical list of those who could be very useful in a conflict.

"Thank you, your Holiness. These are good people. I'll be in contact with them and strategize."

"I have confidence in you, Jorn. Thank you."

"You are very welcome, your Holiness."

Jorn got up, bowed, and walked out. He was on his way to his third meeting with Paul, which he very much looked forward to. Paul was a bright, earnest young man, and had he been Kinder, a perfect candidate for the priesthood. Jorn understood that Paul was on his way to a Casitian version of priesthood and was interested in understanding more. The plethora of belief systems and what the Casitians called "schools" was confusing to him.

As he walked into the room that had been set aside for meetings with the Casitian group, he saw Paul in active but hushed conversation with Dlen, Wlen's daughter, and Ke'lir, another member of the Casitian team. They looked up towards him.

Paul said, "Jorn, so good to see you. Dlen and Ke'lir were just filling me in on the work they've been able to do with the midwives."

Jorn said, "How is that going?"

Ke'lir had a sad look on her face. She said, "We won't have enough time to train them as deeply as we wished to. But they will have a good enough basis to make a really big difference for many women here."

Jorn said, "I'm so glad to hear that. Please let me know if there is any way the priesthood can be of service. Of course, we live in very different spheres, but we are happy to support this effort in any way we can."

Dlen said, "Thank you, Jorn. Just knowing that you support these efforts is important."

Dlen and Ke'lir stood up, gave their goodbye greetings, and left the room.

Jorn could see a worried look on Paul's face.

"You are concerned, son."

"Yes, Father Jorn, I am. I am upset that we are having to leave so soon before so much work we hoped to get done is finished. But we have been given no choice."

"We'll be alright. This will work itself out. There may be a delay, Wlen might lose a challenge, and things might revert for a while. But I have faith that at some time, you and I will be sitting together again, working toward unification. The Exalted King wills this—wills that we all finally come back together again."

# Chapter 13:
## Conflict and Disaster

New Earth: February 2101
Hilcyon: Cfro 1203
Casiti: Hevl 804

*"All humans yearn to understand the universe. Many manifestations of this yearning have been found throughout all of human history. When we finally are in contact again with our siblings on Hilcyon, we will find that they share this yearning with us." Ja'lend'a, 'Spirits Alike'*

### Capital Region, Hilcyon

Ke'lir looked over at Dlen, who was doing the last review of the translation of one of the key texts they would leave behind: a Terran textbook on childbirth. As she looked at Dlen, she couldn't help but think about the last two days, and her complicated joy of being in Dlen's presence.

She would have to leave in less than 14 days. She had no idea whether she could ever return here. She was glad that she and Dlen had this time together, but she could hardly imagine leaving and knowing Dlen was here, possibly suffering and dying, during the inevitable war to come.

She thought of asking Dlen to return with her, but she knew, somehow, that Dlen wouldn't, and couldn't leave her family and the women of Hilcyon behind. Ke'lir couldn't think of asking her to do that, even though she wanted it desperately.

Dlen looked up. "I think we're done for now. My last review of this text is finished. We can start the text on surgical interventions tomorrow?"

Ke'lir nodded. "Yes. And I imagine you need to go and help your mother with preparations?"

Dlen smiled. "No, actually, I have free time until the banquet. My mother relieved me of my household duties when it was clear I needed to focus on this work."

"Well, we could get started on the surgical..."

Dlen took Ke'lir's hand. "No. I can't really focus, and we haven't had a nice break. I want to show you something."

They got up, and went downstairs, and outside. They walked a few blocks, and came to a long wall, which had a gate in it. Dlen opened the gate.

Ke'lir said, "What is this?"

"It's a garden. I've known of it since I was young. It was locked for many years and tended by some priests. Come."

They walked through the gate, and into a small area that was the greenest space she'd seen on Hilcyon. There were many plants she recognized from Casiti, and some she had never seen before.

Dlen said, "This garden was watered and tended even when we all almost starved."

Ke'lir said, "I have really enjoyed my meetings with Jorn. The priesthood are very important allies for us."

Dlen nodded.

They walked around and came across a priest who was watering a patch of soil. The priest looked up.

Ke'lir said, "Hello."

He nodded. "Hello. Welcome to Kinder Home. And welcome to our garden."

"Thank you. It is so beautiful."

"We keep it to remember where we come from. And where we should go."

Dlen said, "I hope for that as well."

The priest nodded and went back to watering. They walked around for a while in companionable silence.

As they were approaching the large, imposing Supreme Chief's mansion, Ke'lir noticed a number of men in specific positions around the mansion, and a few milling suspiciously in front of the set of large doors. She pointed this out to Dlen, who nodded. They also saw several priests who were approaching the men, and saw some heated arguments.

Dlen whispered, "I will tell my father when we get inside. Something is very wrong here."

Ke'lir nodded. They walked into the side entrance of the mansion, and there was the chaos of servants bustling about in final preparations before any guests arrived.

Dlen asked of a passing servant, "Do you know where Supreme Chief Wlen is?"

"He is in his rooms with your ma."

"Thank you." She turned to Ke'lir. "I should go tell him about the men outside."

"I'll join you."

They walked up the stairs, and down a long hallway, and turned into a corridor with several guards stationed. They walked into a large suite.

"Dlen, Ke'lir!"

"Hi Ma."

"How is the work going?"

Ke'lir said, "We are making a lot of progress. Dlen is a very quick study."

Ke'lir looked at Dlen, who smiled, melting more of Ke'lir's heart.

"Ke'lir is too generous. It's hard work, but we have learned a lot. Where's Da?"

"He is in the next room, talking to his aides."

They walked into the other room, to see Wlen talking animatedly with several people.

Dlen said, "Da, we wanted to warn you…"

A very loud bang interrupted Dlen. It was quickly followed by the building shuddering. Men flooded into the room, and another loud bang and shudder followed.

Someone Ke'lir knew knew was a key security aide to Dlen's father said, "Sir, we need to get you all to safety!"

Ke'lir had, like all of the visitors, a small defensive device on her belt. But it couldn't do much in the case of an explosion. She also had

171

an emergency communicator. She summoned a shuttle from the ship. She followed the men out, along with Wlen, Dlen and her mother.

As they went downstairs, all she saw was total chaos. The explosion had completely destroyed the front of the building, and there was dust in the air, and groans and screams. She hesitated.

"Dlen, we need to help these folks..."

Just then a large man wielding a spear came out of nowhere and rushed toward Wlen. He was intercepted by one of Wlen's guards, and a big fight ensued when more and more men came wielding swords and spears.

Ke'lir's first thought was to get them all outside to where she knew the shuttle would land.

"Dlen, what's the quickest way out of here toward the plaza? I've called the shuttle—we'll be safe there!"

Dlen pointed, and Ke'lir got Wlen, his wife, and Tyrin, who had also been with Hril to follow Dlen. The guards helped, and they were intercepted a few times, but they were able to fight off their attackers. Ke'lir couldn't use her defensive tool, because it would render Wlen and the rest unconscious as well, and she needed to get them all to safety.

Finally, they managed to find their way out, and Ke'lir led them to the shuttle, with Te'riol, one of the security team guarding it.

They said, "Ke'lir! Go inside. I'll make sure you're safe."

Ke'lir nodded, and led all of them into the shuttle, where security staff and a pilot sat in front of some equipment.

He said, "Have you seen anyone else from the team?"

Ke'lir shook her head. "No."

"The last thing I heard from Mer'tir was they were doing a last survey of the security details in the mansion. Then the explosion happened. I haven't heard anything at all from her."

The shuttle door opened again, and Paul, who clearly was injured, and covered with soot, dust, and blood, stumbled in, looking shocked.

"They are dead. Everyone else is dead."

*New Orleans, New Earth*

Ro'mer was sitting in his compartment in the passenger shuttle for the trip to orbit, where they would pick up a transport to Casiti. The transport schedule had already been cut back, since the Casitians were reducing travel permits for New Earth residents. This particular shuttle seemed to have a lot of Casitians who were moving back to Casiti after having lived on New Earth.

Ro'mer was no longer surprised, although they were still upset. They knew that eventually, Casiti would try to reduce the influence of Terrans as much as possible. Ro'mer was only one-eighth Terran, but even they was feeling the heat. They hated the current situation, and felt as if it was pulling the process of unification of the human race back further and further. All of the work that their family felt was their mission was turning to dust in front of them, and Ro'mer didn't know that there was much they could do about it.

They were jerked out of their reverie by hearing, "Ro'mer z Kadarin, please come to the front of the shuttle."

Ro'mer got up, walked out of his compartment, and walked toward the front, where one of the flight attendants was standing.

"I'm Ro'mer."

"There is an urgent message for you. You need to go immediately to the Consej headquarters."

They nodded, ran back to get their bag, and then exited the shuttle. They couldn't understand why they were being called back, especially since they were no longer a part of the Consej anymore. Ro'mer left the spaceport, grabbed an automated vehicle, and put in their destination.

When Ro'mer got there and checked in at the desk, they were told that Zrel wanted to see them. They went up to Zrel's office, where there was not a small amount of chaos. Ro'mer made his way through.

"Zrel..."

"Ah, Ro'mer. Glad I caught you. Everyone: please give Ro'mer and me the room?"

Ro'mer watched the assorted staff walk out, and the last closed the door.

"We got a message from Hilcyon. Apparently, some forces that are against the chief we've been in contact with used explosives to partially destroy his mansion. Five team members were killed. I've called an emergency meeting of the Consej, and the Casitians have agreed."

"Who was killed?" Ro'mer thought of Paul, and worried.

"Sandra, the communications expert, Glor, Li'more, and two other team members. A lot of people died and were injured in the attack. Paul, Ke'lir, and Te'riol are the only ones on our team who survived. Reports say that the anti-reformers took over the mansion and the capital."

Ro'mer was shocked. "What happened to the Supreme Chief?"

"He is safe with Ke'lir in orbit."

"What are we going to do?"

"Bring them home. There isn't much else to do at this point."

"So the mission was a failure?"

"Yes, I guess you could certainly say that."


### Hilcyon Orbit, Hilcyon

Ke'lir, Te'riol, Wlen and Dlen sat in the small conference room on their ship. Paul was finally getting his injuries attended to by the doctor.

Te'riol said, "They demand the return of Wlen and his family in exchange for the bodies of our dead."

Ke'lir said, "There's no way we can agree to that..."

Wlen said, "I will not let my family be killed, but I will return. I am really all they want."

Ke'lir could see that Dlen was distraught. "Da, you can't do that! What would it mean for you to die like that? Mrin's death will have been in vain!"

Wlen put his arm on Dlen's. "Daughter, what would it mean for me to be in permanent exile from my home? You and your ma can find a nice, comfortable life with the Casitians."

Ke'lir said, "No. I don't think we can negotiate."

Te'riol replied, "If Wlen is willing..."

Ke'lir was angry. She got up. "How can you say that? We can't negotiate this!"

She started pacing. She was angry and sad all at once and didn't know what to do with the feelings. The families of Sandra, and the loved ones of Li'more and the other Casitian would probably be OK without the bodies. But she wanted to be able to give Glor the Kinder funeral that he would have wanted, but she couldn't do that without his body. But how could she condone offering up Wlen to die in exchange? It just didn't seem right.

She felt Dlen come next to her and touch her arm. She looked into Dlen's eyes.

Dlen said quietly, "My da wants this, Ke'lir. We need to give it to him. I don't want him to die, but I know in my heart he will slowly die of heartbreak in exile. It will be enough. The anti-reformers really just want him. They will exchange him for the bodies of your team."

Ke'lir nodded, feeling tears flow down her face. It was all one—the sadness of losing Glor and the rest of the team, the sadness of leaving Hilcyon, the sadness of a failed mission. They held each other while it all came crashing down on them.

The meeting broke up, and she went to her quarters, while Dlen went with Wlen and her mother for a final goodbye. Ke'lir was at loose ends. She had no idea what was coming next. She suddenly had a sweet image of Dlen and her mother sitting at the dining room table at home. It made her smile. Maybe she could do something, and create a life for Dlen and her mother, a life they could enjoy, even if they were in exile.

She heard Te'riol's voice. "Ke'lir, the Supreme Chief has agreed to the exchange of just Wlen for the bodies of their team. I'm about to leave with Wlen in the shuttle. I imagine you want to say a last goodbye."

"Yes, thanks. Be right there!"

She ran to the shuttle docking area, and saw a knot of people, including Wlen, Tyrin, Dlen, and Hril. Everyone had tears in their eyes, but there was a sense, somehow, of hope alongside the resignation.

Wlen said, "If Msrotl allows me final words, I do certainly have some things to say."

Dlen smiled. "You tell them, da! Tell them what kind of mistakes they are making."

Ke'lir said, "I'm so sorry, Wlen, that we failed you."

He shook his head. "You didn't fail us. It's not yet time. I was impatient. But I do hope that all the work you did with the midwives will help."

Dlen said, "Yes. They have a lot of tools now. We didn't quite finish, but they are in much better shape than they were. And they will train more, and more. More women and children will survive."

They all said their last goodbyes, and Wlen and Te'riol entered the shuttle, and the shuttle undocked. Ke'lir held Dlen, who was crying softly. She looked up to see Dlen's mother looking at them with puzzlement. Ke'lir realized that there was a conversation that they needed to have.

### Capital Region, Hilcyon

Jorn was walking toward the Supreme Chief's residence from a visit he'd had with a parishoner of his temple, who lived at a distance from the Capitol area. He felt he needed a good walk to work out his feelings. wasn't really looking forward to this dinner. He *was* looking forward to the food. His diet over the past weeks had greatly improved. But he wasn't looking forward to spending more time with chiefs. They always treated him with only barely concealed contempt.

He was startled by the bang, and the ground slightly rumbling. He was still almost 1/2 stat away from the residence, but he could tell that the bang came from that direction. He started to run. As he arrived at the square, he could see the rubble that was where the front of the Supreme Chief's residence had been. He also saw a lot of people running around, and a couple of bodies. He found a priest, who was helping someone who was injured.

"Ah, Jorn. It's bad. There are many inside who are injured or killed. Msrotl and his men did this."

Just then, Jorn heard the distinctive sound of the Casitian shuttle take off. Jorn hoped the entire team had been able to get away. He gathered some priests he found who were around trying to help.

"We need to get in there, and see if we can get as many people out of the rubble as possible."

As they were working, a group of men accosted them.

One of them said, "What do you think you are doing. Stop that!"

Jorn said, "There may be injured here. We need to help them."

"Fine, go ahead. We're looking for Wlen's body."

It felt like they were working at cross-purposes. They would look at someone, and if it wasn't Wlen, not bother with them.

Eventually, Jorn and his colleagues found several wounded people, mostly women, and many bodies, five of which were from the Casitian team. Wlen and his family were, thankfully, absent. Jorn wondered if they were able to escape in that shuttle.

After they had tended to the wounded, and tended as they could to the bodies, they were forced away by Msrotl's men. Jorn returned to the temple, went into his cell, and cried. He finally slept.

The next day during prayers, Jorn saw Ylorp sitting in the temple, with tears streaming down his face. After the service was over, Ylorp still sat, and Jorn joined him.

He said, "How are you, son?"

"They killed the Breft, Father! And Msrotl... I hate him. He's now just pronounced himself Supreme Chief. Nobody has challenged him. And he demands loyalty, but got his position without honor! No Kinder chief has ever done what he did."

Jorn said, "Ylorp, he will eventually pay for his sin."

"But I'm on the wrong side! I worked with Msrotl. I know now my father was a hero. I don't know what to do. I have a wife and a child to feed!"

Jorn said, "Everyone is scared, Ylorp. Everyone is doing their best to make sure they end up on the right side. Msrotl is a manipulative and brutal man."

Ylorp said, "I don't know who knows that I've been a spy for both sides. Father, I'm not worried about my life, I'm worried about my soul."

Jorn said, "Son, do not despair."

"How can I not?"

"You are in the Exalted King's hands. All will be well."

"What should I do?"

"I have some people that you need to meet. It will get better."

Jorn later heard that Wlen had agreed to come down in exchange for the Casitian team's bodies. He was to be executed that very day. Jorn resisted internally, but he knew he needed to go to the execution. Msrotl had refused the standard priest companionship for the condemned, so

177

Jorn had to be in the audience. He watched as they brought Wlen out. There was a large crowd, and Jorn could feel the conflict among them.

He watched them pull Wlen toward the block. They made him kneel.

Msrotl said loudly, "Wlen Gnova Jolrs, you have been found guilty of treason. The sentence for treason is death. You have already spoken your last words."

Jorn could see the surprise on his face. Jorn was sad that the people would not hear Wlen's final words.

They pushed Wlen's head down toward the block.

Just as the sword was coming down, Jorn couldn't help it. He shouted, "Heal the wound!"

He could see people around him react. He decided it was best for him to leave, and go back to the temple. As he walked out, he saw, in many faces, not contempt, but appreciation and hope. That gave him solace.

### Hilcyon Orbit

Paul sat in his quarters on the ship, still feeling shell-shocked from the events two days ago. He already missed Glor terribly, and he felt the weight of their failure. He didn't want to think about what would be happening on Hilcyon, now that the anti-reformers were solidly in power again.

He was listening to some messages he'd received from home. One was a video message from his brother in-law. He could see the stress on Franklin's face. The last few months of being the new Bishop had not been especially friendly to him, it seemed. He touched the play button.

"Paul, I'm sorry to hear the news—I know that mission meant a lot to you, and I know it was hard for it to have failed so badly. I also know that you might be at loose ends now, and want you to know that I really you to represent us in the New Earth Authority. Everyone who wants the job wants to use it to tell everyone they are going to hell, and although I do believe it, I am pragmatic—before we all go back to Earth when we die, at least our lives should be better. I want to move the ICS forward in time. Please consider it. Just let me know one way or the other when you can."

Franklin's face faded from view on Paul's tablet. On top of the grief he was feeling, he heard the news that he had lost his position on Casiti, and with his position, he'd lost his housing. Ro'mer and the Ja'lit school had done the best they could, but it wasn't enough. Casiti was closing down. It had started already, but the violent overthrow of the government on Hilcyon had accelerated the process. Some Terrans were being politely asked to leave Casiti, others, like Paul, were unceremoniously fired. No new Terran immigration permits to Casiti had been allowed at all. He doubted any would ever.

He was a little sorry about that. He hadn't learned all that he could learn from his teacher. Second, if he couldn't live on Casiti, his relationship with Ka'li'mo would have to end sooner than he had expected. He knew Ka'li'mo would not move to New Earth to be with him. Ka'li'mo was a true as well as full-blooded Casitian.

Somehow, at what felt like one of Paul's lowest moments, something in the message from Franklin felt promising, hopeful. Perhaps he could be of use, somehow, somewhere. Perhaps he could make a difference in what seemed to him the unlikeliest place. Home.

# Book 2

# Chapter 1:
# Aftermath

New Earth: April 2101 - March 2102
Hilcyon: Cfro 1203 - Cfro 1204
Casiti: Hevl 804 - Paqn 804

*"The Divine is the holder of hope. It is hard for us, those torn from our home with no chance to return, to feel hope. But hope lies in our attention to each other, and our embrace of the love of the Divine." Heart of Carj, Ecologe 123*

### Pa'rai's, NCPIZ, New Earth

Ke'lir, Hril, Dlen, and Tyrin finally arrived at Ke'lir's house in Pa'rai's. It had been a very long two months since the disaster on Hilcyon. Everyone was still unsettled and in mourning. And Dlen was in culture shock—having been immersed in Terran culture for the past two months.

They had landed on New Earth, and spent weeks and weeks in meetings, with everyone trying to get as much information as possible. In addition, there were funerals for Sandra and Glor. Li'more and the Casitian team members had funerals on Casiti, but Ke'lir couldn't get permission to bring Dlen, Hril and Tyrin to Casiti, so they stayed on New Earth, while Paul went back to Casiti to attend those funerals, and gather his belongings, close up his house, and say his goodbyes.

Dlen knew that Ke'lir hoped that a stay at her house, which was remote, and a long rest for all of them would provide some semblance of stability for them. Dlen knew that this life would not be "normal", but she hoped she and the others could get used to it. Ke'lir had been so understanding and generous.

Hril was staring out of the panoramic windows of the house, which had a view of the hills and a bay of Lake Superior. Dlen stood next to her, and Ke'lir joined them.

She said, "I could not even imagine a world like this! So green. And all of that water!"

Ke'lir said, "That is what we call 'Lake Superior', named for a large lake on Earth. It's the second largest on New Earth. What you are seeing is a relatively small bay."

"Bay? What is that?"

"It's kind of like a little part of it. If you were to keep going, it would open up a lot more, and you would see water to the horizon."

Hril shook her head. "I would like to see that someday."

"You can. We can take a boat ride sometime."

"Boat?"

"Um, it's just a vehicle that travels on the water."

Hril just shook her head again. Dlen understood her overwhelm. She felt overwhelmed too.

After Ke'lir had given them a tour of the house, Hril and Tyrin especially, with some help from Dlen, made themselves busy. The house had sat empty for weeks, and needed some attention. Some of the varied features of the house, especially the kitchen and laundry rooms, took some education in their use.

Ke'lir and Dlen had explained their relationship to Dlen's mother and Tyrin during the trip back to the New Earth system. And Ke'lir had decided to explain to them her gender transition. Changing gender, or having a different gender than woman or man was common, both in Casitian culture, as well as Terran culture. Ke'lir had explained that she had become a girl when she was about 4 years old.

They took it in stride, as Dlen had. Dlen later also shared stories of people who had done similar things on Hilcyon—it just wasn't been talked about openly there. Dlen told Ke'lir the story of a man in their hamlet who had been born female, but was allowed to live as a man, and even became a third chief.

The days were full and empty at the same time. Ke'lir said she began to feel a little guilty about how well-run her house had become. Dlen decided to apply herself to studying English and Casitian and felt they all shared a bond both of sadness and hope.

As he walked home from school, Plir felt hopeless and scared. It had only been a few moons since his father seized power from the reformer chief, Wlen. Plir knew that his father had been working and organizing people against Wlen. He had no idea his father would do something like he did.

And being in school was bad. Everyone knew what his father had done. All of the other boys avoided him, even his best friends. He was alone, and felt lonely.

They had moved from their house in the northeastern corner of the Capital region to a house very close to the Capitol. The Supreme Chief's residence was mostly rubble by now, and was being demolished. Plir knew his father planned to build a new residence there.

As he walked in the door, his mother greeted him.

"Plir! You are home from school. How are you?"

Plir put his head down, heading to his room. He didn't want to talk. "Fine, Ma."

"Plir. Stop this minute and look at me. What's going on?"

As he looked up at his mother's concerned and compassionate face, he lost his will to hold it all in. He started to cry.

"They hate me! All of them. None of my friends will talk to me, the teachers no longer call on me. Everyone hates me. I hate being there! I don't want to go back."

She gathered him into her arms, and let him cry. He knew that she knew he could never cry in his father's presence—she was his safety.

He stopped, and wiped his face.

"Let me go get you a cool cloth. Your father will be home soon."

He took the cloth she offered, and washed his face, and stuffed as much of his feelings as possible inside. He didn't want to show any emotion when his father was around.

Later, while his mother was serving dinner to him and his father, she stood next to him and said, "Plir has been shunned at school lately."

Msrotl said, "Shunned?"

"Yes. Students and teachers are avoiding him."

"Why should I care? Plir, be a man!"

"He's not a man! He's just a boy. You didn't think about how your actions would affect your family?"

"Woman, leave us alone! I'll handle this."

His mother left to eat in the kitchen, and he cringed inwardly.

"So, Plir, is this true?"

"Yes, Da."

"You should show your pride in me. Ignore them. Know that someday, you will rule over them."

This statement confused Plir. He knew enough to know that the Supreme Chief is always determined by a battle, or, at least, *was* only determined by a battle before his father took it by force.

Plir said, "I..."

"You will rule after me. Believe that."

Plir said nothing, not really knowing what to say, but knowing, deep in his heart, that the last thing he wanted to be was a Supreme Chief.

### Zwek, New Earth

Kywl sat in his monastery cell, and finished reading the publicly available report about the disastrous mission to Hilcyon. He was sad at the loss of life and that this meant the end of another round of reforms. But he also knew, deep inside, that in his life, he would get to see Hilcyon, the planet he considered home.

Kywl's grandfather was one who had deserted—he had decided life on New Earth was preferable to life back on Hilcyon. He had made a life for himself. He found a spouse, a woman who had been born on Earth, in a country called "Sudan." They had lived in Zwek, had three children, one of whom was his father. Kywl's father was dedicated to fostering Kinder culture on New Earth. He married a woman who had also grown up in Zwek, one of the few who chose to stay. His parents raised him, their only child in their culture, as much as they were able to.

Kywl discovered the priesthood early in life. He'd had questions about spirituality, and his father suggested he visit the temple in Zwek. He was instantly taken with it and had asked about becoming a priest candidate, which he did when he was only fourteen. He was initiated into the priesthood at eighteen, the earliest possible age.

When he was initiated, he learned about the thousands-year effort of the Kinder priesthood to bring about the unification of the Kinder and the Casitians. They worked tirelessly and diligently toward their goal.

He discovered secret writings and rituals—although the few priests who were among the deserters didn't have most of the secret writings. They had tried to recreate some. And one, a book that was at the core of their work, they discovered that the Casitians had a copy of it. One of those priests translated it into Kinder language. One of the things he hoped he could do someday is to compare the two versions of that book, called "The Heart of the Car'j."

He heard the bell for lunch. His stomach growled. He was hungry, and it had been a while since he broke his fast this day. He rose, left his cell, and walked the short distance down the hall and down some stairs to the main part of the monastery.

The monastery had been finished only a few years earlier. There had been a temple in Zwek soon after it was founded, but the priests had felt it important to move to Casiti when Ngellin moved there, so only a few priests remained, and there was no need for a monastery. Once it was decided that all Kinder would return to Zwek, a monastery was built. Kywl had spent a number of years on Casiti in the monastery there but was happy to be back in Zwek, which felt more like home to him.

### Jor'ar'lir, Rel'toro, Casiti

Paul was finished packing. He was sad to leave this house. He hadn't really even had all that much time living in it. And now he had to say goodbye to it.

He'd found a small apartment not far from the Michaelson family house in New Orleans, in New America, which was where he was headed after a short visit with his family and meetings with Franklin Martin in the ICS.

Ka'li'mo had come and gone. They had had a nice cup of tea, he had promised to visit Paul on New Earth when he next had time. Paul knew he would enjoy the visit, but also knew it wouldn't be the same as being Ka'li'mo's companion for a winter.

At least the brief relationship he'd had with Ka'li'mo opened up so much in Paul's understanding of himself. So much that hadn't made any sense to him when he was growing up made perfect sense now.

He didn't know who was going to live here next, but he had cleaned up, made sure the greenhouse beds were covered, and re-painted his front door, so it was plain again.

He heard the quiet sound of a vehicle arriving in front of his door—his ride had come.

He left the house with his stuff and saw Ro'mer get out of the small vehicle. "Good morning, Paul! We should be arriving at the shuttle station in plenty of time."

"Thanks so much for coming so far, Ro'mer. You didn't need to."

"I know, but I feel some responsibility. And I also want to get to spend at least a little time with you before you go. I don't know when I'll see you next."

Paul thought about that as he put his bags and boxes in the back of the vehicle.

As they started the drive toward the shuttle station, Paul asked, "How long do you think this shutdown will last, Ro'mer?"

Ro'mer shook their head. "I don't know. But it might be a while, likely several years at least. When the Casitians get their back up, it takes a while for them to calm down."

"How are you doing?"

"I'm alright. I was born here, and I'm 7/8ths Casitian. Not enough to be in most leadership positions right now, but enough to be employed. I was tapped to be part of a technology transfer team. I'm happy with it."

"I'm glad Ro'mer. I was so upset when you lost your place on the Consej."

"Honestly, I should have predicted it. And our family, for the time being, is a bit on the outs on Casiti. And now that all of the Kinder folk have returned to New Earth, it's going to be an interesting time. Are you looking forward to your work in the ICS?"

"Yes, oddly enough, I am. I actually *like* Franklin Martin, and I think I can do some good work there. I've learned so much in the past four years, or year, for you. I'm happy to be going home. Well, not really home. I'll be living in New Orleans. But I'll be in the ICS a fair amount."

As the vehicle came to a stop at the shuttle station, behind a queue of other vehicles with passengers disembarking, Ro'mer said, "Well, please keep in touch, will you? I do expect to visit New Earth at some point."

"It will be great to see you when you visit! And thanks, Ro'mer for everything. I wouldn't be where I am without you."

"You are very welcome, Paul. I'm glad I got to see your growth into an amazing man firsthand."

Paul felt a little bit of embarrassment at that compliment, but he smiled. They got out, and he put his stuff on one of the convenient anti-grav sleds available. Ro'mer and Paul hugged, and Paul watched Ro'mer's vehicle leave the queue, and go down the highway leaving the shuttle station.

His first meeting with Franklin Martin as the new, official ICS representative to the New Earth Government wasn't going well. Franklin had brought in the leaders, called "deacons" of all 10 states of the ICS, which Paul should have realized would be a mistake. Franklin wanted to make sure Paul heard from the deacons, and understood what their particular issues were. But the deacons took this as an opportunity to complain bitterly about everything, especially including the fact that Franklin had chosen what one deacon called "a Casitian puppet," and another called "a Michealson heretic" as a representative.

Paul had not as yet said anything, and as he let the varied voices in the room roll over him, he stilled his mind using his practices, and then waited for a moment where he could speak.

"Gentlemen, please!" Of course, they were all men in the room.

There was, finally quiet.

"You have all made it quite clear that you don't really like the fact that I was appointed representative by Bishop Martin. I want to take a moment to tell you what my goals and plans are, which may, perhaps put your minds at ease.

"I was born here, in the ICS. My family is here. I care deeply about what happens here, and I also care deeply that the ICS should have the freedom to be as it is. But we have to face reality. We have a crisis—a health crisis, a housing crisis, and an economic crisis. Crises we have not been able to solve on our own. We have to find the right balance between using the support of the global government, and keeping ourselves apart, as we wish to. I'm not here to force the ICS to do anything it doesn't want to do, or adopt any technology it doesn't want to. I'm here to figure out how to make all of our citizens healthy, happy, and free."

He heard grumbles, but no one chose to speak in direct response to that statement. He added, "So if you would, deacons, please each tell me what's most broken in your own state. What are the biggest needs, and what kinds of things have you tried that haven't worked." I'll take that information, spend some time with it, and make some modest proposals as a start. These will be proposals you'll all get to make comments on, and decide whether or not to move forward with them.

He could tell they were still a bit suspicious of him, but the rest of the meeting was informative for him, and he already had a few ideas of things that might be helpful.

### Independent Christian State, New Earth

Joanna was walking home from school, trying to shake off the interaction she'd just had with Lucy. Lucy was one of Joanna's brother's followers, and Lucy was making it her mission to make Joanna's life miserable, since Joanna refused to follow her brother.

Joanna was tired of hearing Lucy talk about how she was going to hell, and was a heretic. Joanna didn't care. She knew Joseph was unbalanced, even though it seemed that most other people in their town didn't seem to get it. And besides, she'd always hated the theology and culture of the ICS, even before Joseph twisted it into his own weird form.

Joseph was ten years older than Joanna, who was coming up on her 18th birthday. He was the eldest, she was the youngest, with two in-between. She had looked up to him until that fateful day when she was 12. He had been groomed to take over their town's church, but somehow, for some reason, when the minister died, the board had chosen someone else. And that day, Joseph became someone Joanna couldn't understand.

He still lived with their parents, running his new church in a large metallic warehouse without plumbing or electricity—because that was what God would want. Many of his followers were purposefully homeless, camped out at their house, and being fed by her parents. Joanna hated the situation, which got more unbearable each day.

But she had plans no one knew about. She was done with the ICS, and was going to make her way out as soon as she could. She'd risked everything, and gotten in touch with the only person she thought she could trust, the man who represented the ICS to the New Earth Agency. And it seemed her trust was well-founded. He was going to help her get settled up in one of the independent zones, and not tell anyone that he was helping her.

As she approached her house, she saw the regular crowd around it, which seemed to grow larger every day. As she made her way through the crowd, she heard Lucy's strident voice.

"She's an apostate! Our beloved leader's own sister doesn't believe!"

Joanna squared her shoulders and pushed her way to the door. She didn't look back as she opened the door and closed it on the crowd.

"Yes, you are an apostate," Joseph said, quietly but insistently.

"Please leave me alone, Joseph."

"Why don't you embrace the truth, Joanna? Mother and Father have. Julie and Mark have."

She walked to her room, and slammed the door, not answering him. Two more months, and then she'd take a bus out of the ICS, and never, ever return.


### Zwek, Kinder Region, New Earth

Ke'lir said, "We're here!" Tyrin wasn't quite sure where "here" was, but she was happy to have arrived.

This trip had been months in the making. Once Tyrin found out that there was an enclave of people who descended from men from Hilcyon, she knew where she wanted to go. She wanted to be among her people or at least the closest she could get.

It wasn't that she didn't enjoy being with Ke'lir and her family and friends. She did. She genuinely liked all of them. But she felt she had this hole in her heart that only other people from Hilcyon could fill.

Ke'lir had explained that these folks were descended from the men who had deserted. There were no people left who had been born on Hilcyon—the last of them had died some time ago.

But these people were their sons, daughters, and grandsons, and that was going to have to suffice until she could someday return to Hilcyon. And she knew in her bones she would return.

They got out of the small vehicle that Ke'lir had rented in the center of Zwek when they arrived via train from Pa'rai's. They were in what felt like a hamlet, with houses close together, around a square. It reminded her immediately of home, even, at the same time as there was verdant green all around her.

An older woman opened the front door of the house they were in front of. She wore clothes reminiscent of those from home, but also different.

Ke'lir said some words to the woman that Tyrin didn't understand, and they hugged. Ke'lir turned toward Tyrin and seemed to be introducing her to this woman.

The woman said, in that strange accent she was familiar with from Glor, "Hello, Tyrin. I'm Grun, Glor's mother. So nice to meet you, and sad for the loss of your father-in-law."

"Grateful to meet, Grun. Sad for the loss of your son."

Grun opened her arms, and Tyrin eagerly embraced the woman.

"We are happy to host you in our house. I also wanted you to know that you have cousins here! The grandchildren of Jrel, who was the son of ..."

"My great-grandfather Hytn! The family story was that Jrel had valiantly died here!"

Grun smiled. "Well, your cousins can tell you Jrel's story—he did die here, but not in battle. He died of old age. Grant is one cousin who lives here, as is Kwyl who is a priest. Janice and Loren, are also cousins, and live elsewhere on New Earth."

The fact that not only were there descendants of those on Hilcyon here but that she had family here was almost more than she could stand. All she had expected of this fate was strangeness and loneliness. To find family instead! She was grateful and happy.

### Capital Region, Hilcyon

Jorn finished the 12th hour prayers and watched the parishioners slowly leave the temple. When it seemed that everyone had gone, he started to clean up after prayers, folding ritual cloths, snuffing out candles, when he heard what sounded like quiet crying somewhere in the room. He looked around, and saw a small figure sitting in the far corner, in the dark.

He put down what was in his hands, and went to the back to sit next to the boy. The boy looked up at him, and Jorn recognized him. He was Msrotl's son, Plir.

"Son, can I help you?"

"I don't know what to do, Father. Everyone hates me; they all avoid me."

"They don't hate you, son. They are scared of your father."

"But I'm not my father!"

Jorn put his arms around the boy, who seemed to settle a little.

"Son, I know that. And that's something you have to hold close to your own heart. You are not your father."

"I don't know what to do! What can I do?"

"Don't do anything, Plir. Just live your life. Be yourself. Go to school, learn as much as you can. Come to services. This is temporary. It will all work out. The Exalted King holds you in His hands. We hold you in our hands. You will be alright."

"How can you have such confidence, Father?"

"I listen to the Exalted King's voice in my heart. I know this is temporary. I know this will lead to something much better. Have faith."

The boy nodded. "Alright. I'll do my best."

"I'm here, son, whenever you need to talk."

"Thank you, Father."

Several days later, Jorn was in conference with Glin and relayed the story to him.

Glin said, "This is good to know. Msrotl's son isn't at all like his father. This may eventually be important."

"Yes, I think so. He's so young—only 10 years, but he seems older than his years, and is a caring boy."

"I just hope his father doesn't corrupt him."

Jorn shook his head. I don't think so, Your Holiness, and anyway, we'll know. I told him to come to services. We can see how he develops.

Glin said, "Thank you, Jorn, for your tireless service."

"Your Holiness, the tasks I have give me joy, and hope for the future. It is my honor to serve you."

Jorn bowed, and left the office of the High Priest.

# Chapter 2:
# Inner Work

New Earth: March 2102 - October 2103
Hilcyon: Cfro 1204 - Sdert 1205
Casiti: Paqn 804 - Klef 804

*"Human beings are naturally contemplative. We see this showing up everywhere. We have learned in many different ways, in many different times, that contemplating our minds, our lives, our faiths, our interdependence to each other and to nature leaves us healthier and more content." Ja'lend'a, 'Spirits Alike'*

### New Orleans, New Earth

The lights in his apartment switched on when Paul opened the front door. It was good to be home. He'd just come back from a meeting with Franklin and some of the deacons of ICS, preparing for the legislative session that would be starting in a couple of weeks. It was late, and he was dog-tired.

As the ICS representative to the New Earth government, he had a seat in its governing body, called the General Assembly. This year, it seemed that the primary issue was going to be how to deal with the Casitians' new round of being closed off. They had eliminated all emigration to Casiti, and limited travel visas to emergency visits only. Trade between Casiti and New Earth had trickled down to almost nothing.

New Earth depended on Casiti largely for technology and medicines. Between the large stockpile of rare earth elements shipped to New Earth during The Event, as well as the mining of some asteroids in the New Earth system, they had all they needed to manufacture this technology, but because Casiti had so much capacity, New Earth hadn't really built up their manufacturing base, they just imported from Casiti.

Now, they had to do the work to build up manufacturing, which, to Paul's mind, wasn't a bad thing. Paul was trying to convince the ICS that manufacturing would be one way to help the economy. The deacons weren't convinced. They were worried about the Casitian influence. Paul was going to figure out what specific kinds of factories might be best. It would probably be low-level technology, household goods, and things that the deacons would understand and see as useful.

And in the meantime, he had started to get messages from kids all over the ICS that wanted to find their way out. They'd heard of him, somehow, and heard he was trustworthy. He sometimes felt like it had just been yesterday that he'd gotten himself out, but it had been four years, and a lot of experiences packed into that. Somehow, he had emerged feeling some stability and willingness to help others like him as much as he could.

As he dropped his bags in the bedroom and got ready for a shower, his message system chimed. He looked at his tablet, to see a message from Kevin Hagill. He vaguely recalled that name, but he didn't remember who they were. He tapped the play icon.

"Hi Paul, my name is Kevin. I'm one of the members of the Ja'lit school here in New Orleans. Gil'ern told me that you had moved here, and might want to be connected to the community. It's small but growing, and I'd love to meet you, and invite you to our weekly gathering. We meet Sunday afternoons at 7:00, at the West End Community Center."

This sounded just the right thing for Paul now. He so missed his access to Gil'ern and the Ja'lit school in Jor'ar'lir. He wondered who made up the Ja'lit school here on New Earth. He imagined a mix of Casitian immigrants and mostly Dlejonese folks. But perhaps there would be others. He looked forward to learning more.

### Zwek, Kinder Region, New Earth

Tyrin had spent a wonderful few months in Zwek, meeting new people, and getting to know the community. After just a few weeks, she'd been able to get her own dwelling in Zwek, which was a lot easier than she expected. Moving hamlets on Hilcyon was a painful and cumbersome process—so much so that few people did it. Here, they found her a small house that was a part of a little compound where mostly single men and women lived.

Because of the emigration of all Kinder who had been on Casiti, back to New Earth, there had been a lot of building in the past few years. Ngellin, leader of the Kinder who stayed on New Earth, had wanted a better understanding between Kinder and Casitians, and so moved, with several hundred Kinder to Casiti. They raised their families there, and ended up numbering several thousand.

One of the things that was so interesting to Tyrin about Zwek was the skewed gender balance. The Kinder on New Earth still shared many of the patriarchal qualities of their society, and so more men raised in Zwek stayed, which was not the same for women, or other genders.

There was so much Tyrin was learning, but she so far felt at home in Zwek. The things that were comfortable about home were here, and the things that were oppressive and scary were not. And she'd gotten to know Tvor, Glor's brother and cousin of Ke'lir. He came to visit his mother frequently, and she and he had started to what they called "date." It was a mystifying process for Tyrin, who was more used to the Kinder way.

Today was a great day—it was the day she was to meet her cousin, Grant, grandson of Jrel, her great-uncle. Grant had been away for business. He worked with the Zwek government on trade with other countries on New Earth, and he'd been on a trade mission. But he finally was home from his travels, and Tyrin was going to visit him today. She was nervous and happy.

She finished her breakfast, and as she was just about done cleaning up, she heard a knock on her door.

"Grun, good morning!"

"Good morning, Tyrin. How are you doing today?"

"Really well. I got some help starting my little kitchen garden, which I can hardly wrap my mind around how fast and big everything is growing!"

Grun smiled, by Tyrin could see in her eyes that she didn't really understand. It was true when she talked to everyone who was born here, this was all they knew, they'd never known how forbidding Hilcyon was.

"Shall we go visit Grant?", Grun changed the subject.

"Yes, I'm ready."

Grant lived on the other side of Zwek, and most people in Zwek either walked or took the small buses that plied the main thoroughfares. Like all of New Earth, transportation was required to be environmentally neutral, so there were some individual vehicles, but few people owned them; they generally borrowed them for specific trips. This trip, it was easy to take a bus. Both Tyrin and Grant lived close to a main street, an easy walk from the bus stop.

As Tyrin and Grun rode the bus, Tyrin thought back on what she'd learned about how things were in Zwek, and in New Earth in general. There were so many cultures here, and some were more insular than others. Even in Zwek, she'd interacted with people with Terran and Casitian ancestry. Though it had been only a year since the fateful events on Hilcyon, Tyrin knew that she could make a home here, even at the same time as she was sure she would see her real home again.

Grun indicated when it was time for them to leave the bus, and with a short walk, they arrived in a cul-de-sac, with a few homes. A group of children were playing an unfamiliar game in the street. It looked like they were kicking a white ball around, trying to get beyond each other.

"It's here." Grun pointed to one of the houses. She knocked, and the door opened. A man who was darker-skinned than Tyrin expected answered the door.

"Are you Grant?" Grun asked.

"Yes!"

"Ah! Nice to meet you. I'm Grun, and this is your cousin, Tyrin."

Grant looked at Tyrin with a smile, and that smile looked so familiar. It reminded her of her grandfather's smile. She recognized the family resemblance.

"It's so nice to meet you, cousin!"

"Nice to meet you as well, Tyrin. Come in, please. My wife has graciously made some food for us."

As they walked into the house, a woman emerged from the kitchen.

"My wife, Lron. Lron, this is Grun, Glor's mother, and Tyrin, my cousin from Hilcyon."

"So nice to meet you." She hugged them both.

As she hugged Tyrin, she said, "So wonderful to meet someone from home."

Grant said, "Lron's great-grandfather was a friend and associate of Ngellin's. He stayed behind on New Earth, and led the Kinder here, while many of the Kinder were on Casiti."

Lron said, "Please, let's sit. As you might imagine, since all of the Kinder who stayed here were men, there is somewhat of a dearth of good recipes, but I've done my best. I hope this tastes just a bit like home."

In truth, Tyrin had gotten used to the food, but it never tasted quite the same. Some of it was more delicious than she could imagine, but it wasn't the food from home. She also sometimes had to remind herself that she grew up during times of famine, and it was likely that the food had been much better and more varied in the past.

As they ate, Grant told her more of his story and the story of her great uncle Jrel. Grant's father also married a Terran, a woman he'd met while working for the New Earth Authority. They lived for a time in a settlement called Dlejon, where she had grown up, and that's where Grant lived until he was in his early twenties. He explained that Dlejon was a Terran settlement originally designed to be a lot like Casitian culture, and there were quite a number of Casitians that emigrated there. He said that their two other cousins lived in Dlejon.

"Although I love living in Zwek, and am glad to be here, unlike my wife, I'm probably more Terran and Casitian than Kinder."

Tyrin was glad to hear his story, and more of Lron's story. They insisted that she come again, and she agreed. She enjoyed their company.

### Pa'rai's, NCPIZ, New Earth

Dlen was alone, for the first time in a long time. Ke'lir was in New Orleans for a series of meetings, her mother Hril was in Zwek, visiting Tyrin and others. She would join her mother in a few days, and they would travel back home together.

Dlen realized that she has spent so little time alone at home. She was always either on the road, traveling to this hamlet or that hamlet to assist with births, or at home with her parents and brother. It was something she wasn't used to but realized she rather enjoyed.

She was looking over her tablet which was helping her learn the language called "English" which was the major language of New Earth, and Ke'lir's first language. Ke'lir also was fluent in Casitian, and Dlen was learning that language too, but English was her focus, as it would help her live here on New Earth without having to depend on Ke'lir or an automated translator for everything.

Even though she had been on New Earth now for more than 6 months, she still had culture shock. It would have been impossible for her to imagine a culture more different than hers. In some ways, what she knew and saw of Casitian culture was almost familiar. Not that it resembled Kinder culture, but because both of their cultures were forged from their shared experience, there were things she understood, and recognized. Earth culture had evolved wholly differently, and so much of it, and the fact that there were so many subcultures, mystified her.

The North Circumpolar Independent Zone, where she lived, was, like many of the Independent Zones, a real mix of subcultures, but had evolved somewhat of a shared culture. Ke'lir told her that a significant number of Casitians had moved here in the initial few years after what they called "The Event." It also housed descendants of people from all over Old Earth, but it was most heavily populated by descendants of those from North America and Europe.

It was fluid, egalitarian, what Ke'lir called "progressive" and had, surprisingly to Dlen, deep compassion for everyone who lived there.

Like Hilcyon, it was comprised mostly of close-knit, small communities, rather than big cities. That was partially due to its climate. It never got especially warm, as the planet had little tilt, and the region was close to the poles. It was similar to the temperatures of Hilcyon in that regard, although much, much wetter.

The hierarchy that existed was, to Dlen's mind, minimal. Communities were governed by small town or city councils, and each town or city sent a representative to the IZ government. Each zone sent representatives to the New Earth government. All positions of power in their IZ were elected, by everyone. This was not true in all of New Earth. Many regions of New Earth, like the state that Paul was from, were governed differently.

A notification appeared on her tablet. She still wasn't completely used to the technology available to her, and she'd had Ke'lir give her the most stripped-down tablet possible. It was an email from Paul. They had been having a conversation about spirituality, and he said he would send her something to read.

She could understand about one word in five that he wrote, but she got the impression that the document that he had attached was one she would want to read. She opened the document, and was surprised to see that it was in her language! It had been translated by his and Ke'lir's great-grandfather Ngellin. She remembered him talking about him. He had translated several Casitian works, with the help of some Casitians, into their language.

A few days later, she was on a train to Zwek, pondering some of what she'd read. She'd read the first chapter of "Spirits Alike", which was a book by the revered Casitian Teacher, Ja'lend'a. She was intrigued by this book, and by the wisdom it held. She looked forward to finishing it and talking with Paul about it.

### Capital Region, Hilcyon

Things had gotten a little bit better. Mostly because Plir's father left him alone, and he had gotten used to being ignored by just about everyone except his mother and the priest, Jorn.

He knew they would take care of him, and he listened to them. Listened about how to be a better, more honorable man than his father would ever be.

At the same time as his father ignored him, he also took him for granted. He assumed Plir was growing up to be the brutal, dictatorial leader he was. And it was a challenge for Plir to never do anything that suggested otherwise. It was a very hard balance, but he managed.

He sat with his mother eating lunch. Today was a day off of school, and his father was, as usual, at the Capitol running things.

His mother said, "You are enjoying going to services?"

He nodded. "It makes me feel better. And Jorn is almost always there. He's very good, and teaches me a lot."

"I'm glad you've found him, Plir. He sounds like a wonderful man."

"He is. And he wants reform, too, like us. He thinks that I will be important someday. But he knows I don't want to follow in my father's footsteps."

"You *will* be important someday, Plir, I know it. And I have confidence in you."

He wasn't so sure of himself, but he appreciated the confidence that she had in him.

She said, "Oh, I should tell you of the meeting I had. As you know, I meet occasionally with the midwives who were trained by the Casitians."

"How is that going?"

"It's going well. They have developed a full training program. The training is spreading, and making a big difference. One midwife said that maternal deaths are already down significantly."

"That's so good to hear, Ma!"

"Remember, Plir, it will be the women and the priests that will make a difference. And your father will never know—he ignores women, and hates priests."

"I know. I just hope he never knows how often I go to services."

She shook her head. "He won't. He doesn't pay you enough attention, Plir."

Which was something Plir was actually glad of.


### New Orleans, New Earth

Joanna finished up her shift at the small coffee shop that was two blocks from the house she shared with several other ICS refugees. All of them were about the same age, and needed to escape from the ICS for one reason or another. They all had totally rejected the religion they were raised with, and most were, like her, completely estranged from their families.

As she walked home, she thought about the year since she'd left the ICS, and how so much had happened to her. She'd learned how much of a backwater the ICS was, and how good life could be outside of it. She'd finally admitted to herself, and then others, that her lifelong feeling that she wasn't a girl, and felt better not being one, was valid, important, and something she needed to listen to.

She didn't totally know what that all meant—it was still a little confusing in her mind, and scary. She had started to visit a therapist, who was helping her sort it all out. But she finally knew, based on meeting so many different people, that she could figure it out, and live her life in a way that made sense to her.

She also discovered an abiding love of politics. It had come as a complete surprise to her. She always enjoyed reading the local news services when they wrote about this bishop, and that other bishop, and how they were chosen and organized. But moving to New Orleans, which was the Capitol city of New Earth, had been a complete revelation to her. So many things were going on. She'd learned about all of the different governments, and how they interacted to form the New Earth Authority, which actually had a lot less authority than she might expect, coming from the ICS.

She started to read the history of New Earth, and the factors that lead to it having the kind of governmental structure it had. She knew that this was what she wanted to study. She'd already applied to New Orleans University, and with Paul's help, she was going to get admitted. She'd need a lot of remedial help, but she knew she could handle it.

She arrived at home, and was greeted by Uther and Jason, who both escaped the ICS before she did.

Uther said, "Hey, how's it going?"

Joanna said, "Alright - you?

Jason pushed in, "He's doing really well."

"Jason! Jeez, let me tell it, OK?"

Joanna wondered what the news was.

"I have a… boyfriend."

Joanna was genuinely pleased for him. He'd really struggled with his sexuality, in the same way as she was struggling with her gender.

She said, "Woohoo! Congrats, Uther. What's he like?"

Uther smiled, pleased. "He's nice. Not from the ICS. He grew up in Dlejon. Lives here because he's going to NOU."

Jason said, "Grew up in Dlejon... I bet he's really good in bed."

Uther turned a very dark shade of red, and everyone laughed.

They ordered pizza, and Ruth and Mary joined them later. Joanna loved her housemates, and loved this life, even with its struggles. It was so much better than before.

### Zwek, Kinder Region, New Earth

Kwyl watched the medium-height woman with the sienna-toned skin and almond eyes that were typical of natives of both Hilcyon and Casiti walk toward him.

He moved forward, putting out his hand in greeting. "Tyrin, so nice to meet you."

She clasped his hand, Kinder-style, firm, fingers curled, no shake.

"It is nice to meet you, Kwyl! Thank you for coming to my humble house to meet."

"I'm glad to. I'm sorry that the Monastery and Temple aren't very useful for casual meetings of this sort."

He entered into her house and could smell the food, especially what smelled like breadmufs.

"I've learned to make breadmufs with the adapted ingredients they have here. They don't quite taste the same as home, but they are close."

"I didn't actually grow up with anything near authentic breadmufs. The golchi flour wasn't available for quite a while. The Casitians don't have a food export process, and it took us a while to figure out the best way to grow it here on New Earth, since the climate is so different than Hilcyon or Casiti. So it's so nice to get them now. I appreciate that you've baked some for me."

Tyrin smiled. "I love to bake them anyway."

She indicated he should sit at her small table, which was filled with dishes with delectable food, and a basket of breadmufs in the middle. She went into the kitchen, grabbed plates, and sat down across from him, placing plates in each space.

Kwyl asked, "How are you finding Zwek?"

Tyrin said, "I like it here. It feels something like home, but missing the stress, and the horrible chief system. But it is also very different. I see things here that would not be present at home. I miss home, I have to admit."

"I hope to see Hilcyon someday. I wish to pray with the priests there, and learn from them."

"I am sure I will get to go home. I just don't know how long it will take. I may be an old woman."

Kwyl smiled. He was glad she had that faith. He wasn't sure he shared it.

He peppered her with questions about Hilcyon, and she generously answered.

After a while, he said, "I'm sorry I'm so curious. Do you have any questions of me? About Zwek, our family? Anything?"

"Being a priest, you might not know this answer, but why do so few women stay in Zwek? There's so much freedom for women here!"

"I do know, actually. It's because Terran and Casitian cultures, by comparison, are so much more free for women than even our pale reflection of Hilcyon's culture. And if you grow up here, it's easy to find out what it's like next door, say, just up north in the North Central IZ. So many women leave when they turn 18. Some women end up returning, bringing their non-Kinder spouses with them. And some non-Kinder women marry into Kinder households. But it's pretty uneven."

Kwyl could see Tyrin thinking. She finally said, "That seems surprising, but all I know is home."

Kwyl said, "Well, if you wish to marry again, you'll have lots of choices!"

They laughed, but Kwyl could see a thread of sadness in her face, and he regretted saying it.

Kwyl said, "Thank you again, Tyrin, for your hospitality. I understand there will be a family gathering at Grant's house in several weeks?"

"Yes, he's invited all of the cousins, and anyone related to me. I am so happy to find family here. I never imagined this. I still want to be home, but this is close, and good."

Kwyl smiled, and got up. "I'll see you there. It's been too long since I've seen my niblings."

Tyrin looked puzzled at the word.

"Ah, I'm sorry. It's a non-Kinder word borrowed from English. It's a gender-neutral term for nieces and nephews."

Tyrin nodded. "I see. Thank you for telling me."

They both rose and hugged. As they parted, and Kwyl made his way back to the monastery, he was pondering what her life here would be like. He hoped she could be happy, given all that had happened to her.

A few weeks later, Tyrin had invited Kwyl to a challenge match that Tvor, the man that Tyrin was currently involved with, was fighting in. In Zwek, the Kinder tradition of chief matches was mirrored in what Terrans would call a "sport", where individual men would fight each other in a ring with wooden versions of the traditional weapons. Kwyl had never really been interested in the matches and had never gone to one, but he decided he'd go for his cousin.

As he arrived somewhat later than he'd planned, he found Tyrin in the audience, he could feel the excitement in the air. He sat next to her.

She looked up at him and smiled as he sat down. She said, "Tvor is in the next match. Thanks for coming."

He watched the current match. Two opponents circled each other. One wielding a curved wooden blade, the other a long staff with a bladed end. It was actually beautiful to watch. In a way, it was a dance. The match ended with a sharp blow to the midsection by the staff, followed by a slash to the chest that was not successfully avoided by his opponent.

The defeated man knelt, and the victor gave a ceremonial tap to the neck, then reached out his hand to let him up. They clasped arms, and then went back to their benches.

Tvor's match was the main event of the evening. He was considered one of the best fighters in Zwek. Tvor and another man, whose name was Brian, by the large display above, entered the ring. They bowed to each other, then started their match. Tvor was using a long sword, and Brian that curved blade.

Tyrin said, "Tvor is especially good at countering the circle blade, he's told me. This should be an easy match for him."

As Kwyl watched, Tvor ducked and lunged, swiveled and jumped, easily avoiding his opponent's blade, while hitting him several times in several places. There would be bruises tomorrow.

Eventually, Tvor landed a "killing" blow to the neck, and Brian surrendered by kneeling. Tvor tapped him on the neck, then helped him up. They hugged.

He looked at Tyrin. He said, "I'd never realized how beautiful this sport was. It was so mesmerizing to watch them fight."

"I've only seen two matches on Hilcyon. It was nothing like this. So brutal and scary. This is such a different way."

"Did you see the match with your father-in-law?"

"No, he forbade us to go, in case he died doing it. I wished I had been able to see it. I'd seen matches at a much lower level: some third or fourth chiefs' challenges."

"How do you feel that Tvor is doing this?"

"I am impressed by it. Tvor is strong and stable. And kind, too."

"It sounds like you are beginning to love him."

"I am. I didn't think it would happen, after losing Mrin. But it has. I'm happy."

Kwyl could feel the smile forming on his face. "I'm so happy for you."

### Capital Region, Hilcyon

Jorn was tired. He felt like he had been holding a lot over the past months.

He was in touch with Ylorp, who seemed a bit more steady than before but was perhaps still spiritually precarious. Plir was also doing better, which was a relief. He felt deeply responsible for making sure that Plir wouldn't get corrupted by his father.

Now, he was at a meeting about the priests' liaison with the midwives group. He had met with one of the midwives, Mirn, who was important in training midwives and spreading the news and strategies of reform. It was his turn to report.

"Jorn, your meeting with Mirn, the midwife?"

"They have been training more midwives, extending to many different regions. They now have at least 3 midwives in each region who are trained, connected to each other, and connected to the hub of their network here in the Capital."

Glin said, "Wonderful! That means we can quickly get word out to them in all regions?"

Jorn nodded, "Yes. They are in good contact with each other."

Another priest asked, "Any noise from the chiefs about this?"

Jorn shook his head. "From what I and the midwives can tell, they are completely ignoring this. At some point, Msrotl was told about the training, and how it was helping women, and he said basically, 'That's women's work, why do I care?' So they can keep growing."

Glin said, "I think *we* should be careful, in terms of our connections with them. I don't think the chiefs would ignore it if they found out how extensive our relationship is with them."

Jorn said, "Agreed, Your Holiness. Msrotl seems to be suspicious of us of late. I don't exactly know why. We do need to be careful."

Another priest asked, "How many women who are not midwives are involved in this network?"

Jorn said, "Very few. They are being very careful. There are pockets of very conservative women, particularly wives of chiefs. We don't want those women getting wind of the reform part of this effort. They are happy fewer women and babes are dying in childbed, but they would alert their husbands if they understood what else was going on."

Everyone nodded. They finished up the meeting, and Glin asked Jorn to stay behind as everyone else filtered out.

Jorn said, "How may I be of service, Holiness?"

"How is Plir, Jorn?"

"He is doing better, Your Holiness. He seems to be gaining a bit more confidence and is not allowing the reactions of his peers to bother him quite as much. He has a strong faith, and trusts me. But I worry about him sometimes."

"As do I. Continue your work with him. I don't want him to be like his father."

"I don't think that's possible. But I do worry that his father might discover how Plir is thinking. Which would be dangerous for him."

Glin nodded. "I appreciate the work you are doing Jorn."

"Thank you, Your Holiness."

# Chapter 3:
# Change is Inevitable

New Earth: January 2104 - December 2104
Hilcyon: Lykl 1206 - Sdert 1207
Casiti: Nird 805 - Hevl 805

*"Ritual seems to be a deeply human phenomenon. We find it everywhere. Casitians of all spiritual schools have rituals, and I have learned that ritual is almost ubiquitous among humans on Earth. Rituals bind us to each other, allow us to explore realms of being, and open ourselves to the Divine, and to our inner heart-minds." Ja'lend'a, 'Spirits Alike'*

### Zwek, New Earth

Tyrin was sitting in the main bedroom of Grun's house, getting ready. She was happy. She was getting married to Tvor, and the marriage ritual would be very different than what she'd had with Mrin. That one just had the priest, four parents and she and Mrin. This time, there would be many, many more guests than would ever be at a marriage at home. And there would be something called a reception, with food, something also absent in Kinder ceremonies at home.

The Kinder on New Earth had evolved more elaborate marriage rituals than ever existed on Hilcyon. Tyrin learned that it was mostly borrowed from the Terran marriage rituals, as Casitians didn't marry. She had to remember she was also marrying into the large, sprawling Michaelson clan, which meant that guests were coming from Casiti, too.

Dlen had made a traditional marriage bltynon for her, the Kinder women's commonest garment. When the Hilcyon women had arrived, they had together given the women of Zwek a series of patterns, because the bltynons they had been using were a bit far from the norm on Hilcyon. Those patterns had become an instant hit, and several small companies were now using them to create clothing for people in Zwek.

But there was a current of sadness in Tyrin today. She had been so briefly married to Mrin before he was taken away from her. She loved Tvor, and, really, knew him better than she'd ever known Mrin. But she couldn't help but think of Mrin today.

Dlen and Hril walked in, both beaming. Dlen said, "You look so beautiful, Tvor."

Tvor turned and said, "Thank you! This is such a beautiful bltynon you made for me. Such a gorgeous color!"

Hril said, "You look so wonderful in it. Are you ready?"

Dlen's face changed. "What's wrong, Tyrin?"

"Nothing's wrong. I'm happy. I love Tvor, I'm happy to be getting married to him. I'm just sad about Mrin. I still miss him."

Dlen came over to Tyrin, and hugged her.

Hril said, "Mrin and Wlen will always be in all of our hearts, Tyrin. And they both would be happy for you right now."

Tyrin nodded and brushed away tears. "I know."

They held each other for a bit, then parted.

Dlen said, "The guests have all arrived! The Michaelsons really show up for weddings. Ke'lir told me that this is the first one in the family in a while. We both will get to meet some of those we haven't met yet—the older ones from Casiti."

"I still can't quite get my mind around what is becoming our family. I'm getting used to it, but there's nothing like that at home."

"I know. I'm learning a lot from Ke'lir, but the fact that it's so varied, and also so famous is a challenge. Frankly, it seems to be a challenge for all of them! Anyway, shall we go and get you married?"

Tyrin smiled, and they walked outside to the generous backyard to see rows of chairs with guests in them. Grant, who was her closest male relative, had offered to "give her away." He said it was an archaic Terran custom that the New Earth Kinder had adopted eagerly in their marriage rituals. Her cousin Kwyl, the priest, had agreed to officiate the ritual. He was standing at the front, in conversation with a few people, including Tvor, who was standing at the front, in a traditional ceremonial belt.

Grant saw her, and moved toward her. "You look really beautiful, Tyrin."

"Thank you."

"Are you ready?"

"I think so."

Grant motioned to Kwyl and Tvor, and everyone took their seat. Grant walked with her down the middle of the rows of seats, and she could see people she knew, and people she didn't know, smiling at her.

She joined Tvor at the front. He looked radiant and happy. She was as well. She had been so lucky, twice, in the men she married. Tvor, like Mrin, was smart and gentle, and deeply respected her and her wisdom. She looked forward to her life with Tvor, here, in Zwek, and she hoped later, at home.

The ritual and the rest of the day passed in a blur to Tyrin. The reception was an unfamiliar practice, and she met so many new relatives from Tvor's family. She realized the sadness she'd felt earlier was gone. She was happy.

### Zwek, New Earth

Paul and Ke'lir sat next to each other in the second row at Tyrin and Tvor's wedding. Paul was struck by how different the ceremony was, even though he knew so much of it was borrowed from Terran traditions.

There wasn't any music, and the prayers that were said by the priest and by the couple were completely different in kind than those he was familiar with. There was no mention of love. Just duty, honor, obedience (well, only Tyrin had to mention that one), and perseverance.

But Paul knew they loved each other, and he could see the happiness in each of them. He was glad of that.

He could feel an undercurrent of sadness. He wasn't sure it wasn't just him, but he suspected not. Glor, Mrin, and Wlen were not present. Yes, it had been almost three years since the disaster of the failed mission, and the loss of Glor and Wlen, but sometimes, like today, it still felt fresh.

Later at the reception, he somehow managed to end up at a table with Tricia, Cassie and their wife, Amadu and his wife, and Liam. Tricia had, surprisingly, decided to move on from being Vice President of the New Earth Authority, to teach at New Orleans University in Political Science. The move surprised everyone. She had been heir apparent to become president, but she hadn't wanted to. She'd tired of politics. She was someone Paul consulted regularly in his role as ICS representative to the NEA.

Politics had the opposite effect on Liam. He had moved from working in the Vice President's office to becoming chief of staff of New America's representative to the NEA, surprising the whole family. The relationship of the Michaelson family to New America had always been rocky, even though Kurt, Leticia and Mira's co-parent, had once been president.

Paul started the conversation, "Liam, how's it going in George's office these days, especially given George's new expanding coalition?"

Liam said, "It's exciting! I'm loving the work. And I will have a call into your staff, by the way, George wants a meeting."

"He doesn't actually think he can get the ICS to join his coalition, does he? Franklin is adamant that we stay out of everything. I can't sway him."

Liam smiled, "He has some ideas, let's just say."

"OK, I'll hear them, but I'm pretty sure it's a waste of time."

Tricia said, "George is surprising. I'd bet good money he's done his research on the ICS, and has some carrots to offer."

"Well, I hope they are carrots that don't have anything even close to a Casitian or Galactic technology smell to them. Franklin is completely allergic to that. You can't believe how much convincing it took me to have him even consider the ICS manufacture clothing using old-school sewing machines, because some of the cloth may have been manufactured using galactic technology."

Cassie said, "You are *kidding* me."

"Oh, no. You have no idea what I'm dealing with, cousin."

"Better you than me, then."

Paul smiled. By now, the splintering-off of his ICS part of the Michaelson family was beginning to rejoin the rest, largely because of him. His family hadn't quite been able to make the leap to come to this wedding, but given how his parents had spoken of it, it was a close thing. They did send a gift.

A few days after the wedding, he was at a meeting at the Ja'lit school, where he was now on a committee that was the liaison between the Ja'lit school on New Earth and the school on Casiti. Since the school on Casiti was the "home" of the Ja'lit school, and the New Earth schools were branches, this committee's job was to coordinate communication.

Makena, a new member of the committee, and someone Paul was getting to know, raised his hand. Kevin, the chair of the committee nodded.

Makena said, "It's been a challenge keeping up with all of the new branches of the school on New Earth. I just heard a rumor of one starting up in New America, believe it or not."

Paul said, "Really? That sounds interesting."

Makena nodded. "I haven't been able to pin down who started it, or how big it is. But I do have some contacts in New America that might know about it."

Kevin said, "I think we should assume that eventually, they will let us know, or at least let the home school know on Casiti. Let's just table this one until we hear more. Paul, did you hear from Gil'ern about the policy changes?"

"Not yet. I think they are just now realizing that their policy changes will likely land differently with folks here than there. If I don't hear by the end of the week, I'll check back with him."

The Ja'lit school was growing much faster on New Earth than it was on Casiti. There was an appreciation for it among Terrans that made a lot of sense to Paul, but had come as somewhat of a surprise to the Casitians.


### Pa'rai's, NCPIZ, New Earth

Dlen and Ke'lir returned home after spending a few days after the wedding in Zwek with Tyrin and Tvor, and others of the family. Dlen's mother Hril had stayed behind in Zwek for a while, because she was feeling homesick. Dlen felt both content and full, and a little overstimulated by all of the people for many days.

They were sitting in their living room, and Dlen was looking out over the view that she had gotten used to, but sometimes struck her as extremely alien, as it did at this moment. Perhaps because she had spent so much time in Zwek, which had so many reminders of home.

"Penny for your thoughts?" Ke'lir asked.

"Hmmm... I was just thinking how familiar and alien this view is at the same time."

Ke'lir nodded. "I can imagine that."

Dlen said, "I was just remembering that boat trip we took a couple of months ago."

Ke'lir chuckled. "I remember how scared you were of the water."

Dlen lightly slapped Ke'lir on the arm. "That was *not* funny."

It hadn't been funny. Dlen still remembered in her body the abject terror she'd felt once they had lost sight of land. She insisted they turn around and go back, and she kept her head in her hands until she was assured that land was close.

Ke'lir sobered. "I'm sorry, you're right. You were really scared. No amount of assuring you you were safe helped."

"Well, I'd never, ever encountered anything like that. No one swims on Hilcyon."

"Do you want to learn?"

"Learn? How to swim?"

"Yes. There's a pool we can use, and you can take lessons."

Dlen thought about it. For a moment, she imagined herself in that big body of water, moving through it easily.

"I like that idea. Let's do that."

### *Capital Region, Hilcyon*

Plir walked home from Jrin's house, feeling pensive, but content. Jrin was the one person from school who was willing to talk to him, and play with him. They had become close friends.

He was scared for Jrin, because he knew Jrin was ridiculed and shunned because he was willing to be Plir's friend. But it felt so good to have a friend.

Plir walked into his house, to see his father sitting in the main room, reading something. He was surprised to see him—usually his father didn't get home until much closer to dinner.

"Ah, Plir, good to see you. We are having guests for dinner tonight."

Oh, how he hated nights with dinner guests. It did happen a couple of times a week. He mostly could stay quiet, but sometimes his father asked him questions meant to impress the guests with his smarts and cunning, or some such. He always managed to answer the questions well. He was smart, but he wasn't cunning or manipulative, like his father. But he had to pretend to be.

"OK. I'll go change."

He went into his room, to find his nicer tunic and pants, with a wide belt already laid out by his mother. These must be important guests, he thought.

He spent as much time in his room as he could, until he heard loud voices of the guests arriving. He entered the main room, and saw two men and one boy, perhaps a year or two older than he. He also heard women in the kitchen with his mother.

"Plir, this is Fril, First Chief of the North Central region, and his son, Kren. And Wysl, First Chief of the Central Valley."

Plir said, "Nice to meet you. Welcome to the Capital."

They sat down at the dining room table, and the women served them. Plir's mother had really made a large, impressive meal. It reminded him of the banquet at what had been the Supreme Chief's residence before his father had destroyed it. He knew that his father refused to return to the same kind of abundance and opulence that Wlen had favored. It was almost as if he was preparing people for the famines to come.

The conversation started out innocuous and boring, and Plir basically ignored it. He almost forgot he was supposed to be acting until his father cornered him with a question.

"Plir, tell our guests what you think about the strategic importance of the North Central region to Hilcyon."

He felt caught for a moment, then his brain kicked in. "Well, it has such a small population, and can't grow much. Although the ulrik hair produced in that region is essential to keep everyone clothed and warm."

Looking at his father, Plir instantly realized his mistake. His father's face looked like stone. He was supposed to have not mentioned the hair.

He added, "But of course, the grythin grasses grown in the Central Valley are a great replacement for ulrik hair."

His father smiled, and said, "Yes, Plir, quite a good answer."

He could see that Fril and his son looked somewhat dejected, and he felt bad for them. He knew his father was playing some sort of game, here, and he hated to be a part of it, but he felt like he had no choice.

The next day, he got up early to go to services before school. As he let the prayers and chants wash over him, and took part in the ritual, last night's dinner kept bothering him. He felt such guilt for having contributed to the game his father was playing.

He commiserated with his priest, Jorn, and was reassured. Later, as he was in the roughhousing wrestle play that he and Jrin did, he allowed himself to get lost in the sensations of his body and Jrin's moving together.

### New Orleans, New Earth

Johan woke a little confused.

"Ah, you are awake, good."

He looked up to see a nurse standing near him, adjusting the IV tube. He began to take in his surroundings. He felt a little groggy, but not too much.

"I'm giving you a dose of the nanoparticles that will help you heal from surgery. They also will flush any anesthesia and their metabolites from your system."

Because of the complexity of sex change surgery, it was one of the medical procedures that used almost exclusively Casitian technology. Johan had read some of the history of this kind of surgery on Old Earth, and in comparison to what the Casitians could do, it was almost barbaric.

The surgery he just went through completely remodeled his mammary tissues to match the male standard without scars, as well as removed his female reproductive organs, and remodeled his genitals. He had functioning testes that released testosterone and a penis that functioned as if he was born with it.

He couldn't produce sperm—that would kind of be magical, but he could have biological children via his harvested and preserved eggs, if he wanted to.

"We're going to wait for an hour or so to make sure you can pee without the catheter. In the meantime, let's get you up and walking, shall we?"

With a little help, he swiveled his legs out from the side of the bed, and stood up. He was a bit unsteady, but then managed to walk up and down the aisle of the recovery room several times. He felt sore all over, especially his chest and between his legs.

After the walk, he was sitting up in bed, and his doctor came by.

"Johan, how are you doing?"

"Doing well, thank you Dr. Martin. I'm feeling good."

"Great. Well, after you're cleared to leave, remember the advice I gave you for post-surgery care?"

"I shouldn't do any vigorous activity for at least a week. And no... no masturbating or sex for two weeks."

"You won't really be able do it anyway. You'll still be sore, and the testosterone won't really kick in for about a month, but just in case you are tempted..."

"I understand."

He would be tempted, he knew himself. The idea that he had a completely functioning organ that he'd dreamt about almost his entire life still hadn't quite sunk in.

After he was cleared to leave, he was picked up by Uther and Mary.

Mary said, "How does it feel?"

Johan said, "Uh, I dunno yet."

Uther said, "He's only been out of surgery for a couple of hours. Give the man some time."

Johan couldn't help but smile.

### Zwek, New Earth

As Kwyl walked toward Tyrin and Tvor's house, he was remembering how happy he had been to honor Tyrin and Tvor as their wedding priest. He loved having a relative from Hilcyon, and everyone in Zwek had learned so much about Hilcyon from Tyrin and the other women.

Tyrin and Tvor had invited him to an informal dinner for the first time as a couple. He always enjoyed Tyrin's company, and was looking forward to learning more about Tvor. At the wedding, Kwyl had learned a lot about Tvor's extended family: a family famous in Zwek, and all over New Earth. He had enjoyed meeting a varied group of family members, even those from Casiti. They were a sprawling, yet close-knit family whose history was so intertwined with the history of New Earth.

He arrived at their front door, and before he could knock, he saw the tall, dark-skinned figure of Tvor open the door.

"Kwyl! Welcome. Glad you could come tonight."

He smiled. "Thank you, Tvor. So happy to be here. I'm sorry I come empty handed. The priesthood doesn't allow much in the way of extras in my life."

"Oh, no worries, my friend. We are always happy to see you no matter what. And we don't need anything, really."

He entered into their house, and could smell delicious food cooking.

"Oh, my, the food smells are getting me hungry already!"

Tyrin came out, wiping her hands on a towel.

"I hope you enjoy what we've cooked up. Tvor makes Gral that is quite good."

Tvor said, "Apparently, my great-grandfather learned to make Gral from his ma, who taught him. He passed on the directions and recipe to my da."

Tyrin said, "It's almost as good as my ma's. *Almost.*"

Tvor smiled.

Over dinner, they talked mostly small talk: how they were settling into their new home, their plans for children, and Kwyl's varied duties at the monastery.

Finally, Tvor said, "Tyrin wanted to have a conversation with you about the priests."

Kwyl looked up from the luscious desert he had been enjoying.

"What do you need to know?"

Tyrin asked, "We think that our priests could potentially be a good connection to the priests on Hilcyon when the time comes to talk about unification. Do you think that's something that would work?"

Kwyl took a moment to gather his thoughts.

"I'll say this: we have been waiting, and praying for such an opportunity, Tyrin. We feel that we can be one of vehicles of unification. The unification of the priesthood could be a very important component to the unification of Kinder, and humans."

Tyrin said, "That's so good to know. I hoped that, but it's nice to hear it directly from you."

Tvor asked, "We're beginning to work with others, like Paul and Ke'lir, on planning for the next contact. Some people, like Tyrin, believe that re-contact will happen sooner than everyone thinks. Would you like to be included in our planning group?"

Kwyl felt elated. "Yes, please, count me in. I am eager to work on planning toward unification."

The next day, Kwyl told Daniel, the head of the Monastery, about this group, and his possible involvement. Daniel gave him his full permission to get involved, and set up a small liaison committee that Kwyl would report to regularly. He looked forward to this work—it felt so meaningful to him.

### Capital Region, Hilcyon

"But I hate having to lie like that." Plir sounded plaintive. Jorn was understanding.

"It's just for now, Plir. You *can't* let your father know how you really feel."

"I know, I know." Plir put his face in his hands, then looked up at Jorn, eyes full of tears. I'm just so tired of it. And people are really suffering."

Jorn put his arm around Plir's shoulders. "Plir, you are doing the Exalted King's work, sticking through this. Your father won't last forever, and you'll be prepared to take his place, but so differently."

"I can't even imagine how that will happen."

"You don't need to. Just have faith, and wait."

Plir nodded, and wiped his face with the sleeve of his tunic. As Plir walked out of the temple, Jorn considered the two conversations he'd had today. The first, with Ylorp, who was having deep doubts about his role inside of Msrotl's organization, and now Plir. These two were essential pieces of the puzzle for the future. Jorn didn't know how this would all play out, but he knew they all needed these two desperately.

The next day, he had a meeting with Mirn, one of the midwives that had been trained by the Casitian team. He wanted to learn more about how their network was growing.

# Chapter 4:
# New Lives

New Earth: January 2105 - May 2105
Hilcyon: Lykl 1207 - Mrontl 1208
Casiti: Hevl 805 - Gont 805

*"Pay attention to the miracle of birth. This miracle is not just that moment when a newborn emerges from the mother's body. We have moments of birth throughout our lives. Watch for the miracle of new things emerging." Heart of Carj, Eclogue 47*

### Pa'rai's, NCPIZ, New Earth

"Oh, my god, you feed me so well when I visit!" Paul pushed back from the table, quite full from the amazing meal, mostly Hilcyon-style food.

Dlen said, "You don't visit often enough, so we have to spoil you when you come."

Paul always felt so at home when he visited Ke'lir, Dlen and Hril. He said, "Yes, you are right, I don't visit often enough. But I'm so busy these days in New Orleans. Between my chaotic job as ICS representative to the government, and my work with the Ja'lit school, I barely have time for anything else."

Dlen asked, "How is that work with the school going?" Paul knew that Dlen had a keen interest in the Ja'lit school, ever since she'd read "Spirits Alike."

"It's really interesting. When I first started, I spent most of my time working on my own spiritual practice and developing my personal theology. But I got recruited early to work on a committee, and now I seem to be on several. It's very satisfying work, and I am learning a ton. The school is good at making sure our administrative and committee work doesn't take away from the spiritual work.

"But it's a new school. It started only 6 years ago, and it's growing fast. I'm quite sure it will be larger than the one on Casiti in a few years. So there are a lot of growing pains."

Ke'lir said, "I guess that makes some sense. The school on Casiti was always small since it had to compete with so many other schools already there for thousands of years. And I think there has always been some reticence to allow Terran influence into Casitian spirituality."

Paul nodded. "All of the Casitians that are part of the school migrated from Casiti specifically because they felt committed to continuing Ja'len'da's work with Terrans. Some of them have described some experiences of ostracism when they joined the Ja'lit school."

Ke'lir said, "The Casitians can be an obstinate bunch, but I guess that goes with the species, eh?"

They all laughed.

Dlen said, "Paul, have you had a chance to talk with Tvor and Tyrin lately?"

"I had a nice long video call with both of them a few weeks ago. Tyrin looks so happy, and I am always reminded of Glor when I talk with Tvor. Anyway, they are so excited about the possibilities of unification. I'm still kinda skeptical we'll get another contact anytime soon, but they are pretty sure we'll hear from someone within a decade or so."

Ke'lir said, "I was doubtful too, but they have really convinced me. I'd like our team to meet with them and talk about what they have been planning—it's quite detailed."

Paul happened to look toward Hril, who had a sad look on her face. He didn't know Hril as well as he knew Dlen, but he felt he could interpret her look as "I won't be here to see this." But Paul knew she wasn't all that old. She'd married and had children young. It didn't feel right to say anything, but he felt sadness in his heart.

### Pa'rai's, NCPIZ, New Earth

Dlen came up for air, breathing hard after her dive in the water. This was her third trip to swim in the bay of the big lake near their house.

As she did the breaststroke to return back to the beach, she marveled at how much had changed in just over a year. She'd gone from being in abject terror on the water, to swimming almost every day and loving it.

She never would have gotten to learn how to swim or learn the joy of the water at home. The only large bodies of water on Hilcyon were the reservoirs that were created by the systems that melted glacier water. No one ever swum in those because they were too cold and remote. Some areas of Hilcyon had streams and small rivers, but there wasn't enough water for lakes, or as she's learned, the oceans of old Earth.

She got out of the water and walked up the beach to see Ke'lir sitting in a chair reading some report or another on her tablet. Ke'lir had gotten extremely busy of late in her role with the NEATac. That had given Dlen lots of time to work on her own projects. Those were honing her English, learning Casitian, and catching up on science and math.

She sometimes missed her old life of being a midwife, and she, with encouragement from Ke'lir, had decided to get a medical education. But she had so much to catch up with, in order to apply to medical school. She was currently taking a chemistry course, which she enjoyed.

Ke'lir looked up from her tablet. "How was the swim? I see you went all the way out to the 1/2 kilometer marker."

"It was good. I'm loving it."

Ke'lir smiled. "I'm so glad you've taken to the water, Dlen. You seem to get such joy from it."

Dlen laughed. "I do!"

As Dlen peeled off her wetsuit, Ke'lir stood and folded her chair. Dlen then put on the robe she used for swimming, and they started their short hike up to the house. Dlen was cold from swimming, but she warmed up as they hiked uphill.

As they walked into the house, they could smell something quite delicious cooking. Hril had been learning some new recipes she'd found. She had decided to try her hand at short ribs. Cattle didn't exist on Hilcyon but were raised in abundance on New Earth, as they had been an important staple of the human diet on old Earth.

Dlen said, "Ma, that smells so good!"

Hril came out of the kitchen. "I hope it tastes as good as it smells. It has to braise for another couple of hours."

Ke'lir said, "That should be perfect timing. I have a short meeting with my group in 10 minutes, and I'll be done in time for dinner."

Ke'lir went off to her office, and Dlen and her mother sat in the kitchen.

"How was swimming, Dlen?"

"Good, Ma, I really love it. It feels so freeing, somehow. I can't really explain it."

"That kind of expanse of water is hard for me to get my head around. But it is really beautiful. I'm glad you're finding pleasure in it."

Dlen looked at her mother. She seemed so sad, sometimes. Dlen knew how heartbroken she was, first to lose Mrin, then her husband, then her home. Dlen was finding her place here. She felt more and more at home on New Earth. But Dlen wondered whether her mother would ever feel at home again.

### New Orleans, New Earth

Johan sat waiting in the anteroom to Paul's office with some anxiety. Paul had been such a help to him in the four years since he managed to escape from the ICS and his fanatical family. He'd been doing odd jobs in New Orleans since he arrived while he got his education at New Orleans University. Paul had been instrumental in getting him enrolled there. His education in the ICS would never have been enough to gain entrance normally.

The door to his office opened, and Paul smiled at Johan, and opened his arms for a hug.

"Johan, it's good to see you!"

They hugged, and Johan said, "It's good to see you too, Paul."

"I see you're growing a beard! Looks good on you."

"Thanks!" Johan was a little shy about it, although he did like the way it looked.

"Come in, have a seat."

They sat down in a small comfy seating area Paul had in his office.

"Thanks so much for coming by, Johan. I really appreciate it."

"I don't know how I can be helpful, Paul, but anything you need, I'm happy to help in any way."

"I'm sorry, but it's about your family. In particular, your brother. I need some information."

"My brother? Joseph? Oh, no, what has he done now?"

"He just became the deacon of the North Western state of the ICS."

"Oh, no!"

"Yes, he did."

"Well, honestly, based on how things were going when I left, I'm not utterly surprised. I'm imagining he grew his followers, and started strategizing."

"Well, yes. He got enough followers that he was easily chosen by the local council of elders. He now has enough followers in the ICS that Franklin Martin's leadership there is threatened. Already he has the backing of another three deacons. Two more, and he'll have a majority. "

"Wow. He really moved fast!"

"Yes, enough that Franklin is worried, and wants to find out as much information as possible. Your brother's newfound power makes it possible that all of the progress we've made in the last few years might go up in smoke."

"What do you need to know?"

"Well, we need to know what his weak spots are. Does he have any skeletons in the closet, so to speak?"

"Not from when I was there. He's one of those people who actually practices what he preaches. He was spotless, I suspect mostly because he was so obsessed with leadership and power. Power is definitely his drug of choice. He was hoping to become the minister of our local church, but the church elders chose someone else, mostly because at the time Joseph was too young. It was then he started on his purity thing, but he's always had a desire to have power over people ever since I remember.

"Between his charisma and the fact that he does really have the purity he preaches about, he's going to be hard to beat."

223

Paul said, "Thanks. I was sort of suspecting this. Anyway, when did you last talk with your family?"

"It's been over four years. I don't have the courage yet to tell them about my life. They periodically send me messages, but I have not replied to any of them, especially since they are always full of 'we're afraid for your soul' et cetera."

"I understand. I hope they come around sometime, but I can understand if you aren't waiting. How's the University?"

"Challenging, but good. Because of taking remedial math and writing at the beginning, I'm a little behind, but I will graduate next year."

"What's your specialty?"

"Political science. I'm thinking of heading to graduate school after I'm done. I should have the grades for it."

"That sounds like a great specialty, and right for you. Let me know if you need a letter of recommendation. I'd be happy to provide one."

"Thank you! You have been so helpful to me!"

"I know what it's like to be from the ICS, and feel trapped. I am happy to help folks find their own ways away from there."

Johan walked out of the office, feeling happy: happy that he was on a good path and happy that he had a real ally and mentor.

### Capital Region, Hilcyon

Plir hated to be duplicitous. But he had learned, over time, to act one way around his father, and his father's loyal chiefs, and a completely different way around those he knew he could trust.

He'd learned to be tough-sounding, mocking weak people like his father did, and he felt like a little part of him died inside each time he did it.

But when he talked with his mother, or Jorn, or Ylorp, or a few others who were in the reform movement that he knew he trusted, he could be himself, and show himself, and that part of him that had died seemed to come back to life—a little.

He didn't know how long he was going to be able to continue this charade, but he knew he had to keep going, at least for a few years. Jorn had arranged an escape plan, just in case. There was a monastery in the Upper Highlands he could join anonymously, and blend in. He was relieved that he had a way to safety if his father discovered the truth.

He was on an errand for his father. He was to speak to a second chief in charge of farming equipment in the Central Valley. As he sat in the tram watching the landscape go by, he thought about his approach. Jorn knew this chief as potentially interested in reform. His father knew him as one who had never shown any loyalty. Ostensibly, Plir was to extract a pledge of loyalty from him. In reality, Jorn was going to assess where this chief stood.

The tram stopped at the transit center in the center of the region. Plir made his way to the factory section, where the farm equipment warehouse was.

As he walked into the large building, and saw people walking to and fro, he called out, "Where can I find Chief Dryl?"

One man pointed toward the back of the building.

"He's in an office on the left side in the back. He's in a bad mood, though, I'd be careful, young one."

"Bad mood? Why?"

"Apparently, the *Supreme Chief* is sending some lackey to try and get him to be loyal, or some such."

The man said "Supreme Chief" with enough disdain that Plir knew right off his job would be easier than he thought.

"Thanks for the warning."

He walked toward the back and could see the office appear out of the dim light. He saw sitting at a desk, a short, stocky man, with a surprisingly large mustache.

Plir said, "Hi, I'm looking for Chief Dryl."

The man looked up, and said, "Who's asking?"

"My name is Plir. Are you Dryl?"

"What if I was?"

Plir smiled his genuine, friendly smile. "I would want to talk with you. Nice mustache, by the way."

The man looked puzzled. "Who are you? Aren't you a little young for this?"

"I said, my name is Plir. I come from the Capital region."

The man frowned. "You don't like my mustache, do you?"

"No, really I do like it! I don't think facial hair is a sign of disloyalty to Kinder."

He sat up, looking at Plir.

He asked, "What else do you think doesn't show disloyalty to Kinder?"

"Hard work, helping others, and wanting things to be a little different."

The man peered at Plir, still looking puzzled.

Plir said, "I am the Supreme Chief's son. He sent me here, to ask you for a loyalty pledge."

Plir didn't include the part about the loyalty being to Msrotl.

"So I'm asking, can you say you are loyal? You seem like a loyal type."

"I am loyal to the Kinder way. And the Kinder way has to be different."

It was completely clear what he meant.

Plir nodded. "I will relay your loyalty to my father." Plir knew that Dryl knew what he meant. His face seemed to relax, and he smiled.

"Thank you, Plir."

Then, another expression of puzzlement came across his face.

"How... how are you doing this, son?"

Plir sighed. Then he said, "The best I know how, Chief. It's touch and go, sometimes. My father thinks one thing, I do another. I trust you will not betray my confidence."

The man shook his head. "Never. You will be in my thoughts, son."

"Thank you."

"Look, do you have any plans this evening? I'd love you to come meet my family and stay the night. You can go back home tomorrow."

Plir smiled, grateful for the invitation.

"I'd love that, thank you."

On the tram home, Plir reflected on the wonderful evening he'd had with Dryl, his wife Jren, and his two sons, Ywl and Cmir. He enjoyed their company. And he would maintain contact with them, to keep track of the reform movement in the Central Valley. It turned out that Jren was a midwife, and was connected with the midwife network. Plir was glad of the trip, and accomplished far more than his father knew.

### Capital Region, Hilcyon

After the service ended, Jorn saw Ylorp sitting in the back, his head in his hands. Ylorp was one of the most faithful men he knew, and he also knew how much Ylorp struggled with his position, and what was happening now.

He walked toward the back, and sat down next to Ylorp, and just waited. Eventually, Ylorp looked up toward Jorn, and Jorn could see the tears in his eyes.

"Father, I don't know how long I can do this."

"Ylorp, you are faithful, brave, and strong. You can make it."

Ylorp sighed. "Have you heard, Father?"

"Heard about what?"

"The new loyalty oaths."

"No. Tell me."

"Msrotl has decided to demand signed loyalty oaths all over the world. If someone is moving, starting a new position, or getting a travel permit, they are required to sign a loyalty oath. If they don't they won't be able to do anything."

Jorn sighed. He knew this would make for hardship for some people.

"He's also going to track who gets the most oaths signed, and have that be a measure of how loyal we are. I can't force people to sign those things, Jorn."

"It's alright, Ylorp. Just keep doing what you can."

"He's going to know..."

"He has so many people he's trying to keep track of. Don't worry."

"I guess you're right. But it's hard to keep going."

"You can do it, Ylorp. You are doing the Exalted King's work, here."

"I know, I know. It's just... anyway, I do have some good news for you from my wife."

"Ah, go ahead."

"They predict that there will be a reform cell in every section of each region in a year. They also hope that in five years, there will be a cell in every hamlet."

"Five years. That's great."

"Can I survive this for five years, Jorn?"

"You have survived this long, Ylorp. Yes, you can do it. I know it."

As Ylorp left, Jorn still had that rock-solid feeling that Ylorp was going to do something important.

### Zwek, New Earth

"Push!"

She heard Dlen's voice loudly. Tyrin didn't know if she had the energy. She'd been in labor for what seemed like eternity. Her husband, Tvor, stood at her head, and seemed to give her strength.

She pushed, and felt something change—a big shift, and a release.

"Ah, it's coming!"

After a while, she heard the bawling sound of a baby crying after their first breath.

Dlen said, "It's a healthy boy, Tyrin."

Dlen put a swaddled baby into Tyrin's arms. Tyrin could feel exhaustion mixed with exquisite joy.

Tvor said, "There's Mrin, Tyrin. Our son."

A few hours later, after Dlen and the dula had helped Tyrin clean up, put her to bed and let her nap for a little bit, Tyrin woke to a crying baby.

Dlen said, "I think he wants his mama."

Dlen took the baby and directed Tyrin on how to get the baby to latch for the first time. Mrin latched on to her left breast and fed hungrily. Dlen softly helped Tyrin to switch breasts, and after a little false start, Mrin seemed to be fine with the left as well.

Dlen said, "It might be a challenge at first, Tyrin - don't feel bad if he doesn't latch right away. You might also end up getting a bit bruised. I'll leave you with some medicines that can help. I've learned the Casitians really have figured this one out."

Tyrin was so happy to have Dlen attend her birth. She knew it was the first birth Dlen had attended since their exile.

The next few days and weeks were a blur for Tyrin. Hril, who Tyrin had come to relate to like a mother, stayed around like a new grandmother, doting on Tyrin and Mrin alike. She felt the love of her larger family, as members of Tvor's family came from far and wide to visit and meet the new member. Her own family was also present here. The kitchen was full of food, and their living room was full of gifts for Mrin and the family.

She and Hril were sitting in the living room during a rare quiet moment, where Mrin was napping, Tvor was away working, and there were no visitors.

Hril asked, "How are you feeling, Tyrin?"

"Tired, but good. I'm so happy to finally be a mother. And at the same time, I'm sad. I love Tvor, I really do, but I somehow feel the sadness of losing Mrin again. As if I was meant to carry his child, somehow. It feels strange to say that, but..."

"I understand, Tyrin, I do. I know this place isn't home for you, and it's not home for me."

"We will see home again, Hril, I know it."

Tyrin looked at Hril's sad face, who said nothing in response. She could feel tears forming again, as the grief of their losses had faded but never went away.


### Zwek, New Earth

Kwyl felt uneasy, entering the house empty-handed. He knew the traditions of Terran, Casitian, and Kinder to bring food or gifts to a family with a newborn. But as a monk, he had nothing to give or buy anything with. Ultimately, he knew that Tyrin and Tvor wouldn't care, and would have enough, but he wished it could be different somehow.

"Kwyl, so good to see you." Tvor greeted him at the door.

"Glad to come visit and see your new child."

Tvor beamed and had that combination look of pride, joy, and sheer exhaustion Kwyl had seen before.

He looked around and saw Hril in the kitchen. She came out to greet him and gave him a hug.

"So nice to see you, Kwyl. I'm glad you came to visit."

"How could I not? A new member of our family has arrived."

Tyrin came out of the bedroom, carrying a swaddled bundle.

"Kwyl, so glad you are here. Here's Mrin!"

She walked close to him, and he looked down at the little baby. His eyes were open, and Mrin looked at him smiling.

"He looks happy."

Tyrin said, "He seems to be a mostly happy baby. He smiles and giggles a lot. Here, do you want to hold him?"

Kwyl was a little nervous—he never spent much time around babies, but he was game to try.

"Sure."

"Just make sure you support his head."

Kwyl took Mrin in his arms and held him while Mrin gurgled a little.

"He's very cute."

He handed Mrin back to his mother, and Mrin promptly started to wail.

"Ah, I think it's feeding time…"

Tyrin went back into the bedroom.

# Chapter 5:
# Information

New Earth: April 2108 - June 2108
Hilcyon: Cfro 1211 - Mrontl 1211
Casiti: Hevl 806

*"It is often hard for human beings to embrace complexity. We want simplicity, and so many human spiritual traditions have given the illusion of simple truths, when life, the universe, and, especially, human culture are far from simple." —Ja'len'da, "Spirits Alike"*

### New Orleans, New Earth

He had been sent a senior thesis by one of the "kids" he'd helped escape the ICS some years ago. It had been sitting in his inbox for weeks, but he finally had gotten around to it. Johan always struck him as an amazingly smart young man, but this senior thesis bordered on genius.

Johan had taken the task of looking at the different political systems of humans—the Casitian system, a few specific New Earth political systems, including the ICS, Dlejon, New Aard, and the NCPIZ, and used the Kinder system as a kind of cipher. The idea was to find a path from that system to a system that they might be able to adopt with the least amount of friction.

It was brilliant, and he absolutely had to show it to everyone on his old team, and in addition, with Tyrin and Tvor, who were actively working on building structures for unification from the Kinder direction.

His message system chimed, interrupting him from his thoughts about where to take these ideas.

"Play message."

"Franklin Martin is requesting a video conference as soon as possible."

"Acknowledge the request; we can start the conference when he's ready."

Paul had a sense of what this was probably about. Several seconds later, Franklin's face was on the screen. Paul had gotten to know Franklin over the years; he looked devastated.

"You look like it's bad news."

"It *is* bad news. Joseph Miller is now Bishop of the ICS."

He tried to act completely surprised.

Paul said, "What?"

Franklin said, "Yes, Paul, I am no longer Bishop of the ICS. He is. I am also no longer the deacon of the South Central state. I was replaced by one of Joseph's acolytes, as have all other deacons who have not pledged loyalty to him."

Paul had been warned recently by Johan, who was monitoring things from afar, although he was a little surprised this happened so soon.

Franklin said, "I'm assuming you'll get a message soon. Last I heard, he didn't want the NEA to have an ICS representative. All our work is gone, Paul. He and his followers don't care how poor the ICS is or how many of its citizens are in poverty."

"I know. Poverty is a virtue in his eyes."

"Yes. There's nothing we can do now except find other jobs. I imagine you'll have a much easier time of it than I will."

Paul remembered the offer he'd been sitting on for a long time—waiting for this day. He had been asked to lead the Ja'lit school on New Earth full-time, instead of the part-time, squeeze things into the small spaces of his schedule kind of thing he'd been doing for the past couple of years. It was time for him to move on.

### Zwek, New Earth

Tyrin finished the dishes while Tvor played with Mrin on the floor with toys. After they both saw Mrin to bed, they sat in their living room, returning to the detailed planning they had been working on for years.

Tyrin said, "What did you think of that thesis that Paul sent over—have you had a chance to read it all?"

"Yes, I have read it. It's amazing, and pretty convincing."

"I thought so, too! I think it helps our planning quite a lot. One of the biggest gaps we have has been governance. We knew we needed to eliminate the chief system, but we hadn't come up with a replacement yet. This gives us the path to a good solution. I'd make some specific changes and suggestions, but I think it's such a good start."

Tvor said, "Yes, I agree. I guess part of the question for me is how stable the reform movement will be when they contact us. I imagine it will be just as tenuous as before, which makes the governance question difficult."

Tyrin replied, "But what if it's not so tenuous? The priests have been working toward this slowly for perhaps hundreds of years. In addition to the influence we had seven years ago, it might not be as tenuous as it was last time."

Tvor nodded, "Also, everyone has felt the benefits of water and food. Paul thinks the priests will agree with this potential political structure since it includes them in ways they haven't been included before."

Tyrin replied, "Yes, and making sure more people can feel the positive effects of the technology we can bring there."

"I'd like to have another team meeting, in light of this new idea. And we should definitely invite... Johan was his name? ...to the meeting."

"Yes, let's do that. Perhaps we can include Ro'mer for a Casitian perspective. I know it will be a while before many Casitians want to be involved in this planning, but I think having a connection with them would be good."

Tvor said, "I'll send messages, and see if we can get this meeting on the calendar. I don't know whether Ro'mer will be willing or able to travel for it, but let's try to do it in New Orleans. I can commandeer some meeting space in my NEA office area."

Tyrin said, "OK, dear, it's time for us both to go to bed. You have your big match tomorrow!"

"I'm ready, Tyrin. I've fought Hwol several times now, and won all but one match."

Tyrin was proud of her husband, who was considered the best fighter in Zwek. What was so interesting to her was how the fighting "sport" in Zwek was completely divorced from any power. They did it for fun, although it seemed very serious fun. She thought of a question she'd never asked him.

"Tvor, how do you think your fighting relates to the fighting tradition on Hilcyon?"

"I think it was a way that our forefathers could honor their heritage and tradition while, at the same time, setting it aside because it wasn't good for the people. I think it was a wise decision: not to abandon fighting altogether, but weave it into the culture in a different way."

She nodded. "Yes, this does sound wise. And sounds like something we should talk about introducing to Hilcyon."

He smiled. "Yes, we should!"


### New Orleans, New Earth

Johan had been a bit intimidated navigating his way through the NEA Technology Administration building, but he finally found the conference room where the meeting was going to happen.

The door was open, and he paused a minute in front of the door, to look in. He was nervous, and he figured it probably showed. He saw Paul, who smiled widely and motioned him inside.

Paul said, "Johan, thank you so much for being willing to be part of this process."

Johan said, "Um, I'm happy to, although I'm having a hard time understanding why."

Paul wrapped his arm around Johan's shoulders. "Johan, your work is brilliant and has added a very important piece to our puzzle. I'm glad you are here to contribute."

Johan felt himself relax a bit, feeling good about the words Paul said.

"How are your grad studies going?"

Johan replied, "Really great. I'm loving the work. My major professor is the best-regarded expert in Hilcyon governmental systems. One of the deserters was her grandfather. I've learned so much from her so far."

"Has she read your senior thesis yet?"

Johan could feel himself blushing, "It's how I got to work with her. I was told she is extremely selective about her graduate students. I'm the first one she's ever taken who wasn't a Kinder descendant. She hasn't said much to me about it so far, but she's asked me many questions, and we're beginning to design some interesting research around it."

Johan heard someone speak, "We're all here; let's get started."

Paul and Johan sat down next to each other. Johan didn't know anyone except Paul. He'd been in email contact with a variety of people but hadn't met any of them yet.

A broad-shouldered man with a shaved scalp, small goatee, and what looked to Johan like Kinder features, which shared much in common with Casitian features, started to speak.

"Hello all! For the sake of our visitor, who hasn't met most of us yet, let's each introduce ourselves, shall we? I'm Tvor, and have been involved in working on this issue since soon after my brother, Glor, was killed on Hilcyon."

As part of the research for his senior thesis, Johan read the report from the team that visited Hilcyon six years ago. He was familiar with the story, and how the disaster had unfolded. As he somewhat belatedly realized that most of the people in this room had actually been there, he got nervous again, feeling intimidated. He had just been a confused teenage girl, trying to figure out how to get out of the horrible life was leading in the ICS. Being in the same room with all of these folks seemed almost unthinkable.

The person next to Tvor, who also looked like they were Kinder, said, "I am Tyrin, an exile of Hilcyon, here with my husband Tvor, happy to be working toward unification, and seeing my home again." Johan remembered her story from the reports as well.

Paul introduced himself next, then it was Johan's turn. He was at a moment's loss for words, then said, "I'm Johan, honored to be here. I'm studying Kinder government systems in graduate school. I feel a little overwhelmed." He got embarrassed, then felt Paul's comforting hand on his arm.

The person beside him said, "I'm Ke'lir, I was born and raised on New Earth and was a member of the original team that visited Hilcyon."

"I'm Dlen, also, like Tyrin, an exile of Hilcyon."

"I'm Ro'mer, from Casiti, and I used to be on the Consej, representing Casiti. I now am doing technology transfer work on Casiti, and hope that work can start to include Hilcyon as well as New Earth."

From his research, Johan knew that most of these folks were all related to each other, and part of the great Michaelson family. And he knew why there weren't any other officials here. Basically, no one thought that re-contact with Hilcyon would happen anytime in the next 50 years. Not even his mentor thought that. But based on his research, he thought things might happen much more quickly.

Tvor said, "OK, thanks, everyone, and let's get started. Johan, you said you'd be willing to present the basic outlines of your thesis to us and what might be a good starting place for new governance. Are you still able to do that?"

Johan nodded. "Yes. I sent my presentation to Paul..."

Paul nodded, looking at his tablet. The 3D display lit up above the conference table.

"OK, much of this is going to be old hat, especially for those of you who grew up on Hilcyon. Please forgive me, and also feel free to correct anything I got wrong.

"Hilcyon has been governed by a hierarchical chief system that was inherited from the system that was created when the Tud'scla captured humans. There have been many waves of reform, each followed by a time of retrenchment. Our research, based on information gleaned from deserters from Hilcyon, and your visit six years ago, suggests that each time reform happened, the retrenchment was less effective, and there was less time between reform efforts.

"The two most recent waves of reform, the first over 80 years ago, during the time of The Event, and starting seven years ago, from what we can tell, have left the most lasting effects on the society of Hilcyon. In addition, the current supreme Chief, Msrotl, was elevated to that post in a way that no supreme chief in the history of Hilcyon has—by force instead of single combat. This suggests a deep instability of the governmental hierarchy at this time.

"You can see from this graph what we know of the time frames between the six waves of reform, as written about in the history by Ngellin. Each retrenchment period is shorter: from 1000 years to 820 years, 650 years, 250 years, and finally 80 years. Although most people seem to imagine that it will be another 80 or more years before we are in contact with Hilcyon again, these two factors, the base instability of the current regime, and the fact that the high likelihood of a new reform wave soon, means that planning now is important. Even though the repairs made when you visited will allow food and technology sustainability for over 100 years, this government won't last that long.

"Of course, there is the possibility that a chief who is not reform-minded will successfully challenge Msrotl and win—and this may already have happened. But it seems unlikely, and another reform wave is inevitable, and, based on historical precedent, is most likely to happen in the next 30 years."

Johan took a breath and waited for any questions or corrections. There were none. He nodded to Paul, and the diagram of the current governmental system appeared.

"From what we can gather, the governance completely excludes two key constituencies, the priesthood, who may account for as much as 5% of the population, and women, who consist of approximately 55% of the population. And there is good evidence, based on your visit, that the priesthood is quite reform-minded. Any planning we do must incorporate them, as those two constituencies are a majority of the population."

He nodded to Paul again. "Here is a diagram of the hamlet, village, and region system, also inherited from the time of slavery by the Tud'scla. This system is an important core. We must find a way to incorporate that into any system we wish them to consider.

"I think it would be good for me to stop here for now. I'm happy to take any questions as we consider the next steps. I don't think it's quite time for me to dive into the details of my proposed governmental system, but I'm happy to outline it if it seems useful."

Dlen said, "I agree with all of this, and I'm also wondering if Msrotl is preventing challenges in his position. He was, honestly, never an especially strong man. He got to his position entirely by appointment. I'm not sure he'd ever been in the ring."

Johan nodded, "Based on Earth's historical precedent, authoritarian leaders who get into power by circumventing normal government processes generally have much more unstable governments and hold onto power by violence. And given the high value that is placed on honor in Kinder society, Msrotl's kind of authoritarianism is likely to be unstable and short-lived."

Tyrin said, "It would be so good for us to know what's happening now. How can we make that happen?"

Tvor said, "The only way we can do that is to return to orbit around Hilcyon. We do still have many extant listening devices there, and they all are recording currently, but the Consej refused to let us leave a satellite to transmit that information through the wormhole."

Johan said, "What would it take to get permission to send a satellite?"

Ro'mer said, "The Casitians are finally getting a little less tight these days. I'm willing to send out some feelers to folks I know still on the Consej. If we frame it simply as sending a satellite that allows us to feed that listening info through the wormhole so we can know what's happening and do some planning, they might be amenable."

Paul said, "But do we need the Consej? Can't we just get the NEA Space Authority to build and send a satellite on our own?"

Ro'mer looked to Johan like they were thinking, and a smile broadened on their face. "Why Paul, what a good idea! I'm pretty sure we've already transferred all the tech New Earth needs for the satellite, and New Earth has its own wormhole. You can have the data sent here!"

There were murmurs in the room, and they Johan heard Tvor's loud voice, "OK, everyone!" The murmuring stopped.

Tvor said, "I think we're probably all in agreement that the next step is connecting with the NEA about getting a satellite. Ke'lir, is that something you can spearhead?"

Ke'lir said, "Yes, I think I know the team to talk with. We'll probably have to get the NEA Space Authority director's OK for this, but I don't imagine we'll need to go any higher than that. They can OK the funding for a small project of this size. And even if we did need to go higher, our cousin Tricia has connections. I think she'd be amenable to helping with this."

The meeting continued for a while, largely including things that weren't going to involve Johan. But he did end up being put on a small team with Dlen and Tyrin to talk more deeply about the kinds of new governments possible and how to plan to implement them. He looked forward to working with both of these women. He knew he could learn so much from them.

Dlen had just returned from a visit to Zwek, where she spent time with Tyrin and Tvor. She treasured time with both of them—it almost could feel a little like home, and it was so good to visit after the tragedy of losing her mother.

Her mother had been feeling a little ill for a while, and it got steadily worse. Ke'lir suggested she be admitted to the local hospital. After her admission, they learned that Hril had a fatal, inoperable brain tumor—even incurable with the high-tech Casitian medicine available to them. She lived for a few months after that, cared for by both Dlen and Ke'lir. She died quietly at home just two months ago.

The visit to Zwek was partially to give her time away from the place where her mother died, a change of scenery and pace. It was also partially working with Tvor and Tyrin on more planning - the satellite was due to launch in a few weeks, and they were looking forward to the data it would send back.

Dlen would be home alone for a few days. Ke'lir was involved in committee work in New Orleans and getting all of the necessary agreements and permissions for the satellite launch. This would give Dlen time to work more on her part of the picture for unification planning: medical care.

Dlen could, in some ways, extrapolate from her work with the midwives. She and Ke'lir had been able to train about 20 midwives, and were preparing those 20 to train more. Conservatively, if each of those midwives were able to train five more each year, that would be almost 800 midwives trained: a good number of them. That would mean thousands of women saved from death in childbirth, and more of their children would survive as well. Dlen remembered that many more children would also survive because of the assistance given to fix the water systems fifteen years ago.

And plugging back into that network of midwives should be easy, and expanding it to other healers, largely women. This would allow them to very quickly show the populace the benefit of access to galactic-level medical care.

At first, a few years ago, she was sure she would never see her home planet again. But now, she felt almost certain that she would. And her big question was: would she go home and stay there, or stay here? She knew Tyrin and Tvor planned to move permanently to Hilcyon to help steer the new government. Dlen wasn't sure what her role might be, and she'd come to love New Earth, and, of course, she doubted that Ke'lir would want to live on her home planet permanently. Her home really was wherever Ke'lir was.

Several weeks later, Dlen stood with the team in the back of the crowded room. It was the control room assigned to gather the data from the satellite sent through the wormhole, orbiting Hilcyon and sending it back to New Earth.

There was a dizzying array of screens, and the team was craning to see as the data began to trickle in and was analyzed by the system.

Trysha, Jake, and Marie were the engineering team that had been assigned to work on the satellite and its data.

Trysha, who was the data analyst, said, "It's going to take several days for the translators and data aggregators to analyze the years of data. But the current listeners seem to show that someone named Msrotl is the leader."

Dlen said, "That's the man who took power from my father."

Ke'lir asked, "Any other chatter that arises from the noise?"

Trysha shook her head. "No, there doesn't seem to be, so far."

Jake said, "Not sure about that: look over here."

They were pointing to a graph of the frequency of words used over time—and it was populating as they watched it, but words relating to priests seemed to be trending up.

Dlen said, "That sounds very interesting. Can we hear any of those conversations?"

Dlen couldn't tell what Jake was doing with their display, but it seemed they were trying to find specific conversations in the capital related to priests.

They said, "Here's one. I'll play it, it's short."

Tinny voices started, "... chief, respectfully, people like priests. People respect priests. I think it's important to befriend..."

"You don't seem to understand. The priests are plotting reform, and I will not tolerate their traitorous behavior."

The voices then seemed to move out of the range of the listening device and could no longer be distinguished.

Dlen said, "That conversation sounds like it might be with Msrotl himself."

Ke'lir asked Jake, "Would isolating all conversations regarding Msrotl be too much to analyze?"

"How common is that name on Hilcyon?"

Tyrin said, "Most people try to use names by generation - so there won't be many Msrotls alive now, even though that is a somewhat common Kinder name."

Jake said, "Because he's apparently the leader, it would be impossible to *listen* to all those conversations. But we will be analyzing word and phrase usage, which should give you some good data."

Trysha said, "The population data is coming in. It looks like there has been an increase in the population, particularly in the younger age brackets."

Dlen said, "That makes sense. Less maternal and infant mortality since we left."

Tvor, who, by recent consensus, had been made team leader, said, "OK, let's let these folks work. I look forward to your report in a few days. Let's reconvene... Secondday, Trysha? Would that give your team enough time to get us a preliminary report?"

Trysha nodded. "Yes, Secondday is great."

They all filtered out of the room. Ke'lir, Dlen, Tvor, Tyrin, and their son Mrin were staying at the Michaelson house, which had plenty of room for all of them.

Paul said, "Let's go get some dinner, shall we? I know a good, supposedly authentic Old New Orleans restaurant with some nice, big tables."

# Chapter 6:
# Unfolding

New Earth: January 2109 - August 2109
Hilcyon: Lykl 1211 - Wtler 1212
Casiti: Gont 806 - Paqn 806

*"Obedience is important, but never at the expense of care for each other. Deep honor is found in obedience, but honor without compassion isn't true honor." Heart of the Carj, Eclogue 943*

### Hilcyon, Cfro 30, 1210 (January 6, 2109, New Earth Time)

Plir knew his father hated that he sometimes went to services. He'd first come for solace as he tried to figure out how to please his father. After several years of being connected to Jorn, his priest, he came for information.

When he was a young child, he wanted to be just like his father. But as he grew up, he realized that his father was a violent, brutal man, even though he'd never seen that side of him at home. He couldn't and wouldn't follow in his footsteps. But everyone, including his father, expected him to be his heir, to take over the supreme chief position when his father died.

So he pretended, as best he was able. So far, his father hadn't asked him to do anything he had been unable to do. He hoped that continued.

He felt the familiar movement of the bench as Jorn sat beside him.

"How are you today, Plir?"

"Alright, I guess, Father. My father is frustrated with the lack of people signing the loyalty oath outside of the Capital and North Central regions."

Jorn nodded. "That doesn't surprise me."

"I think he'd like to use drastic measures but knows they will get nowhere. So he's just frustrated."

"He probably is beginning to see that he has only so much ability to force people to do things."

"Agreed. I've spoken with Ylorp. He says there are even a good number of chiefs in the Capital region who are being easy on people and not forcing them."

"That makes sense. Is Ylorp in touch with those chiefs?"

Plir nodded. "That's my sense. I can get..."

"No need, Plir, we are also in touch with Ylorp. I don't think we need it... yet."

He said his goodbyes and went toward home. His father had asked him to give a message to a particular second chief in the capital village of Koln, whose house was on his way home, as the capital was officially in Koln. He liked this second chief. He seemed like a good man, and he'd been chief there for many, many years.

He knocked at the door, and the chief's wife answered.

"Plir! So good to see you. I just took some breadmufs out of the oven. I'm sure you'd like one!"

Plir was happy—she made some amazing breadmufs—even better than his mother's.

"Thank you! Yes, I'd love one to eat on my way home!"

"My husband Sadre isn't home yet; he's doing some errand. But he'll be back soon."

"I just have a message for him - you can just relay it for me."

Suddenly, She seemed tense, but handed him the breadmuf in a nice cloth napkin.

"Thank you. I'll return this, I promise. Anyway, the message is that my father needs to see the chief as soon as possible. I don't know what it is about, but..."

The color drained from her face, and Plir was confused.

"Are you alright?" he asked.

"Will he disappear?"

Plir understood then what her fear was. And he then realized something important. This chief had been in place since long before his father became supreme chief, and he hadn't been challenged for a very long time. Thus, people liked his leadership. He wasn't one of his father's close allies, and Plir had never seen him in the capital, even though he was in the same village. That added up to Plir that he was reform-minded.

He hated that he'd been the bearer of this message. He didn't quite know what to say, but he tried his best.

"I'm sorry to have been the one to bring this message. I have an idea. Have your husband come to my father's office at sixth hour tomorrow. I'll make sure to be there. I don't know if I can prevent anything from happening, but I'll try."

Plir could see tears in her eyes.

"Thank you, son. You are a blessing."

He felt terrible. He left, the breadmuf feeling like ash in his mouth.

The next day, he got to his father's office just before sixth hour. He noticed, as he walked in, that his father looked terrible. He had circles around his eyes, and his skin was sallow.

"Da, you alright?"

"I'm fine, son, fine. Did you talk with Sadre?"

"He wasn't there, but I left a message with his wife. He should be here soon."

"What?"

"I told him to show up first thing."

"Ah, I see. Fine." His father seemed out of breath.

A knock on the door, and his father's attache stuck his head in the door.

"Supreme Chief, a Sadre from Koln is here to see you."

"Send him in. Plir, you can go."

"I'd like to stay if you don't mind."

"Suit yourself."

An older man with a very slight goatee that skirted the norms of the Kinder walked in.

"Supreme Chief Msrotl, you asked to see me?"

The man turned toward Plir. "Is this your son?"

"Yes, that is my son. I didn't call you here for small talk, Sadre, and shave that chin of yours."

"Why am I here?"

"You have a very bad attitude, Sadre. Anyway, your village is last in loyalty oath signatures."

"With all due respect, Chief, my village has an older population than most. So few travel, and there are fewer people seeking housing or job changes than in other villages."

"Given that, you should have taken the initiative and asked for loyalty oaths more generally."

Sadre shrugged. "That wasn't what you required."

His father rose from his chair on his arms, red in the face.

"What I require, Sadre, is loyalty. You have shown none to me since the beginning. I should have had you removed a long time ago, but your village is full of cowardly men, none willing to challenge an old man for leadership. It's shameful!"

"Is that all, Chief? I have a village to run."

"Get out of here." His father coughed several times and sat down heavily.

Sadre looked at Plir with a look of gratitude. Seeing that his father wasn't looking at them, he nodded to Sadre, and Sadre nodded back. This was an ally Plir could depend on.

"Da, really, are you alright?"

He didn't expect the explosion he got. His father yelled, "I'm *fine*. Get out of here, now!"

He left. As he walked out, the attache caught his elbow.

"Your father is very sick. He's been not feeling well for days now."

"Did you suggest a healer?"

"I did. He refused."

"Thanks. I'll talk with my mother."


A few days later, Plir was at home. He looked at his mother, who was repairing one of his tunics.

"How is Da?"

"Not well, Plir. He finally agreed to see a healer. The healer thinks it's something fatal. He's been in bed for the past few days."

"Why won't he let me or anyone except Bkon and his attache see him?"

"He's afraid of what will happen when people know he's sick."

"There are already rumors going around..."

"It's time for you to start your plans, Plir."

Plir nodded. "I've already been speaking to some of the folks I've made connections with. But I can't quite see how I will pull it off. And then there's Bkon. I think he has his own designs on being Supreme Chief. I can't possibly beat him."

"It will work out. You don't have to beat him; just maneuver around him."

Plir took a breath. If it wasn't for his mother, he felt as if he would be lost. He had no idea what his father would do if he knew how he felt, but he could never let that happen.

"Thank you, it's helpful to talk with you. I have a meeting with Bkon that my father arranged. I should go now."

"Take care, my son. You are in the right, you know."

Plir nodded. "I know. I love you."

"You know I will always love you, Plir, my heart."

Plir left the house across from the capital building and walked across the square. He knew that the Supreme Chief's house used to be very large, but it had gotten largely destroyed during an uprising, so they built a new, smaller, more modest house, the one they moved to when he was ten.

As he entered the building, he noticed eyes following him, as usual. He was always watched; some were eyes for his father, but he knew most were eyes, knowing his father had him in mind to take over for him. The meeting was supposed to happen in his father's office, even though his father was in bed at home.

Bkon was standing at the window, turned, and came closer to him, a little too close. His breath smelled of sweet herbs, surprising Plir.

Bkon said, "There is someone your father wants you to follow. His name is Ylorp. He's Great Chief Willm's grandson."

Plir did his best to keep his face completely neutral.

"Alright. What are you looking for?"

"We think he is a traitor and is working against us. But so far, no one has been able to figure out how. He does do his job, but something is not exactly right."

Plir nodded. "I can do that. I'll report back if I find anything. Anything else?"

Bkon said, "Yes. I'll be straight with you, Plir. Your father is dying. I am going to take his place—you are too young. If you are loyal to me and follow me, you will be next in line after me to take the Supreme Chief's spot. Don't even think of crossing me. You are not my son, and I have no use for a traitor this close to me."

Plir wasn't even surprised. At the same time, his skin was crawling with fear. He did his best not to betray his feelings. He also felt that saying nothing would be the best strategy at this point, so he nodded and walked out.

As he walked back to the house and calmed down, his head was formulating what he and Ylorp could fabricate to ease this situation and perhaps turn it to their advantage. Plir knew it was likely that there were eyes on him, even as he was supposed to be putting eyes on Ylorp. He would have to be very careful. This could be a trap Bkon was setting for both of them.

### Pa'rai's, NCPIZ, February 10th, 2109

Paul put the mug down, smacking his lips appreciatively and enjoying the tartness on his tongue. He said, "That apple cider is amazing. I've never tasted anything like it."

Ke'lir lay back on the couch, smiling. "It took so long to figure out why apple trees did so badly on New Earth, but those agronomists were amazingly persistent. We've now got many apple orchards up in the NCPIZ, with four different varieties. It's definitely the better climate for them."

Dlen said, "I still, even after all of these years, find it fascinating how wonderful Earth foods taste to me. A few years ago, I read an account written by one of the Casitians who was responsible for first making contact with Earth. And she described how delicious Earth foods were to all Casitians who had tried them."

Ke'lir said, "They theorize that because we evolved tasting Earth food, that no other food would taste quite as good to human taste buds. Makes sense to me."

Paul always enjoyed his visits to Ke'lir and Dlen. Ever since that fateful mission, he and Ke'lir had been close. And he had gotten to know Dlen well over the past 9 years as they all worked together to plan for unification.

Ke'lir put her hand on Paul's arm. "Tell me, how is Makena?"

Paul smiled. Makena was a new romantic interest in Paul's life. He was steady and a part of the Ja'lit school, like Paul.

"He's fine. We are enjoying each other's company."

Dlen said, "So when will we meet this man, Paul?"

"I'll try to get him to come up with me next time. He's incredibly busy in the New Earth Agency, but I know he needs some time off!"

Ke'lir said, "I read his rather long report on the economic development of the Eastern Europe region. It was fascinating."

"He's become the NEA expert on economic development. I wish I had known him when I was still the ICS representative."

Ke'lir nodded. "I can imagine. I have been hearing some really horrible stuff coming out of there lately."

"I don't even want to think about it. They now call Joseph Miller 'The Prophet,' which is way worse than 'Bishop.' Anyway, they have managed not only to wipe out the modest GDP gains Franklin and I had made, but go backward! They are worse off than they were when I was a kid. But it's their choice. However, the good news is that my family has left the ICS and moved to New Orleans. There's a small ICS ex-pat community there, and since Franklin is now *persona non-grata*, he's likely to join them."

As Ke'lir got up, she said, "Your mother's trip to Casiti a few years ago helped her attitude immensely. I hope that they settle in OK." She went into the kitchen, and Paul realized he could smell something delicious and sweet cooking.

He said, "There's dessert?"

Dlen grinned. "Apple pie and ice cream. My favorite!"

"Apple pie. Wow, it's funny. It's such a common idea, but I don't think many of us have ever had it."

Dlen said, "Yes, I've come across that term in many of my history readings, and I understand that it was quite common in America on Earth. The phrase 'As American as apple pie' seems common—but no one understands what that means anymore."

Ke'lir returned with three plates holding a slice of pie and a scoop of ice cream each. They dove in, and all conversation stopped for a while as they enjoyed the dessert. This gave Paul a moment to reflect on his life and on how far he had come since he first left the ICS almost 12 years ago. He was happy and felt that he was not only being of service but he was following his calling in life.

He spent a few days with Dlen and Ke'lir, with many more conversations about spirituality, culture, and unification, as well as their personal lives and family. As they were driving back to the shuttle station, he remembered that in a week, Paul had a date for dinner with his family, who had just moved from the ICS.

That next week, Paul looked around the restaurant to see his family seated near the back. He and Makena walked back to where they were sitting and saw two seats open for them.

Seated at the large table were his parents, his brothers and their wives, his sister, and Franklin Martin, his sister's husband, as well as ex-bishop of the ICS. It was hard to even imagine him in this setting.

Paul had chosen a conservative-ish restaurant that was very family-oriented, which he hoped would make them feel more at home. But they had all just moved from the ICS a week ago and looked almost shell-shocked.

"Paul!" his mother saw him approach.

Everyone got up, and hugs were given all around. Even Makena got hugs from some of his family.

"Mom, Dad, everyone. So glad to see you. How has settling in been?"

His father's face sort of screwed up, and he could see the tension at the table rise.

His mother said, "It's been a challenge, Paul. We didn't feel at home in the ICS, and we don't feel at home here."

Franklin said, "Well, the church here is quite good, I think I rather like that pastor."

His sister said, "And he's quite intimidated by you, Frank."

Paul laughed. "I'm not surprised in the least. Is the ICS expat community alright?"

His father said, "There are quite a number of our friends who also left and have settled here. So it will do. But it's hard, Paul, to be surrounded by..."

His sister filled in, "...a different culture. We used to be all there was, in the ICS, and our differences seemed large. Now, we are only a few in this soup of so many other cultures. We do stick together more."

Paul thanked the spirit that, for the most part, the evolution of the religion of the ICS had eschewed evangelism. Otherwise, they would definitely have created tension with their neighbors.

The conversation moved to what Paul and Makena were doing, and they settled into a nice conversation until his mother said, "I'm going back to Casiti for a bit to visit. Mother is sick and likely dying. I need to mend some fences."

Paul could see his father's face and body tense, and he knew it had been a point of great contention between his mother and father. But his mother could be strong and decisive when she needed to.

"I'd heard grandmother Marianne wasn't doing well. It's about time for me to visit as well. I probably could drag Ke'lir and Dlen along. Dlen has yet to visit Casiti. Have you made shuttle arrangements yet?"

"Yes, I'm leaving on the 20th."

"Hmmm, that's a little soon, but I'll see if I can swing it or a shuttle soon after. It would be good to go back and visit."

He turned to Makena. "Want to come? You haven't been in quite a while."

Makena nodded. "Not for more than 10 years. Yes, I'd enjoy that and meeting some of your Casitian family."

Paul looked at Franklin. "You know, Franklin, it might be quite educational for you to visit Casiti once in your life."

He shook his head. "Paul, that's a bridge too far, I'm afraid, even though there are no ramifications if I visit right now. I can't see myself doing that."

"I understand."

After a bit of uncomfortable silence, they got back to more comfortable topics of their new housing, job opportunities, and general life in New America.

Dlen sat at her favorite window, looking out on Lake Superior. It felt like such a privilege to her, even after all these years, to have so much space and to get to see such an amazing view. She thought back on a moment several years ago when she and her mother sat in this very place, looking over this very view, talking about that feeling of privilege. And they talked of missing home.

Her mother's death had left a hole in Dlen that she was sure would never be filled again. She was glad she still had Tyrin, who was her only connection to her homeworld, at least now.

She felt the touch of Ke'lir on her shoulders and looked up into Ke'lir's smiling face. She had been thinking for quite some time, and hadn't even heard Ke'lir entering the house.

"How was the drive?"

"A little more traffic than usual. Pa'rai's is growing again."

"That's a good thing, right?"

"Yes. The welfare of Pa'rai's has been so tied to how much exchange there has been between New Earth and Casiti—and now that it's opening up so much, we're doing a lot better. And now, perhaps, it might be time for us to visit. It's been too long since I've been back."

"You'd like me to see it, wouldn't you?"

"Yes! I think you'd like it - it's like Pa'rai's, except, well, more of it."

"I'm looking forward to it!" Dlen was, truly. Going to see the planet her people called "The Breft," which meant "accursed," would be an experience she'd never imagined when she was home.

When she thought again of her home, some sadness and inner determination she didn't realize she had came to her. Ke'lir noticed her emotional change.

"Are you still sad about home?"

"Yes, and no. Sad about home and Ma and wondering what's happening. I also remember the conversations I've been having with Tyrin and Tvor. It's confusing sometimes. And there is so much we would have to do if I went home again.

"In Kinder, we have the word 'hlrpet.' There isn't an English equivalent. It's basically a word that incorporates grim determination with moments of satisfaction and uncertainty."

Ke'lir said, "Sounds like a very Kinder concept. So different than the Casitian word, that is close to the English word 'equanimity.'"

"Equanimity is a word I've always struggled with."

"I'm not surprised, love. I don't know if equanimity is possible for Hilcyon."

Dlen nodded, knowing her culture deeply. Yes, there was no room for equanimity.

Ke'lir asked, "Have you considered the question of the priesthood that Paul and Johan have?"

Dlen answered, "I have. I think I have an answer. I think we need a specific structure for the logistics and details of unification. And that structure should include all three constituencies—chiefs, women, and priests. I was reading some of the histories and was struck by the idea of creating a group of 12, 4 from each constituency."

Ke'lir said, "Hmmmm. That sounds like an interesting and good idea. I wonder what the chiefs will think of it."

"Based on what we've been hearing, I think the chiefs are pretty fragmented right now. I'm not sure they will care much."

### Hilcyon, Wtler 20, 1211 (June 26, 2109, New Earth Time)

Jorn rose from prayer, blowing out the candle and covering the altar. The coal fire in the small stove had long gone out, as it was late at night. Many priests found getting up in the middle of the night for midnight prayers too burdensome, but Jorn loved praying over the hours. It soothed him in these uncertain times.

A few days later, as he was finishing the ritual in the chapel, he saw Ylorp sitting in the back with his eyes closed. These days, he risked coming to services less often as the priesthood became less and less favored by the chiefs. Jorn knew that Ylorp was walking on a very fine wire. He was now a Second Chief, working quietly, but on the outside still following the "Kinder Way." That had lately become shorthand for the brutal, restrictive reign of the chiefs—something they both were working to end.

He walked back toward where Ylorp was sitting and slid next to him on the hard stone bench. He opened his eyes and looked at him with a smile.

"How are you doing, Ylorp?"

"Alright, I guess. It's rough sometimes."

"I understand. We have some news for you."

"Good news, I hope." Jorn saw Ylorp shift in his seat.

"Yes. Very good news. Four more hamlets, including Brun in the South Central region, have enough support to easily overthrow their chiefs. That leaves only two regions where we don't have a majority of villages yet. But we're thinking that we can act soon."

"The capital and..."

"North Central."

Ylorp shook his head. "Ah, North Central has Fril as First Chief. He's loyal to Msrotl forever."

"And he rules the villages and hamlets with an iron fist: making sure all of his chiefs are loyal. He's even disbanded the last two remaining priestly orders there in the past year. We will probably never be able to overturn him, but we can weaken him significantly."

"How? If you don't have any priests?"

Jorn smiled. "You don't need to know."

Ylorp nodded. "Understood. I hope this will turn out... I have been intensely training."

Jorn was puzzled. "Training?"

"Yes. You know Msrotl is sick. I'm sure he will die soon. Bkon will try to take his place. I will challenge Bkon to the ring."

Jorn felt a pang; sadness that Ylorp would have to enter the ring, but then relief. Perhaps this was the role Ylorp had to play.

Jorn put his arm on Ylorp's shoulder. "The Exalted King is ever with you. You are on the right path. We will prevail."

The next week was time for Jorn's favorite ritual. It was held once a year, on the day that is mostly celebrated on Hilcyon: the day that the Kinder and Breft split. But for him and his fellow priests, it was a day of mourning and a ritual to re-kindle their dedication to reunification.

The Kinder priesthood had an old secret society - it was as old as the priesthood itself. The first priest, Jyrl, had founded it. An increasing number of priests belonged to the society, and his entire order belonged.

The society was dedicated to the eventual reunification with the Breft, although in secret, they all called them by their proper name: Casitians. Since the events of 80 years ago and the introduction of people from Grier Nro, their home, the mission has been expanded to include the reunification of all humans.

From what Jorn knew, both from the fated mission 12 years ago and historical records from the visit of Grier Nro humans 80 years ago, humans from Grier Nro were now an essential part of the picture, as they almost represented a middle ground between Casitians and Kinder.

A singsong voice brought him back to the present. "May we heal the wound that bleeds us."

"May we," was said in unison by all of them.

"May we be instruments of the Exalted King."

"May we."

"May we heal the wound that hurts us."

"May we."

"May we hear the Exalted King's compassionate voice."

"May we."

The next part of the ritual was a reading from the book, "The Heart of the Car'j." It was one of the secret books, apparently written by a man who had been born on Grier Nro and one of his students thousands of years before.

The leader of the ritual, one of the high priests, opened the book and started to read.

"He who is compassionate reflects the will of Divine Love. She who shouts the names of the Divine for all to hear is blessed. They who sit in silence, with ears open, will hear the quiet voice of Love. She who gives what she has to her neighbor will be given more. He who lays down arms for the sake of peace is Peace. They who work for the good of all will be given All."

They all said, "It is so. So it is."

The priest closed the book, closed his eyes, and raised his arms toward the ceiling. "May the Exalted King guide us in our work. May He see us, may She bless us, may They know our hearts."

"It is so. So it is."

A kind of relief and strength washed over Jorn. He treasured these rituals so much. They all got up and embraced each other, and they would share a meal before many of them had to go on their way to other locales.

Various small conversations drifted around the large kitchen as they cooperatively prepared the meal. As he was chopping some vegetables for the stew, a priest he knew well came to assist him. Jrot had been a priest in the North Central region and had been forced to leave with all the other priests.

Jorn looked up and said, "Jrot, it is so good to see you. I'm sorry that you lost your hall."

Jrot started chopping. "It's good to see you too, Jorn. We knew it was a risk. We knew that they would find us a threat. But the movement is in very good hands there."

"Yes, I heard. I must admit I can't wait until they find out they had been undone by women!"

Jrot chuckled. "Women and priests—they mostly ignore us both, and that will be their undoing."

### New Orleans, New Earth

Johan looked over the last trove of data on his tablet. They were meeting again soon, and it would be a long meeting. Johan wanted to have a good, solid grasp of what the data said before going into the meeting. He wanted to make sure that some of his ideas would work in the way he hoped. The data was going to help that.

He'd talked with his mentor over the past few months about the satellite and the team. All of the team members agreed that his mentor would be a welcome addition, but she demurred, and Johan didn't really understand why, as this data was so valuable for her work. He did get permission to share all of it and the team's analysis with her, so that was good. He hoped she had some insights.

Based on what he was seeing, Msrotl was still in power and held it fairly well, particularly in the North Central and Capital regions. But the increased chatter about the priests was really interesting.

Also particularly interesting was their analysis of the usage of one particular English word included in the midwife training with no Kinder equivalent. It was "hypervolemia," which was apparently related to ectopic pregnancy. Johan had had to look that up.

Ke'lir and Dlen had said that the training on ectopic pregnancy had come last, and they had run out of time to translate some terms, so the English terms for those words remained in the training manuals. Over time, the usage of that word went from nonexistent in the year after the visit to over 100 this year.

This meant that the training Dlen and Ke'lir spearheaded during the visit had expanded further than they had expected. The listening devices could only hear one conversation out of tens of thousands. So, 100 uses in a year meant the word was likely used thousands of times.

Johan knew this meant that many more women's attitudes would be in the reform direction, as they had first-hand knowledge of how medical information and technology benefited them.

His basic premise was that a system built upon the region, village, and hamlet model they had lived with for several millennia was the most likely to stick, and a modification of the chief system based on election by men rather than single combat or appointment. Each hamlet would still have a fourth chief, each village a third, each precinct a second, and each region a first. The supreme chief would be chosen by the entire population of men. Other chief positions, those relating to specific functions by village, region, and planetwide, as was the current practice, would be by appointment by the supreme and first chiefs.

His proposed system included a parallel leadership structure for women who would be in charge of health, children, housing, and food policies. These two parallel systems, both hamlet, village, and region-based, would work for probably a generation or two, with increasing blending until a whole system, including everyone, could arise.

What Johan thought might be problematic was that the women would, in fact, be in leadership over the most important policies. In Dlen and Tyrin's estimation, this was the brilliant part because men in Kinder society thought mainly of those things as women's work anyway and had always had difficulty managing policy regarding them. So, ultimately, women would be in charge of the bulk of the work regarding unification early on, as the most important tasks would be theirs.

Johan didn't know how long it might take the men to realize this, and he did worry a little about what might happen when they did. Dlen thought it might take a couple of generations, and by then, the men would just laugh about it.

Johan's major challenge had been the priesthood. They had been working quietly for unification for a long time and were much more active presently. Unlike Earth and New Earth with its multitude of religions, and Casiti, with its many schools of faith, Hilcyon had only one unified religion. Dlen had said she suspected that different orders of priests had different cultures and theologies, but it was a much more unified system than either Casiti or Earth had.

On New Earth, following the model of Old Earth, some religions were tightly integrated with the government, some casually connected, and some set apart. On Hilcyon, the priesthood was definitely set apart from the government. But given how long the priesthood had been working toward unification, it seemed problematic to just leave them out of things.

Johan realized that a long conversation with Paul on this topic would be a good idea.

As Johan looked over the latest tracking data from the satellite, and noticed something... off. He wasn't sure exactly what it was, but something clearly was changing. He spent a few hours diving more deeply, and getting help from some algorithms he'd sicced on the data.

Mentions of Msrotl had slightly increased, but the words and phrases used were changing. Words translated as "absent", "missing", "illness" were popping up with a frequency that suggested something was definitely amiss.

Further, there seemed to be a lot more chaotic movement of people in the Capital region especially. A weird combination of less movement in some places and times, and much more movement in others. He saw an increase in movement between the Capital and North Central

Regions, particularly groups of people moving toward the capital from that region.

He sent a message to the team outlining his findings, and they would review the data at their meeting tomorrow. There wasn't anything they could really do—because the Consej had quite clearly prohibited anyone from proactively contacting Hilcyon in any way. But perhaps they could be more prepared.

# Chapter 7:
# Death, and Life

New Earth: September 2109
Hilcyon: Wtler 1212
Casiti: Paqn 806

*"The approaches different spiritual traditions have on what happens after death are quite varied—but many have in common a sense that what happens during life influences what happens after life in one way or another."*--Ja'len'da, "Spirits Alike"

### Capital Region, Hilcyon

Plir was with his mother in their kitchen, talking about next steps.

"Bkon has declared himself Supreme Chief. I am waiting—I've been talking with the priests and some other chiefs. We are gathering our people, and should be in a position to take over from him in a few days. But we want to do it without violence. I'm not sure how to accomplish that."

"I'm not sure you can, son. Bkon seems the kind of man to only go out swinging."

"I know, Ma. I'm not sure..."

At that moment, the man Plir knew as Msrotl's attache ran into their house shouting "Ylorp is fighting Bkon!"

Plir ran out of the kitchen. "What?"

"Ylorp came into the office. I overheard some of their conversation. He came to challenge Bkon. They are fighting."

"Let's go!"

Plir and the attache ran back toward the Capitol, which was still mostly deserted. They came to what had been his father's office, and they heard nothing. Plir tentatively opened the door, to see two men on the floor in a large pool of blood. They both looked quite dead.

Plir felt both a sense of sadness to see Ylorp lying on the floor and relief because Bkon was also dead, clearly at Ylorp's hands. But then followed a feeling of overwhelm. What was he going to do? How could this be handled? He was, far and away, the most obvious choice for someone to take over, yet not only did he not feel ready, he didn't want it. He didn't think it made any sense for him to take charge. And if he did, the next thing that would happen was he would be challenged.

He knew he needed help. Fast. He decided the priests would have to be the ones he called upon.

He turned toward the attache, who was still seemingly in shock.

"Remain here, please. Stay outside the door; I'm going to lock it. Recruit a guard if you need one, but don't let anyone break in, if at all possible. If you have to, lie and say Bkon cannot be disturbed right now. I will gather some help to deal with this."

The man nodded, clearly happy to be leaving the room. Plir found the key to the room in its expected place in the desk, and as they left, he locked the door, and pocketed the key.

His first trip was back to his mother to tell her the news, and get her to find women to deal with the bodies. He gave her the key.

"You are going to the priests?" she asked.

"Yes, Ma. And I'm going to tell Ylorp's wife."

"No. Let me. I know her, and she'll need a woman's care right now."

Plir nodded. "Alright. I don't know when I'll be back."

"Be careful, my son."

"Always, Ma."

They embraced, and he ran out of the house to the main temple in the Capital, where Jorn lived.

### Capital Region, Hilcyon

Jorn had been in the meeting with Glin and others inside the Capitol building, and Glin had asked him to go to the back Capitol gate, and check on the priests guarding the gate.

As he was there getting detailed information from the priests guarding the gate, a man approached him. He looked quite determined. He then recognized him as Rtlir, who had been the attache for Wlen.

260

"Rtlir! What are you doing here? You should go back home!"

He said, "Ah, Jorn. Good to see you. I need to tell you that I have the Breft communication device."

Jorn was amazed, and the other priests around him began to mutter and shuffle.

He quieted them, and said to them, "Stay here and keep guard."

He said to Rtlir, "Please, come with me."

He and Rtlir walked to the Supreme Chief's office. Jorn realized that the office would look quite different to Rtlir, as they had removed all of the memorabilia, and made it more like a temple space than a supreme chief's office. He gestured to the large table that now sat in the middle of the room.

Jorn said, "Your Holiness, this is Rtlir. I knew him as the attache for Wlen. He has the communications device!"

Glin said, "I am Glin, High Bishop, please, sit down." He pointed to others around the table.

"This Wren, Tyr, and Plir. Also, Mirn, the leader of the midwives in the Capital region, and Hjirn, also an important leader of women, and the wife of the man who killed Msrotl. Please, sit. Explain what you have."

He sat. "As you remember, Wlen, when he was supreme chief, contacted the Breft. That visit culminated in Msrotl's takeover. He contacted the Breft using this device..." he took the device out of his bag, and placed it on the table.

"All we need to do to activate it, is push this button." He pointed.

"What will happen?"

Rtlir said, "I'm not sure, but I do know that when we did it, some sort of artificial person answered, and relayed our message to the Breft. They responded some days later, when a group of them arrived here."

Glin looked at the device, and moved it toward him. Glin looked up. "Are we all agreed that contact with the Casitians at this moment in time is the right thing? Or do we want to wait?"

Mirn spoke first. "Father, we need more medical training and equipment. What they left with us when they were here last helped, but we still need more. There is still so much suffering in our hamlets and villages."

Plir said, "I know, Father, that your priests have done a good job of quelling the fighting. But who is going to be chief? I'm certainly not, even though my father wanted me to."

Rtlir said, "I do want to make sure we prevent happening what happened before. How can we do that?"

Tyr, who had a low, booming voice said, "Almost every order of the priesthood is outside of their temples, in the streets. We are keeping order, and assisting people as necessary. We can maintain a perimeter around the Capitol complex that no one can get through. What happened then will not happen again."

Jorn saw Rtlir nod. Everyone around the table looked at each other, and nodded. Glin pushed the button, and paused.

"Hello, I am a messaging system. Do you have a message?"

Glin said, "This is Father Glin Hrosta Knor, High Bishop of the priesthood. I am here with a group of leaders. We would like to invite the Casitians back to Hilcyon."

"Message relayed. There is an approximately 1.5-day delay before you will receive a message back."

"Thank you."

"You are welcome."

There was silence in the room. Plir then said to Rtlir, "Do you have a place to stay? If not, please accept my hospitality. My mother would love to meet you."

Rtlir nodded. "Thank you."

Jorn felt a sense of hope and wonder at the Exalted King's work.

### New Orleans, New Earth

An insistent alarm woke Paul from his slumber. He wondered what time it was. As he swam to the surface, he realized it was an emergency communication from the satellite team.

He got up, and grabbed his tablet, poking at the message reception icon.

"Team, this is Trysha. There has been an activation of the communications device. It followed several days of intensive activity, particularly in the Capital and North Central regions. The North Central region is still quite active, but the Capital is quiet.

The message is apparently from the High Bishop of the priesthood. He said he was with 'a group of leaders' and invites us back. Please come to the satellite offices as soon as possible."

Paul looked at the time. It was toward the end of second sleep period, which meant he'd have time to shower and have breakfast before leaving. He and Johan would be first, followed by Tyrin and Tvor, who were in Zwek, then last by Dlen and Ke'lir. It would take them a while to get to New Orleans. Paul knew they all would be staying at the Michaelson house in New Orleans.

Johan sent a message suggesting that he would pick up breakfast for both of them, which they could eat while meeting. Paul appreciated that, and sent a message agreeing.

As he was dressing, he realized that they absolutely would have to contact the Consej, and get permission to visit. Their satellite mission had not been received happily by the Consej. They grudgingly agreed that New Earth had the right to send the satellite on their own, but they wished they had asked permission first.

Paul knew that they couldn't really visit again without the Consej's blessing. He sent a message to Zrel, letting them know what was going on, and guidance for next steps.

He arrived in the conference room, seeing Trysha, Johan, Jake, and Marie, all drinking coffee and eating breakfast sandwiches. Johan pushed a sandwich toward Paul, and Trysha said, "Coffee and tea are over there."

Paul gathered his breakfast, then said, "So tell me about the activity before the call."

Jake said, "We definitely saw violence, although surprisingly not in the Capitol building itself. That seemed super quiet. It was isolated to a number of villages in the Capital and North Central region. I can't say for sure how many people died, but I'd guess in the hundreds."

Paul said, "I wonder why the Capitol itself was quiet."

Johan said, "Jake, if there was, say, only one or two fights inside the Capitol, we would not likely hear that, correct?"

Jake shook their head. "No, we wouldn't hear it. We've got I think one or at most two listening devices around the Capitol, but none of them are close to the center.

Johan said, "So I can imagine one or two fights that ended the rule of Msrotl, then created a vacuum that the priests and others entered."

A message indicator on Paul's tablet lit, and he saw a message from Ke'lir.

He said, "Ke'lir and Dlen are on their way—they should be here by 20th hour. Tvor and Tyrin told me they will be here by 12th hour, just in time for lunch."

Trysha said, "I've ordered catering for the next few days."

"Thank you, Trysha. We'll be pretty busy."

Johan asked, "Have you contacted Zrel?"

Paul nodded. "I have. He hasn't gotten back to me yet. I don't have any idea how the Consej will react to this—or, shall I say, the Casitian members of the Consej. The Terran and Kinder members will be more predictable.

### Hol'venif, Rel'toro, Casiti

Romer was busy working on a report about technology transfer of information about medical equipment to New Earth when their messaging system spoke, "A message from Zrel."

"Play, please."

"Hey, Ro'mer—I have news! The communications device on Hilcyon has been activated again! I've been tasked to be the liaison between the team and the Consej, and I'd like you along as a staff member for that. I'll get myself down to New Orleans later today. I'd suggest you book yourself a shuttle as soon as you can. In the meantime, I sent Paul a message we can send to those on Hilcyon to get more information.

"First, we need way more information about who exactly is in power on Hilcyon, how that happened, how they got the device, and who these leaders are. Of course, every single Kinder, and likely most of the Terran representatives will want to send a team down there as soon as possible. But the Casitians are gonna get their backs up unless we can argue that what happened last time won't happen again. I don't know that the Casitians, honestly, are ready for even the idea of unification."

The Casitian representatives to the Consej, including Holt'eron, were still staunchly against any intervention. Had they not been outvoted by the Kinder and Terran representatives, they would have invoked sanctions against the NEA for doing the project without their consent. As it was, technology trade between Casiti and New Earth, which Ro'mer was closely involved with, had become much more contentious since the satellite was launched.

It felt good to Ro'mer to be Zrel's assistant. They saw the next shuttle was in a few hours—he could easily make it. Before they made that shuttle they wanted to make one visit: to get a pulse on what the Caraj's perspective might be.

It was late fall, so the walk to Trel'or'li's house was colder than Ro'mer was quite expecting. They and Trel'or'li had a very tumultuous relationship. They had moved from close friends and allies, to almost enemies, and then back to a friendly companionship again. Trel'or'li was fiercely loyal to Casiti—almost to a fault, which had lead to much of the tumultuousness in their relationship. The other factor was that they'd spent a winter as companions when they were both young, and the bond they'd forged that winter seemed to be unwilling to loosen, even after all of these years.

Ro'mer knocked on Trel'or'li's door, and after a little while, a familiar tall figure opened the door.

"Ro'mer. So nice to see you!"

As in the tradition of coming winter, Trel'or'li let Ro'mer in first, keeping the cold out. They hugged once Ro'mer was safely inside.

"Here—let me take those coats. And sit. I just started a pot of yellis tea, and I know what this visit is about."

Trel'or'li was no longer a member of the Caraj, but she kept her ears wide open and connected to many people.

They sat at a small table near one of the windows. The table seemed to be an art piece of some sort. Trel'or'li was not the creative type—she was too analytical.

Ro'mer asked, "Trel'or'li, this is a gorgeous table! Where did you come by it?"

"My companion last winter was an amazing furniture artist. They made me all sorts of wonderful, creative things during our time last year."

"Oh, wonderful! I should look them up—I'd love to have some of this. I'll be leaving our family house in a year or so, once my youngest joins a youth house."

"Ah, time does fly, doesn't it?"

"Yes, it does. How have you been? I'm sorry I've been a terrible friend. It's been months since we've been in contact."

"I've been good. I've become one of the teachers in the Casitian data analysis unit. Fascinating and, honestly, fairly sobering work. But I'm enjoying it."

"Sobering?"

Trel'or'li gave Ro'mer one of those sidewise smiles, which generally meant a combination of concern and chagrin.

"We are stagnating, Ro'mer. When we went through that last round of working to eliminate non-Casitian influence from our lives and culture, we re-started a downward trend that began well before The Event. I have come to realize that we actually need New Earth and even Hilcyon if we are going to survive as a culture. And other leadership members here are coming to that conclusion."

"So many of us who are part of blended families have seen it. We feel made outsiders, yet can see the stagnation—we've been trying to fix that."

"I know, Ro'mer. I never completely apologized to you for my behavior after the failed mission. I was so wrong, and I can see that now. I'm sorry for the pain I caused you and your family."

She reached out to them, putting her hand on their arm.

"I know what was fueling that. You have such a fierce love of Casiti and its culture. I do, too, you know."

She smiled. "Yes, I know, beloved."

She sat back. "So. You are hunting for information about how the Caraj will respond to this new situation?"

They smiled. "Yes, indeed."

"Well, they haven't yet met to give their final determination, but my bet is that they will agree to... step back. To not interfere in the work that New Earth is doing. And also, to not contribute."

"Not contribute? Not send anyone?"

"Correct. I think it's about finding a common denominator. Some think that Terrans and Kinder are better suited to be a bridge to Hilcyon. Others don't want to risk any more Casitian lives on Hilcyon. So that means they aren't going to send anyone as part of the team."

Ro'mer nodded. "That makes some sense. I know that, in general, the loss of Casitian life in the disaster of the last mission was greatly felt."

"Honestly, Ro'mer, I would say that one big thread that is part of our decline is that we are cowardly. We've been cowardly for a very long time. I don't quite know when that happened; we were so brave in the beginning. And the loss of connection to the Galactic Community only fueled that cowardice."

Ro'mer had read their history. He might even argue that Casitian cowardice caused that disconnection in the first place, but he and Trel'or'li had had that argument, and he wasn't going to start it again today.

"Thank you for telling me this—it helps us. I'm on my way to New Earth in a few hours. I've become attached as staff to my cousin Zrel, who is acting as the liaison between the Caraj and the New Earth team."

"Ro'mer, I wish you and the team the best. I trust you to do the right thing. I look forward to seeing how this unfolds."

They talked for a while about life and plans for the coming winter. Ro'mer wouldn't have a companion this winter—they were still engaged in raising their children. But next winter, the idea of perhaps rekindling their connection to Trel'or'li was quite tempting.

As they watched the late, deep fall landscape go by on their way to the shuttle port, they pondered how this all might play out. The Casitians choosing to step back might actually be the best thing they could have hoped for.

## Zwek, New Earth

Kywl was basking in the sense of peace he found after weekly prayers. As he walked back to his monastic cell, he contemplated how the priests of New Earth had adopted a different schedule for the major and minor prayers. They had to compensate for the different day length, as well as the fact that New Earth had no moons. The cycles of prayers had been very geared toward the nine moons and their cycles. Instead, New Earth priests used the weeks and months of the Terran calendar.

As he walked by the main gathering area on his way to his cell, one of the other monks caught up to him.

"Kywl, there is an email message for you in the monastery's email system."

"Thank you, Bryce. I'll go check it."

Monks didn't have their own devices. Everyone used a central system, and personal messages were sent care of the monastery. He wondered who was contacting him. Perhaps it was Tyrin, with a babysitting request, something he enjoyed greatly.

As he sat down in front of the screen and read the message from Tvor, he was amazed and excited. It was about Hilcyon! The leader, Msrotl, had fallen, and a leadership group had formed, headed by the priesthood. Tvor requested his presence in New Orleans to be part of a large team that would hopefully go to Hilcyon.

He needed to get permission from his Abbott, but he didn't think it would be a problem.

A few days later, as he traveled on the night train from Zwek to New Orleans, he wondered what it would be like to be on Hilcyon and pray with the Monks there. He wondered whether he might be able to stay for a while.

## New Orleans, New Earth

Johan rubbed his eyes. He'd been up far too long looking at the data, and thinking about the North Central region. Last they'd heard, one of their leadership team, who had been born there and spent the bulk of the last 8 years there, was going to go back and see what he could do.

Johan was working on the report to the Consej, with the attendant list of recommendations. Yesterday, in their meeting, the team had decided they were going to request intervention, even with the uncertainty of the North Central region. Johan was crafting the argument that waiting for that region to work itself out was going to delay the process of re-working the governmental system on Hilcyon, possibly endangering the whole endeavor.

Johan knew that although Fril, the First Chief of the North Central region, was the only traditionalist First Chief in power, that didn't necessarily mean he would stay the only one. Traditionalist chiefs could use his example to challenge chiefs in regions that weren't close to the Capital region, like the South West, or Southern regions. Johan felt they needed to act quickly.

His argument was that unification was a process that would ultimately take hundreds of years, given the differences in culture and government. Terran and Casitian cultures were not as far apart as Casitian culture was from Kinder culture. It helped that there were Terran subcultures that resembled both Casitian and Kinder cultures. Terran culture was an essential bridge that made unification possible.

The Casitians tended to have a longer view than Terrans. Johan was reminding the Casitian members of the Consej that they only had 900 or so years to get this done. His argument was that any delay now might delay the process by a hundred years or more. He hoped this argument would sway them.

### New Orleans, New Earth

Dlen hadn't slept well. She was still dog-tired between the long shuttle to New Orleans and sleeping in a new bed. But for the first time in a long time, the actual reality that she would see home again struck her. She'd been convinced, finally, of it several years ago, but facing it so squarely as she was right now was jarring.

She was sitting along with the team that had worked together for a while, as well as Ro'mer and Zrel. Zrel was going to be their liaison to the Consej, and Ro'mer his assistant. Dlen understood that they couldn't go to Hilcyon without its permission. Zrel, however, seemed quite sure that they would get the permission.

Paul said, "OK, now that we are all finally here, let's outline what we know, and how we will frame our request to the Consej. Johan?"

Johan's role had grown. He had become the person who kept track of most of the leadership and governmental status on Hilcyon based on what they heard directly and what their surveillance data had gleaned. Dlen had been so impressed with this young man, and how he'd grown into the authority and responsibility as the project progressed.

Johan said, "We don't know all of the story, but somehow, Msrotl died. And when he died, one of his close aides assumed power by fiat. Then, someone challenged that aide and killed him, but he died in the process. This left a power vacuum that the priests quickly filled.

"The priests say they are in complete control of the Capital region. All other regions except the North Central region are currently in the hands of First Chiefs, who agree with the priests in wanting contact with us. The North Central region is currently governed by a traditionalist First Chief who rejects the leadership of the priests and, I think, by inference, does not wish contact with us.

"The priests have assembled a leadership team, including several priests, the son of Msrotl, who is a reformer, the previous attache for Wlen, Rtlir, who is known to us, and also two women, Hjrin and Mirn, also known to Dlen.

"From my perspective, this is somewhat expected, and also a perfect setup for us for a successful introduction. I don't quite know how to deal with the North Central region, though."

Zrel said, "The Casitian members of the Consej may suggest we wait until that has straightened itself out. Some Terran members might, too. But the messages I'm getting from the Casitians is that they are likely to allow this."

Paul asked, "Johan, what percentage of the population lives in the North Central region?"

"It's tiny. Less than 5%. It's far north, closer to the poles, the coldest region. They can only grow utility grasses and ulrik, whose hair they use for clothing."

Zrel said, "So it's hard to imagine that region will make that much of a difference."

Johan said, "Apparently, the priests were removed from the North Central region some time ago. We could ask what they think it would take to settle that region."

Dlen thought it important to talk to the women in that region. She said, "Can we ask Mirn about the midwives of that region? Johan, you said that the fighting in that region had stopped."

"Yes, it has, but I assumed that the reformers lost."

Dlen said, "That might not be the only interpretation of that data. The first chief there might be more isolated than we think."

Paul said, "We have a few other questions we'd like to ask. Why don't we send a message this morning, take a break for a while, and reconvene in a few hours?"

Everyone seemed to agree this was a good idea. Paul, Johan, and Trysha stayed behind to craft the message.

Ke'lir said, "I've always wanted to try that new Iranian restaurant - wanna go there for lunch?"

Dlen nodded. "Sounds wonderful. And nap after?"

Ke'lir put her arms around Dlen, which felt so good. "Yes, sounds perfect."

# Chapter 8:
# A New Vision

New Earth: September 2109
Hilcyon: Wtler 1212
Casiti: Paqn 806

*"Human beings have the same desires and the same weaknesses. But we all differ in how we go about getting those desires met, and our relationship to our weaknesses." Heart of the Carj, Eclogue 142*

### New Orleans, New Earth

Johan had not bothered to sleep during his day sleep period, and here he was, up at 47th hour, still working. He'd better get some sleep tonight, or he'd be a wreck in the morning.

But he couldn't let go of one big problem. The problem of Zwek. A few days back, he'd had a long conversation with Dlen and Tyrin because this had been nagging at him. One of the things he'd learned about in researching the Kinder on Hilcyon was their concept of honor. From Johan's perspective, their concept of honor was mostly about obedience. One gained honor by continued obedience to those above you. There wasn't any room for honor without obedience—something quite different than most traditional Terran concepts of honor.

Tyrin told him of her late husband, Mrin, who had been executed for contacting the Casitians. She explained that although obedience was the essence of honor, saving the lives of others was a highly revered act, and because of this, Mrin was respected but was not considered honorable.

Johan had a hard time wrapping his head around that one.

Tyrin also thought that Msrotl managed to still be honorable by forcing obedience and obfuscating his rise to power. Johan figured that the extremely brief rule of Msrotl's colleague could not have stood long in any event because of a profound lack of honor.

Zwek was a big problem of honor. It was a community founded by a large group of people who would be considered, by Hilcyon standards, to be completely without honor. How would the Kinder on Hilcyon receive Zwek? Neither Dlen nor Tyrin had a definitive answer, but they both were worried about it, which worried Johan.

He knew that people in Zwek had family on Hilcyon they wanted to reconnect with. And Johan wasn't sure that this desire would be returned. He realized he wasn't going to solve this tonight by himself. It would just have to emerge as it would, and they would all have to deal with it in time.

### New Orleans, New Earth

Paul entered his apartment and experienced wonderful, rich smells. Makena clearly was outdoing himself in cooking dinner tonight. He was exhausted—a day full of meetings, planning, and writing up his final report and recommendation to the Consej regarding the mission to Hilcyon.

He was hopeful. His last conversation with Ro'mer suggested they would have enough votes to make the mission a reality. The question might be in some of the details. The Casitians seemed to be thinking about taking a back seat for once—something that Paul found both troubling and promising. But in the end, the Casitians stepping back might be the best thing they could hope for.

He stepped into the kitchen and saw Makena stirring something on the stove.

"Smells heavenly. What's for dinner?"

Makena answered, "African groundnut stew."

"Wow, that sounds interesting!"

"It's a recipe that was passed down from my great-great-grandmother. It has been a long time since I've made it."

Paul smiled. "I'm so looking forward to trying it."

"It will be done in about 20 minutes."

Paul hear the telltale chime. His messaging system spoke, "Gil'ern has returned your message."

He said, "I need to address this. I'll be back in time for dinner."

He walked into his small office nook and sat at his desk.

"Play the message, please."

He looked to see Gil'ern's face, looking a little more aged than the last time he saw him.

"Paul, thank you for your message. I agree with you. I believe it is time for the Ja'lit school, especially here on Casiti, to get fully involved in the spiritual aspects of unification. I've sent you a document with the team I have in mind and a little bit about each of them and their connection to the school. You've met most of them. I also suggest that you act as what we call a 'bridge' between your team and this team, given your high role in our school. Because of your conflict of interest, you won't be able to join in consensus, but you'll be present for our deliberations."

That sounded to Paul a lot like what they called "ex-officio" role in an organization.

"Further, I had a very long conversation with Tor'elto. I don't know if you've met him yet. He's the newest Casitian representative to the Consej, and he's been a part of the school for about 2 years or so. He shifted from the You'l Selo school, which I think you know is one of the more isolationist Casitian schools, due to a change of heart. He is fully committed to unification, even at the risk of loss of life. That is something most Casitians find very difficult. So of the five Casitian representatives, at least one will vote to send another team right now."

Paul could feel a sense of relief. Based on what he'd known about the Casitian representatives, he didn't think any of them would vote to send a team based on the current realities. But knowing there was one meant that even if there were one or two Terran holdouts, they could still get a team approved.

"I'm assuming you can arrange housing for this team. Although two of the members are already on New Earth, relatively close to you, so you'll only need to find housing for four. I believe they can arrive on New Earth between 91 and 93 Paqn.

"I look forward to hearing more as things progress. And I also realize I still have not congratulated you on the growth of the Ja'lit school on New Earth. I am not entirely surprised—you are a gifted young man. It is gratifying to see Ja'len'da's work spreading so broadly. Blessings to you, my friend."

Paul felt warmth in his chest from Gil'ern's unexpected compliments. He had come so far from his confused days first discovering the school. Sometimes, it was hard to believe it completely.

He looked at his Casitian/New Earth calendar guide - the team would be here within 15 calendar days or 7 New Earth days from now. He had his work cut out for him.

### Zwek, New Earth

Tyrin looked into the audience in the auditorium, seeing many people she'd not met. They had organized a meeting with the entire Kinder leadership. At the front were the four Kinder representatives to the Consej, the human governmental council. When Tyrin first learned of this council, she was quite intrigued by it and had found a history of the Consej in Kinder language she could read.

It surprised her that the Casitians, and now increasingly Terrans, adopted governmental bodies of 12, something the Kinder didn't have. She was amazed to learn that the origin of that number was the number of fingers of the Tud'scla—the species the Kinder think of as their parents and mentors and Terrans and Casitians think of as their enslavers.

The four Kinder representatives to the council, one of whom was Tvor's uncle, were mostly older. One, Clen, was quite old, the son of one of the deserters. He had served on the council at a time when there were still Kinder from Hilcyon alive.

In the front row were the village leaders of Zwek. Zwek had been divided into villages and hamlets, and each hamlet voted on a representative to the village council. Each village voted on a representative to the Kinder Council. There were 18 villages in Zwek, each with about 20 hamlets. The rest of the audience were hamlet representatives, other functionaries, and leaders in the Zwek government.

Tyrin was used to the cultural differences by now, but at times, they still struck her after all these years. First, there were many women in the audience. A leadership conference of this sort on Hilcyon would only be attended by men. Second, even though virtually all men shaved their heads, many men here sported facial hair of one sort or another. In Zwek, it was considered disrespectful of Kinder culture for men to grow hair on their heads unless one was a priest. But somehow, facial hair had not been considered disrespectful. On Hilcyon, even a thin mustache or tiny goatee could get one disciplined.

She would make a note to tell Tvor, who had his own modest facial hair, to suggest the entire Kinder team remove all facial hair before they landed on Hilcyon.

Zrel, who was the current leader of the Kinder representatives, spoke loudly into his microphone. "Please, everyone, let's get started."

The room got quiet, with only a few murmurs.

Zrel said, "I want to thank you all for showing up today. This is an extremely important meeting. As I think all of you are aware, the Kinder on Hilcyon have again been in contact and are in a moment of enormous change. We are working to get the Consej to send a team to Hilcyon, and it is unclear when that might happen, but it is almost certain to happen in the next few weeks. We need to begin to talk about how we will be successfully connected to them, and they can become integrated into the human family."

"Of course, this means some big changes for us. We knew we have strayed from the Kinder cultural norms and learned from our more recent Kinder refugees how far that has been. We know we aren't going to go back—that isn't possible for so many reasons. The question remains for us is how to move forward."

"There are several items on our agenda today. First, we will talk about Kinder's representation of the Consej in the future.

"Second, we, on the whole Consej, need to communicate our thoughts about Zwek's responsibility for Kinder emigres from Hilcyon. We have no idea how many Kinder might want to immigrate to New Earth, and to Zwek in particular, but we need to begin thinking about that and how we might build and accommodate them.

"Third, we need to begin to gather a list of people who might be willing to live on Hilcyon for extended periods of time, to re-introduce ourselves, continue to learn more about the Kinder on Hilcyon, as well as provide technical assistance as we bring their technology levels on par with those on New Earth and Casiti."

"I'm handing the floor to Clen to talk about representation."

Clen was one of the oldest Kinder Tyrin had known. His 85th birthday had been a big event in Zwek earlier in the year. He had been one of the first children of the Kinder deserters, or refugees as many chose to call them. His mother had been a Terran woman who was born on Earth.

Clen started slowly. "We set up the initial Consej with four representatives for Kinder, knowing that we held space for the 'real' Kinder when they were ready to join us. Thinking about that now, it was, perhaps, a foolish idea. We have become our own culture: a mix of Kinder, Terran, and Casitian, and I'm sure we would be unrecognizable to Kinder from Hilcyon.

"I know we don't want to lose our representation - but we must. We MUST. We will continue to govern ourselves in Zwek, and if Kinder from Hilcyon join us here, they would need to understand that we have become different than them. And there will need to be a transition period. But these four seats need to be given as soon as possible to Kinder on Hilcyon. We must make this sacrifice now."

The room erupted, with people standing up and moving around. Tyrin heard several angry shouts. She saw many heads shaking. Somehow, she was surprised at this.

Zrel said loudly, "Please be quiet and sit down. We are willing to hear comments. But understand that the original charter for the Consej is clear: when Hilcyon joins us, those seats will be theirs. Four seats per planet. We have no choice."

The crowd quieted down some.

"We will take a few comments. Please enter the queue."

Tyrin looked down at her tablet to see if she knew anyone who wanted to speak. So far, she didn't. The first speaker's name was Jwel."

"Jwel, please speak."

Tyrin saw someone dressed in conservative Kinder women's clothing rise and start to speak.

"Hello, I am Jwel, granddaughter of Mbirn, a refugee. I understand the hesitance to lose our representation in the Consej. But I want to remind everyone that we govern ourselves in our daily lives. We are subject only to our own governance and, to some extent, the governance of the New Earth Agency. The Consej is designed to bring humanity together so that in 900 years, the Galactic Community will welcome us back with open arms. If we aren't willing to make this sacrifice, we are jeopardizing the future of humanity."

She sat down.

"Herrel, you are next."

Seeing Herrel, Tyrin remembered she'd met him. He was a schoolmate of Tvor's, and from what Tvor said, was always jealous of Tvor and his family connections. He had also been somewhat of a bully.

"Well, I'm not so worried about 900 years from now. We have created our own place here, and if we give up our representation, I think we'll just kind of disappear into Terran culture as some sort of weird offshoot like Dlejon. I'm not interested in that. Dlejon has absolutely no power in the human community, but we do. We can't give that up!"

Tyrin had heard about Dlejon. It was a community on the other side of the planet that had originally been designed to be a lot like Casiti, and had a large number of Casitian immigrants in the early years. Zwek wasn't actually all that much bigger than Dlejon—perhaps twice its size. She could completely understand why Herrel felt that way. She assumed that this was exactly what would happen. But she didn't think that was necessarily a terrible thing.

"Dvir, you're next."

Dvir stood and said, "So what if we become like Dlejon? We are a lot like Dlejon, really. I spent a lot of time there, and my aunt lives there. Autonomous, self-governing, but also part of New Earth. That's what we are, especially when Hilcyon re-joins us. And I don't think that's terrible."

The comments continued, some completely rejecting the idea of giving up the seats and others more willing to relinquish them. By the end, it seemed most people were getting used to this idea. The meeting then went on to talk about immigration and emigration, and several people volunteered to collaborate on committees to deal with details and logistics when the time arose.

Tyrin felt that this meeting had been a success. In general, there was reluctance to give up their representation, but also some recognition that it was exactly the right thing to do.

### Capital Region, Hilcyon

Plir was impatient. He didn't understand why the Casitians were asking all of these questions. But the group of them were doing their best to respond with all the information they had.

There was one order of priests who had been in residence in the North Central region - High Bishop Glin had asked them to find out whether they could possibly return and to see what the conditions were there. They were still waiting to hear back. And Mirn was trying to contact some midwives in the region for more information.

He was sitting in the living room of his house, now shared with Rtlir and another man who had been a reformer ally of Wlen years ago. His mother had moved to live with a group of women leaders, and he was grateful for her role in all of this.

He was thinking back on a conversation he had with her just yesterday.

"Ma, one thing I don't understand. When you learned Da was who he was, why did you stay with him?"

"Plir, for all of his brutality, he never was brutal to me. And given that I would have nowhere to go if I left him, I tolerated his actions on others. And I did my best to raise you with a different set of ideals. It was hard some days. Particularly the day I learned he'd killed so many to gain the Supreme Chief position. That was a sad day for me."

Plir remembered that day well. He had been a lot younger then, and what had happened was bewildering to him. He remembered when his father returned triumphantly to tell them they would be moving to better quarters because he had become Supreme Chief.

His mother had said, "Msrotl, what did you do?" in a tone that was cold and devoid of any approval. His father had dissembled. Plir didn't hear more details about that day until his mother told him several years later. She learned from other women whose husbands and sons had died. He'd stopped looking up to his father years before, but at that moment, he knew he had to be different than him.

Rtlir walked in, a grim look on his face.

"What's wrong?"

"Glin heard back from the priests from North Central. It's as I suspect. Fril is keeping an iron grip on the region. The priests can't re-enter. Fril has eliminated all reform-minded chiefs, including the one I used to work under. Mirn says that the women who have organized in that region aren't able to flex their authority now that Fril has clamped down, and I'm considering going back, to reconnect with them. I'd been working with them before I came back."

"Wouldn't that be dangerous? Especially since you're known to have worked for a reformer?"

"It might be. But I don't think we'll get help from the Casitians unless we can bring North Central along."

"Perhaps a group of us..."

"No, Plir. I have to go alone. I'll be back, I promise."

A week later, Plir was waiting for the leadership meeting to start, but it had been delayed because the High Priest had been called to an emergency meeting—something about the North Eastern Region.

Ever since Rtlir got back from his unsuccessful trip to the North Central region, they'd been getting news from several regions that the anti-reformers were gaining some pockets of power. He worried that it all might fall apart before the Casitians got here.

The first to arrive was Jorn, and close behind him was Glin and other priests. Rtlir followed, along with Mirn and Hjirn. They filtered into the room, and all sat down.

Glin said, "Let's start. I think we need to hear some reports. I'll start. The reformer chief of the North Eastern Region has been ousted by a competitor chief aligned with Fril. However, he has been unable to do much because our networks of priests and women are extremely strong there. He's isolated in his house and can't go anywhere. Both of the anti-reform second chiefs of the region have been likewise neutralized. Jorn?"

Jorn looked up from something he was reading. "All regions except for the North Central region are currently peaceful, but we don't know how long this will last. I'm confident we can keep the peace in the North Eastern region. I'm less confident of the Upper Highlands. They have been out of the loop for many reasons, and the priests there are the most conservative we have. They are reform-minded but less enthusiastic about unification. That said, it is a tiny population and not likely to spread anywhere."

Plir heard an insistent beeping sound coming from somewhere. Glin got up and took the communications device off the shelf it was on. Plir could see several lights blinking. As he recalled, this meant a message waiting.

Glin said, "We seem to have a message waiting. Let's play it, shall we, and finish our reports afterward."

He pushed a button, and a small 3-dimensional person who they had seen before appeared. Plir remembered learning that he was a direct descendant of someone born on Hilcyon, who had defected during the invasion of Nyet Grier Nro, and the brother of one of the men killed during Msrotl's takeover.

"Hello again," Tvor spoke in his strange accent. "We wanted to update you on our status and what to expect. We have gotten full authorization from our governments to send a large team to Hilcyon with the intention of creating a permanent establishment there. We should arrive in orbit in about 3 days. This team will largely be descendants of Grier Nro and Hilcyon. The Casitians have decided we are better suited to provide support and begin negotiations about unification."

Plir could see Rtlir raise his eyebrows.

"We will need housing for 15 to begin with, alongside five others who will be in liaison specifically with the priesthood. We will have with us the capacity to help build a new building which will eventually house a larger team dedicated to the support and unification effort."

### New Orleans, New Earth

"We're getting a rather larger ship than I expected," Paul said.

Ke'lir smiled, "Well when the Casitians make a decision, they make it big."

Dlen had been quite amazed at what had unfolded over the last few days. The team had been almost sure that the Casitian members of the Consej would vote against a team returning to Hilcyon. Instead, the newest member of the Consej had schooled the Casitians, and all but one agreed, with the entire Terran and Kinder contingents also agreeing, to send a team with a lot of resources and equipment for an extended trip. The ship was easily ten times the size of the ship they'd gone with last time.

Paul, Makena, Dlen, and Ke'lir sat in an informal Mexican restaurant in New Orleans, sipping Margaritas and discussing the trip that would start tomorrow.

Dlen said, "I'm happy we'll have a large team. And the Ja'lit school team is amazing."

Paul said, "I know, aren't they?" I've been really enjoying being a part of their work. And I think they will be a fantastic connection to the Kinder priesthood."

Ke'lir said, "And I'm really glad the Casitians are letting the Terrans and Kinder take the lead on this. Them not choosing to send a defense team is kind of amazing."

Paul said, "I think they wanted to reduce the risk to Casitian life this time around. And also, I think they realized that we, Terrans, plus our New Earth Kinder, were the best interfaces for this. Ro'mer told me that the growing consensus among Casitians right now is to take a back seat to all of this and let it play out. To let us, the Terrans in particular, lead the effort."

Ke'lir said, "It kinda makes sense, really. I think perhaps they realize that their decision to pull support helped to create the conditions of the disaster last time. And if they are in the background, they will always be in the position of saying 'told you so' if things go awry."

Dlen said, "I don't think things will this time. Something tells me this is really the right moment."

Paul said, "But there are going to be some bumps. We just need to be ready for them."

Ke'lir was worried in particular about how they would handle the more conservative regions and wanted support and help but had no interest in a long-term commitment to communication with them, nor real unification. The priesthood had been working toward that end for hundreds of years, but it was a very new idea to most people on Hilcyon.

A few days later, the whole team was in the conference room. Johan, Dlen, Tvor, Kywl, and Tyrin were leading a team discussion about how to describe to the Kinder on Hilcyon the difference between a long-term commitment to communication and support and "unification": the idea of shared governance by the Consej.

After Johan's presentation on his final tweaks to the proposed governance structures on Hilcyon, Tyrin noticed that his only comment at the end was that he still didn't feel comfortable proposing how to bring those Kinder into human government.

It was Tvor's turn to give his comments.

"It's going to be a challenge for the New Earth Kinder to give up their representation, but there is now a consensus that we must."

Dlen knew this was a sore spot for Tvor.

She turned to Tyrin and said quietly, "One of the things that was hardest for me to get used to in Zwek was how, well, free I felt. The strictures of our culture are so deep. I don't know what it will be like for people on Hilcyon even to begin to think about giving them up. And, they will look at the New Earth Kinder as unrecognizable."

Everyone around the room nodded.

Johan added, "And it doesn't help that all of the Kinder on New Earth are descendants of deserters. They might well be considered traitors. I don't know what the political effect of that might be. I don't know the extent to which they know about how many Kinder deserted and why. This part has been worrying me for a long time."

That led to a moment of quiet as people realized the ramifications of that reality.

Kywl said, "The priests there have been thinking and working on unification for so long. I think our priesthood and theirs can work together to mitigate some of the issues here."

Johan said, "Another question is how we will handle potential immigrants. Once people on Hilcyon discover how warm and hospitable New Earth is, I'd be astonished if there wasn't a rush to move here."

Paul said, "Thankfully, that won't be our job. The nitty gritty, or even bigger picture of unification, is far beyond the jurisdiction of our team. Our job is to gather all the information we can, get the primary players in the room together, and then let the Consej handle it. Let's start by finding out as best we can what the Kinder on Hilcyon need and want."

# Chapter 9:
# Landing

New Earth: October 2109
Hilcyon: Wtler 1212
Casiti: Paqn 806

*"In all of my studies of human spiritual traditions on Earth, the similarities to the traditions, the kinds of questions they are trying to answer, dwarfs the differences."--Ja'len'da, "Spirits Alike"*

### Capital Region, Hilcyon

Plir watched alongside the other leaders as the shuttle landed in the middle of the square. The priests had done a remarkable job of keeping people away from this part of the capital. There was a lot of curiosity about this new team and what would happen.

One of the things he felt was real relief. He had felt uncomfortable taking part in the leadership team and was glad to become just a small part of this process. His mother teased him. She felt he was too reticent to bring his ideas forward. He just felt he was too young and not sure leadership was what he wanted.

As the door to the shuttle opened, he saw people file out and move forward toward them. They had been told the team would be large, twenty in all. Five would be working directly with the priests, and fifteen would be working with the rest of them.

Glin, who had become their de facto leader, stepped forward. He was greeted by a tall lighter-skinned man with a full head of brown, curly hair.

Glin said, "Hello, I am Glin, High Bishop of the priesthood."

The man said something Plir didn't understand, then from somewhere came, "I am Paul, leader of this liaison team. I am from Nytt Grier Nro. I would like to introduce you to Tvor, a descendant of Kinder on Nytt Grier Nro."

Plir understood they had some sort of translation device. He looked at Tvor, whose skin tone was closer to that of his own and completely bald and clean-shaven, as were at least 5 of the other members of their team. He also noticed two men in priestly garb.

He said in the accent he recognized from the previous visit, "It is an honor to meet you, High Bishop. I am so glad you have invited us here to support you."

Glin said, "I'm sure you'd all like to get settled. We have a large welcome dinner planned. Tomorrow, we'll start our meetings. The priesthood liaison team can come with me. The rest of you, please follow Plir, who will get you settled."

Tvor and Paul nodded. Glin started in the direction of the main temple and monastery, about a 10-minute walk from the Capitol buildings.

Plir said, "Follow me, please."

The Capitol building had a large wing that had been used for housing government staff but had fallen out of use during the rule of Msrotl, who purged career staff members, replacing them with people beholden to him. Those people largely were chiefs and already had housing elsewhere.

Plir's mother and other women had been busy making it more hospitable, and there was plenty of room for this group. He led them into the Capitol building, then down hallways to the north wing of the building. He met three of the women who had been working with his mother at the entrance to the wing.

"There are more than twenty rooms and suites in this wing on two floors. Some are suitable for singles, and others are small suites for couples. The suites have their own bathrooms. For the single rooms, there are bathrooms here and at the far end of the hall on both floors. There is also a large living area over here, also on both floors. We've left snacks and drinks for you in both living areas."

Tvor said, "Thank you so much, Plir and the rest of you, for your hospitality. I think we can wander around and sort ourselves out."

Plir nodded. "This is Hwen, Jryb, and Cirn. They will stick around and will be happy to answer any questions or get anything you need. We'll convene for dinner at sunset."

Paul and Tvor nodded to the women in thanks, then nodded to him. Plir decided this would be a good time to take his leave. He smiled, turned, and walked toward home. It would be good to get a rest before dinner.

Before he could leave the hallway, a slim man, not much older than he, with dark skin and abundant facial hair, stopped him and spoke haltingly with an accent.

"Hi, Plir, I'm Johan. Do you mind if I ask you a couple of questions? It can be now, or it can wait until later."

Although he wanted to rest, something about this man intrigued him.

"Now is fine. Do you..."

"Can I walk with you?"

Plir hesitated, then realized there really was no problem with it.

"Sure. I'm on my way home..."

"I'll walk you there, then walk back. It would be good to... ugh, sorry, I'm still not quite... fluent. We have a saying, 'stretch my legs,' but I can't think of a way to say that exactly in Kinder."

"I would say it will be good to be out in the air."

"That works. Shall we?"

Johan followed Plir down the stairs and out the door.

Johan asked, "I have a particular question you might give me insight into."

"Go ahead." Plir was curious. Johan seemed to be in some tension about whatever he had on his mind.

"What exactly happened to your father? When we asked for more information, you told us the broad outlines, but we were more focused on the group who had come into leadership and the status of some of the other regions rather than the events that led up to that."

"Well, my Da got really sick and died. His attache, a man with a brutal reputation, took his place by fiat. A different man, Ylorp, challenged him that same day and killed him, but also died in the process. I discovered their bodies and called in the priests."

"Ylorp - was that Hril's husband?"

"Yes. He had been working underground for years. He and I knew each other. We both worked with Jorn, the priest."

"Thank you for this information. It's really helpful."

"Why?"

"First, my specialty is political science. I am interested in how power can be wielded and shared in societies. And one of the things that is interesting about Hilcyon is how the chief system works, and in this case, broke down."

"From my perspective, Wlen was brave and honorable, my father cowardly and dishonorable. But so many people thought my father had honor because he demanded obedience and got it."

"The honor thing is important, isn't it?"

"Yes, it is, although I don't understand why so many people gave my father obedience, given how he took control."

As they walked, they talked about honor, what it was, and how it was different for Johan, and those from Casiti. They also talked about other things. Talking with Johan was easy, even when he struggled with the language. Finally, when they arrived at Plir's home, his mother unexpectedly opened the door.

"Plir, welcome home! Who is this?"

"Ma, this is Johan. He's one of the team from Nyet Grier Nro."

"Welcome, Johan. Would you like a snack?"

"Thank you, ma'am, but no. I should stop bothering Plir and get back to my team. Thank you so much, Plir, for all the information."

Johan's smile warmed Plir's heart.

"You are welcome. See you at dinner!"

As Johan walked away, Plir turned towards his mother, who had a broad smile on her face.

"He seems like a good man, doesn't he?"

Plir nodded.

### Capital Region, Hilcyon

One of the first things Tyrin noticed was the gaping space where the Supreme Chief's residence used to be. Seeing it was odd, a stark reminder of the events that led to her exile from her home.

She was both joyful and worried about being back home. She had no idea how this process would play out, and she knew that if she wanted to stay on Hilcyon, which was her desire, they needed to be successful.

Tvor and Paul were both confident, as was Dlen, but she still wasn't convinced this would be entirely smooth. But she certainly hoped it would be. There was a lot of complexity, and they still weren't sure what exactly the Kinder leadership wanted.

As they walked to the Capitol, she noticed how few people were about—it was almost eerie. But she imagined the priesthood had been good at keeping people away from the Capital square.

She and Tvor found a lovely little suite right away. It was sweet. A small bedroom with a standard-sized Kinder couple bed, smaller than their generous bed at home, was behind a nice living area with a few comfortable chairs and a table. Off to the side was a bathroom. Tyrin thought that changes had been made to this room. She suspected extra chairs and that a small kitchen had been removed.

As she and Tvor were unpacking in the bedroom, she heard a "Hello!" coming from the entry. She walked out to see Dlen poking her head inside.

"Dlen, did you and Ke'lir find a nice suite?"

"Yes, we did, just down the hall. It looks a lot like this one. They added furniture, didn't they?"

Tyrin laughed. "You caught that, too?"

Dlen smiled. "I'm not surprised. When I helped to set up the quarters in the Supreme Chief's residence, we also added a lot of furniture. Now we really know that makes sense."

Tyrin nodded. "How are you feeling?"

Dlen said, "Strange. It was strange to see that there was no evidence of the old Supreme Chief's residence except its absence. It had been such a big building. And it feels strange to be in a familiar climate, even though it's much less comfortable. I did remember to pack warm clothing!"

"I noticed you switched back to our traditional dress." Tyrin had tried wearing different kinds of New Earth clothing, like pants or even skirts, but generally enjoyed the traditional Kinder women's loose, long bltynon.

"I did. I felt we needed to be gentle in our introductions. Just like the Kinder men being clean-shaven. But I will miss wearing pants."

Tyrin smiled.

Dlen said, "How are you doing?"

"I'm happy to be home, but I'm also nervous. I want to stay, as does Tvor, but we both know that this process has to be successful for that to happen."

"Yes, I understand."

"You aren't coming back to stay, are you?"

"No. First, Ke'lir doesn't want to live here—no surprise there. I don't think it's wise for us as a couple to live here. Also, I have come to love New Earth. It's home to me now."

Tyrin nodded. "That makes sense to me."

Dlen said, "I think a small nap is in order before dinner. I think it's going to be a very busy few days."

### Capital Region, Hilcyon

Jorn was walking behind the small team walking to the main temple and monastery. They had set aside five cells close together, which required moving some grumpy monks who had had those cells for years. Jorn's own cell was on the same hallway, and he was acting as the hospitality coordinator. Except for the welcome dinner, the team would take their meals with the priests.

He was fascinated by the makeup of this team. Apparently, two of them were Kinder priests from Nytt Grier Nro, who had been trained by people who had been trained by priests who had, for some reason, been part of the invasion force and then deserted. Jorn so wanted to hear their stories. The other three were part of a religious order started by the Casitians but had spread to Nytt Grier Nro and had even spread to the Kinder there. One of these three was of Kinder origin, and one was Casitian.

They all had requested to be allowed to partake in some of the rituals of the priesthood. Glin, Jorn, and others had spent a lot of time determining which ones to finally conclude that they should allow their guests to choose. They could go to as many as they wanted to.

First moon prayers would happen in two days. Second moon prayers in 5 days. The conjunction feast, when the first and second moon were in the sky with the fifth and eighth, would happen in about 10 days. And, of course, each day has the six praying hours. Jorn wondered how many of this team would choose to pray at deep night.

They arrived at the monastery, and Jorn gave them a cursory tour, showing them places they would get to know intimately during their visit. They walked up the stairs to the hallway with the cells assigned to their guests.

Jorn said, "These five cells on the right here have been assigned to you. They are likely smaller and simpler quarters than you are used to, but we hope they are adequate. There are 12th-hour prayers quite soon. A bell will ring. I'll meet you in the hall, and we can go to the temple from there.

Their guests nodded and found their way to the empty cells. Later, when they gathered in the hallway for 12th-hour prayers, Jorn noticed a sense of quiet curiosity from the group.

He said, "I'm happy to answer any questions you have about the service after it's over. Please follow me."

He led them down to the temple, where monks were collecting for the prayers. 12th-hour prayers during the Second full moon rise were public, but given that the Second moon was not full, the temple only had priests in attendance.

He led the group to some benches on one side of the temple, and they all sat. He let the chanting and prayers wash over him. Usually, he helped officiate these prayers, but he had been relieved of that duty because he was hosting these guests. He was grateful for that; it allowed him to be fully present in the prayers.

After the service was over and the other monks exited the temple, he turned toward his guests.

"Do you have any questions?"

One, named Kywl, who was one of the priests in the Kinder community on Nytt Grier Nro, asked, "I'm struck by one difference in this prayer compared to the one we have. There is a verse chanted from Secrets, Utle verse 4. We have always chanted from verse 6."

"Many orders do chant from verse 6. I believe our order switched to verse 4 about a hundred years ago. Do you know which order your predecessors came from?"

"I believe it was a mix of orders. I don't know the details. It might be recorded somewhere. Verse 4 is so much more... compassionate, I think. Less focused on obedience."

Jorn nodded. "Our order is considered the most focused on the compassion, forgiveness, and love of the Exalted King. Some orders have disdain for our approach."

Another man, Brian, asked, "I would love to have a conversation with you about the history of your faith. Monotheism didn't develop on Earth until a thousand years after Capture."

Jorn said, "I'm actually not the expert. That person is in another order. But I'm sure I can arrange a meeting for you to talk. He's very interested in the religions of Grier Nro. But the short answer is that our faith developed a hundred years or so after we settled on Hilcyon. The priesthood really started before the faith was fully developed. We depended on our parent species for understanding."

He sensed a bit of tension arising from these men but didn't understand it. Perhaps, at some point, they would have a deeper conversation.

"Well, it's time for us to return to the Capitol for the welcome dinner."

### Capital Region, Hilcyon

Johan was castigating himself for his feelings. Something about Plir was tugging at his heart, but Johan kept reminding himself that one, Plir was Kinder and not Terran, and two, who knew how he would react to hearing that Johan was born a woman. Johan didn't even know whether Kinder even acknowledged the attraction between members of the same gender.

He tried to push Plir out of his head and into the tasks ahead. He had transcribed the conversation with Plir as much as possible in his notes. He felt good at having the completed information about the process of transfer of power to the current leadership team.

He'd gotten a little more information from Plir about issues of honor and didn't feel like their honor problem would go away anytime soon.

He heard Paul's voice, "Time for dinner!"

He got up, left his room, and walked into the hallway just as Ke'lir and Dlen were leaving their room.

Dlen said, "Hi Johan. How has your afternoon been?"

"Good. I spent time with Plir and got more information about what happened with this father."

Ke'lir said, "Oh, good."

"And we talked a lot about honor. It's still gonna be a sticking point."

Dlen said, "Yes. It is. I've been thinking a lot about it, too. We will have to figure out a way to address it somehow. We can't just try and sweep it under the rug. I think that might have been part of what happened last time."

Plir was surprised. "I thought no one here had really learned about the origin of the Kinder on New Earth."

"When you raised the issue at the last meeting, I remembered a conversation I overheard with my father and other chiefs. They had talked about Glor's lack of honor because of his ancestors. I didn't have a context then, but I understand that conversation now."

Johan saw the pieces of the puzzle fit.

"Perhaps Msrotl, thinking about Glor's lack of honor, felt that using explosives wasn't any worse."

"Yes, that's my thought now."

They walked downstairs and down a few hallways, following others, until they reached a large room, now specially arranged with many tables, all at the same level.

Ke'lir said, "Ah, no dias this time."

Dlen turned toward her. "I think that's quite wise of them."

Mirn, who was one of two women on the leadership team, walked toward them.

"Welcome! We have decided to split up your team—so you'll be sitting at different tables. Ke'lir, please sit over there, Dlen, over here, and Johan, that table on the far side."

Johan nodded, realizing that Mirn had no idea Ke'lir and Dlen were a couple. It probably was best, Johan realized.

Paul let the conversations at the table drift in and out of his consciousness. He was most engaged in a set of problems in his head. He had been gratified by the welcome they had received so far, and he was generally fairly optimistic about the future.

But as he had observed the people he'd interacted with so far, and his memories of the previous trip, he was, again, struck by how different their cultures were. And culture would likely be a sticking point, and present all sorts of issues in the future. And the honor question bothered Paul ever since he heard Johan talk about it.

He made himself leave his brain behind and focus on what people at the table were talking about. Directly on his left was Glin, who was a hearty eater. On his right was Mirn, one of the midwives Dlen had trained. Directly across from him was Rtlir, Wlen's old attache and a key leadership team member. Rtlir and Plir were the two men who weren't priests who were part of the core leadership.

Glin said, "I never get to eat this well at the monastery. This is wonderful food!"

Mirn laughed. "Glin, you need some women priests!"

Glin looked at Mirn with what seemed to Paul to be mirth in his eyes.

"We're working on that! This dinner might well smooth the way."

Everyone laughed.

Glin said, "There are several orders, including my own, that have been considering allowing women to be priests."

Paul said, "How popular is that?"

"It's a mix. Some priests are afraid that would create too much temptation since priests are celibate. But from my perspective, I don't think that would be the case. I think there is temptation enough. I think women would be a welcome addition. A new perspective, one that would be quite useful, I think."

Paul asked, "Would that change the attitude of the chiefs toward you?"

Glin laughed. "There is nothing we can do to make the chiefs think *less* of us."

Even though Glin thought it funny, Paul had to think about it. It was an important piece of the complex puzzle of power they were trying to put together.

### Hol'venif, Rel'toro, Casiti

Ro'mer was monitoring the daily reports the team on Hilcyon was sending, and all seemed like it was going well. The Casitians had, in choosing to step back, entered what seemed to be a more relaxed phase. It was as if they had relinquished their leadership role.

In fact, Ro'mer could see evidence of this everywhere. The technology transfer process was going more smoothly than it had in years. They were again allowing some limited immigration, particularly to Jul'when and Loc'de'her, areas already populated with many Terrans. It was still almost impossible to immigrate to Rel'toro, but Ro'mer could see that changing soon.

He'd even heard of some Casitians figuring out how to prepare for visitors from Hilcyon! They reflected on their conversation with Tre'lor'li, where she talked about the stagnation of the Casitian culture. It seemed that perhaps this relaxed stance and the ability to be in dialogue with other cultures had a good effect.

Zrel had asked them to write an outline for the process of technology transfer to Hilcyon. It seemed pretty likely, given Ro'mer's experience, that they would be tasked with overseeing that process. Health care and agriculture were first, communications next, and then after that, whatever priorities the Kinder had. They knew the Kinder had a dearth of personal luxury items—things most Terrans, and even Casitians took for granted. They wondered how long it would take for them to decide that was something they wanted.

Ro'mer decided it was time for them to take a break. They also remembered it was their turn to check in with Gor'eli, one of the elders in the house. They enjoyed their time with Gor'eli. Gor'eli was very old, more than 40 Casitian years old. Even though Casitians were generally relatively long-lived, compared to Terrans, very few Casitians made it past 40.

They walked toward the elder hallway and knocked on Gor'eli's door.

They heard a quiet "Come in."

They opened the door and saw Gor'eli sitting in her chair with a tablet in her hand. She was always reading one thing or another.

"Gor'eli, how are you today?"

Her halting, quiet voice said, "I'm... good today, Ro'mer. You?"

"I'm alright. Busy with work."

"Yes, yes... I hear you are working on... what is it? Getting technology to the Za'... no, to the Kinder?"

Ro'mer knew that Gor'eli was old enough that her habit would be to call the Kinder the old Casitian name for them. Za'aref, or "accursed." There had been an active campaign, really since the time of Ja'lend'a, but more urgent now, to eliminate that word from their vocabulary.

"Yes. I'm responsible for the overall plan. It's fairly daunting."

"I... can imagine."

Ro'mer sat in the chair across from Gor'eli.

She said, "How... how are the children?"

"Growing fast! It's amazing. The eldest just entered a youth house. I haven't heard from him in a while, but I expect he's having a good time. My youngest is doing well. They are especially enjoying their art lessons."

"Ah... will we have a new... artist in the family?"

"Perhaps, Gor'eli. We'll see how it unfolds."

"Well... tell them it's been a long time... since they visited me. I'd... I'd love to see them."

"I'll definitely tell them."

Ro'mer spent time with Gor'eli, hearing stories, telling her about their work, and answering her questions about the Kinder. At one point, she started to nod off, so they took their leave, remembering the request to include Terran chocolate pudding in their dinner that evening.

# Chapter 10:
# Upending

New Earth: October 2109
Hilcyon: Wtler 1212
Casiti: Paqn 806

*"Killing to gain and hold power is ultimately fruitless. If you kill to gain a position, you must be willing to kill to keep it. The Exalted King does not demand death; humans do." Heart of Car'j, Ecologue 445*

Plir had just spent the day running from village to village, making sure each village chief in the capital region would make it to the meeting tomorrow.

He had also been tasked to track how many regional First Chiefs would make it and had been surprised to get messages suggesting that all of them would be present.

That was satisfying to Plir. He knew that there would likely be conflict and controversy, but he felt that the fact they would all be in the same room together meant progress, and he hoped that they could come to some sort of agreement.

He was on his way back to the Capital to pick up Johan, who had accepted his offer for an invitation to dinner cooked by his Ma. The few times his Ma had met Johan, she had really taken to him and was happy to be cooking for him.

He saw Johan in a hallway, talking animatedly with the team leader, Paul. Johan turned when he saw Plir approaching and smiled. Plir's heart did a little flip when he saw the smile.

"Plir, hello. Paul and I were just talking about the meeting tomorrow. Is it true? Even Flir is coming?"

Plir nodded. "Yes. Every First Chief will be there. I'm a little surprised but certainly happy this is happening."

Johan said, "I'm wondering how much they've been in contact with each other. My theory is they are planning something."

"Really? What could they be planning?"

"I'm not sure, Plir. But I sense something is going on."

Paul nodded. "Yes, Plir, I agree with Johan here. There is going to be something we don't expect."

Plir asked, "What can we do to plan for it?"

Johan said, "I'm not sure we can. We just have to be prepared for a... in English, we would say 'curve ball,' but you don't have an equivalent idiom. What's your idiom for something unexpected that someone can do?"

"The closest I can think of is 'wild challenge'."

Johan nods. "That works."

Plir said, "Ma probably has dinner waiting. Johan, are you ready?"

Plir saw Johan look at Paul and saw a broad smile on Paul's face. Plir felt a little exposed in that moment.

"Yes, Plir, let's go."

Johan then said three words to Paul, which he could not understand. Plir didn't have one of those translators most of the team had in their ear, so he couldn't understand when they spoke the Terran language. He wondered what Johan had said.

As they walked toward his house, Johan seemed pensive.

But then, he said, "Plir, I have something I need to tell you. I feel like we've become friends, and it seems to me this is something you should know. I..."

Plir stopped walking and turned toward Johan. "I know your culture is different than mine, Johan. But I can't imagine you could tell me something about yourself that I would reject."

"I appreciate that, Plir, but... Alright, let me just get it out. I wasn't born a boy, Plir."

Plir was surprised, but he realized he was more curious than disturbed.

"You look like a man. How did that happen?"

"I realized some years ago that I wasn't a girl. So, I changed my sex. This is something we can do."

Plir had to admit to wondering what was involved in that change. But it didn't really matter all that much to him. He liked the Johan that existed right now, and how Johan got that was interesting to him, but it didn't bother him.

"Sometime, when we have more time, I'd like to hear more about what was involved, but it doesn't bother me, or make me like you any less. We have some people here who do that. Girls who grow up to be men and even become chiefs. Boys who grow up to take women's roles."

Plir heard Johan's sigh of relief.

"Someday, I'd like to hear more about those people if you are willing to tell me about them."

Plir smiled. "I'll introduce you to one of the people I know. He was a part of the resistance."

It had felt like a long day for Kwyl. He had spent much of it with the priests, preparing for tomorrow's meeting. He spent the rest of the time strategizing with the Terran team. Finally, after the last meal, he was settled down in his cell.

He had been given a copy of one of the primary prayer books, and he had been interested in seeing what differences there were between the books he had been working with and trained with in Zwek. Clearly, the priests who had been conscripted and ended up on New Earth had copies of some of the books, but not all of them. And printed editions of the Zwek versions had some subtle, and some dramatic differences from the ones used by this order.

He wished he knew how much of this was that different orders had different versions and how much of it was what the New Earth Kinder priests had changed.

He heard a knock at his door.

"Yes, come in."

The door opened, and Kwyl saw Jorn's head with his tousled hair peek in.

"Hi, Jorn, please enter."

Kwyl moved from his chair to his cot, allowing Jorn to sit.

"Kwyl, I'm sorry to bother you..."

"It's no bother, Jorn. How can I help you?"

"I was going over the final seating arrangements with Glin, Paul, and Johan. They feel strongly that all five of you here should sit with the priests and not with the Terran team up front."

"Yes, I agree with that. Do you have an issue with it?"

"No, not really, and I understand the signal it is meant to send to the chiefs. I think Glin underestimates the signal it will send to the priesthood."

Kwyl said, "I don't know that I quite understand."

"If the five of you sit with us, this would signal to the priesthood that Glin and other priestly leaders consider you a part of our priesthood."

"Oh." Kwyl pondered this. "I see."

"I do know that Glin is just about ready to bless the monks on Nyet Greir Nro as an order."

"He is? I hadn't heard that!"

"He told me so. He's not quite ready to make it public, though."

"I see. But having us sit with you would suggest it to the priesthood."

"Exactly. I just wanted you to be prepared—you might hear from some priests."

"Thank you, Jorn. I can see how this could create ripples in the priesthood."

"It *will* create ripples. I just hope we can control them."

### Capital Region, Hilcyon

Tyrin looked around the large room that had been set up for this meeting of many leaders from all over Hilcyon. This had taken a monumental effort and many hours of messages and movement from region to region to make this happen.

All of the First Chiefs of each region had decided to be present, even Fril, the chief of the North Central region, which was surprising, as it had been clear that he was bitterly opposed to the presence of the team from New Earth.

Tyrin had heard from Tvor that when this chief had heard that the only Casitian member of the team was one of what he considered the "priesthood," he had relented, and, he said, came primarily out of curiosity, although both Johan and Tvor thought there were some other motivations. The team knew he wouldn't be interested in a long-term connection to the other planets and definitely not unification.

Alongside the chiefs were priest representatives, as well as representatives from the midwives from the regions.

Strategically, they had placed the chiefs all in the front of the room and included only the male non-priesthood members of the New Earth leadership, including Plir, Rtlir, Paul, Tvor, and Johan at the front. She, Dlen, Mirn, and Hjirn were on one side apart, and the priests were apart on the other side. She knew that the men and chiefs would be the main event at this meeting.

Rtlir, who had been tasked with leading this meeting since he was the eldest and closest to a chief in the leadership team, had, rose and motioned to the crowd to be quiet.

"Welcome, chiefs of Hilcyon! I am Rtlir, past attache to Supreme Chief Wlen, the last Kinder chief chosen in the traditional way."

There was a murmur in the audience, but it quickly died down.

"We are here today to talk about the future of Hilcyon. There are many questions to answer and many topics to consider. Many of you have already met and talked with Paul, the team leader from New Earth."

Rtlir pointed to Paul, who rose.

"This is a momentous time in your history. We are here to support you, provide technology and resources, and help you through this unstable time. As Terrans, we have a somewhat different perspective than the Casitians and will be the ones most involved. The Casitians have decided to let us lead."

There were again some murmurs and conversation in the audience.

"We've heard from many first and second chiefs already—there are differing opinions as to how much connection you are interested in with Terrans and Casitians. We're here to help you figure that out."

Someone rose and said, "I have a question!"

Tyrin didn't know who this person was.

Paul said, "We can take questions now. What is your question?"

"I hear any help you provide depends on us ending our way of selecting chiefs!"

Paul took a moment and shook his head. "No, our help and support does not depend on your way of choosing leadership. We will provide you with technology, training, medical support, etc., regardless of your leadership decision. That said, if you wish to join us in collaboration—in trade, immigration, and joint leadership over all of humankind, your method of choosing leaders is incompatible with ours, so that would not be possible."

The man sat down, seeming to be satisfied.

Tyrin saw Flir rise.

Flir said, "I have a different question."

Paul said, "Go ahead."

"I understand that Tvor there and all the New Earth 'Kinder' are the descendants of traitors." Tyrin noticed the way he said the word "Kinder" was full of acid.

Tvor rose. "First Chief Flir, my great-grandfather's name was Ngellin. He was a relatively low-level soldier conscripted to fight in an invasion of New Earth started by a Supreme Chief who kidnapped children from New Earth to work in the mines of Hilcyon. He could see the injustice of the invasion, and he decided, alongside about 2000 of his peers, to abandon it and settle on a verdant planet that welcomed them. I know that to you, that there is no honor in disobedience. But to us, there is great honor in choosing justice and compassion."

Flir said grimly, "All of you have no honor, and we will not follow people who have no honor. As far as I am concerned, this endeavor is tainted by your lack of honor."

Tvor said, "What would you need to know that we have honor?"

"The honor we find in obedience has its pinnacle in the ring. You, Tvor, fight me in the ring, and if you win, your honor will be proven, and my supporters will follow you. Lose, and you all must leave."

The room erupted. Tyrin could see a sense of superiority and confidence on Flir's face. Tyrin felt two things at once: a feeling deep in the pit of her stomach of fear of losing Tvor. And the clear knowledge that Flir had absolutely no idea how good Tvor was at fighting. She knew Flir would likely live to regret this challenge.

She looked at Tvor's face as chaos reigned in the room. She had only been married to him for five years, but she knew that face. Grim determination joined with a kind of certainty. He would do it.

Ke'lir said, "Are you out of your mind, Tvor?"

Paul was sitting slumped in the couch in their living area, where they all had decamped after the disaster of the meeting with the chiefs. He was despondent and at a loss for what to do.

Johan said quietly, "It makes perfect sense. They need something that can help them put this issue aside. Honor is *everything* to them, Ke'lir."

Ke'lir said, "But he could die, and then we'd have to leave!"

Tyrin said quietly, "Did you know that Tvor is considered probably the best fighter in Zwek?"

Paul turned to look at her.

He said, "What?"

"Tell them, Tvor, please."

Tvor took a big breath. "Yes, I have been fighting in the Zwek form of matches since I was probably five. My father introduced me to it because, frankly, I was a nightmare kid to deal with. He thought I would be easier to handle if I got tired out of training. I was very unlike my brother.

"Anyway, I've been a champion fighter at every level since I was 11 or so. I was given what is called the 'Chief Crown' two months ago because I've won against every other fighter."

Ke'lir said, "How is it none of us in the family knew this?"

Tvor shrugged his shoulders. "I just never talked about it."

Paul chuckled. "I always wondered why you were so ripped."

Johan said, "Holy shit. This is perfect."

Paul said, "Please elaborate, Johan."

"Look, this thing with the ancestors of Zwek is not going away. It is, obviously, the roadblock to anything moving forward. As you can see, the chiefs, even the ones who support connecting and potentially unifying, need something. If we don't do this, we might as well pack up and leave. But if Tvor wins, this will absolutely pave the way for us."

Ke'lir said, "IF, that's the thing, IF!!"

Dlen put her arm on Ke'lir's arm and said, "Love, you are not listening. Tvor will most likely win - think about it a minute. Here is someone who fights regularly and wins regularly, compared to Flir, who probably hasn't had a challenge fight in years. He thinks Tvor is weak, but Tvor is about as far from it as Flir could imagine."

Ke'lir started to cry. "I can't stand the idea of losing another cousin, and I can't imagine going home and having to tell Aunt Grun Hilcyon has taken her second son!"

Tvor walked over to Ke'lir and knelt beside her. "Ke'lir, I won't lose, and I won't die. And I know that this is the only way we can do this. We have no other choice."

Paul felt a new energy in his body and felt Tvor's certainty. He also knew and felt Johan's. They had no choice.

"OK, Tvor, we will agree to do this."

### Capital Region, Hilcyon

Johan looked around the arena, which held about 5,000 people. He was sitting with the Terran team, with the midwives on one side of them and the priests on the other. The rest of the space was filled with chiefs from all over Hilcyon. They had erected huge screens in the Capital Square, and other screens were scattered around the Capital region broadcasting the fight. Hilcyon didn't have the same kind of network New Earth had, so people would have to congregate at those places to see the match.

Tvor and Flir were wearing the traditional fighting garb, which was new to Tvor. He had chosen a long sword and Flir, the circle blade. Johan smiled, remembering the conversation with Tvor about his ability with circle blade-wielding opponents.

But Johan also knew that these blades were not wooden, as were the weapons Tvor was used to.

Plir was sitting next to Johan, and Johan took a moment to look at his face as he concentrated on the crowd. When Johan had met Plir, there was a sense of immediate connection. The third evening they were there, he and Plir spent hours talking about their lives, childhoods, and what had shaped them. Plir took Johan's change in sex in stride, which had surprised him. When he looked at Plir, his heart did a little extra beat. Johan didn't know what was next, but he knew he wanted to stay on Hilcyon for a while and see what emerged.

Plir said, "See Flir's loyalists over there?"

Johan nodded. "Yes."

"They look a little concerned, don't they?"

Johan looked again and could see the concern. They were watching Tvor. He wondered whether or not they had just assumed that Tvor couldn't possibly match Flir. He wondered whether Flir assumed that, too.

Flir and Tvor entered the ring and bowed to each other. Tvor stepped back, dancing and moving his sword as if warming up.

Flir lunged in a move that might seem to catch Tvor off-guard, but Tvor easily stepped aside and tapped the flat of his blade on Flir's exposed side.

This enraged Flir, who went in swinging. Tvor danced and continued to avoid Flir's swings and lunges easily. He tapped the flat of his blade several times on Flir's legs and side.

Instead of slowing down and considering things, Flir just got angrier. He started to shout as he lunged, and finally, Tvor took the butt of his sword and hit him squarely on the temple. Flir was disoriented and stumbled.

Plir said breathlessly, "This is the end. Tvor is going to end Flir."

But Johan knew better. He watched as Tvor took the flat of his blade and smacked Flir on the head again. Flir crumpled to the floor, then struggled to get up.

Tvor said loudly, "I could easily kill you now, Flir, but that's not how we fight."

Flir didn't say anything but struggled to get his blade in front of him and attack Tvor with it. Tvor grabbed the blade, yanked it out of Flir's hand, and tossed it out of the ring.

"You have lost."

Flir lunged at Tvor, who again used the butt of his sword to hit him on the head. Flir was down, unconscious. The crowd roared.

# Chapter 11:
# Unification

New Earth: October 2109 - March 2113
Hilcyon: Wtler 1212 - Cfro 1215
Casiti: Paqn 806 - Paqn 807

*"A desire to understand and the desire to control are two driving factors in human behavior. Every spiritual tradition has, at its core, values or practices that serve to limit those driving factors. Spiritual traditions help us to accept what is and embrace complexity and the unknown."--Ja'len'da, "Spirits Alike"*

### Capital Region, Hilcyon

The New Earth core team gathered in one of the lounge areas close to their rooms late the next day after the match. They had all spent most of the day in meetings with various stakeholders. Everyone was both elated and thoughtful.

Paul said, "So, I talked with Plir. Flir is still out of it, but his attache and other chiefs of the North Central Region have said they will not stand in the way of continued communication and connection with us. Tomorrow, we meet with all of the First Chiefs of each region, and it's time to introduce the idea of shared governance with women and priests."

Johan said, "I've been working with their leadership team, introducing them to our ideas on governance here. They all favor including the priesthood and women, although Rtlir is not sure how it will actually go over with the chiefs. He thinks telling them up front that the suggestion that women be in charge of managing food distribution, education, and medical care will make automatic sense to them, as these are things women are already doing here."

Tyrin said, "The challenge is that so many of them don't want women at the table, with any power—this will be problematic for them."

Johan nodded. "I think it will take them a while to get used to it, but I think if they think the women are really delegated to 'women's work,' they won't notice the women are actually taking on the most important tasks."

Paul turned to Dlen. "How have the conversations with the midwives been going?"

Dlen said, "Very well. We've already planned in detail the medical training we'll put in place, not only for midwives but also for medics, who are also largely but not entirely, women. We've also begun recruiting leaders in education and agriculture. Many of the latter are men, but so far, we haven't had any problems in meetings with them."

Paul was feeling really hopeful about how this process might unfold.

He turned to Kwyl. "Any news to share?"

Kwyl said, "I have been having long conversations with Jorn, Glin, and other priest leaders. The priesthood is ready to take their place in leadership. Glin already had plans in place to unify the priesthood by blessing the monks in Zwek as a new order that would be supervised by Jorn and Glin. Jorn and a few other monks will be traveling to New Earth."

Paul said, "That's wonderful to hear. I'm putting together a report for NEA and the Consej, outlining what has happened and what our next steps are. They will want a timeline for this mission and a list of experts and partners who should come before we leave. What I'd like to hear from each of you is what your medium-term and/or long-term plans are in regard to being on a local team."

Johan started. "I want to stay a while. I've built some really good relationships here, and I also would like to be involved in helping to create the governance structures."

Paul nodded.

Tvor said, "Tyrin and I are staying. This is our home. We are going to have Mrin join us."

Paul knew that that had been their hope from the beginning.

Dlen said, "Ke'lir and I are planning to go home soon. It's been wonderful to be here and get a chance to be a part of this process, but other medical experts will be better at the training process than I am, and I'm due to start medical school in the NCPIZ in a couple of months."

Kwyl said, "I'll be staying as a representative of the priesthood on New Earth. I don't know how long. I might stay permanently."

Paul nodded. "Thank you all. I will stay for a few months to see some of this through, then go home, back to the Ja'lit school."

They conversed casually for a while, and Paul could feel how tired he was. This was a long, tense stretch, and he was glad things were getting easier. He was looking forward to being home with Makena.


Johan could hardly believe it. It had only been ten days since the match between Flir and Tvor. Ten amazing, incredible days. He briefly thought back on so many things that happened, but the one thing that stood out the most was the first afternoon he had spent in bed with Plir. He had been so busy working on New Earth that he hadn't had time to find a boyfriend. Plir was everything Johan could imagine and more.

Paul's voice brought Johan back to the present. "Johan, what's the current status of elections?"

He looked down at his tablet. He *had* prepared for this meeting.

"So far, all regions have elected their First Chiefs. Without exception, all remain the same. Most hamlets and villages have also held elections, and it's about 70% of the same chiefs. Hamlets seem especially interested in electing someone different."

"So next time..."

"I expect that the next round of elections will replace most of the chiefs. I could be wrong, but..."

Tvor said, "Well, leadership looks different when you don't have to kill to get it. I expect a new generation of leaders who would never have been in power without this change."

Paul said, "Speaking of not killing, Tvor..."

"Yes, the sport matches are catching on. I've asked several coaches from Zwek to come, and they have agreed."

Paul said, "We've gotten permission to build on the southeast edge of the capital region, in some open land that hadn't been used in a while. The building team expects to have the infrastructure built in the next few weeks and the structures finished and furnished soon after. We've also set the schedule for regular shuttle service between New

Earth and Hilcyon, although we'll be carefully vetting the passengers for a while."

Paul looked at Dlen. "Dlen?"

"We're doing well, Paul. Mirn and Hril are really amazing leaders and have assembled a crack team. By the time Ke'lir and I leave, they will have everything they need to keep going."

Paul said, "OK, folks, really good work here. I think we can adjourn for today."

Johan was tired but in a good way. He was going to spend the evening with Plir and was elated. He walked out of the meeting room, down the stairs, and to the shared office where Plir usually worked. As he walked in, he could see Plir on the far side. He hadn't noticed that Johan was in the room, so Johan had a moment to observe him. Johan could feel a wide smile forming on his face.

Plir looked up and toward the door, recognizing Johan. He got up and walked toward him. There were others in the room, so they needed care.

"Johan. Nice to see you."

"Good to see you, Plir."

Johan did have work he needed to discuss with Plir but didn't want to. But it was a good excuse.

"Plir, I have some questions for you. Do you have time?"

"Of course."

"Can we go up to my room?"

"Sure, let's."

They walked back upstairs and down the hall to Plir's room. Well, rooms. He had commandeered a couple's suite a few days ago when he realized he would want a bigger bed. No one was using it.

When he closed the door, Plir grabbed him and kissed him fiercely. Johan melted into Plir's touch and kisses. Somehow, they made it to the bed, tangled in their clothes, in a great hurry to experience as much of each other's bodies as they could.

After, Johan looked at Plir, whose eyes were closed, even though Johan knew he wasn't asleep.

"Johan?"

"I'm here."

"I know you want to stay here."

"For a while. But that's because I want to be here for you."

"I want to leave."

"Huh?"

"I want to go to New Earth. I don't feel like I belong here. I've never felt like I've belonged here."

"You've told me of that feeling. Like I felt I never belonged in the ICS."

"Right. Let's leave. Take me to New Earth. Please?"

Johan held Plir's cheek in his hand. "Yes. Plir. I'll take you there."

They kissed deeply and found more solace and joy in each other's bodies.


### Capital Region, Hilcyon

Tyrin watched the large shuttle land. It was the second shuttle to arrive on Hilcyon after they had finished the first stage of their work here. The first shuttle was full of experts and leaders. This shuttle was the first with just civilians.

Many people from Zwek wanted to visit, and they had to carefully vet them for the first group. But Mrin was on this shuttle, and Tvor's mother, Grun, was traveling with Mrin and would stay with them for a few weeks before returning home.

Tvor was at her elbow. He had changed, subtly, in the moons since the match. He always seemed a man with confidence, but winning the match with Flir meant that the people of Hilcyon almost considered him akin to Supreme Chief. He refused that power, of course, but he had taken on some of the stature, which she thought looked good on him.

Tvor yelled, "Mom, Mrin!"

Tyrin also spotted Grun and saw the little boy of theirs next to her. They walked quickly through the small gathered crowd, and everyone hugged.

Tvor picked up Mrin, and Mrin said loudly, "Dada! Ma!"

Sometimes, she worried about how Mrin would like it here. He was only 5 years old, and this would be a new experience for him. But they both wanted to make Hilcyon their home and although it might be challenging, they were up to it.

They picked up the baggage and walked the few blocks to Tvor and Tyrin's new house.

Tyrin said to Grun, "We were able to get a dwelling close to the Capitol—mostly because of Tvor's new status. Most folks coming here are going to live in the new section that was built on the far east side of the region set aside for staff and visitors from New Earth and Casiti."

The home they had been able to get was a little larger than many and quite adequate. It had three small bedrooms, a living room and dining area, and a kitchen. Tyrin had done her best to make it as home-like as possible. She gave Grun a tour and showed her the guest room.

A few hours later, they sat around the dining area table.

Tyrin said, "Welcome, Grun. We are so glad you are here and brought Mrin. I want you to meet some of the women I've been working with. They are so brave. And a couple had met Glor and remembered him fondly."

Grun said, "Thank you, Tyrin, I hope to. I have to admit it's a little hard to be here, remembering one of my sons died here. Although I fully embrace our culture, it's hard for me to imagine this planet as home."

Tvor said, "I can understand Ma. And I also know that if it had not been for the work Glor had done, we wouldn't be here right now."

Tvor looked at Tyrin with love, reaching out and holding her hand. Unsaid was that he and she would have never met.

Grun smiled, hearing and seeing the unsaid.


Jorn left his new cell, closing the door behind him. It was more spacious and comfortable than just about any cell he had ever seen. Of course, to the monks here, these cells were austere and small compared to the typical dwellings of people in Zwek.

He had arrived in Zwek some days ago and was still working to get used to days that were twice the length of the days at home. The priests had been clever in how they re-ordered and re-arranged the prayer hours. He appreciated the flexibility and comfort of the schedule.

He had a meeting with the head monk, named Daniel. All the monks had been very welcoming and open with him, although

Jorn could sense some tension and apprehension, which he could understand. He was here to supervise them, to bring them together with all of the other orders of the priesthood.

He arrived at Daniel's office and saw the door ajar. He knocked.

"Please, come in!"

He opened the door to see Daniel sitting in a comfortable chair beside a bookshelf. Daniel indicated Jorn should sit across from him in a similar chair.

"Jorn, how have you been so far?"

"Well, I've finally got the sleeping thing. It's challenging to take a nap during the day—we never get that luxury at home."

"I can imagine getting used to such a long day and night could be a challenge. I know it took some of the priests who came back from Casiti months some years ago to get used to it. I hope you are giving yourself room with it."

Jorn had to smile. There were so many differences in culture between the Kinder in Zwek, and on Hilcyon, but one thing that kept jumping out at him was the ease they had with their own comfort. It was sometimes disturbing, but Jorn realized it made a lot of sense. They had luxury and ease that those on Hilcyon could not even imagine.

"I am, yes. Thanks."

"Good, good. So I know you plan to spend time observing us, what we do, and how we do it."

"Yes. I don't think I'll have a sense of how best to work with you until I have a real sense of what you are doing and how it's different."

"Some priests are afraid you'll want us to change things."

Jorn shook his head. "No, that's not how it works. You have already been blessed by Glin as a separate order of the priesthood. As such, you have tremendous freedom in both praxis and theology. There already is a wide range of that within the orders on Hilcyon. My role is just to figure out the best way to integrate you into our networks and systems so you'll have a voice and a role."

"Thank you for that clarity. I think it will ease some minds and hearts."

"One of the things we often do is priest exchanges. A few priests from one order will go and spend time with another for a year or so.

I think it would be very interesting for your order to engage in that—have some priests come here, and you send some elsewhere. I can start with some ideas for the most compatible orders."

Daniel nodded. "I think we would like that. I already have a long list of priests who want to go to Hilcyon."

"We can accommodate that—I think any priests here who want to experience orders on Hilcyon should be allowed to do so. It will be healthy for both sides."

Daniel nodded.

Jorn said, "If I may ask, how did you get your name? It's quite unusual."

Daniel smiled. "It's a Terran name. My mother was half Terran; it was her maternal grandfather's name. He had emigrated here from Earth."

"Ah, I see. I have seen that many seem to have Terran names."

"Yes, because all of the Kinder who deserted were, of course, men. So they had to have children with either Terran or Casitian women. Most were Terran."

Jorn said, "It's been very illuminating to be here. I hope to stay for a while."

Daniel smiled again. "I'm glad, Jorn. I hope we can get to know you well."


Plir walked with Johan out of the spaceport into the bustle of central New Orleans. Even though they were in the middle of the city, there was greenery everywhere.

Johan said, "Let's grab a cab to my apartment."

Plir watched Johan look at a device he had fished from his pocket. Johan noticed him looking.

"It's called 'phone,' which is kind of a relic. It doesn't really do what old 'phones' did on Earth from what I understand. But I have messaged a cab. They will be here momentarily."

Plir nodded, allowing the mysteries that were piling up just to be for now.

In a while, a small vehicle that didn't seem to have a driver pulled up to them.

Johan said, "Here it is."

Johan opened the back of the vehicle, put their bags in, then opened one of the doors on the side.

"Get in. It'll be alright."

Plir nodded and got in. Johan followed, and the vehicle zipped off, winding its way through traffic. Plir relaxed.

Johan said, "You alright?"

Plir nodded. "Everything feels new, which is both scary and fun."

"I understand."

They were silent during the rest of the taxi ride. Finally, it slowed down and stopped in front of a squat building with lots of greenery around it.

Johan got their stuff and directed Plir around a bush to a door.

"It's a nice building. All of the apartments kinda feel like their own little cottages."

Johan pushed some numbers into a keypad with unfamiliar characters on it.

"The code is 4543. I'll write it down for you. You press this 'lock' icon to lock it when you leave, then the numbers and the lock icon to unlock it when you come home."

Plir nodded, sort of understanding, and entered a spacious apartment. A small animal was sitting on a piece of furniture, and Plir watched Johan go to it, surprised.

"Cooper! I missed you so much!"

The animal made a weird yowling sound, followed by some low-pitched rumbling. Johan was stroking its back and head.

"What is that???"

"It's a cat. Oh, right, you don't have pets."

"Pets?"

"Animals that humans keep for company."

Plir smiled. He had so much to learn.

Ro'mer got up and realized they had sat in a strange position for too long. They stretched and walked around their room. They had just spent the last few hours reading the latest report from Tvor, who had now been on Hilcyon for almost a Casitian year. It was the last official report of the transition team. In just a few days, the Consej would meet for the first time with four representatives from Hilcyon.

In some ways, the progress at that time was astonishing. Matches for chief status had been halted only days after Tvor's fateful match with Flir. Chiefs were now chosen by election, and, of course, as of yet, only men could vote. Although there had been an attempt to draft Tvor for Supreme Chief, he refused because he felt the first elected chief should be from Hilcyon. Rtlir was elected by a wide margin.

The women in charge of almost everything were doing an incredible job. Two medical schools had been started, and hundreds of people were being trained. Food production was up significantly, and many foods that had been lost during the drought period were re-introduced.

Sheep and goats had been imported to the highlands and provided milk, meat, and wool. Tvor had requested Alpaca, and one of Ro'mer's tasks was to make that happen.

And, in general, the people of Hilcyon went on with their lives. There had been a few emigrants, but most of those were people who were connected somehow to the Terran teams. Ro'mer considered Plir, Msrotl's son, who emigrated to New Earth with Johan.

They needed to get dressed and ready. They had an appointment for tea with Trel'or'li this evening. They were very much looking forward to it. Their youngest was getting prepared to leave to join a youth house, which meant that in a month or so, Ro'mer would be leaving the family house to live on their own again. Ro'mer and Trel'or'li had some very sweet interactions, and they both thought that the next Musb might find them together again.

# Epilogue

*Hilcyon Orbit, Hyril 45, 802 Unified Date (January 3, 3038 New Earth Date)*

Jerrold stood at the front of the large orbiting platform, looking down on the verdant planet he grew up on. Beside him stood two of the other members of the Consej—Jerrold represented Hilcyon, Gor'el'e represented Casiti, and Rosalind represented New Earth.

They had just finished their presentation to the small team of galactic representatives sent through the wormhole two days ago to assess the status of humankind and the possibility of their return to the Galactic Community. Of course, there would be more assessments and meetings. Jerrold would go with a team to Upsilon Andromedae to the Galactic Council for their meetings and final vote.

Based on what Jerrold knew, it was unlikely that the Galactic Community would reject them—they had been peacefully unified for more than 800 years. They had terraformed Hilcyon, making it similar to old Earth. Casitian, Terran, and Kinder cultures thrived and happily co-existed on all three planets, most notably on New Earth.

Later that day, he visited his grandmother to tell her what happened. He sat at her table, drinking a cup of fuge, smelling the breadmufs baking in the oven.

"You are confident, Jerrold?"

"I am, grandmother. You should have seen the reactions of their team when they saw Hilcyon from orbit. They were clearly impressed at how much had been done in so little time."

"So little time! Huh! 1000 years. So little time..."

"Anyway, we'll get the notice in a few months about when we're expected at the Galactic Council."

"Shall I show you what I've been working on?"

"The newest family tree? Yes, I'd love to see it."

A three-dimensional display appeared in front of them. His grandmother used her hands to manipulate what was displayed, which looked a lot like a tangle of tendrils. She eventually reached the very top, which included three sets of parents.

"Here's the beginning, Jerrold. Beatrice and Ngellin, Leticia and Mira, Krely and Sadre. Our ancestors during the time of The Great Closing. Connecting the historical records with the birth and family records took a while. And, particularly, it was difficult to track the Hilcyon side of the family for a hundred years or so."

Jerrold spent some time with the display. He could see the color-coded threads, often interweaving and blending. Historical events were connected with specific people, like his ancestors Tvor and Tyrin, and their pivotal role in the unification of all three branches of humanity. This display went back 40 generations.

"This is amazing, grandmother! Our family has been through so much in all of these years."

"And we've finally come full circle. We're witnessing the re-entry of our human family into the Galactic Community. I wish all of those before us could witness this. They would be proud of what we've managed to accomplish."

Jerrold knew that even if they could witness this moment, they wouldn't completely understand it. First, the languages spoken by his ancestors were mostly non-existent. Once all three branches were united, a new language emerged, one everyone eventually adopted. Second, the unification of humanity caused an extraordinary technological growth spurt. Even in the absence of technological influence from the Galactic Community, humankind had developed so many new technologies, all sustainable and geared toward human well-being. And last, they had made Hilcyon a paradise planet, one that now could sustain a thousand times more people than before.

Jerrold could not say what lay ahead for his species, but he was glad to be alive now, to witness this moment in its history.

# About The Author

Maxwell Pearl is a science fiction and multi-genre writer. His novels are largely hard science fiction, but incorporate social, political, and spiritual topics. He lives in Northern California and Seattle, Washington.